Massacre at Bear Creek Lodge

A Kodiak, Alaska Wilderness Mystery Novel

Robin Barefield

Alaska Wilderness Mystery Author
Author Masterminds Charter Member

PUBLICATION
CONSULTANTS
WE BELIEVE IN THE POWER OF AUTHORS

PO Box 221974 Anchorage, Alaska 99522-1974
books@publicationconsultants.com—www.publicationconsultants.com

ISBN 978-1-63747-083-1
ebook ISBN 978-1-63747-084-8

Library of Congress Catalog Card Number: 2022903321

This is a work of fiction. Names, characters, businesses, places, events and
incidents are either the products of the author's imagination or used in a
fictitious manner. Any resemblance to actual persons, living or dead, or
actual events is purely coincidental.

Manufactured in the United States of America

CHAPTER 1

Saturday, September 6th

7:40 a.m.

Sergeant Dan Patterson arose early, looking forward to a leisurely day at home with Jeanne. He hadn't taken a Saturday off in weeks, and he planned to make the most of this one. Jeanne was a radiology technician at the local hospital, and she had the day off as well, so they could spend the day together for a change.

Lately, Kodiak had been a hotbed of crime. The island, plunked like a jewel in the North Pacific, boasted a population of 13,500 humans and 3,500 Kodiak brown bears. Kodiak saw its share of crime, but over the last few weeks, one major incident after the next had demanded Patterson's attention. Things seemed to have been under control when he'd left the office on Friday. He'd told Brie Davis, the weekend dispatcher, "Don't call me unless you receive a report of an alien invasion, a big explosion, or a mass murder."

Patterson's phone rang at 7:23 a.m. "Sergeant? This is Brie. I'm sorry to bother you, but we have a problem."

Patterson banged his coffee mug on the kitchen counter. "This better be good, Brie."

"Yes, sir."

"Go ahead, then. What do you have?"

"Eight people dead, sir. Murdered."

Patterson slid onto the nearest stool by the kitchen counter. Out of the corner of his eye, he saw Jeanne enter the kitchen, still wearing her blue bathrobe. They wouldn't have a moment to themselves anytime soon.

"Eight people?" Patterson asked. He'd seen nasty crime scenes in his years as an Alaska State Trooper, but he'd never investigated a massacre.

"Yes," Brie said. "A young woman called me on a sat phone. She sounded rattled, and I'm not sure I understood everything she said, but she told me she's the cook at a lodge in Aktuvik Cove, and she discovered the owners of the lodge dead in their bed early this morning. While she tried to resuscitate them, she sent the camp helper up to the guest cabin to check on the six guests, and the helper found the guests also dead."

"Where was this again?" Patterson asked.

"Aktuvik Cove."

The name sounded familiar, but he couldn't place it. He'd only been stationed in Kodiak for eighteen months, and he still found he often needed to consult a map to locate the spot where a hunter went missing or a crime occurred. The Kodiak National Wildlife Refuge covered two-thirds of the island, and no roads crossed the refuge. Humans could only access most of the large island by float-plane or boat.

"Where is Aktuvik Cove?" he asked. "Did I pronounce it right?"

"Not quite, sir," Brie said. "The first syllable rhymes with 'yak.' It's on the southwest side of the island."

Patterson tried to shake the cobwebs from his head. "It's a wild-life-viewing and fishing lodge, right?"

"Yes, sir, Bear Creek Lodge. The Bartletts own it. I went to school with their daughter." Brie's voice cracked over the phone.

"Good job, Brie," Patterson said. "You've handled this perfectly."

"Thank you, sir. What should I do now?"

"Call Mark and Sara. I know they both have the weekend off, but see if they can meet me at the plane at Trident Basin." Patterson rubbed his head. "We'll need another plane too. Call Kodiak Flight Services and find out if they can spare their turbine Beaver. Also, get ahold of the crime scene techs. We'll need at least four." Patterson sighed as he thought of their blown budget for the next six months.

"Sir," Brie said, "our techs all have the weekend off, and I know at least two of them planned to go fishing early this morning."

"Find who you can," Patterson said. "If you can't find techs, then send more troopers. If what the cook reported to you is true, then we'll have a massive crime scene to investigate."

"Yes, sir."

"Have everyone meet at the basin in an hour. I'm heading there now to warm up the plane."

After he hung up, Patterson offered Jeanne an apologetic smile. "This is a bad one, hon. I need to cancel our plans for the day."

"So I gathered," she said with a sigh and then handed him a sack lunch.

CHAPTER 2

Saturday, September 6th

8:53 a.m.

Sixty-seven minutes later, Patterson was manning the controls of the Alaska State Troopers' de Havilland Beaver. He circled the town of Kodiak and flew toward Sharatin Pass. A twenty-knot wind buffeted the plane, but other than the brisk breeze, he had perfect flying weather. Not a cloud marred the pale-blue sky, an unusual occurrence for September, one of the rainiest months on the island. As the plane soared over the mountains, Patterson admired the patches of deep-red fireweed separated by cow parsnip, alders, willows, and other green vegetation. The random pattern of red and green reminded him of the Christmas quilt Jeanne's mother had given them several years before.

He shook his head. How could he think about fireweed and Christmas quilts when he was on his way to what was sure to be the most brutal crime scene he had ever witnessed? Trooper Mark Traner sat in the passenger seat next to him, and Troopers Sara Byram, Peter Boyle, and Gary Reeves occupied the rear seat of the plane. Two crime scene techs and two more troopers would follow in an hour on a Kodiak Flight Services plane.

No one spoke during the hour-long flight to the far side of the island. Patterson understood the tension in the plane, and he felt it, too, as he tried to prepare his mind for what they would see when they arrived at Aktuvik Cove.

Patterson circled the small cove and noted the beautiful sport-fishing boat anchored in front of the lodge. He landed on the choppy waves and idled up to a long dock, where two young women stood. As the plane approached the dock, he changed his appraisal. The tall, thin figure with muscular arms, short brown hair, and an apron cinched tight across her waist must have been in her midtwenties. The woman standing beside her wore a long floral skirt and a billowing blouse. She appeared to be in her midteens.

As they pulled alongside the dock, Mark and Peter jumped from the plane and secured the Beaver to the cleats. Patterson shut down the engine, and he and the other troopers emerged from the plane.

The tall, thin woman wrapped her arms around herself, apparently trying to control her violent shaking. Her red nose and streaked, pale face indicated she'd been crying. The girl stood quietly beside her.

Patterson introduced himself and the other troopers, and when neither woman said a word, he asked them their names.

"I'm Elle," the older one said, "and this is Susan."

"Let's go up to the lodge and sit for a few minutes," Patterson said. "I want you to walk me through your morning, and then we'll take a look at the crime scene."

After noting the lodge's rustic exterior, Patterson was surprised by the interior. High-beamed ceilings showcased beautiful wildlife paintings and other local artwork, and expensive-looking woven rugs covered the hardwood floors. The furniture looked costly but practical, with wooden frames and overstuffed cushions in mottled grays and browns.

Elle opened the front curtain to let daylight spill from the large picture window, and then she flipped on the light switches, flooding the great room with a soft light. She and Susan sat beside each other on one of the love seats, and Patterson sat in a chair across from them. Mark Traner also sat down and then pulled his notebook, pen, and tape recorder from his pocket. He placed the recorder on the table in front of Elle and Susan.

"You don't mind if we record this conversation, do you?" Patterson asked.

Elle and Susan both shook their heads.

Patterson noticed a shotgun resting against the love seat near where Elle sat. He motioned to the gun. "Is that loaded?" he asked.

Elle looked down at the gun as if surprised by its presence. She reached a hand toward the barrel, but Mark told her to stop. He grabbed the gun by the barrel and placed it near the door.

Elle seemed flustered. "I loaded it for protection while Susan and I waited for you to arrive," she said to Patterson.

"Smart move," Patterson said, "but you don't need it now."

He watched tears trickle down Elle's cheeks. She swiped at them with a tissue and took several deep breaths.

While Patterson and Mark conducted the interview, Peter, Sarah, and Gary remained standing, their attention focused on Elle and Susan.

"Why don't you start, Elle," Patterson said. "Begin by telling me when you got up and what you did this morning."

"I woke up at five this morning," she said.

"Can you speak up a little, Elle? I can barely hear you," Patterson said.

Elle cleared her throat and spoke again. "I woke up at five. That's when I get up to bake the rolls for breakfast. Bob usually gets up at seven a.m. and turns on the generator, and Jules is out here by seven thirty at the latest."

"Bob and Jules are the Bartletts?" Patterson asked.

"Yes," Elle said. "At seven twenty, when Bob still hadn't come out to turn on the generator, I figured he'd overslept. We're all tired by this point in the season, so I wasn't surprised they'd slept through their alarm clock." She paused and seemed to fight back the tears. "I knocked on their door, but they didn't answer, so I opened the door a slit and called their names several times. When they still didn't answer, I took a few steps into their room." She paused again. "I was about to call their names again, but I saw all the blood." The tears flowed, and Elle used her apron to mop her face.

Patterson waited for her to stop crying. "What did you do next?" he asked.

"I tried to do CPR on Bob, but they were already dead. They were cold."

The questions were building in Patterson's mind, but he wanted to keep Elle on track. "Then what did you do?"

"I went back to the kitchen and told Susan to go up and check on the guests. I wanted to make sure they were okay. I didn't know what else to do." Her face flushed red.

"Of course," Patterson said. "You did the right thing, Elle. Don't second-guess yourself." He smiled at her. "I just have one more question for now. I don't see any blood on your clothes. Didn't you get blood on you when you tried to give Jules and Bob CPR?"

The question seemed to confuse Elle. She looked down at her apron and black leggings. "I did get blood on me," she said. "I changed my clothes."

"We'll need to take your bloody clothes with us to the lab," Patterson said.

Elle nodded. "I don't want them back."

Patterson focused his gaze on Susan. "Why don't you tell me what happened next, Susan."

Susan seemed outwardly calm, but her pupils appeared dilated, and she sat rigidly, hands gripping her knees and feet planted firmly on the floor.

"I walked up to the guest cabin," she said, her voice low but controlled. "I knocked on the door several times, but when no one answered, I went inside. They were all dead."

"Are you sure?" Patterson asked.

"I'm sure. When you see them, you'll know."

"All the guests are in one cabin?"

"It's a big cabin with three bedrooms and bathrooms and a great room," Elle said. "We have"—she shook her head—"or *had*, three couples here. One couple was from Germany, one from England, and the other was from Atlanta, Georgia."

"Did they know each other before their trip here?" Patterson asked.

Elle shook her head. "No, but they seemed to get along fine."

"The couple from Atlanta was rude," Susan said.

Elle gave her a sharp look. Susan quickly looked down at the floor.

"Where do you two sleep?" Patterson asked.

"Upstairs," Elle said. She shivered. "I guess the killer didn't think to look upstairs."

"Do either of you have any idea what happened here?"

Elle and Susan shook their heads.

"You didn't hear anything?"

"I went up to my room early last night," Elle said. "The Bartletts' son and daughter were here. He's a commercial fisherman, and his fishing boat is anchored near here. Deb, the daughter, works at the cannery. Jules told me they were having dinner together because they needed to have a family conversation, so I gave them some space."

"What about you, Susan?"

"I always go to bed early."

"And neither of you heard anything suspicious?"

Elle and Susan again shook their heads.

"You're out here in the middle of the wilderness," Patterson said. "Do either of you have any idea who could have done this?"

Elle and Susan glanced at each other and then turned to look at Patterson and again shook their heads.

"Who, besides the Bartletts' son and his fishing crew, is out here near the lodge right now?"

"There's Sammy," Susan said, and Elle graced her with a dark look.

"Who is Sammy?" Patterson asked.

Susan looked down at her hands, apparently intent on not drawing more of Elle's wrath.

After a few moments, Elle said, "Sam Lutz. He's a guy who lives out here in a little cabin. He's nice, though. He'd never hurt anyone."

"Okay," Patterson said. "Who else?"

Susan glanced at Elle again. "Tell him about the Fairweathers."

"Sure, I didn't think about them," Elle said. "A few nights ago, we heard Georgie Fairweather on the VHF. She said she and her husband, Tim, had had a fight. At first, he pulled a gun on her, and then she said he grabbed every gun he had plus several boxes of ammunition, jumped in his boat, and took off. She didn't know where he was going, but she announced the situation to everyone over the VHF and warned people to be on the lookout for her husband, because she thought he was planning to kill someone, or maybe several people."

"I don't remember anyone calling the troopers," Patterson said.

Elle shrugged. "Tim Fairweather always seemed nice to me, but Bob said he's a nutcase. He made sure we stayed in the house all evening."

"But you never heard anything else about it?"

"No," Elle said.

"Does this couple live near here?"

"They have a cabin close to the mouth of the bay," Elle said. "Several miles from here."

"What about Deb?" Susan asked.

Susan and Elle shared a long look.

"You mentioned Deb earlier," Patterson said. "Tell me more about her."

After a long pause, Elle said, "Debbie is the Bartletts' daughter. She works at the Aktuvik Fresh Seafoods Cannery."

Patterson tried to picture the location of the cannery in his mind. He knew it was several miles from the lodge, even though it bore the name of the cove in front of the lodge.

"Do you think Deb murdered her parents?" Trooper Sara Byram asked.

Elle looked up at Sara, who stood a few feet behind Patterson. Elle seemed startled by the question.

"No." Elle shook her head. "I don't know," she said and then started crying again.

"Ladies," Patterson said to Elle and Susan once Elle's sobs had quieted, "I know this has been a terrible morning for you both. Let's take a break from the questions. Elle, would you mind showing Sara where you put your bloody clothes? She'll bag them, and then we'll take them back to town with us." He turned his gaze to Susan. "Are any of your clothes bloody?"

Susan shook her head rapidly. "No," she said in a small voice.

Patterson stood and looked at Sara. "Peter and I will start in the Bartletts' bedroom. Once you get Elle's clothes bagged, I'd like for you and Mark to go up to the guest cabin and take photos. Don't touch anything until the crime scene techs arrive, and then assist them until they finish." Patterson glanced up at Mark. "Does that work for you?"

"Yes, sir," he said.

"Gary," Patterson said to the least-experienced trooper in the group, "you stand outside the front door and make sure no one enters the house without my permission."

"Yes, sir." His reply sounded so sharp that Patterson expected a salute.

"Remember," Patterson said, his eyes locked on Gary's, "we have a murderer running loose. Don't let down your guard."

"No, sir," he said and then exited the front of the lodge, closing the door behind him.

CHAPTER 3

Saturday, September 6th

10:20 a.m.

"The Bartletts' bedroom is down this hall?" Patterson asked Elle. He pointed to the narrow walkway leading from the great room.

Elle nodded and watched Sergeant Patterson and another trooper walk down the hall. She shuddered, knowing what they would find when they entered the bedroom. She would never forget the gruesome scene she'd discovered a few hours earlier. Someone had beaten Jules and Bob to death. She had not recognized them. She couldn't even tell that the bloody forms in the bed were human. Blood spatter covered the walls, the beamed ceiling, the comforter, and the throw rugs. Everything in the room was painted scarlet. She shook her head, willing the image out of her mind.

"Elle?"

She looked up, startled. *How long has the lady trooper been calling my name?* Both officers and Susan stared at her.

"Sorry," Elle said. "Did you ask me something?"

"Yes," the trooper said. "Would you take me to your bloody clothes, so I can bag them? Once we get them out of here, you won't have to look at them again."

"Okay," Elle said. She stood, but her knees buckled and she nearly fell.

"Whoa," both troopers said in unison. The woman hurried to Elle and held her arm to steady her.

"I'm okay," Elle said. "My bedroom is upstairs."

"Can you make it up the stairs?" the female trooper asked.

"Sure," Elle said, but her vision kept fading to black, and she worried she would faint at any moment. As soon as they reached the stairs, she gripped the handrail.

"My name is Sara," the female trooper said. "I know Sergeant Patterson introduced us, but I'm sure you're overwhelmed right now."

"Okay, Sara, got it," Elle said.

"How long have you worked for the Bartletts?" Sara asked as she followed Elle up the stairs.

Elle welcomed the trooper's question. She wanted to think about anything other than the bloodbath in the Bartletts' bedroom.

"This is my third year," Elle said. "The Bartletts are good to me. I especially like Jules." She couldn't bring herself to refer to Jules in the past tense.

"What about Susan?" Sara asked. "How long has she been here?"

"This is her first year," Elle said. As they reached the top-floor landing and walked down the hall out of earshot from anyone sitting in the great room, Elle looked at Sara and said in a soft voice, "Susan is only seventeen years old, and this is her first real job." She shook her head. "What a way to start."

"Where is she from?"

"Her family has a farm somewhere north of Palmer. Actually, I think it's more like a compound. The entire family, including Susan's grandparents, aunts, uncles, and cousins, all live in this one little area. The kids are homeschooled, and their parents brainwash them."

"How do you mean?" Sara asked.

"I don't like to judge," Elle said, "but Susan has some crazy ideas about how the world works."

Elle led the way. Her bedroom was the second small room down the hall, and a bathroom occupied the space at the end of the hall.

Elle stopped just inside the bedroom door. The bloody pile of clothes on the floor brought her back to the moment. She pointed at them and stood back while Sara donned gloves and gently dropped each article of clothing into a garbage bag. Elle had earlier stripped off everything, including her underwear, and she stood and watched Sara collect each piece.

"What sort of ideas?" Sara asked.

"What?" Elle had lost the thread of their conversation.

"You said Susan has crazy ideas about how the world works."

"Oh," Elle said, no longer in the mood for small talk. "It's just that she's been taught that women should stay at home and take care of their husbands and children. She can't wait to get married and start a family."

"And you said she's only seventeen?"

Elle nodded. "She's engaged to a guy who's in his midtwenties. I've never met him, but he sounds like a loser. His name's Stan. He has Susan mail her paychecks to him."

"Wow!" Sara said.

"It makes me so crazy I can't even talk to her about it," Elle said, "but Jules tried. I think she considers Susan her project. Jules told me once that she felt she needed to save Susan from herself."

"Did Susan listen to her?"

Elle shook her head. "Susan is in love. She doesn't listen to anyone except Stan."

Elle led the way out of her room and down the hall to the top of the stairs.

"What about you?" Sara asked. "Where are you from originally?"

"Here and there," Elle said. "My family traveled a lot when I was young."

When they reached the great room, Sara continued to the front door, carrying the garbage bag full of clothes. She opened the door, spoke briefly to the trooper stationed on the porch, and handed him the bag of bloody clothes. She then looked over her shoulder at the other trooper. "Are you ready, Mark?" she asked.

The trooper named Mark nodded and followed Sara out the front door.

Elle reclaimed her seat on the couch next to Susan.

They both sat quietly for several minutes, the ticking of the large wall clock the only noise in the room.

Finally, Susan said, "I think Snowball is dead."

Elle jerked away from Susan at the mention of the cat. "Why would you say something like that?"

15

Susan reached her hand to Elle's arm. "I'm sorry," she said. "I haven't seen her all morning, and you know how she liked to sleep with Jules and Bob. I'm worried. Have you seen her?"

Elle began to cry softly, but her sobs grew in volume to a wail. She didn't think she could handle more bad news. She'd always thought of herself as tough, but right now, she couldn't hold herself together, no matter how hard she tried.

"Maybe Snowball will show up in a while," Susan said as she patted Elle's hand.

Elle wondered how Susan was coping so well. She was just a kid; Elle should be comforting her, not the other way around. Elle took several deep breaths. "Who could have done this, and why didn't I hear anything?"

"Why did the killer leave us alive?" Susan asked.

"Maybe he or she didn't know we were upstairs."

"Or maybe he likes us and didn't want to kill us."

"You think the killer knows us?" Elle asked.

"Of course," Susan said. "Don't you?"

Elle couldn't imagine anyone she knew doing something this terrible, this evil. "Who?"

"I don' know," Susan said. "I'm probably wrong. Maybe the only reason we weren't murdered was because the killer didn't know we were upstairs, but if the killer only wanted to murder Jules and Bob, why did he go up to the cabin and shoot the guests?"

Elle whipped her head toward Susan. "The guests were shot?"

Susan nodded. "When you sent me up to check on them, I could see they were all dead, but they looked peaceful. They must have been asleep when the killer shot them." She shrugged. "Maybe it would've taken too long to beat them to death."

Elle shuddered. *How could someone bludgeon another person to death?* "Why not just shoot Jules and Bob too? It would have been simpler."

Susan shook her head. "I don't know. Maybe whoever did it hated Jules or Bob."

"Who hated them?" Elle couldn't even think straight. She knew Sergeant Patterson wanted her to list possible suspects, but she couldn't imagine anyone doing something this horrible.

"I know you like Sammy," Susan said, "but he and Bob had a terrible fight. Do you know what it was about?"

Elle shook her head. "Not for sure. I asked Jules, but she said she didn't know."

"Did you believe her?" Susan asked.

Elle shook her head again. "No, I think she knew, but she didn't want to talk about it."

"I heard Bob caught Sammy window peeping on Jules," Susan said.

Elle nodded. "I heard that rumor, too, but I don't believe it."

"Did you talk to Brian after the family meeting last night?" Susan asked.

"Why would I talk to Brian?" Elle felt her face grow hot.

"Come on, Elle. I saw you and Brian kissing down by the dock a few days ago. I know you have something going on with him."

"It's none of your business." Elle kept her voice low and controlled.

"I don't care what you do with Brian," Susan said. "I just want to know if he said anything to you about the family meeting."

"We didn't talk," Elle said. "What are you getting at, anyway? Brian wouldn't hurt his parents."

"He might if he thought they were planning to sell the lodge to someone else. He's supposed to inherit it," Susan said.

"How do you know that?"

"It's not a secret," Susan said. "I heard him and Bob fighting about it the other day. I heard Brian tell his dad that he couldn't sell the lodge because it was supposed to be his someday, and Bob said he and Jules need money now, and they'd sell it if they wanted to sell it."

"If anyone in the family hurt Jules and Bob, it was Deb," Elle said. "I heard them tell her if she didn't get her act together, she wouldn't inherit anything from them."

"Or her crazy boyfriend," Susan said. "Jason is scary."

"Listen," Elle said, "we don't know what happened, so don't tell the troopers any of this."

"Don't you think they should know who we suspect?"

"I don't suspect anyone," Elle said. "I can't believe anyone I know could do something like this."

"I guess the killer could be a stranger."

"Or it could be Tim Fairweather."

"Or the fisherman who got into a yelling match with Bob the other day," Susan said.

"You didn't tell me about him." Elle liked the idea that the murderer was a stranger.

Susan shrugged. "Bob told me not to mention it because he was afraid it would upset Jules."

"What happened?"

"It was after Bob returned one evening," Susan said. "He brought the guests into shore and then took me back out to the boat to help him fillet fish. We were working when a commercial salmon seiner pulled up beside us, and the captain started screaming swear words at Bob."

"Why?"

"He said Bob dropped anchor and started halibut fishing right in his way when he was making a set."

Elle thought it sounded like something Bob might do. He didn't like most commercial fishermen and seemed to enjoy flexing his muscles in front of them to let them know he thought he belonged here, and they didn't.

"What did Bob say when the guy yelled at him?" Elle asked.

"He laughed and told him to get lost."

Elle stared at Susan for several moments. "I think you should tell the troopers about the encounter," she said.

Susan sighed. "I guess. I can see why the captain might want to punch or maybe even kill Bob, but why would he kill everyone else?"

"You don't know anything about the guy," Elle said. "Maybe he's a psychopath and enjoys killing people."

Elle and Susan sat quietly for several minutes. Elle listened to the big wall clock tick while she wondered if she knew the person who had committed these horrible crimes. Finally, she said, "Who do you think killed Bob and Jules?"

Susan's gaze dropped to the floor for several seconds, and then she looked at Elle, her eyes wide. "I don't know," she said, "but I have to ask you something."

"What?"

"Why did you have so much blood on you?"

"What do you mean?"

"Why did your clothes have so much blood on them?"

Elle stood and took several paces away from the couch. She turned and faced Susan, tears streaming down her face. "Just say it, Susan. You want to know if I killed them, don't you? Say what you mean." Elle's voice quivered.

Susan said nothing but looked straight into Elle's eyes.

"I was bloody because I went into their bedroom and touched them," Elle said. "Bob was on his back, so I started CPR on him to see if I could save him." A sob escaped her, and she quickly covered her mouth with her hand. "Why weren't you bloody? Didn't you try to help the guests when you went to the cabin?"

Just then, the front door opened, and four troopers, their arms laden with gear, entered the great room. One of the troopers (his name tag said Reeves) followed them into the house and pointed toward Jules and Bob's bedroom. "Sergeant Patterson is in there," he said. "I think he'll want the two of you to go up to the guest cabin. We have more bodies up there."

One of the other troopers shook his head. "This is a massacre," he said.

CHAPTER 4

Saturday, September 6th

10:27 a.m.

Patterson and Peter Boyle stood in Jules and Bob's bedroom, afraid to move. There was so much blood in the room that they couldn't take a step without contaminating the crime scene. Patterson snapped several photos of the room from his vantage point by the door, but he needed to move closer to get photos of the victims. Both he and Peter had donned boot covers and nitrile gloves before entering the room, and now, he stepped carefully toward the bed, attempting to avoid the blood spatters.

The killer had beaten the heads of both victims so severely that they were barely recognizable as humans. He could only assume the couple in the bed were Bob and Jules Bartlett. Nothing he'd seen yet contradicted this identity of the victims, but what if Bob had caught Jules in bed with someone else and had beaten them both to death? He needed to keep an open mind at this early stage in the investigation.

Patterson fought back nausea while he photographed the victims. Blood matted the woman's long, dark hair. She lay on her stomach, with her smashed-in face turned to the side on the pillow. Much of the left side of her head and face were missing. Elle said she'd touched the bodies, so he would need to check with her and find out how the bodies had been positioned when she found them. From the looks of the damage to Jules Bartlett, though, Patterson guessed she'd been sleeping in this position when someone bludgeoned her with a sharp object. She must have been murdered in her sleep. *At least she never saw what was coming.* Patterson guessed she was the first victim. The man lay on his back with his arms over his head as if he had tried to fend off the blows.

"Do you see a murder weapon?" Patterson asked Peter.

"No, sir," Peter said. He still stood by the door, and when Patterson glanced back at him, he noticed how pale he looked.

"You okay?"

"Yes, sir," Peter said. "It's just that …" He paused. "I've never seen anything like this."

"Me either," Patterson said. "These two don't even look human. I'd say the killer used an ax. It's the only weapon I can think of that could inflict this much damage."

"Yes, sir," Peter said again.

Patterson continued to snap photos, and then he and Peter stood in the room, trying to move as little as possible while still getting a feel for the crime scene.

A knock sounded on the bedroom door, and Peter opened it. "Crime scene is here, sir," he said to Patterson.

Patterson let out a long breath, relieved to have an excuse to get out of this room for a while. The crime scene crew consisted of two techs and two young troopers. He'd rather have all crime scene specialists for a scene this big, but most of the techs had the weekend off.

"Jill," Patterson said to Jill Clafflin, the senior tech in the group, "I'd like you to take charge of this scene. Andy," he said with a nod to one of the young troopers, "you assist, and Peter, I want you to stay and help as well." He looked Jill in the eyes. "We can't afford any mistakes here. Take your time. This scene will require at least the rest of the day to analyze."

Jill's spine straightened. "Yes, sir," she said. Her eyes swept the room, and she turned back to Patterson. "I've never seen anything like this," she said.

"None of us has," Patterson said. "We need to put the monster who did this in a jail cell, and I'm counting on you to find crucial evidence in this room. I took some photos, but I want you to take more.

You're good at what you do, so take this scene apart piece by piece. Be thorough and take your time."

"Yes, sir," Jill said.

"I'll be back in a few minutes. Joe and Patrick, come with me," Patterson said, referring to another crime scene tech and a state trooper. He left the room and carefully shut the door.

Patterson felt guilty about leaving Peter in the room. Patterson wanted fresh air, and he knew from observing his pale face that the other trooper could also stand to step outside and catch his breath. Still, Patterson wanted an observer to stay in the room from the moment the crime scene techs began their analysis until they finished, and poor Trooper Boyle was the person tasked with this responsibility. He would give Trooper Sara Byram the same job in the guest cabin.

Patterson removed his gloves and boot coverings. He pulled a garbage bag from his pocket and unfolded it, then stuffed his soiled gloves and boot coverings into it. He left the bag outside the Bartletts' bedroom door and then nodded to Joe, the other crime scene tech, and motioned to Trooper Patrick Little. "The rest of the victims are in the guest cabin."

Patterson noted that Elle and Susan were sitting quietly on the long couch in the great room. He opened the front door and asked Gary Reeves how things were going.

"Quiet so far, sir," he said.

Patterson followed the marked trail around the side of the main cabin and up a small hill. The trail wound through the trees and into an opening that revealed a log cabin with large windows and two porches on the front. Patterson and the techs stopped on one of the porches and donned clean boot covers and nitrile gloves.

"Mark, Sara?" Patterson called as he opened the door and stepped into the cabin. He stood in front of two twin beds, each with a human form under the covers.

"Sir," Mark Traner called from one of the other bedrooms, "we're in here."

Patterson heard footsteps as Mark crossed to their side of the cabin. "No pulses. They're all dead, sir. We checked."

Patterson nodded at the two beds. "This scene looks much cleaner than the scene in the house. How were they killed?"

"Single gunshot wound to the head," Mark said. "Three through the side of the head, two through the back of the head, and one through the front. I think the killer shot them on whichever side was convenient."

"In other words," Patterson said, "three were sleeping on their sides, two on their stomachs, and one on his or her back."

"Yes, sir, and that's not all," Mark said.

"What else?" Patterson asked when the trooper failed to continue.

"I think the killer shot through a pillow to muffle the sound. In the third bedroom, we found a pillow with several holes and gunshot residue. Except to check for pulses, I didn't touch the victims, but I saw feathers in at least some of the wounds."

"Interesting," Patterson said. "A pillow would muffle the sound of the gunshot. Maybe that explains why no one heard the shots and woke up."

"Still," Trooper Little said, speaking for the first time, "they must have been sound sleepers not to hear something."

"Were the doors to the bedrooms closed when you entered the cabin?" Patterson asked.

"No, sir," Mark said. "All the interior doors were open."

"From what Elle told me, these three couples were strangers," Patterson said. "I have to think they must have closed their bedroom doors for privacy."

"Maybe the killer opened them," Patrick said.

"Or Susan," Sara said as she entered the room. "Elle sent Susan up to check on the guests, and she probably walked through the cabin and opened the bedroom doors."

"I'm not sure it matters," Patterson said, "but I'll ask Susan if the doors were opened or closed when she entered the cabin this morning to check on the guests. If they were closed, and I assume they were when the killer entered the cabin, then the guests in the second room might not have heard the shots in the first room."

"Possibly," Mark said, "but the second victim in each room should have heard his or her sleeping companion get shot."

"If they didn't, they sleep better than I do," Sara said with a grim chuckle.

"I'll leave you guys to analyze the scene," Patterson said. "Joe's in charge, so please carefully follow his instructions, and don't forget to dust for prints on the doorknobs. Sara, I want you to stay here to observe and help where needed. Joe, take plenty of photos, and as I told Jill at the other scene, take your time. We must do this right so it'll stand up in court. Whoever did this needs to spend his or her life in a jail cell, and our crime scene analysis must be beyond reproach."

"Mark," Patterson added, looking at the trooper, "I want you to come with me and help me hunt down some possible suspects."

"Yes, sir," Mark said, and Patterson knew he was happy to be relieved of crime scene duty.

When Patterson and Mark rounded the corner of the main cabin, Patterson heard Gary arguing with another man. As they got closer, they saw a tall, muscular young man facing off against the trooper.

"It's my house. You can't keep me out of it," the man said.

"Sir, if you'll just wait until my sergeant returns," Gary said. He glanced up and nodded at Patterson. "Here he is now."

The man turned toward Patterson. "What's going on here. What happened?" he asked.

The young man was no more than twenty-five. He towered over Gary, and Patterson guessed he must have been at least six foot three. His lean, muscular frame suggested a physical occupation.

Patterson held out his hand, and the man shook it. Patterson calmly introduced himself and Mark. The man's pale-blue eyes darted back and forth between the two troopers.

"I'm Brian Bartlett," he said. "My parents own this lodge. Where are they? What happened here?"

Brian seemed confused by the situation, but Patterson watched his reaction as he gave him the bad news about his parents.

Brian ran his fingers through his short and curly blond hair but said nothing and showed no emotion of any kind. *Is he in shock, or is he trying to decide how he should react?* Patterson knew people handled bad news in various ways, but a lack of emotion always made him suspicious. Brian's eyes locked on Patterson's for several moments before his gaze dropped to the ground.

"Are you okay, sir?" Patterson asked.

Brian seemed to suddenly remember Patterson was there. He looked up and shook his head as if trying to clear his thoughts. "I'm okay," he said. "How were they killed?"

"We're not sure yet," Patterson said, "but their six guests were also murdered."

"What about Elle and Susan? Are they okay?"

Patterson nodded. "They weren't harmed."

"Who would do something like this?"

"We're hoping you can help us answer that question," Patterson said. "When was the last time you saw your parents?"

"Last night," Brian said. "My sister and I had dinner with them, and then we had a family meeting."

"Your sister Debbie?"

Brian nodded. "I left about eight p.m. Debbie was still here when I left. I'm a commercial fisherman, and I anchored my boat near here."

"Did your sister spend the night?"

"No," Brian said. "I saw her leave in her skiff around eight thirty or nine. She works and stays at the cannery."

"The Aktuvik Fresh Seafoods Cannery?"

Brian nodded. "I'd better go there now and tell her the bad news."

"We'll give her the news, sir," Patterson said. "We'd like you to come in and sit down. We have more questions for you."

Patterson was about to usher Brian into the lodge's great room when he heard the outboard motor of an approaching boat. He walked toward the dock, leaving Mark, Gary, and Brian Bartlett standing by the front door.

Patterson reached the dock just as a heavyset man in his fifties awkwardly crawled from his aluminum skiff and tied it to the cleats on the opposite side of the dock from where Patterson's plane sat.

The man stood straight, stretched his back, and noticed Patterson. He held out his hand, and Patterson recognized him.

Patterson nodded. "Bart," he said. "I'm glad you're here. I assume you heard about our little problem." Bart Miller was the Village Public Safety Officer, or VPSO, of nearby Kanuk Bay, a small Alutiiq village of approximately one hundred people.

Bart nodded. "I called into the trooper station in town to report a domestic dispute in Kanuk Bay, and Brie told me about the murders here at the Bartletts' lodge. Is it true? Are there eight people dead?"

Patterson blew out a breath and nodded. "I'm afraid so, and I sure hope you can point us toward a possible killer."

"Have you talked to Sam Lutz yet?"

"The neighbor?" Patterson asked, recalling Susan's comments about Sammy, their neighbor.

Bart nodded. "He and Bob had quite an argument a few weeks back. Bob caught Sam spying on his wife, Jules. Bob said Sam was watching Jules with binoculars when she was in the bathroom showering. Bob reported it to me, and I talked to Sam. Sam, of course, denied he was spying and said he was watching a buck up behind the cabin. I asked Bob if he wanted to file a report, but he declined. He did say he'd press charges against Sam if it happened again, though." Bart shook his head. "He told Sam to stay away from the lodge. I know Sam was quite upset because he and Bob had been good friends, and Sam even worked at the lodge as a fishing guide part-time when Bob needed him."

"How far away from here does Sam live?" Patterson asked.

"Not far—a little over a mile by boat, but less than that if you walk through the woods. I'll give you a ride if you want to interview him."

"Just a minute," Patterson said. He walked up the trail several steps and called to Mark.

The trooper quickly joined Patterson and Bart on the dock, and Patterson asked the VPSO to repeat his story to Mark about the conflict between Bob Bartlett and Sam Lutz.

"I'd like you and Bart to head to the Lutz cabin and interview Sam," Patterson said. "Be on your guard, though. Anyone crazy enough to murder eight people won't hesitate to kill a VPSO and an Alaska State Trooper."

"Yes, sir," Mark said.

Patterson heard the outboard motor start as he headed back up the trail to the main lodge. When he arrived at the front door, Brian Bartlett and Gary Reeves stood watching him.

Patterson nodded to Gary to open the door, and Patterson and Brian walked into the lodge.

As soon as Elle saw Brian, she jumped up from the couch and hurried toward him. She started to put her arms around him, but Brian stopped her. He grabbed her by both biceps and held her away from him. Patterson found the interaction curious. He didn't yet understand the relationships between the people, dead and living, at this lodge, but he would dissect these bonds until he found the person or persons who'd hated the Bartletts enough to bludgeon them to death in their bed.

CHAPTER 5

Saturday, September 6th

11:28 a.m.

"Why don't you sit down, Brian," Patterson said. "Elle and Susan have already given me some background information about your parents, but if you're up to it, I'd like to hear what you have to say about your mom and dad and their lodge."

"I guess," Brian said. He lowered his frame into a chair by the large window. "What do you want to know?"

Brian still seemed oddly unemotional, but Patterson tried not to read too much into his behavior. He'd seen investigations go sideways because the responding officers thought the victim's supposed loved one had exhibited inappropriate behavior. Maybe Brian internalized his emotions, or perhaps he was a psychopath. For now, Patterson mentally filed away Brian's lack of tears.

"When did your parents start this business? Did they build the main lodge and the cabins themselves?"

Brian nodded. "Yeah, my dad is—or was—a workaholic, and he expected Mom and Deb and me to work as many hours as he did. They bought the land in the late nineties, and it had a small cabin on it. My dad worked at a car dealership in town, and Mom was a teacher. She taught high school English. They originally bought this place so we would have a family getaway in the summer." Brian shrugged. "Like everything else in his life, though, Dad had to turn this into a business, and both Debbie and I hated coming out here when we were kids."

"Why is that?" Patterson asked.

Brian sank back into the overstuffed chair. "Instead of fun, this place was work. As soon as we were old enough to carry a two-by-four, Dad had us hauling lumber. We'd finish one building, and he'd start the next. When we completed the guest cabin, he started booking guests. He booked sport anglers and wildlife viewers in the summer and hunters in the fall. Debbie and I looked forward to the start of school every year, so we'd have time to play."

"What about your mom? Did she continue to teach?"

"Oh, no," Brian said. "Dad made her quit teaching so she'd be here to cook for the fall hunters. She did some substitute teaching in the spring, but she missed teaching her own class, and she didn't like cooking."

"When did they start hiring a cook?" Patterson nodded his head toward Elle.

"About ten or eleven years ago, I guess," Brian said. "The business started doing well, and once Dad ran out of things to build and had a boat he liked, they began putting money in the bank. Mom flat out told him she wasn't cooking anymore, and they hired a cook. A few years ago, they started hiring a camp helper too."

"What about guides?" Patterson asked. "Did your dad do all the guiding?"

"No," Brian said. "He hired three guides for the hunting season. I helped him as a fishing guide for a while, but he didn't think he needed to pay me much, so once I turned eighteen, I started working as a commercial fisherman."

"When you left, who did he hire?"

"Mom helped him on the boat when he needed it, and sometimes he'd hire Sam Lutz. He lives a couple of miles from here." Brian motioned toward Susan. "The camp helper is supposed to help fillet and package the fish the guests catch."

"Were your parents happy running this business?" Patterson asked.

Brian gazed off into space and remained quiet for so long that Patterson wasn't sure he planned to answer the question.

"I think they were fairly happy with the business for several years," he finally said, "but Dad was not a people person, and this place was never Mom's dream. They were talking about selling."

"When you say your dad was not a people person, what do you mean?"

"Dad had a short fuse and thought his opinions were the only ones that mattered." Brian laughed. "He'd argue with the guests sometimes and mortify Mom."

"Did he lose his temper with your mom?"

Brian nodded. "Yeah," he said. "He could be a total jerk to Mom. To be honest, I don't know why she didn't leave him a long time ago."

"Was he ever physically violent with your mother?"

"No, no," Brian said, "nothing like that. He'd just yell at her and put her down. He made her cry regularly."

"Was she considering a separation or divorce?" Patterson didn't see how the relationship between Bob and Jules could weigh on this investigation. He knew what he'd seen in the Bartletts' bedroom was not a murder-suicide, but he also knew marriages often involved more than two people, and he was still too near the beginning of this investigation to foresee the twists and turns it might take. At this point, he needed to listen and learn about the victims.

"I don't know." Brian shrugged and looked at the floor. "She didn't say anything to me, but maybe she talked to Debbie about it. Although I doubt it. They haven't been close in a few years."

"Why weren't they close?"

Brian's eyes widened, and Patterson could feel him withdraw. "Just teenage stuff," he said. "Nothing serious."

"What about you?" Patterson asked. "How did you get along with your parents?" He knew he'd erred by asking Brian about any issues between Debbie and their mother. He had hoped to smoothly transition into questioning Brian about his relationship with his parents, but now, Brian was on guard.

Brian sat forward in his chair, a frown on his face. "We didn't have problems," he said. "I was planning to buy the lodge from them."

Interesting. "You want to run this place? I thought you hated it."

"I told you that when I was a kid I hated it." Brian's voice rose a notch. "We all grow up and realize we love what we thought we hated, right? Besides, this is much easier work than commercial fishing. If I raise a family out here," he continued, "I won't make them work all the time."

"Do you have any idea who hated your parents enough to murder them?"

"No," Brian said. "No one would do this."

"Sir," Trooper Andy Marrs said as he stood in the hallway leading to the Bartletts' bedroom, "Jill would like a word with you."

Patterson nodded and excused himself. He glanced down at the young trooper's feet and felt a wave of relief to see that he had remembered to remove his boot covers. Jill had probably reminded him. Now, Andy handed Patterson a clean pair of boot covers, and both men donned them as well as nitrile gloves before pushing through the door and into the crime scene that Patterson wished he'd never have to look at again.

Peter Boyle was dusting the bedroom surfaces for prints while Jill photographed the now-exposed bodies in the bed. They had placed the bloody top sheet in an evidence bag.

"Sir," Jill said as she looked up from her work, "we found this." She pointed to a bloody ball in the center of the bed between the two bodies.

"What is it?" Patterson asked.

"I think it's a cat or a very small dog."

"The murderer killed the cat?" he asked. The bizarre act added another level of brutality to this crime.

CHAPTER 6

Saturday, September 6th

11:47 a.m.

Brian stared straight ahead as Sergeant Patterson followed the other trooper to his parents' bedroom. Elle waited until Patterson had left the room and then hurried to the chair where Brian sat. She didn't care if Susan saw her showing affection for Brian because her heart ached for him. She knelt on the floor beside him.

"Are you okay?" she asked.

Brian slowly turned his head to look at her. "I'm fine," he said. "I just need time to think."

"This is so terrible. I'm sorry."

Elle placed her hand on Brian's arm, but he shook free from her grasp. "Leave me alone, Elle. This isn't the time."

Elle remained kneeling for several seconds while tears cascaded down her face. Finally, she stood and returned to her spot on the couch. She could feel Susan's eyes on her, but she didn't look at the girl. Elle pulled a tissue from her apron pocket and wiped her tears and blew her nose.

Elle, Susan, and Brian sat in a strained silence, punctuated only by the ticking of the large wall clock.

Ten minutes later, Patterson returned to the great room, a frown clouding his face.

"Did your parents have pets?" he asked Brian.

"A stupid white cat," Brian said and then shook his head. "Dad showed that cat more affection than he ever showed his kids."

"Why do you want to know about the cat?" Elle asked in a small voice.

"The crime scene techs found a bloody white animal in the bed with Jules and Bob," Patterson said.

This news was too much for Elle to bear. "Not Snowball," she said. Her tears turned into gulping sobs, and she could barely breathe. Next to her, she heard Susan softly crying. They both loved Snowball.

Elle didn't realize Patterson had left the room until he was forcing a glass of water into her hands a minute later.

"Are you okay?" he asked.

"No," Elle said, but she sipped the water and fought to get her emotions under control.

"Snowball never hurt anyone," Susan said.

"Are you suggesting Bob and Jules hurt people?" Patterson asked as he sat on the arm of the couch beside Elle.

Elle glanced at Susan's wet face and runny nose, and she dug a clean tissue from her apron pocket and handed it to the girl.

"I didn't mean that," Susan said. "I just meant Snowball was an innocent animal."

"The crime scene tech thinks, and I agree with her," Patterson said, "that Snowball was in the wrong place at the wrong time. The killer likely had no idea the cat was under the covers."

Elle recalled Susan's earlier statement about Snowball and turned to her. "How did you know Snowball was dead?" she asked.

"What?" Susan said.

"You said you thought Snowball was dead," Elle said. "How did you know?"

"I didn't know," Susan said. "I just hadn't seen her this morning, and she's always here for her breakfast."

As Elle's and Susan's sobs subsided, Patterson slowly stood and walked back to sit in the chair across from Brian.

Elle looked at Brian. He seemed lost in thought, oblivious to Susan's and Elle's reactions to the news about Snowball.

Patterson stared at Brian for several seconds and then said, "Brian, you were about to tell me about issues you had with your parents."

Brian focused on Patterson and seemed to pop back into the room. "No," he said, his voice level and controlled, "I told you I got along great with my parents."

Elle watched Brian's hands tighten on the arms of his chair and wondered why he was lying to the sergeant. *Does Brian think Sergeant Patterson suspects him of the murders? Or is he lying because he did kill his parents?* Elle immediately pushed the last thought from her mind. Brian couldn't kill anyone, and while she knew he and his dad sometimes argued, he loved his dad and was even closer to his mom. He would never kill them.

Patterson said nothing for several moments. Elle expected him to continue to press Brian on his relationship with his parents, but the sergeant suddenly switched to another topic, one that made Elle queasy.

"We won't know until the medical examiner performs the autopsies on your parents' bodies," Patterson said, "but our crime scene tech told me she believes the murder weapon was an ax or something similar. Do your parents have an ax?"

"Of course," Brian said. "They need an ax to chop firewood and clear trails."

"Do you know where they keep it?"

Before Brian could answer, Susan said, "It's by the woodpile; I can show you."

Patterson nodded to Susan. "Okay, why don't you take me to it."

Susan stood, smoothing her long skirt before crossing to the door. Patterson followed behind her, and the two left the lodge.

Elle hoped Brian would talk to her once they were alone, but he seemed lost in his own world.

"Are you okay?" she asked.

He whipped his head in her direction, his eyes dark and angry. "Don't tell the troopers anything."

"I didn't," Elle said.

"We need to keep our distance from each other now, okay?"

"Why?" she asked. Her voice trembled, and she fought back the tears.

"It's just best."

"Okay," Elle said. She wiped her eyes and stared at her lap. She felt as if she were having the worst nightmare of her life, and she hoped she would wake up soon.

The door opened a few minutes later, and Patterson and Susan walked into the great room. Patterson held an ax by the handle, his hands clad in nitrile gloves.

"I'll be back in a minute," he said. "I need to give this to the crime scene techs to bag."

"Does it have blood on it?" Brian asked Susan once Patterson was out of earshot.

"I didn't see any," she said, "but Sergeant Patterson said they could do tests on it in a lab and find the tiniest traces of blood."

"What about the ax with the blue handle?" Brian asked. "Do you know where Dad keeps it?"

Both Susan and Elle shook their heads. "I've never seen an ax with a blue handle," Susan said.

"You should tell Sergeant Patterson about the other ax," Elle said.

"I'm not telling him anything," Brian said, "and neither should you."

CHAPTER 7

Saturday, September 6th

11:46 a.m.

VPSO Bart Miller and Trooper Mark Traner climbed from the small aluminum boat and stood on the rocky shore. "The tide is high about now," Bart said to Mark. "The boat should be okay here for a bit, but I'll have to put it out on the running line if we stay here long." He grabbed the anchor out of the boat, placed it on the bow, and shoved the boat away from shore while holding on to the anchor line. Once the boat had floated several feet from shore, the VPSO jerked the line and pulled the anchor from the bow into the water. He then tied the anchor line to a tree. He nodded to Mark and led him up a set of wooden stairs to the top of a bluff. Mark saw Sam Lutz's small, brown cabin sitting nearly hidden by the yellow alders and willows.

Sam didn't seem to notice their arrival, and they heard him before they saw him. He and Bart headed in the direction of the whacking noise, and they found Sam busy splitting logs behind the rear of the cabin.

"Sam!" Bart called over the crack of the ax.

Sam stopped chopping and slowly turned to face the two men.

"Bart," Sam said. "I didn't hear you. You need to be careful, sneaking up on a guy like that."

Sam wiped his right hand on his Carhartts and then extended it to Bart, whom he seemed to know. Sam had removed his red plaid shirt and baseball cap for the sweaty job of chopping wood. He'd draped the shirt over a nearby stump, and the cap sat squarely atop

36

the shirt. Sam's naked torso exposed well-formed muscles and little body fat. His head was bald, and a jagged scar spanned the width of his forehead.

"This is Trooper Mark Traner," Bart said.

Sam and Mark shook hands, and Mark noted Sam's dark-brown eyes and full black beard and mustache.

"What brings an Alaska State Trooper out here?" Sam asked, frowning at Mark. "I've heard quite a bit of air traffic this morning and wondered what was going on."

"Yes, sir," Mark said. "I'm afraid we have some bad news about your neighbors."

"The Bartletts?"

"Yes," he said. "They were murdered sometime during the night."

"No." Sam took a step back. "Bob and Jules?"

Mark nodded. "And their six guests."

"What about the kids?"

"Brian and Debbie weren't there," Bart said.

Sam locked eyes with Mark, and he saw tears snake down his cheeks. "Elle and Susan?" he asked.

"They were upstairs," he said, "and the killer didn't harm them."

"My God," Sam said. "Who could do such a thing?"

"We hoped you could help us answer that question."

"I don't know what I can tell you."

"We understand you and Bob Bartlett argued recently," Mark said.

Sam glared at Bart and then looked at Mark and let out a long breath. He grabbed his shirt, slid his arms into the sleeves, and buttoned it, then popped his hat on his head. "Let's go in my cabin and have a cup of coffee."

Sam's cabin was small but tidy. Mark noted a sink and a compact stove and oven in the tiny kitchen. Wooden pegs jutting from the wall held coffee mugs, and Sam grabbed two of the cups and filled them from a coffeepot sitting on the stove.

He nodded to the mug as he handed it to Mark. "Should still be hot. I made it a little while ago." He gave Bart another cup of brew and told the two men to take a seat.

An oil stove sat in the corner of the other room of the cabin, and Mark thought about how little oil it would take to keep a place this size warm. A couch and two stuffed chairs filled most of the room. The furniture appeared worn but comfortable. A small table and wooden chair were tucked under the lone window in the room, and a laptop sat open in the middle of the table. Mark took the stuffed chair nearest the door, and Bart sat in the other chair. Sam carried his cup of coffee into the room and sat on the couch.

Sam glanced at Bart and then at Mark. "I don't know what Bart told you, but I wasn't peeping on Jules." Sam shook his head. "The idea is preposterous, and I told Bob he was acting ridiculous. I like Jules," Sam said, not seeming to notice his mistake at using the present tense. "Jules is sweet and funny and smart, and yes, she's good-looking. I sometimes feel like a schoolboy in her presence, but I'd never watch her through binoculars in her bathroom. How could Bob think such a thing?"

"What *were* you looking at, sir?" Mark asked.

Sam lowered his coffee mug to the small table by the couch and put his hands over his face. He said nothing for several seconds. Then he dropped his hands, picked up his coffee mug, and took a long swallow. "It's like I told Bart," he said with a nod toward the VPSO, who remained silently listening. "I was watching a big buck behind the Bartletts' cabin. Bob wouldn't believe me, though. He wanted to think the worst of me." Sam shook his head and added, "And after all the years we've known each other."

Sam didn't appear to put much effort into making his lie sound credible, and Mark felt Sam had been on the verge of telling them something, but what was it, and did it pertain to the murders? Sam seemed to have decided to stick with his lie, though, and Mark didn't think he would get the man to change his mind at this point.

"How do you make a living out here?" he asked.

"I'm retired," Sam said.

"From what?"

"This and that."

"Who do you think murdered the Bartletts?" Mark asked.

"Me?" Sam asked. "I have no idea. None at all."

Sam's reply seemed too quick and certain, and again, Mark felt he was holding something back. "What can you tell me about the Bartletts?" he asked.

"They're nice folks," Sam said. "I've lived out here nearly twelve years, so I knew Brian and Debbie when they were kids. I always got along great with them until"—he huffed out a breath—"recently."

"What about the family dynamics?" Mark asked. "Did Jules and Bob have problems? Did they fight with the kids, that sort of thing?"

Sam shrugged. "All families have problems," he said, "but I don't think theirs were any worse than most. Bob could be an ass, and I thought he talked down to Jules at times. I often wondered what she saw in him."

"Did they argue?"

"Not in front of other people," Sam said, "but I could tell when Bob made Jules mad, and she was no shrinking violet. I'm sure she told him what she thought when they were alone."

"How did Bob treat the kids?"

Sam nodded. "He was tough on them. When I first moved out here and met the family, I couldn't believe how hard Bob worked those kids, and they didn't dare talk back to him, at least not then."

"What do you mean by 'not then'?" Mark asked.

"When they got older, neither one of them held back. They'd mouth off to both Jules and Bob, but mainly to Bob. I think they were tired of him working them so hard, and Debbie ..." Sam chuckled. "That girl can swear like a sailor. She's made me blush a time or two. By the time Debbie was fifteen, her parents had lost control of her, and I know they both felt helpless about what to do."

"Did she get into trouble?" Mark asked.

"Oh my, yes," Sam said. "When they were in town, she'd skip school, stay out all night, use drugs and alcohol, and she even got picked up a few times for shoplifting. She's cleaned up her act quite a bit, but she has a ways to go. I don't know what this news about her parents will do to her."

"What about Brian?"

"Brian's a good kid, or I guess I should say a good man," Sam said. "He went through a wild time, too, but he's beyond all that now, I think, and he's looking forward to the future."

"How did he get along with his dad?"

"Not bad," Sam said. "They both have tempers, but I know Bob is proud of Brian." Sam stopped speaking for a moment. "I mean, he was proud of him." Tears spilled from his eyes, and he pulled a handkerchief from his Carhartts and mopped his face. "I can't believe Jules and Bob are gone."

"I'm sorry for your loss, sir."

"I don't want you to get the wrong idea about Bob," Sam said after he'd collected himself. "Most of the time, he was a good guy, but he had a temper. He tended to say what he thought, and he made some enemies. He'd even yell at his paying guests at times. I occasionally worked on his charter boat, and I couldn't believe how he treated his guests."

"But you can't think of anyone who disliked him enough to kill him?"

"I don't know anyone deranged enough to kill Bob and Jules and their six guests."

Mark and Bart shook hands with Sam and thanked him for his time. Sam promised to contact the troopers if he thought of anything that might be useful to the investigation.

Mark and Bart walked down the path to the shore. Mark looked up and saw Sam standing on the edge of the cliff, watching him and Bart as they climbed into the skiff and pulled away from the shore. Mark offered Sam a wave and then sat on the wooden plank seat in the boat.

"What do you think about Sam?" Bart asked a few minutes later.

"He was holding back something."

"Yeah," Bart said. "He wasn't watching a buck behind the Bartletts' lodge."

CHAPTER 8

Saturday, September 6th

12:20 p.m.

Patterson returned to the great room and told Elle and Susan they would not be able to stay at the lodge, at least not for the next few days. "The crime scene techs will need to process the entire lodge."

"Where will we go?" Elle asked, tears again trickling down her cheeks.

"We'll find someplace for you to stay in town," Patterson said. "You don't have to take all your belongings. Take what you'll need for a few days. Once we release the cabin as a crime scene, we'll either let you come back out here and pack your stuff, or we'll pack it for you and bring it to town."

"I want to go home," Susan said.

"We'd like you to stay in Kodiak for a few days," Patterson said, "until we finish our preliminary investigation. You and Elle know more than anyone about what happened at the lodge this summer. We'll need to get separate statements from both of you, and I know we'll have many other questions as the investigation progresses."

"But we still have three more groups of bear viewers scheduled this season," Elle said.

Patterson wasn't sure how to respond to Elle's remark. Her thinking must not have been clear if she thought tourists would want to stay in the lodge so soon after eight brutal murders had taken place there. He doubted anyone would stay in this lodge until the murderer was apprehended.

41

Brian responded to Elle, his tone sharp: "The lodge is closed for the year. I'll contact the remaining guests, and I guess I'll have to scrounge enough money to pay back their deposits."

"And pay us," Susan said.

"Yes, Susan," Brian snapped. "Thank you for reminding me."

Elle began to cry again, and Susan patted her back.

"Once you've packed what you'll need for the next few days," Patterson said to Elle and Susan, "bring your bags back to the great room and wait for me." Patterson glanced at Brian. "I'd like you and your sister to fly to town with us, too, Brian."

"What?" he said. "I'm the captain of a fishing boat. I can't leave and fly to town."

"Brian," Patterson said, not bothering to mask the annoyance he felt, "I'm sure you want to help catch the perpetrator who murdered your parents."

"Well, sure, but ..." Brian began.

"Then we need you to come to town with us," Patterson said, "and I will escort you out of the lodge now. I can't leave you in here until the techs process the building. You can run back to your boat and tell your crew you'll be away for a few days. I'll have the plane warmed up and ready to go in two hours, so you'll need to be back here then."

Patterson expected Brian to object to all or part of what he had just said, but he stood and quietly walked out the front door. Patterson escorted him to the dock and watched him climb into his skiff, untie from the dock, and speed away.

Patterson turned and started back to the lodge, planning to walk up the path to the log cabin and check on the progress of that crime scene investigation. He took several steps, but when he heard an approaching outboard engine, he returned to the end of the dock. As soon as the boat had motored around the rock outcrop that formed the cove's entrance, Patterson saw it was Bart Miller and Mark Traner, returning from their interview with Sam Lutz.

Bart pulled alongside the dock, and Mark jumped from the skiff to tie the boat to the cleats. Patterson offered Bart a hand and helped pull the large man up onto the planked surface.

"Did you talk to Sam?" Patterson asked.

"Yes, sir," Mark said.

"What was your impression of him?"

"He seemed genuinely shocked to hear someone murdered the Bartletts," Mark said, "but neither Bart nor I thought he was telling us the full truth."

"About?" Patterson asked.

"For one thing, about who or what he was looking at when Bob accused him of spying on Jules in the shower."

"Do you think he was looking at Jules?"

"Possibly, but I got the feeling he was watching someone else. I thought for a minute he was going to confess what he was doing, but then he clammed up."

"Interesting," Patterson said. "Was there anything else?"

"I also got the impression he suspected who might want to kill Bob and Jules, but I could be wrong."

"Okay," Patterson said. "We need to keep a close eye on Sam Lutz, and soon, we'll hit him hard with more questions. Except for Brian and Deb Bartlett, Sam Lutz is our most likely suspect."

"Yes, sir," Mark said.

"Right now, I think we should inform Deb Bartlett about the deaths of her parents. Do you mind giving us a ride to the cannery, Bart?"

"At your service," Bart said, and all three men climbed into the skiff. Patterson and Mark untied the boat from the dock, and Bart edged the vessel out into the bay.

The boat ride to the cannery took thirty-five minutes, and after pounding through choppy seas for over half an hour, Patterson's back complained when he stood and jumped from the skiff to the steep cannery beach. Today, he felt older than his forty-five years, and he wondered how old he would feel before he found someone to arrest for the brutal murders at Bear Creek Lodge.

Bart stayed with the skiff while Patterson and Mark trudged up the steep beach to the cannery office. They stepped off the beach onto a wooden walkway and followed it around the building to the office's front door. Patterson pushed open the door, and the young woman sitting at the reception desk in the front office stopped keypunching and looked up expectantly at the two troopers.

"We need to talk with Deborah Bartlett," Patterson said.

"Uh, sure," the woman said. "They're on mug-up—that's coffee break—right now, so she's probably in the mess hall, but she could be in her room or wandering around outside. Just follow this walk to the end, and you'll see the mess hall."

Patterson sighed. The woman could have offered more help with hunting down Deb Bartlett, but how hard could she be to find in a small, isolated cannery?

Fifteen minutes later, he wished he had demanded help from the woman in the office. Deb was not in the mess hall, and he had yet to find anyone willing to tell him where her room was in the dormitory.

He was about to suggest to Mark that they head back to the office when a man in his midtwenties marched up to them and demanded to know why they were looking for Deb Bartlett.

"And who are you?" Patterson asked.

The young man stood about five foot ten and had greasy, shoulder-length black hair secured in a ponytail. He pulled himself up to his full height and strutted up to Patterson. Up close, Patterson noted his mean, beady, black eyes and the large pores on his crooked nose. Muscular arms covered in tattoos protruded from the short sleeves of his black T-shirt. "I ain't got to tell you nothin'," he said.

Patterson reminded himself to breathe. He'd had a bad day so far, and nothing would make him happier than snapping a set of handcuffs on this punk and tossing him into the bottom of Bart's skiff. While it might make him feel momentarily better, though, such a move would not get him any closer to finding Deb Bartlett.

"Deb isn't in trouble," Patterson said, "but I need to pass along some bad news to her."

"Tell me, and I'll tell her," the punk said.

Patterson was quickly reaching his breaking point. "I tell you what," he said to the young man. "You tell me right now where I can find Deborah Bartlett, and I won't arrest you for impeding a police investigation."

Like most bullies, the young man quickly backed down when challenged. He led Patterson and Mark to the small room he apparently shared with Deborah Bartlett.

Deb sat on one of the two beds in the room, reading a book. She sat straight when she saw the troopers enter her room.

"What?" she asked.

Patterson took two steps into the room. "I'm Sergeant Patterson with the Alaska State Troopers, and this is Trooper Traner."

"Look," Deb said, scooting across the bed as far away from Patterson as she could get, "I don't know what my parents told you, but they lied. I didn't steal anything from them."

A bandana secured Deb's shoulder-length blonde hair. She had a thin nose, big, green eyes, and a spattering of acne on her face. The lack of makeup made her look younger than Patterson knew she must have been. Deborah Bartlett wasn't beautiful, but she was pretty. Patterson wondered if she still took drugs. From a quick scan of the room, he didn't see any drug paraphernalia, but she'd need nothing more than a glass of water to swallow pills.

"Is that what this is about? Your parents called the cops?" the young man asked. "Don't say anything, Deb."

Patterson turned on the man. "This conversation is none of your business," he said. "We need to talk to Deborah alone."

"Oh, no," the young guy said, his face turning bright red. "I'm not leaving you alone with her."

"It's okay, Jason," Deb said. "This won't take long."

"I'm not leaving you alone," Jason said.

"Wait outside the door, Jason." Deb kept her voice calm but firm.

Jason's face again blushed scarlet, but he said nothing while he exited the room and shut the door.

"Ma'am," Patterson said, "I have bad news for you. Your parents are dead. Someone murdered them at the lodge."

"Seriously?" Deborah Bartlett asked.

"I'm afraid so," Patterson said. "They were killed either sometime last night or during the early-morning hours."

Patterson expected Deb to cry or exhibit some other expression of grief. Her roar of laughter caught him off guard.

"Ma'am?" he asked and then exchanged a puzzled look with Mark.

"I won't lie," Deb said. "I'm glad they're dead. My brother probably did it. Neither one of us liked them much."

Patterson was so confused by Deb's gleeful response upon hearing about her parents' murders that he wasn't sure what question he should ask next. Finally, he said, "I understand you had dinner with your family last night. What time did you leave the lodge?"

"Oh, I get it," Deb said. "Dear brother Brian pointed the finger at me by making sure you know I left the dinner after he did. They were still alive when I left, and Brian easily could have gone back ashore and killed them."

"Did you argue with your parents last night?" Patterson asked.

"Of course," Deb said. "Arguing is the only way Dad knew how to talk, and Mom was such a little bunny rabbit, she'd never say anything against His Highness."

"What did you argue about last night?"

"You name it," Deb said. "My job, my life, my boyfriend, my hair, my clothes. Everything."

"Is Jason your boyfriend?"

Deb nodded. "Yeah, he's my boyfriend."

"What is Jason's last name?"

"Caine," Deb said. "Jason Caine."

"Did Jason go to dinner with you last night?"

"No." Deb shook her head. "He wasn't allowed in the house. He dropped me off and picked me up when I left."

"Why didn't your parents like Jason?"

"They thought he was a loser. They accused him of giving me drugs, but Jason doesn't do drugs, and I haven't taken any since I've been with him. If my parents ever listened to me, they would know Jason is a good influence, not a bad influence."

"How old are you, Deb?"

"Twenty-two."

"And Jason?"

"Twenty-six. Why?"

"No reason," Patterson said. "We need the information for the report." His answer was only partially true. He wondered why a twenty-six-year-old man was working as a fish processor. While there was nothing wrong with the job, it paid minimum wage. Patterson suspected Deb's parents disliked Jason's lack of initiative as much as anything. Still, he knew cannery work was an honest job, and it certainly beat sleeping on the street.

"Do you have reason to believe your brother might have harmed your parents?" he asked.

Deb shrugged. "Not really. No. Brian couldn't kill anyone. He punched Dad a few months ago, but he would never hurt Mom." Deb's emotions took a 180-degree turn from earlier, and she began to cry.

Patterson glanced at Mark, who shrugged. Patterson felt bone-weary. This investigation was quickly turning into his worst nightmare.

Mark found a box of tissues and handed them to Deb.

"I can't believe they're gone," Deb said. "Dead." She dabbed at her eyes and then said, "I don't think Brian would hurt them."

Jason, who had obviously been standing outside Deb's door, must have heard her crying and burst back into the room. "What is it?" he asked.

The intrusion irritated Patterson, but he forced himself not to respond, and instead, he watched the interaction between Deb and Jason.

"My parents are dead!" Deb wailed.

"What?" Jason pushed past Patterson, sat on the bed beside Deb, and put his arms around her.

"Murdered," Deb said.

"When? You were just there last night," Jason said.

"Sometime during the night, I guess."

Patterson watched the melodrama play out in front of him, but the act seemed over the top to him. Had Deb and Jason murdered her parents when Jason came to pick her up the previous evening? Or perhaps they'd returned to the lodge in the middle of the night to kill them.

"What was the subject of conversation during your family dinner last night?" he asked.

Jason turned his beady eyes on him. "Can't you see she's upset?"

"It's okay, hon," Deb said. "Would you get me a bottle of water?"

Jason glared at Patterson as he stood and then walked out of the room.

"He's a little overprotective," Deb said, sniffling as she wiped her eyes. "My parents wanted out of the lodge business," she added. "A few years ago, when I was in rehab for the umpteenth time, and Brian's future looked shiny and bright, Dad told Brian that he and Mom had decided to leave the lodge to him in their will. They should never have told Brian he would inherit the lodge. This summer, Dad decided he wanted to sell the lodge and retire. He wanted Brian to buy the lodge, but Brian thought they should hand the lodge to him." She shrugged. "I was never going to get anything, so I thought it was only fair Brian should pay for the business."

Did your parents change their wills?" Patterson asked.

"You mean would Brian get the lodge free and clear if he murdered Mom and Dad before they had the chance to sell the lodge to someone else?" Deb shook her head. "I have no idea, but it would certainly give him a motive to kill them, wouldn't it?"

"I get the feeling you don't much like your brother."

"We were close once," Deb said, "but not for several years."

"Deb," Patterson said, "we would like you to fly to town with us and stay there for a few days until we can get this all sorted out."

Just as Patterson was finishing this statement, Jason returned to the room and handed a plastic bottle of water to Deb. "You can't make her go to town," he said. "Hon, you don't have to go with them."

"It's okay," Deb said. "Brian and I need to make funeral arrangements anyway."

"I'm coming with you." Jason looked at Patterson when he said this, and Patterson knew he expected to meet resistance. On the contrary, Patterson wanted Jason in town, where they could get him into an interrogation room by himself. Even if Deb hadn't returned to the lodge to murder her parents, Jason could have gone back to the lodge by himself. It sounded as if there was no love lost between Jason and the Bartletts.

"Do you want me to pick you up here," he asked, "or would you prefer to meet at the lodge?"

"At the lodge," Deb said. "I have one of the skiffs from the lodge, and I don't want to leave it at the cannery."

They said goodbye and went on their way.

"Wow," Patterson said to Mark as they descended the steep beach to the skiff, where Bart stood waiting.

"I think we can conclude the Bartlett family is dysfunctional," Mark said.

Patterson shook his head. "I'm surprised they didn't all kill each other before now."

"There's one thing, though, sir," Mark said. "I can see why Brian or Deb might kill Bob and possibly even Jules, but why did the killer shoot the guests? They were apparently in their cabin asleep, so it wasn't as if the murderer needed to eliminate witnesses."

"Good question," Patterson said.

CHAPTER 9

Saturday, September 6th

12:30 p.m.

Elle sat on the edge of her bed and sobbed. She knew she needed to pull herself together and decide what to pack for the trip to town, but she couldn't think. *Who murdered Bob and Jules and the guests? And Snowball? Why is Brian acting so cold? Did he get into a fight with his parents and beat them to death with an ax?* She didn't believe Brian could murder his parents, but she'd never seen him behave the way he had earlier. Maybe he was just in shock. She wondered what had happened during the family dinner. She'd prepared the food for the guests and then the family, but after the guests had eaten, Jules asked Elle to go to her room so that the family could have a private dinner. Jules said she would clean up the dishes, and she had. The kitchen was spotless when Elle had started making breakfast this morning.

Elle wondered what time the killer murdered Jules and Bob. *Why didn't I hear anything?* She tried to remember what she did after going to her room the previous evening, but her mind drew a blank. Did she watch a movie, or read, or listen to music? Maybe she just went to bed. Why couldn't she remember?

It can't be happening again. She'd been doing so well. Elle grabbed a tissue and scrubbed her face. She refused to doubt herself. She felt fine, and none of this was her fault. Susan must be right, though. Unless the fishing boat captain who'd argued with Bob killed them, or Tim Fairweather with all his guns killed them, then the murderer must be someone she knew well. But the more she thought about

Tim Fairweather and his lunatic wife, the more she believed one of them must be the murderer. No one else could have done something this brutal. Several people might have had a motive to murder Jules and Bob, but no one in this bay had any reason to walk up to the guest cabin and shoot the six guests. Beating Bob and Jules to death and then shooting the guests must have been the work of a psychopath. But if it was Tim Fairweather, then he knew she and Susan were sleeping upstairs. *Why didn't he kill us too?*

Elle rubbed her face again. None of this made sense. She slowly stood and began filling her pack with clothes and other items she'd need in town. She wondered if she would ever return to this lodge. If Brian took over the business, would he rehire her as the cook? *Do I want to work here again?* She loved it here, but she didn't think she'd ever rid herself of the memory of Jules and Bob massacred in their bed.

Patterson had said he would find a place for her and Susan to stay in town for a few days, and then he'd either fly them back to the lodge to pack their gear, or he'd have one of the troopers pack their stuff for them. She knew she should pack all her stuff now so it would be ready to go, but Elle wasn't sure she wanted any of her things. Of course, she would need her computer and phone, and she'd pack her art supplies, but she didn't care about her clothes or aprons or cooking knives. She doubted Patterson would let her remove anything from the kitchen until the crime scene people had looked at it.

Once she'd stuffed her pack with her essentials, she carried it down the stairs and dropped it on the floor by the couch. She wanted a cup of coffee but didn't have the energy to pour one from the carafe in the kitchen.

Elle settled on the couch and waited, wondering where Patterson was. The great room felt huge and lonely. She threw on a jacket and pushed open the front door of the lodge.

"Ma'am," Trooper Reeves said as she pushed past him. "Sergeant Patterson wanted you to stay here."

"I need some fresh air. I'll be right back," Elle said and then hurried down the path and away from the lodge before the trooper could stop her. Once she'd walked into the woods and breathed in the sweet odors of high-bush cranberries and aging vegetation, her mind calmed. As with the other struggles in her life, she would get through this nightmare.

CHAPTER 10

Saturday, September 6th

2:10 p.m.

Patterson didn't try to talk to Bart and Mark during the skiff ride back to Bear Creek Lodge. He had a headache and no desire to make it worse by screaming over the wind, waves, and outboard motor. Once they reached the dock at the lodge and secured the boat, he asked Mark to check on the progress of the crime scene techs.

Patterson turned to Bart. "What can you tell me about Brian and Deb Bartlett?"

Bart blew out a breath. "Brian keeps his head down, and I don't think he's ever been in trouble with the law. Bob was hardheaded, and I think Brian has a stubborn streak too. I know the two of them butted heads occasionally, but I don't think it was anything serious. Deb Bartlett is a different story, though."

"How so?" Patterson asked.

"She's done time for drug possession, shoplifting, and I believe she was picked up once for solicitation in Kodiak, but I don't think she was ever charged for the solicitation. You'll need to check with your buddies at the Kodiak PD to find out for sure, though."

"According to her, she had problems with her parents."

Bart nodded. "Bob and Jules kicked her out and made her get a job. I think the tough-love approach was just what she needed, because I hear she's now clean and sober."

"She claims her boyfriend, Jason, is responsible for getting her off drugs."

53

Bart snorted a laugh. "Jason is the reason she'll probably start using again. He's a loser."

"Does he have a record?" Patterson asked.

"A long one. Check it out when you get back to town. Caine's done time for dealing drugs, robbery, and assault. The next time he goes down, it'll be for a long hitch."

"Do you think he could kill his girlfriend's parents? Deb told us her parents disapproved of Jason."

Bart nodded. "I'd put Jason Caine at the top of your list of suspects. I think he could kill them simply because he hated them, but he'd be more likely to murder Bob and Jules if he thought Deb would inherit money from them. Jason Caine is all about easy money."

"What about Deb?" Patterson asked. "Could she kill her parents, or possibly ask Jason to do the job for her?"

Bart stared at the dock for several seconds and finally shook his head. "I don't know," he said. "Maybe."

"Elle told me she heard a woman on the VHF radio a few nights ago announcing that her husband was armed, dangerous, angry, and looking for someone to shoot. Do you know anything about the incident?"

Bart nodded. "Tim and Georgie Fairweather." He chuckled. "What a pair. I admit, though, at the time, I was worried Tim might head to Bear Creek Lodge to shoot Bob."

"What happened?"

"I don't know. Tim is crazy, but I think Georgie is even crazier. They had a fight, which is nothing new, but it got out of hand. I suspect Tim had too much to drink and hit Georgie. She pulled a gun on him and told him to get out, and then she got on the VHF radio on the frequency everyone in the bay listens to and announced her husband was armed and dangerous."

"And was he?"

"According to Georgie, Tim loaded his boat with guns and ammunition. When I met him as he pulled up to the beach at the cannery, he had two guns and two boxes of ammo. By then, he'd cooled down and seemed fine."

"Do you think his wife wanted to frighten area residents, hoping someone would shoot him?"

"I think it's a good possibility."

"Why didn't you call us in town to request help with the incident?"

"There was nothing to call about, and if I called you every time Tim and Georgie Fairweather got into a fight, you'd never get anything else done," Bart said. "I talked to Tim, and he told me it was just a squabble. He denied hitting Georgie, but I didn't believe him. I told him to stay at the cannery while I headed to their cabin to interview Georgie."

"Was she still angry?"

"She was in the process of cooling down when I got there, and I didn't see any bruises or cuts on her face. I'm sure Tim is an expert at hitting his wife in places where the marks don't show, though. I asked her if she wanted to press charges, but she declined. She said it was a misunderstanding, and she'd already forgiven Tim and wanted him to come home." Bart shrugged. "I wrote an incident report, but there wasn't much else I could do."

"Why did you worry Tim might head to the Bartletts' lodge?" Patterson asked.

"Tim and Bob hated each other," Bart said. "Mind you, most people in the bay dislike Tim, but they keep their distance. I think we're all a little afraid of Tim and Georgie, but Bob wasn't the kind of guy to avoid a confrontation, and neither is Tim. They butted heads several times. The other day when both men were at the cannery, Tim said something to Bob, and Bob slugged him and knocked him down. This confrontation happened two days before the radio incident, so I was concerned Tim might take his guns to Bear Creek Lodge and confront Bob."

"Do you think Tim could be responsible for these murders?"

Bart exhaled a long, slow breath while he stared at the bay past the end of the dock. "Sure," he finally said. "I think Fairweather could have done it. This"—he waved his hand at the Bartletts' lodge—"is the work of a madman. Right? I mean, anyone who disliked Bob could have killed him, but it takes a deranged individual to murder eight people, and Tim Fairweather definitely has a screw loose."

"What about his wife?" Patterson asked. "Do you think she could either help her husband murder eight people or commit the murders on her own?"

Bart slowly shook his head and rested his arms on his big belly. "I don't know, but I don't see her murdering anyone except her husband."

At the sound of footsteps, Patterson looked up to see Mark walking down the dock toward them. "How's it going up there?" he asked.

"Fine, sir. Jill and Joe both said it's slow work, but they're making progress."

Patterson nodded. "I'm flying Elle, Susan, Brian, Deb, and Jason to Kodiak, and then I'll return with camping gear. The techs can process the scene late into the evening and then continue tomorrow. Hopefully, they'll finish it tomorrow. They'll need to spend some time in the other rooms in the lodge, but I think they can get away with lightly processing those rooms."

"Yes, sir," Mark said. "Do you want me to stay and help them?"

"No," Patterson said. "I have another job for you. If Bart doesn't mind, I want him to run you and Gary to the Fairweather cabin, where I'd like you to detain Tim Fairweather and fly him to Kodiak. You, Gary, and Bart should be able to restrain Fairweather, and once you have cuffs on him, you can escort him to town."

"Yes, sir."

"What time is the afternoon mail flight out of the cannery?" Patterson directed the question at Bart.

"It leaves the cannery at five thirty p.m. We should be able to make it."

"Good," Patterson said. He looked at Mark. "If you don't need Gary's help, I'd like Bart to bring him back here. I think someone should guard the lodge all night, and I'll ask the troopers to trade guard shifts through the night."

"Sir," Mark said, "what should I charge Fairweather with?"

"Tell him you're holding him as a material witness," he said. "I know we won't be able to hold him long, but I want to interview him in town at trooper headquarters. I want him to feel the heat and see if he has anything to hide."

"What about Georgie?" Bart asked.

"We might have to interview her separately too," Patterson said, "but for now, I'm just interested in her husband."

"Should we head out now?" Mark asked.

"The sooner, the better," Patterson said. "It might take you a while to find Fairweather."

"I'll get Gary," Mark said, heading up the dock at a trot.

Patterson turned to Bart. "Is there anyone else you can think of who might have committed these murders?"

No," Bart said. "The murderer must either be insane or someone who has something to gain. Don't you think? No sane person batters two people with an ax while they sleep in their bed."

CHAPTER 11

Saturday, September 6th

3:15 p.m.

Patterson sat in the great room of the lodge and listened to the ticking clock. Elle, Susan, and Brian were ready to fly to town, but Deb and Jason had not yet arrived.

Brian stood and paced. "Let's leave them," he said for the third time.

Patterson didn't respond. He'd already twice explained that he wanted Deb to fly to town with them because he felt she and Brian could provide vital information for their investigation. In truth, he wanted Brian and Deb in town so he could interrogate them further to determine if they were involved in murdering their parents. If Brian hadn't already deduced this was Patterson's true intent, though, then Patterson didn't plan to enlighten him.

Patterson was curious to see how Brian and Deb would respond to each other. He doubted they would collapse into a hug and weep for their parents, but would their demeanors be hostile or merely indifferent?

Brian paced the perimeter of the great room, staring at the walls, the paintings, and the shelves of photographs and books. He stopped abruptly at a large walnut gun case and studied it for several seconds.

"Where is Dad's .44 Magnum?" he asked. He turned his gaze on Elle.

Elle shrugged. "I don't know guns."

Patterson stood and walked over to stand beside Brian. The case held twelve long guns, including both shotguns and rifles. Three handguns hung on pegs on the back wall. Patterson noted there was enough room for three more handguns to fit in the case.

"Was the .44 usually mounted on the pegs?" Patterson asked.

"It was right there." Brian pointed at an empty spot on the back wall of the case. "It's a Ruger—a beautiful gun."

"Was it there last night when you were here for dinner?" Patterson asked.

"I didn't notice," Brian said. "It could have been missing for months, and I probably wouldn't have noticed. Maybe Dad put it in the drawer in his nightstand by his bed." Brian shrugged and looked at Patterson. "You'll probably find it there or out on his boat."

Patterson realized they needed to add the Bartletts' charter boat to their list of places to search. If these murders were related to the Bartletts' business, then the charter boat might hold some clues.

He was staring at the gun case, lost in thought, when Susan said in her soft, meek voice, "I forgot to tell you something."

"What?" Patterson's thoughts were so focused on the missing gun that he nearly forgot Susan and Elle were sitting on the couch. "I'm sorry, Susan, what did you say?"

"Earlier, you asked if Bob and Jules had any enemies, and I forgot about something that happened the other day."

"What?" Patterson asked again.

"The other day, after Bob and our guests returned from a day of halibut fishing, Bob brought the guests into shore and then took me back out to the boat to help him fillet fish. We were working when a commercial salmon seiner pulled up beside us, and the captain started screaming at Bob."

"Why?"

"He said Bob dropped the anchor and started halibut fishing right in front of him when he was trying to make a set with his seine. The guy was furious. His face looked bright red, and he was yelling obscenities."

Susan told her story in a monotone, and Patterson wondered if she had exhausted her emotions.

"What did Bob do?" he asked.

"He told the guy to get lost. Bob thought it was funny."

"Did the guy leave?"

Susan nodded.

"Do you know the skipper's name?" he asked.

"No, but the boat was the *Rising Star*," she said.

Patterson looked at Brian. "Do you know the skipper of the *Rising Star*?"

Brian shook his head. "No, I've seen the boat in the bay, but I'm not familiar with the owner or the crew."

"Thanks, Susan," Patterson said. "We'll run down the boat and talk to the captain. I appreciate you telling me about this."

Susan started to say something, but she was interrupted when the lodge's front door burst open.

Patterson walked toward the door, and Jason Caine nearly mowed him down.

"It's about time," Brian said.

Deb marched up to her brother, hands on her hip as she looked up at his face. "Well, they're dead. This precious lodge is yours now."

"Yeah," Brian said, "and they're conveniently dead—hacked up with an ax, no less—before they had time to write you out of their will."

Deb's hands flew to her mouth, and she took a slow step back from Brian. Patterson saw her already pale complexion lighten a shade. "An ax? Someone killed them with an ax?" Her eyes left Brian's face, and she turned a questioning gaze to Patterson.

Patterson nodded. "I'm afraid so."

"I need to sit down," Deb said.

Jason rushed to Deb and guided her to the chair where Brian had been sitting. She bent her head into her hands, and Patterson saw her legs trembling. If this was an act, it was a good one.

"I bet you know how they died, don't you, Jason?" Brian said.

Jason left Deb's side and strode over to Brian. Both men were muscular, but Brian stood several inches taller than Jason. Patterson bet that Jason was the more experienced brawler of the two, though.

"Knock it off," Patterson said. "If everyone's ready to go, let's head down to the dock."

"Wait," Deb said. "I want to see them."

"No," Patterson said. "That's not a good idea, and the crime scene techs are still working in your parents' bedroom."

Jason helped Deb out of the chair and supported her as the pair followed Patterson out of the lodge. Brian, Elle, and Susan followed the rest of the group down to the dock.

Patterson asked Brian to crawl into the front seat, and he put Jason in the sling seat in the rear of the plane. Deb, Elle, and Susan sat on the middle row of seats. Patterson didn't want Brian and Jason to get into a physical altercation in the plane, so he separated the two young men, seating them as far apart from each other as possible.

Patterson handed each of the passengers a headset to protect their ears from the loud engine noise, but he didn't turn on the plane's internal communication system. He'd wait until they were back in Kodiak before he started asking and answering questions. For the next hour, he only wanted to concentrate on flying, and he'd give his five passengers time to think about who had killed Bob and Jules. Was the murderer one of these five young people? Patterson didn't know, but he hoped to catch the killer before he or she struck again.

As they neared Kodiak and flew back into cell phone range, Patterson called Brie at trooper headquarters and asked if she knew of any place in town where Elle and Susan could stay for a few days.

Brie was silent for a few seconds and then said, "They can stay at my place. I have two bedrooms in my little home. I'm taking care of my parents' house while they're on vacation, so my place is empty."

Patterson thanked Brie and asked her to get someone to take over for her for a few minutes so she could drive down to Trident Basin to meet their plane and take Elle and Susan to her house. He told her also to send another trooper to the basin to give Brian, Deb, and Jason a ride to their home.

Once they landed, Patterson secured the plane, and he and his passengers walked up the ramp from the floatplane dock to the parking lot. Patterson would have liked to interview Brian and Deb immediately, but he needed to get back to the lodge. The interviews would have to wait until the following morning. He asked Brian to come to trooper headquarters at 9:00 the next morning, and he set up a meeting with Deb for 10:00 a.m.

"I'll be with her," Jason said.

Patterson looked at Jason and took in his dirty, long hair, sweaty forehead, and beady eyes. He knew psychopaths came in all shapes and sizes, but this guy looked like someone a Hollywood director would cast in the role of a mass murderer.

"I'll interview Deb alone," Patterson said firmly, "but I'd like to schedule your interview for eleven a.m."

"I've got nothin' to say to you," Jason said, hands on hips.

"You're welcome to bring your attorney," Patterson said, turning abruptly and walking toward his trooper SUV. He needed to go to headquarters and grab enough camping gear for the crime scene techs and troopers who'd be spending the night at the lodge. He also needed eight body bags. He planned to bring the bodies back to town with him this afternoon and get them on the plane up to Anchorage to the medical examiner.

CHAPTER 12

Saturday, September 6th

3:00 p.m.

The aluminum skiff pounded against the waves, and Mark felt his spine compress. He'd probably be three inches shorter by the time they reached the Fairweathers' cabin. Mark watched Gary continually shift positions on the rigid boat bench and knew the young trooper was also in pain. As they motored toward the mouth of the bay, the waves grew in size and the beating got worse. Mark glanced at Bart, but the big man seemed oblivious to the conditions. Bart stared straight ahead while his left hand firmly grasped the tiller of the outboard. Thick, gray clouds rolled toward them, obliterating the blue sky. Mark hoped Patterson would make it back to the lodge before the weather got too bad to fly.

After they'd bounced off the waves for fifty minutes, Bart slowly steered the boat ninety degrees to the right and headed up into a small bay. Once the boat was turned sideways to the waves, the pounding stopped, but then it slowly rolled back and forth. After a few minutes, Mark's stomach began to churn, and he feared he would vomit. He stared at the horizon and tried to concentrate on the questions he would ask Tim and Georgie Fairweather. As Bart motored into the bay, the rocking lessened and finally stopped. Mark released a long breath when Bart idled up to the beach, but then he looked at the steep, rocky shoreline and saw a man rushing toward them, a shotgun in his hands.

Mark glanced toward the rear of the skiff to see Bart's reaction to the approaching man, but Bart stood hunched over the outboard engine, busy lifting it so the prop wouldn't hit the rocks.

Mark stood and held up his hands in a gesture of supplication. The man continued to approach, both hands firmly on the shotgun. "You are not welcome on my private property!" he yelled.

Bart turned and faced the man. "Come on, Tim. You know you don't own the beach, and we're just here to talk to you. Put down the gun."

Mark knew they were there to do more than just talk to Tim Fairweather, but he thought it best not to offer this information. Bart was trying to defuse the situation, and his calm, measured tone seemed to be doing the trick. Tim stopped about ten feet from the skiff and lowered the gun. He held the shotgun by the barrel and rested the base of the stock on the beach.

"What do you want, then?" Tim Fairweather asked, his tone still gruff but the volume a notch or two lower.

Mark kept his eyes on Fairweather and climbed over the side of the boat. Gary and Bart followed him, and Bart grabbed the anchor out of the skiff's bow and stomped it with his boot, firmly embedding it into the rocky beach.

"Can we go up to your cabin for a few minutes?" Bart asked. "We'd like to talk to you and Georgie about something."

"What?" Tim barked.

"Something bad happened last night, and we want to tell you and Georgie about it and get your take on it."

"What happened?"

"Please," Bart said. "Let's go up to your cabin, and we'll tell you."

Fairweather glared at Bart for several seconds and then turned and walked toward his cabin.

Fairweather presented an imposing figure. Mark guessed he stood at least six two, and his raincoat didn't mask his muscular physique. From his worn face, Mark placed him in his late forties or early fifties, but not a streak of gray invaded his jet-black hair. He wore his hair short and combed straight back from his forehead. Fairweather's eyes warned Mark of his potential for violence and made him wary of the man. Mark could not distinguish Fairweather's black irises from his pupils, and he could imagine fire shooting from Fairweather's orbs when the man lost his temper.

Bart, Mark, and Gary followed Fairweather to the top of the beach and down a short trail to a large, green cabin. The cabin surprised Mark because it looked more like a home than a place to escape to for a few weeks a year. A wood-planked deck spanned the front of the building, and several large plate glass windows offered a view of the woods and the wind-tossed ocean. Fairweather led the men to a side door that opened onto the mudroom.

While Mark, Bart, and Gary removed their boots, Fairweather called to his wife: "Georgie, we have company!"

A moment later, a small, plump woman appeared from the recesses of the cabin. She wasn't at all what Mark expected after hearing the story of her pulling a gun on her husband and then announcing over the radio that Tim was armed and dangerous and on a possible rampage. Georgie Fairweather had bleached blonde hair with gray roots. Her soft, gray eyes seemed friendly and inviting, and her face showed few wrinkles except around her mouth, where she had the tell-tale lines of a smoker. When she spoke, her quiet voice added to her image of a meek, subservient housewife.

"Hello, Bart," she said. "How are you today?"

"I'm fine, Georgie," Bart said. "These are Troopers Traner and Reeves, and they'd like to talk to you and Tim, if you don't mind."

"Can I get you gentlemen a cup of coffee?" Georgie asked.

All three men gladly accepted the offering of a warm beverage, and once they had their cups of coffee, Tim led them to the main sitting room, where they each settled into a chair.

"Beautiful view," Mark said.

Tim glanced at the window as if he had never noticed the sight of the boiling ocean through the trees.

"I love it here," Tim finally said as he settled on a couch facing Mark, Gary, and Bart. Georgie followed behind Tim and sat on the sofa beside him.

The furnishings in the cabin looked inexpensive but comfortable. Mark noted the cleanliness of the place. The Fairweathers were good housekeepers, but Mark bet the spotless interior had more to do with Georgie than Tim.

"Do you live out here year-round?" Gary asked.

Tim shrugged. "As much as we can. We have a house in town too."

Mark cleared his throat as he prepared to tackle the reason for their visit. "We have some bad news about some of your neighbors," he said.

"We don't have neighbors," Tim said, "and that's the way we like it."

"I am using the term loosely," Mark said. "The Bartletts were murdered last night."

Mark carefully watched Tim and Georgie as he delivered this news. Their reactions would have been comical if the situation weren't so grim. Their responses mirrored each other's. They both sat back, opened their eyes wide, and then slowly turned their gazes on their partner. If he hadn't been watching closely, though, he would have missed what seemed like mutual suspicion of each other.

Neither Tim nor Georgie said anything in response to Mark's words.

Mark let the pair think about the news for a moment and then asked, "Were you two here together last night?"

Again, Tim and Georgie exchanged a look. "I spent the night at the cannery," Tim said.

"Aktuvik Fresh Seafoods?" Mark asked.

"That's the only cannery near here," Tim said.

"Why did you spend the night there?" Mark asked.

"Not that it's any of your business, but I had a problem with my outboard, so I took it over there to have Jim Chase, one of the mechanics, help me fix it. Jim was tied up with some other stuff, so he didn't get to it until after dinner. We worked on it until ten p.m., and I bunked at the cannery for the night."

"They'll let anyone stay there?" Mark asked.

Tim shrugged. "Sure, if they have an empty room. I sometimes beach-seine salmon and sell to the cannery, so they take care of me."

Mark turned his attention to Georgie. "You were here alone?" he asked.

"Yes," Georgie said. "It was nice and quiet."

"Neither of you went near the Bartletts' place?" Mark asked.

Again, Tim's and Georgie's gazes met for only a fraction of a second before they both looked at Mark. "Why would we?" Tim asked.

"I understand you and Bob Bartlett had some misunderstandings," Mark said.

"I hated the guy," Tim said, "but then, I don't like many people." He rubbed his hand through his hair. "Just because I despised Bob doesn't mean I killed him."

Mark observed Tim, but the man betrayed nothing in his expression. "If you were at the cannery last night, you weren't far from the Bartletts' lodge."

"So?" Tim said. "What are you trying to say?"

"Can anyone vouch for you being at the cannery all night?"

"I was with Jim until eleven. We had a drink of whiskey after we finished working on the outboard. Then I went to my room, and I assume Jim went to his. I had an early breakfast at the cannery this morning, and then I came home."

Mark knew he would have to go back to the cannery and question as many people as possible to find out if anyone had seen Tim Fairweather sneak away from the cannery in the middle of the night. Fairweather had just admitted that he hated Bob, and he'd been in the vicinity of the Bartletts' lodge at the time of the murders. Did his wife suspect him? From the glances Georgie gave her husband, Mark thought she might.

"Mrs. Fairweather," Mark said, "did you talk to your husband last night?"

Georgie nodded. "He called me on the radio around nine thirty or ten last night to tell me he wouldn't be home until morning."

"Ma'am," Mark said, "I understand you recently announced over the radio that you and your husband had a fight, and you told the entire bay he was armed and dangerous."

Tim Fairweather jumped to his feet, his face deepening to a dangerous shade of red. "That was nothing," he said. "Just a misunderstanding. Bart and I straightened everything out. Right, Bart?"

"Please sit down, sir," Mark said. He watched Tim until he'd lowered himself back onto the couch. This man had a quick temper, and Mark did not doubt he could be violent if angered. "Mrs. Fairweather," he said, again looking at Georgie, "I'd like to hear your version of the fight."

Georgie stared down at her weathered hands, folded in her lap. "We fight sometimes, but we made up and forgave each other. I don't want to talk about it."

"How did you feel about Bob and Jules Bartlett?"

Georgie's face turned pink, and her hands tightened in her lap. Her words did not match her actions. "They were nice. I'm sorry to hear they're dead," she said in a voice barely above a whisper.

"Sir," Mark said as he reached for his handcuffs and prepared for a physical altercation, "my sergeant wants me to escort you back to Kodiak."

"What, why?" Tim asked as he stood. He looked as if he planned to bolt at any minute. Gary, who'd been sitting and listening intently, jumped from his chair and took a step toward Tim. Bart struggled from his chair and walked to the other side of Tim Fairweather.

"Sir," Mark said, "we only want to ask you more questions, and I'll escort you on the afternoon flight from Aktuvik Seafoods. We can do this the easy way or the hard way. I would prefer not to handcuff you, but I will if you resist."

"You can't force me to go to town."

"Yes, Tim, he can arrest you and hold you for a day or two for questioning," Bart said.

"I don't want to arrest you," Mark said. "I would like you to volunteer to come with me."

Tim punched the back of the couch so hard that Mark was surprised he didn't put a hole in it. After a litany of swear words directed at Mark, he finally agreed to accompany him to the cannery. Mark noticed that Tim didn't even tell Georgie goodbye as they left the cabin.

CHAPTER 13

Saturday, September 6th

5:10 p.m.

Elle ran her fingers through her short hair and then wrapped her arms around herself. Brie's house was small but nice. When Brie had first let them into her home, she ran around the rooms tidying things, but other than being a little cluttered, the place looked clean. Brie had handed Elle a stack of sheets and showed her to the larger of the two bedrooms.

"This is where I usually sleep," Brie said, "so you'll want to change the sheets." She walked to the attached bathroom and sighed. "Let me clean in here a bit, and then I'll go back to work and leave you alone."

"Thanks for letting us stay here," Elle called from the bedroom. "Your home is beautiful."

Brie exited the bathroom a few minutes later and laughed. "My home is tiny, but it's perfect for me. My parents have a beautiful home overlooking the ocean, so while they're away, I'm staying there and watching their two dogs."

Brie led Susan into the other bedroom, and Elle followed. This room was smaller than the master bedroom, and it had no bathroom. The second bathroom was only a few steps down the hall from the bedroom, though, so Susan wouldn't have to walk far to use it.

"Luckily," Brie said, "I recently had company, and I haven't had time yet to pile a bunch of stuff in this room. The sheets are clean, and the bathroom should be relatively clean." She flipped on the bathroom light, looked around the room, nodded, and turned off the switch.

"There's quite a bit of food here, so help yourself," she added. "Either one of my colleagues or I will take you grocery shopping soon."

Brie told Elle and Susan goodbye and gave them her phone number. "Call if you need anything," she said.

When Brie closed the door, silence enveloped Elle, nearly suffocating her. She looked at Susan, who stood mute, also looking lost.

"There's a TV," Elle said, nodding to the corner. They had no television reception at the lodge, so the device seemed like a luxury.

"What do you want to watch?" Susan asked as she began looking for the remote.

"Nothing," Elle said. "I think I'll take a nap. This day has exhausted me, and I want to escape for an hour or two."

"Okay," Susan said.

Susan's head dropped, and Elle could tell she was disappointed to be left alone. Elle didn't care. She had to get away for a while, and she knew what she needed to do to calm her nerves and help her cope.

Elle picked up her pack, retreated to her bedroom, and shut the door. She dropped the bag and leaned against the door. She exhaled a long breath and then inhaled slowly. Elle liked Susan, but the girl always wanted something from her. She was not Susan's mother, nor her sister. Elle's own family wanted nothing to do with Elle, and for a while, Elle had considered Jules and Bob her adopted parents. She'd stopped thinking of them as a family more than a year ago, though. Still, she liked them, and they certainly didn't deserve to be bludgeoned to death. A vision of their bloody bedroom entered her mind, and she quickly pushed it away. With shaking hands, she unzipped her pack and rummaged through the contents until her hand closed around a small, hard leather case. She pulled the case from the bag, hurried to the bathroom, and closed and locked the door.

Elle kicked off her jeans and then sat on the closed toilet seat. She unzipped the leather pouch, and inside, she found her tools. Elle carefully removed the package of razor blades and slid a blade from the pack. She chose a spot on her upper thigh next to other scars from previous sessions. Elle hadn't cut herself in months, but the craving never stopped, no matter how hard she fought against it. Today, she didn't feel guilty about giving in to her desire. She had to cut herself so she could cope with the situation.

Elle placed the blade on her thigh and pushed on it, pulling down her leg for two inches. She didn't hesitate to push the sharp instrument into her flesh; she craved the pain. Elle then removed the blade from her leg, quickly wrapped the blade in toilet paper, and then threw the bundle in the trash can. She placed another wad of toilet paper on her leg to sop up the oozing blood before it dropped onto Brie's bathroom floor. She slid to the floor and leaned against the wall.

The pain felt wonderful and healing. Elle let out a long breath and then softly began to cry. *Why can't I remember what I did last night?* She remembered cooking dinner and serving the guests. She and Susan ate in the kitchen and then began cleaning the pots and pans. They'd placed the dinner plates in the dishwasher, and she recalled Jules asking her to give their family some privacy while they ate dinner together and discussed a few things. Elle agreed, and she and Susan went upstairs to their rooms. *At least, I think I went to my room.* The last memory Elle had was of walking up the stairs, and even her trip up the stairs seemed hazy.

Jules had hurt her feelings by basically telling her to get lost, but she'd complied. *Did I go straight to bed?* It would have only been around 8:30 p.m. when she and Susan cleaned up the kitchen, and while Susan always went to bed early, Elle was a night owl and liked to read or surf the internet. She usually stayed up until at least 11:00 p.m., even though she had to start her day early. Elle did remember feeling tired, though, so maybe she'd flopped on her bed and passed out. She awoke the following morning wearing the same clothes she'd worn the previous day. She hadn't even changed into her pajamas.

Elle dropped the bloody wad of paper in the toilet and grabbed another handful from the roll. She checked her leg. The bleeding had slowed, and soon she would be able to bandage it. She leaned her head against the cool wall and dozed, her mind momentarily calm.

Elle jerked awake several minutes later, confused by the pounding on the bathroom door.

"Are you okay?" Susan called.

Elle looked around and tried to remember where she was. The terrible memories from the day returned in a flash. She looked down at the toilet paper now stuck to her leg and sighed. She'd thought her cutting days were behind her, but here she sat.

Susan pounded harder. "Elle, are you there?"

"I'm here; why?" Elle yelled back and instantly regretted her flash of temper.

Susan let out a ragged sob. "I was just worried about you," she said.

"Sorry," Elle said. "Sorry, sorry, sorry. I didn't mean to yell, but I need some time alone. I think I'll take a nap."

"Okay," Susan said.

Elle thought she heard Susan leave the bedroom. She picked up her small leather case from the floor, found a Band-Aid, and covered the cut on her leg. Then, Elle pulled on her jeans, flushed the toilet, and washed her hands. She walked into the bedroom, quietly shut the door again, and stretched out on the bed. She fell asleep in seconds.

Elle awoke screaming two hours later.

Susan ran into the bedroom, eyes wide. "What's wrong?"

Elle sat on the bed and pulled her knees up tight to her chest. "Nothing," she said. "I just had a bad dream."

"About Jules and Bob?"

Elle nodded but said nothing.

"Do you want to come out into the living room and watch TV with me?"

"In a minute," Elle said.

"Brie called and asked if we wanted to go to the grocery store, but I said no, as long as she didn't care if we ate her food. She said Sergeant Patterson told her he would reimburse her for what we eat. Did you want to go to the store?"

"No," Elle said. "I don't want to go anywhere. I'll come out and watch TV with you in a minute."

Susan nodded and left the bedroom.

Elle leaned against the wall and tried to process her nightmare. She remembered little of it except the part where she was wielding an ax. Elle shuddered as she remembered the dream. She was standing in the middle of the kitchen at the Bartletts' lodge. Blood spattered the cabinets and floor, but she couldn't seem to stop butchering the white, furry cat in the middle of the floor. She put her hands over her face. *How could I dream such a thing? No.* Why *would I dream such a thing?*

CHAPTER 14

Saturday, September 6th

5:25 p.m.

The weather was beginning to deteriorate, and Patterson didn't want to get stuck at Aktuvik Cove in a storm. The forecast called for forty-knot winds tonight, and Patterson knew if he stayed at the Bartletts' lodge, he'd be awake all night, sitting in his plane while it gyrated and pulled against the cleats on the dock. He had planned to spend some time with the troopers and crime scene techs, but because of the approaching storm, he decided he'd load the bodies into the plane and get them back to town as soon as possible. He wanted to ship them up to Anchorage to the state medical examiner's office on the evening jet. Patterson had already called Dr. Libby, a medical examiner he'd worked with in the past and greatly respected. Libby said he would personally do the autopsies on Bob and Jules Bartlett, and he would oversee the posts on the other victims.

Patterson reminded himself to find the contact information for the six guests. The Bartletts must have the details either on their computer or in a file. He needed to contact the relatives of the guests before they heard the news about the murders some other way. So far, the press didn't seem aware of the massacre in an isolated cove on Kodiak Island, but the news would find its way to the media soon enough.

The wind worsened as Patterson flew toward the south end of the island. When he reached Aktuvik Cove, the muscles in his shoulder and neck relaxed a fraction. Wind gusts ruffled the water's surface, but the mountains protected the cove from this wind direction. Only small waves lapped the shore. Patterson maneuvered through the variable gusts as he touched down and then idled up to the dock. Trooper Gary Reeves pulled the plane into the dock and tied it securely.

Patterson stepped out of the cockpit onto the float. He opened the cargo door and "How did it go with the Fairweathers? he asked.

"Fine, sir. Bart just dropped me off back here."

"Did Tim Fairweather give you any trouble?"

Gary smiled. "He wasn't happy about going to town, but he didn't put up a fight."

"Did they make the evening flight?"

Gary nodded. "With time to spare."

"Good. I'll be able to interview Fairweather as soon as I get back to town. How are things moving along here?"

"Fine, sir. Joe said they're making good progress in the cabin, but Jill told me a few minutes ago that their scene will take more time."

"Are they done with the bodies?" Patterson asked as he and Gary carried the body bags up to the lodge.

"I think Joe is, but I'm not sure about Jill."

"I want to get them bagged and back to town so that I can ship them up to the ME's office on the evening jet." Patterson glanced at the sky. "This weather is rapidly deteriorating, and I don't want to get stuck here."

Once they'd stacked the bags inside the main cabin, Patterson told Gary to go back to the plane and unload the camping gear for the crime scene techs and the troopers. They would need to spend the night and carefully look through the rest of the main lodge and other surrounding buildings. Patterson hoped they would finish by the following afternoon, but he didn't want them to rush the job. Precise evidence collection remained essential for convicting the monster who'd murdered these eight people.

"Brie picked up some pizza and sweet rolls for all of you for dinner and breakfast," Patterson said. "I doubt any of you have eaten since this morning. The food's on the front passenger seat."

"Thank you, sir," Gary said. "I don't think any of us have had an appetite, but I'm sure we'll be hungry by evening."

Patterson nodded. He took two steps toward the crime scene in the Bartletts' bedroom, but then he stopped and retraced his steps out the front door. While in a hurry to get back in the air and head toward the town of Kodiak, Patterson wanted to step back from the crime scene and view the big picture. He'd circled the lodge from the air, but he wanted a ground-level perspective.

The Bartletts had cleared the trees and weeds surrounding the lodge and had planted a lawn. Patterson walked around the outside perimeter of the yard and viewed the main lodge and guest lodge from various angles, even stopping to snap a few photos with the official trooper camera he always carried in his pocket. He wanted to reference these photos when considering how an intruder or intruders could have entered and left the grounds. How did he, she, or they kill eight people without awakening Elle or Susan?

Bob Bartlett appeared to have defensive wounds on his hands and arms, but everyone else seemed to have slept soundly through the murders. From the positions of their bodies, the guests had remained undisturbed while the murderer walked among them, shooting them one at a time. Even if the killer fired through a pillow to muffle the sound, the noise should have awoken at least one of the guests. Had they been drugged? He would ask Dr. Libby to run tox screens on the victims.

Patterson examined the outside of the main lodge as he circled it. He stopped when he spotted a small window that he assumed was a bathroom window. Was this the bathroom Bob Bartlett thought he caught Sam watching? From his earlier walkthrough of the main lodge, he'd noticed two bathrooms on the ground floor. One was attached to the Bartletts' bedroom, and the second was situated off the kitchen. The bathroom next to the kitchen only had a sink and toilet, no shower or bathtub. He assumed the master bath had a shower, but he hadn't inspected it because he didn't want to disturb the crime scene.

The window for the Bartletts' bathroom must have been the small window on the ground floor on the right side of the house. Patterson noted an identical small window on the second floor and guessed it was the bathroom Elle and Susan used. Blackout curtains covered the lower window, so if Jules took a shower and closed the window curtains, Sam Lutz would not have seen her in the bathroom. The curtains on the upper window, though, were sheer enough to let light enter the room even when they were closed. Patterson looked around him. Only a narrow strip of lawn ran along this side of the house. He backed into the thick woods, crowded with cottonwoods, alder, willows, and birch. The leaves of the cow parsnip plants had yellowed, and the stalks were beginning to sag. In the middle of summer, though, this would be a jungle of trees and wild plants. The lodge would only be visible a short distance into the woods. Had Bob Bartlett caught Sam spying on Jules while he stood this close to her bathroom window?

According to Mark, Sam indicated he'd been watching a big buck go past the lodge, but you couldn't see past the lodge from this vantage point. For Sam to be within sight of the bathroom window, he would've been so close to the lodge that all he could have seen was the wall of the building in front of him. Patterson wanted to interview Sam Lutz as soon as possible, but the job would have to wait until tomorrow.

Patterson returned to the lodge's front door and found Gary assembling tents and setting up a camping area.

"I think it will be calmer if you camp behind the main lodge," Patterson said. "If the wind shifts a degree or two, it'll funnel through the cove and blast the front lawn."

"Yes, sir," Gary said. "I'll start hauling gear to the rear of the building."

"When you finish moving the camping gear," Patterson said, "I'll need your help carrying the bodies to the plane."

Patterson entered the front door and covered his boots with shoe liners, then donned nitrile gloves. He grabbed two of the body bags, walked to the Bartletts' bedroom door, and knocked twice. Peter Boyle opened the door, and Patterson saw a wave of relief flash across the trooper's face before he reined in his emotions and retained his passive demeanor.

"How's it going in here?" Patterson asked.

Jill Clafflin, the crime scene investigator, glanced up from her examination of the open chest drawer. "We're getting there, sir," she said. "This is a very messy scene."

Trooper Andy Marrs crouched on his hands and knees, carefully combing through the carpet for forensic evidence. Patterson doubted any fibers the young trooper uncovered could be used in court, but he might discover something to point them toward the murderer or murderers.

"Are you finished with the bodies?" Patterson asked. "I want to get them to town and on the evening jet up to Dr. Libby."

Jill nodded. "We're ready to move the bodies," she said. "I want to do a thorough search of the bed, and I can't do that until the bodies are gone."

"I have two bags here. If you three will package them, I'll get the other troopers down here, and we can move them to the plane. Then, we'll need to move the bodies from the guest cabin."

"You'll have room for all the bodies on the plane?" Peter asked.

"It'll be tight, but I think we can do it," Patterson said. "I'm more concerned about weight than I am space."

Patterson asked Gary to take the remaining bags up to the guest cabin and told him to help Joe, Sara, and Patrick put the bodies in the bags. Once they were ready, everyone could work together to take the bodies down to the plane and secure them.

Patterson walked into the small office past the stairway. The space was barely large enough for a desk, a computer, and a printer. He hoped he wouldn't need to boot up the computer to find the contact information for the six guests. If the device was password-protected, he would need expert help to access the information.

Patterson sat in the desk chair and noted the large family portrait on the wall in front of the desk. The painting seemed too large for the small room. The picture portrayed the Bartlett family in happier days, when Deb looked about six years old and Brian might have been eight or nine.

The top of the oak desk held nothing except a cup of pens and pencils. Patterson slid open the top drawer and found paper clips, rubber bands, spare change, and a cell phone. With a gloved hand, he slid the phone into an evidence bag. Patterson saw only stationery and envelopes in the next drawer, but the large bottom drawer offered what Patterson wanted. He placed the leather notebook on the desk and opened it.

Inside the notebook, Bob or Jules Bartlett had neatly listed the names, addresses, and contact information for each of their summer guests. Patterson knew the Bartletts never thought someone would use this information to advise their guests' next of kin of their deaths. Patterson found the relevant information for the current guests, copied it onto the small pad he carried in his pocket, and placed the leather notebook in an evidence bag.

Before he contacted the guests' relatives, he would make sure the names he'd copied were the actual dead guests in the cabin. By now, Joe Wilson, the crime scene tech, and the troopers processing the cabin should have found IDs of some sort for each guest.

It took nearly an hour to carry the body bags to the plane and secure them with straps. The ride to town would be bumpy, and Patterson did not want dead bodies flying through his plane. He also had to be careful not to inflict postmortem injuries to the bodies.

Patterson told Peter Boyle and Sara Byram, the two lead troopers on the scene, to oversee the remaining evidence collection. "Don't forget about their boat on the mooring," Patterson said. "In particular, search for the missing Ruger handgun."

"I found a .38 in the bedside table, but I haven't seen a Ruger," Jill said.

"It's a .44," Patterson said. "It's missing from the gun case."

Sara nodded. "We'll look for the gun, and we'll search the boat."

Patterson reminded them the killer or killers could still be out here somewhere. They needed to remain vigilant and take turns guarding the scene.

The wind ripped through the mountain passes on the flight back to town, and Patterson fought to find smooth air. If he'd had passengers, he would have flown around the outside of the island, a longer route that would have produced a smoother ride. He was fighting the clock, though. He wanted to get these bodies on the late-evening jet up to Anchorage.

Pain clutched Patterson's shoulders as he gripped the yoke. The ache moved through his neck and into his head. The headache he'd been struggling with all day ratcheted up a notch. By the time he touched down in Kodiak, all he wanted to do was go home and crawl into bed.

Mark Traner and two other troopers met the plane at the dock. They quickly loaded the bodies onto a forklift and transported them up the ramp to three trooper SUVs.

Patterson looked at his watch. The plane was scheduled to depart at 10:10 p.m., and it was already 8:40 p.m. "We'd better hurry," he told the other troopers. He jumped into the vehicle with Mark Traner, and the three SUVs sped toward the airport.

"Did you have any trouble with Tim Fairweather?" Patterson asked.

"He's not happy about sitting in a holding cell," Mark said. "Are you planning to book him?"

"No," Patterson said, "not unless he gives me a reason. What did he say to you?"

"He and his wife both seemed surprised when I told them someone murdered the Bartletts, but he's a hard guy to read."

"Did he have an alibi for last night?" Patterson asked.

"He said he was at the cannery working on his boat with the cannery mechanic, Jim Chase," Mark said. "Fairweather said he and Chase were together until eleven p.m. While Gary watched Fairweather, I had time to run to the cannery and talk to Chase, and he said he and Fairweather were together until around ten p.m. He didn't see Fairweather after that."

"Was his boat operational last night? Could he have used it, and would anyone have heard him?"

"I asked Chase those questions," Mark said, "and he told me that Fairweather's boat was usable, but most of the fishermen have closed down their operations for the season and are coming and going from the cannery all the time. He doubted anyone would notice a skiff leaving from the dock."

"Did anyone else at the cannery see Fairweather after ten p.m.?" Patterson asked.

"I asked around the office," Mark said, "but I didn't have much time before the plane left for town. No one I talked to saw him, but I think we need to question all the workers. Maybe someone saw him leave."

Patterson nodded. "I agree. We'll send someone out to the cannery to interview the workers, and I'll talk to Fairweather as soon as we get these bodies on the plane."

The jet landed twenty minutes late, and Patterson and the other troopers oversaw the transfer of the bodies to the plane. Once he'd returned to his office at trooper headquarters, Patterson immediately called the trooper office in Anchorage and made arrangements for someone to meet the plane and transfer the bodies to the medical examiner. Next, he called Dr. Libby's personal number to inform him the bodies should be at his office in two hours. Libby promised to begin the posts first thing the following morning.

Patterson called Jeanne to let her know he was safely back in town but wouldn't be home for a while. Next, he asked Mark to escort Tim Fairweather to the interrogation room, and then he told Mark to go home. "I'll need you at full speed tomorrow, so get some rest."

"Yes, sir," Mark said.

CHAPTER 15

Saturday, September 6th

11:10 p.m.

Patterson watched Tim Fairweather through the observation window of the interrogation room while the man paced back and forth, his black eyes flashing with anger. He was big and muscular. Patterson stood six two and guessed Fairweather was an inch or two taller than him. His biceps bulged under his tight black T-shirt, and his short, straight black hair was swept back from his forehead and stuck up in spikes as if he had been running his fingers through it.

Patterson rolled his neck to ease his headache, and then he turned the door handle and entered the room.

Fairweather stopped pacing and faced Patterson, his eyes narrowing. "You have no right to hold me here," he said. "I've done nothing wrong."

"Please take a seat, Mr. Fairweather," Patterson said.

"I have nothing to say to you." Fairweather remained standing.

Patterson strained to remain patient. "The faster we get this over with, the sooner you can leave."

Fairweather stayed on his feet, his face turning an ugly shade of red.

"Sit!" Patterson said, jerking his head toward one of the two chairs on either side of a small table.

Fairweather pulled the chair away from the table and sat with a thud.

Patterson let out a long breath and sat in the other chair.

"You are here, Mr. Fairweather, because I understand you had an ongoing feud with Bob Bartlett, and you have no alibi for last night, when someone murdered the Bartletts and their guests."

"I have an alibi," Fairweather said. "I was at the cannery. Ask Jim Chase, the mechanic there."

Patterson nodded. "Mr. Chase says he was with you until ten p.m., but he could not account for your whereabouts after that time. You were in the vicinity of the Bartletts' lodge, and you had a boat at the cannery. You could have traveled to the lodge at any time during the night and committed the murders."

Fairweather ran his fingers through his hair and kicked the table so hard that it banged into Patterson's leg.

Patterson considered escorting Fairweather to a cell and continuing this interview in the morning. The day was beginning to catch up with him. He'd witnessed the aftermath of a gruesome mass murder, and now he was tasked with finding the murderer before he or she could strike again. Still, he knew he had no reason to hold Tim Fairweather, and he couldn't blame the man for being upset. The troopers had plucked him from his home and transported him eighty miles to a jail cell. Patterson could see this man as their potential suspect, and this interview was important. Patterson knew he needed to clear his head, rein in his temper, and do all he could to appease Fairweather's anger.

"Mr. Fairweather," Patterson said, "I know we've ruined your day, and I apologize, but we have a mass murder on our hands, and we need your help trying to figure out who killed the Bartletts and their guests."

"I don't see how I can help you."

"Tell me about your relationship with Bob and Jules Bartlett."

Fairweather said nothing for several seconds, and Patterson could almost see his brain working on what he should say.

"Bob was a pompous ass," Fairweather said. "He thought he knew everything about everything. Ask around." Fairweather leveled his charcoal eyes on Patterson. "I'm not the only one who hated Bob Bartlett. No one liked the man."

"I'm interested in why *you* didn't like him, sir," Patterson said.

Fairweather slid his fingers through his hair several times in rapid succession. "I can't remember what event tipped off our mutual dislike, but I think it had something to do with our skiffs." He paused for a moment and then nodded his head. "Yeah, that's right. One day I got to the cannery, and the tide was falling, so I tied my skiff on the running line and pulled it out a ways. I just needed to make a quick trip to the store, so I didn't pull it out far. Bartlett arrived a few minutes later and anchored his boat on the beach, right next to mine." Fairweather shook his head. "By the time I got back to the beach, our boats were banging against each other. I went back to the store and gave Bartlett a piece of my mind." Fairweather shook his head. "The jerk punched me."

"You got into a fight because your boats bumped into each other on the running line?"

Fairweather shrugged. "I had every reason to yell at him. A man should respect another man's property."

"What did you do after he punched you?"

"Nothing," Fairweather said. "I was groggy for the next hour. He walloped me."

"Did you have any other disagreements?" Patterson asked. He didn't believe Fairweather. It would have taken more than a complaint about their boats banging to cause Bob Bartlett to punch the man.

Fairweather let out a long breath. "Every time we see each other, we argue," he said. "I guess we're both wound too tight. I didn't like the guy, but I didn't dislike him enough to kill him."

"How did you feel about Jules?"

Fairweather's hard eyes softened and glistened with moisture. He sat back in the chair and stared at the floor. "Jules was a fine lady," he said in a low, hoarse voice. "She deserved better than Bob Bartlett. I can't imagine why anyone would hurt her."

"Do you know anything about the Bartletts' relationship?"

"No," Fairweather said too quickly but then added, "I'd see them at the cannery in the summer, and he was very impatient with her. He talked down to her, and she had twice the brains he did."

"Did you know Jules Bartlett well?" Patterson's mind sharpened. He'd expected Tim Fairweather to tell him about Bob Bartlett, but it seemed as if the man had known Jules at least as well as he'd known Bob.

Fairweather said nothing for several seconds, and then he shrugged. "No, I didn't know her very well, but she seemed like a smart, classy lady. She was too good for Bob Bartlett."

Patterson felt Fairweather knew Jules Bartlett better than he claimed, but for now, he let the topic drop. "What about your wife?"

Fairweather's head snapped up, and he again looked Patterson in the eye. "Georgie? What about her?"

"Was she alone at your cabin last night?"

"Yes," Fairweather said. "Why?"

"Did she have access to a skiff?"

Fairweather nodded slowly. "We have a second skiff at the cabin."

"How did she feel about the Bartletts?"

"Wait a minute," Fairweather said. "Are you asking if she could have motored from our cabin to the Bartletts' lodge, murdered eight people, and then boated home again before I arrived at seven a.m.?" He shook his head.

Patterson shrugged. "What do you think?"

"I think the idea is silly. Besides, Georgie had no beef with Bob Bartlett. Leave her out of this."

"What about Jules Bartlett?"

"What about her?"

"You said Georgie had no beef with Bob, but how did she and Jules get along?"

Patterson noticed Fairweather's neck begin to turn red, and the color slowly traveled up his face. *Why did this question rattle the man?*

"They didn't know each other well," Fairweather said. "I mean, we didn't socialize with the Bartletts, but Georgie and Jules chatted whenever they saw each other. They were fine."

Patterson didn't believe him. *Was there a rift between Jules and Georgie?* He felt his headache worsen. He now needed to spend the time and resources to question Georgie Fairweather. When he talked to Mark the following morning, he'd get his take on Georgie.

"You have a home here in town?" he asked.

Fairweather nodded.

"You can stay there for the night, then. What's the easiest way for you to get home?"

Fairweather shot Patterson a dark look. "Since I'm in town now, I might as well pick up some supplies. You can charter me home tomorrow. I hope you plan to pay for my plane ride."

Patterson nodded. "Yes, sir, I'll call the airlines and have them charge your fare to our account."

Patterson watched Tim Fairweather leave the interrogation room. Muscles rippled under his T-shirt as he stepped through the doorway. Patterson had no trouble imagining this man with his toned body and explosive temper wielding an ax to murder Bob and Jules Bartlett. But why? *What am I missing?*

CHAPTER 16

Sunday, September 7th

5:00 a.m.

After Tim Fairweather had left trooper headquarters the previous evening, Patterson undertook the grim task of notifying the next of kin for the Bartletts' English and German guests. He spoke to the German couple's son, and while the man spoke English well, Patterson struggled to understand his words due to his strong accent. He felt foolish asking him if his parents had had enemies. How likely was it that someone would follow them to a remote Alaskan lodge and murder them, plus nearly everyone else at the lodge? Still, he needed to ask the question because experience told him that a good defense attorney would grill him on the stand about why he hadn't considered that the killer might have been related to one of the guests.

He repeated his notifications with relatives for the English couple but waited to call the family of the Atlanta couple until 5:00 a.m. Kodiak time the following morning. It would be 9:00 a.m. in Atlanta and a more considerate time to deliver bad news. The daughter in Atlanta morphed from grief to rage in record time and railed at Patterson for not protecting her parents.

He promised all the relatives that he would keep them apprised of the investigation's progress and let them know when they could ship the bodies of their loved ones home.

Patterson got dressed after his call to Atlanta. He wanted to get to the office early and prepare notes for his interviews with Brian and Deb Bartlett and Deb's boyfriend, Jason. Then he planned to fly out to the Bartletts' lodge and pick up the troopers and crime scene techs. At the top of his to-do list, however, was making arrangements to fly Sam Lutz into town. Not only did Sam know the Bartlett family well, but he and Bob Bartlett had also argued this summer. Sam could provide background information on the Bartletts and the nearby residents, and Patterson considered him a person of interest in the murders.

Without even talking to the man, Patterson placed Sam Lutz near the top of the list of suspects based solely on where he lived. Sam could walk to the Bartletts' lodge. According to Elle, a rough trail ran between Sam's cabin and the lodge, and the hike only took about twenty minutes. Sam could have hiked to the Bartletts' place in the middle of the night, committed the murders, and then walked home, and no one would have seen him come or go. Patterson wanted to talk to Mark again and get his take on Lutz.

Trooper headquarters was blissfully quiet when Patterson arrived a little after 6:00 a.m. Helen, the night dispatcher, told him she'd answered only a handful of calls, and they had been typical. A bear broke into garbage dumpsters in Bells Flats, but no one saw the animal. A domestic dispute in Chiniak resolved itself before an officer could respond, and she'd dispatched a trooper to a minor fender-bender near Monashka Bay.

"No calls from reporters asking about the murders?" Patterson asked.

Helen shook her head, her gray curls bouncing. "Not yet. I hope to finish my shift before the vultures descend," she said.

Patterson asked Helen to send Mark to his office when the trooper arrived. He then walked into his office, closed the door, and shut his eyes, breathing in a few moments of silence. Patterson knew he needed to savor the early-morning quiet because the remainder of the day would be loud. His superiors in Anchorage already wanted to send down specialists to help with the investigation. He'd reminded them, though, how he and his officers had solved the recent murder of a floatplane pilot. But he knew his bosses were viewing this investigation under a microscope, and if he didn't catch the murderer soon, he would lose control of the case.

He opened a notebook and thought about his 9:00 a.m. interview with Brian Bartlett. The Bartlett children topped his list of suspects in these murders. *What happened at their last family dinner? Did Bob and Jules announce their plans to sell the lodge, or were they planning to change their wills somehow?* Patterson hated to do it, but he felt the best way to uncover the family secrets was to turn the brother and sister against each other. The bond between the two already appeared tenuous, so he hoped to find a way to get them each to spill family secrets about the other one. He also knew Elle and Susan could give him a clearer picture of the family bonds and tensions. They were the invisible servants in the household and had probably heard more family business than any of the Bartletts realized.

Patterson worked in silence for an hour before he heard a soft knock on his office door. He looked up from his notebook. "Come in," he called.

Mark Traner opened the door. "Sir, Brie said you wanted to speak to me?"

Patterson looked at his watch in surprise. It was 7:10 a.m. Helen had departed, and Brie was on duty. He motioned to Mark. "Yes," he said. "I want to talk to you about a couple of your interviews yesterday. Please, shut the door and take a seat."

"Is there a problem?" Mark asked as he slid his thin frame into the chair in front of Patterson's desk.

"Nothing like that," Patterson said. "Things were moving fast yesterday, and I didn't have the chance to get your feel for some of the people you interviewed. Tell me more about Sam Lutz—not only what he said, but how you felt about the man."

Mark shrugged and then shook his head. "It's funny you should ask about him," he said. "I dreamt about Sam Lutz, or I guess I should say I had a nightmare about him."

"What do you mean?"

"Sam didn't hear Bart's outboard when we arrived at his place, and we found him chopping wood. At the time, I didn't realize the Bartletts were murdered with an ax, so I didn't think anything about watching him expertly split the logs. Later, when I heard the killer hacked the Bartletts to death, I couldn't get the image of Sam swinging the ax out of my mind." Mark expelled a dry laugh. "Last night, Sam Lutz chased me through my dreams while swinging a huge ax at my head."

"We need to get ahold of his ax."

"Yes, sir. I agree."

"Sara's supposed to call on the sat phone at eight a.m.," Patterson said. "I want to bring Sam back to town for questioning, and I'll have her hike over to his place and bag the ax. I want to know before I interview Sam, though: How do you feel about him? Could he be our murderer?"

Mark stared at Patterson's desk and blew out a long breath. "He seemed shocked when we told him about the murders, and I felt his reaction was sincere. Still, he was evasive about why he was watching the Bartletts' lodge when Bob Bartlett caught him." Mark lifted his eyes to Patterson's face. "Even if Sam didn't kill everyone at the lodge, I think he might have an idea who did."

"Why do you think he knows who the killer is?" Patterson sat forward in his desk chair.

"It's just a feeling, sir," Mark said. "It's nothing Sam said, but he hesitated far too long when we asked the question."

Patterson nodded. "One thing I've learned over the years, Mark, is never to ignore your gut instincts. I'd like you to sit in on Sam's interview when we get him back to town."

"Yes, sir," Mark said.

"What about Georgie Fairweather? What was your impression of her?"

A slight smile creased the corners of Mark's lips. "She's the opposite of her husband. She's short, plump, and quiet. They seem like a strange pair."

"According to Bart, Georgie can be volatile."

Mark slowly shook his head. "Maybe, but she seemed like a sweet little old lady to me."

Patterson shrugged. "Thank you, Mark. I appreciate your observations. That's the important information we don't put in our written reports."

Patterson had told Sara to call him on his cell phone instead of calling the dispatcher. Satellite phone calls tended to drop easily, so he wanted to cut out any extra steps in the process of communicating with her. At 7:55 a.m., Patterson's cell phone buzzed.

"Sir," Sara said, "everything's fine here. We had a quiet night, and the techs think we'll finish by midafternoon."

"Good," Patterson said. "I'll try to be out there around three p.m., and I'll charter the turbine Beaver from KFS. Will two planes be enough for the six of you and the evidence?"

Sara paused so long that Patterson thought he'd lost her. "Yes, sir. I think so."

"We can make another trip out there if we have to," Patterson said. "Can you get away for a couple of hours this morning?"

"Sir?" Sara asked.

"I'd like you to walk over to Sam Lutz's cabin. According to Elle, there's a trail between his place and the Bartletts' lodge. I'd like you to ask Sam to fly to town with us this afternoon. I want to interrogate him here."

"Do you want me to bring him back to the Bartletts' lodge?"

"If possible, but if he insists, I'll stop at his place and pick him up." Patterson paused for a minute. "I guess we'll have seven passengers for town, but I still think everyone plus the evidence will fit on two planes."

"I have to finish up a few things here, and then I'll start hiking toward his camp," Sara said.

"One more thing," he said. "I want you to bag Sam's ax and bring it back as evidence."

"Yes, sir."

"And Sara," Patterson said, "remember to stay on your guard. We don't know who murdered the Bartletts and their guests, and Sam Lutz had the means, opportunity, and a possible motive."

CHAPTER 17

Sunday, September 7th

8:58 a.m.

At 8:58 a.m., Brie buzzed Patterson to let him know that Brian Bartlett had arrived. Patterson asked Brie to have one of the lab techs fingerprint Brian, Debbie, Jason, Elle, and Susan when each arrived for his or her interview. He told her to escort Brian to the conference room once they had his prints. Patterson thought the conference room would serve better than the interrogation room for this interview. Yesterday, he'd become acquainted with Brian Bartlett's prickly personality, and he hoped to disarm him today. He wanted to understand Brian better and gain some insight into the Bartlett family dynamics.

When Patterson entered the conference room, Brian sat on the table's far side, staring down at his hands. He looked up when Patterson entered the room, but he didn't stand or offer his hand. He simply gave a slight nod of acknowledgment.

Patterson pulled back the chair at the head of the table and sat. "Thank you for coming in this morning, Brian."

"I didn't have much of a choice, did I?" Brian looked Patterson in the eyes.

Patterson ignored Brian's comment and decided to start their conversation with a softball question. "Where is Bear Creek?"

"Excuse me?" Brian frowned.

"Bear Creek," Patterson repeated. "The lodge is named Bear Creek Lodge, but I didn't see much of a creek anywhere near it."

Brian slowly nodded and smiled. "Dad didn't let a little thing like the truth get in the way of his promotional ideas when he named the lodge. We get our water from a small stream near the lodge, but there is no Bear Creek. Dad just thought the name sounded rustic and 'Kodiak.'" Brian made air quotes with his fingers. "I know he never stopped to think that most of his guests were going to ask him the question you just asked me."

"Now you'll be the one answering the question."

Brian sighed but said nothing.

"Your parents' bodies are in Anchorage at the medical examiner's office," Patterson said. "I'll let you know when the ME releases them."

Brian's gaze fell to the table, and for a minute, Patterson thought Brian displayed an emotion resembling grief.

"Again, I'm sorry for your loss. This must be very difficult for you."

Brian remained quiet for a moment, but then he inhaled and sat back in his chair. "I don't know how I can help you," he said. "Despite what Deb told you, I did not kill my parents."

"Brian, you need to help me see the full picture. Who hated your parents enough to murder them brutally and then kill their guests?" Patterson considered his words for a moment and then decided to lay out the facts for Brian. "The murder scene in your parents' bedroom was far different than the scene in the guest cabin. The person who killed your parents hated them. The killer used brute force and violence to murder your mother and father. We're looking for someone who despised one or both of your parents. Who hated them enough to murder them with an ax while they slept? You must have your suspicions."

A tear trickled down Brian's cheek. He wiped it away, grabbed a tissue from the box on the conference room table, and blew his nose. "Jason," he finally said.

"Jason Caine? Deb's boyfriend?"

"That's right," Brian said. "You wanted to know my thoughts." He sat forward again, placed his elbows on the table, and rested his chin on his folded hands. "That's who I think did it."

"What about Deb? Do you think she was involved in the murders?"

Brian slowly shook his head. "To be honest, I don't know what to think. One minute I feel she either helped Jason or at least put him up to it, and then the next instant, I don't believe there's any way she would hurt Mom and Dad. She fought with them all the time, but I can't imagine her murdering them."

"Do you think Deb could have killed the guests while Jason murdered your parents?" Patterson asked. From the moment he'd first viewed the two murder scenes, he'd wondered if they were looking for two murderers. While one scene appeared bloody and violent, the other seemed organized and sterile.

"I don't know. The guests were shot, right?"

Patterson nodded. "Yes, the killer shot each guest once in the head."

"Deb's a crack shot. She's been the best shot in the family ever since we were kids. We used to do a lot of target shooting. Deb knows guns, and she's good with them."

Patterson knew you didn't need to be an expert marksman to shoot someone in the head at point-blank range while they slept, but on the other hand, someone familiar with guns would be more apt to use one. "What did Deb and your parents fight about?" he asked.

"Mostly her lifestyle," Brian said. "Deb started using drugs in her early teens, and ever since then, she's been on a roller coaster. She gets clean for several months, and then she falls off the wagon. When Deb's on drugs, you can't trust her. She'll do anything to get money to buy her drugs. She's stolen a lot of stuff, including money, jewelry, tools, and even Dad's laptop once." Brian shook his head. "I thought Dad was going to kill her when she took his computer, and I think his reaction even rattled Deb because she managed to get it back for him." Brian remained silent for a moment and then added, "One time, she took my credit card, and I didn't catch it until she'd charged nearly five hundred dollars. I told her I was going to report the card stolen and send the police after her, but she begged me not to call the authorities and promised to pay me back."

"Did she pay you?"

Brian snorted. "Of course not, and now, I try to keep my distance from her."

"Do you think she's on drugs now?"

Brian shrugged. "Deb says she's clean, but she's dating a dealer, so I doubt she's telling the truth."

"She says Jason has nothing to do with drugs."

"Well, she's either a liar or a fool," Brian said. "Everyone at the cannery and all the fishermen know Jason is the go-to-guy if you need drugs. Deb has to know he's dealing."

"Tell me about your family dinner two nights ago."

Brian rubbed his hand across his face and stared at the table. Patterson waited several seconds for Brian to speak, but the young man seemed in a trance.

"Brian?" Patterson finally said.

Brian looked up at Patterson, his pale-blue eyes rimmed with red. "It isn't a good last memory," he said. "Dad and I yelled, Mom cried, and Deb laughed."

"What was the fight about?"

Brian exhaled a long breath, and his shoulders slumped. "My parents promised the lodge would be mine someday." He shrugged. "I didn't expect them to give it to me, but they said I could pay it off slowly over time. When the time came, I planned to sell my fishing boat to make the down payment. Commercial fishing is okay, but I don't want to do it my entire life, and I have plans to make the lodge bigger, hire a couple of extra fishing guides, and make some money with the place."

Brian's words again trailed off, but Patterson waited this time for him to continue. He knew he should let Brian determine the course of this story. Any question he might ask him could divert Brian's train of thought.

"They caught me by surprise," Brian finally said. "Dad's like, 'Pass the peas, and, oh yes, by the way, your mother and I have decided to put the lodge on the market and try to sell it this winter.'" Tears spilled from his eyes, and he furiously wiped at them. "I thought I'd misheard him, and he just kept eating as if he hadn't just dropped a bomb in the middle of the meal."

"What did you do?" Patterson finally prodded after several more seconds of silence.

"Deb laughed and looked at me, and I lost it."

Patterson wondered if Brian realized he was setting himself up as a prime suspect for the murders of his parents. He waited patiently for him to say more.

"Dad and I talked about the lodge several times this summer. He told me a few weeks ago that he and Mom were thinking of selling it, but I thought I'd talked him out of it." Brian paused a beat. "During our last dinner, after Dad said he and Mom were planning to sell the business, I told Dad I wanted the lodge, and Dad said they couldn't afford to give it to me or wait until I had enough money to pay them back. He said they needed the money now."

"What were your mom and Deb doing while you and your dad discussed the sale of the lodge?"

"Deb loved it. She's always resented the idea of me getting the lodge, so she thought it was funny that they were planning to sell it to someone else."

"And your mom?"

"Mom started to cry, but she sided with Dad and said she was sorry, but they needed the money now."

"Why did they need the money?"

Brian shrugged. "I don't know."

Patterson didn't believe Brian, but for now, he didn't challenge his reply. "What happened next?"

"I lost my temper," Brian said in a voice barely above a whisper. "I called Dad and Mom all kinds of names I'm not proud of, and then I stormed out of the place and went back to my boat."

"Were your crewmen on your boat?" Patterson asked. "Can they vouch for when you returned, and can they give you an alibi for the rest of the night?"

Brian shook his head. "Unfortunately, no," he said. "They went to the cannery with the crew of another boat. They played poker half the night, and I heard them return around two thirty a.m."

"So, you were on the boat alone most of the night?"

"I didn't realize I'd need an alibi."

"Your boat was anchored near the lodge," Patterson said. "Did you see your sister leave?"

Brian nodded. "I left around eight p.m., and I saw Jason pull up to the dock around nine. Deb must have been waiting for him because they left again a few minutes later. It was dark by then, so I couldn't see Jason, but I know he dropped her off and was supposed to come to get her when she called him on the radio."

"Jason wasn't invited to dinner?"

Brian laughed. "No," he said. "My parents disapproved of Jason. The first and last time Deb brought Jason to a family meal, Dad punched him in the nose when Jason got mouthy with him."

"And you think Jason hated your parents enough to kill them?"

"I think you need to talk to Deb," Brian said. "I believe something happened after I left. Deb and my parents probably got into it, like usual, and Deb told Jason. I don't know any of this for a fact," he quickly added. "I'm just telling you what I think."

"Speaking of punching someone, Deb told me yesterday that you recently punched your dad. Is this true?"

Brian huffed out a breath. "Deb," he said and shook his head. "No, Sergeant, I did not punch my father. We got into an animated argument out on the boat once this summer, but I didn't touch him, and Deb wasn't there. I don't know what she's talking about, but you can't believe everything Deb says."

"What were you and your dad arguing about?"

"The lodge, of course," Brian said. "By the end of the argument, I thought I'd talked Dad out of selling it to a stranger."

"Do you know if your parents had a will?"

"I know they made wills a while back, but I don't know what was in them," Brian said, breaking eye contact with Patterson and looking down at the floor.

"I'd like you to stay in town for a few days. I'm sure I'll have more questions for you."

"I knew you'd say that," Brian said. "I got someone to run my boat for a few days, so I'll be here until the end of the week."

Patterson nodded. "Is there anything you'd like to ask me?"

"Did you find the missing .44 Magnum?"

"I don't know," Patterson said. "I haven't talked to the crime scene techs yet today."

"I looked for it at my parents' house, but I couldn't find it."

"Did your parents usually bring the gun to town with them?"

"No," Brian said. "They have other guns in town. When they left the lodge for the winter, they hid the guns at the lodge. They left them there."

Patterson nodded. "If the techs haven't already found the Magnum, we'll keep searching for it."

"What about the ax? Was the red-handled ax the weapon used to kill my parents?"

"I didn't see any obvious signs of blood or tissue on it, but we'll send it to the crime lab in Anchorage for a more thorough analysis. Even if the killer cleaned it, the lab technicians should be able to find traces of blood on it."

"It's not the only ax my parents had," Brian said.

"Really? Where is the other ax?"

Brian shrugged. "I don't know. It should have been near the woodpile with the red ax. It's slightly larger than the red one, and it has a bright-blue handle."

"Do you remember when you last saw it?"

Brian shook his head. "I used it last fall to chop wood, but I don't remember seeing it since then. It probably broke, and my dad got rid of it, but I thought you should know about it."

"Yes, we'll look for it. Thank you."

Despite what he'd said, Patterson did not think the red ax was the murder weapon. He hadn't seen any blood on the red ax, and the tool didn't look as if anyone had recently cleaned it. Perhaps the killer had used the larger blue ax and then gotten rid of it or stashed it somewhere.

CHAPTER 18

Sunday, September 7th

9:40 a.m.

Trooper Sara Byram laced up her hiking boots and exited the front door of the lodge. Gary Reeves was standing guard, pacing back and forth on the path.

"Sergeant Patterson wants me to hike over to Sam Lutz's place," she said. "I'm not sure how far it is, but I should be back in an hour or two."

"Are you going alone?" he asked.

"Yes," Sara said with a laugh. "I hope I don't get lost. Sergeant Patterson said the trail should be obvious."

"Be careful," Gary said. "Watch out for bears and crazy humans."

Sara patted her sidearm and the canister of bear spray she wore on her belt. "I'm ready for anything."

She found the path and began hiking through the alders, birch, willows, and cottonwoods. No one had maintained the trail lately, and Sara guessed there had been little traffic on it ever since Bob Bartlett had told Sam to stay away from the lodge. As quickly as the vegetation grew on Kodiak, it wouldn't take long for the wilderness to reclaim the trail.

Ten minutes after Sara started her hike, a soft drizzle clung to her hair. She pulled up her hood but then pushed it down again a few moments later. The hood would not only cause her to overheat but would also block her sense of hearing. When walking through the Kodiak woods, hearing was nearly as important as vision. She knew that more than three thousand giant bears roamed this island, and she wanted to be able to hear a bear coming before it appeared in front of her on the trail.

The rain steadily increased in intensity, and before long, it was pelting her head and drowning out the sounds of the woods. Sara fought the urge to sprint down the trail and instead slowed her pace and maintained her vigilance.

Sara expected to see a bear at every twist and turn of the trail, and when branches snapped to her right, she reached for her can of pepper spray and fought to breathe evenly. She squinted her eyes, attempting to see into the dense foliage. Despite the yellow leaves littering the ground and the sagging cow parsnip plants, the vegetation remained dense.

A moment later, a Sitka black-tailed deer popped out of the brush. The wary doe seemed more startled than Sara. A fawn slowly followed its mother onto the trail. The fawn's spots had nearly faded, and it soon would be on its own. Both animals stopped and stared at Sara for several moments before the mother bounded into the woods, the fawn on her heels.

A burble of laughter exploded from Sara's mouth, and she snapped the pepper spray back into the pouch on her belt. *Get it together, girl. You're a state trooper. You can handle a walk in the woods.*

The rain continued in a steady barrage as she followed the poorly defined trail to what she hoped would be Sam Lutz's cabin. At one point, while she pushed through the brush, she wondered if she was following a deer trail leading nowhere.

After nearly a half hour of tromping through the woods, she finally exited into a small clearing. In front of her sat a cabin, and she assumed she had finally reached her destination.

A stack of logs covered by a blue tarp lay twenty feet in front of her. Next to the logs, she saw a chopping block and an ax. She didn't have a warrant, so she'd have to attain Mr. Lutz's permission before she could bag the tool as evidence.

Sara reminded herself to be careful. She unsnapped her holster and put her hand on the butt of her gun. Although they had little information, Sam Lutz sat near the top of their list of suspects in the horrific murders at the Bartletts' lodge. She approached the cabin from the side, eased along the front of the small building, and crouched under the one small window. She knocked on the door and stood to the side, hand firmly on the revolver still in its holster.

She waited as seconds and then a minute passed. She knocked again, harder this time. Perhaps Sam was out in his boat or off on a hike. This didn't seem like hiking or boating weather, but Sam Lutz had chosen to live in the wilderness. Perhaps rain and wind didn't bother him.

When Sam didn't answer Sara's third and then fourth knock, she thought perhaps she should walk to the edge of the cliff to see if his skiff was on his running line. First, she reached down and turned the doorknob. The door swung open, but why wouldn't it? Sara doubted Sam's door even had a lock. Why lock your door in the middle of the wilderness? Bears never knocked before entering, and they were rarely courteous enough to use the door. Instead, they broke through windows or walls.

Sara warily stepped into the small cabin. She pulled her gun from her holster, on high alert for an ambush. She took in the small kitchen with one glance, but she saw nowhere for someone to hide in the tiny alcove. She looked up as she entered the main room. The darkened loft concerned her. She listened but heard no sounds. Her eyes dropped to the main room, and she slowly scanned the perimeter. When she reached the table and chairs to her left, she gasped at the sight, and the gun began shaking in her hand. She held her breath and quickly backed out of the room.

Sara put her hands on her thighs and bent her head toward the floor. She forced herself to breathe evenly for several seconds. She should have brought another trooper with her on this assignment. *You can do this. You're an Alaska State Trooper.*

She holstered her revolver and returned to the main room of the cabin. Her eyes again focused on the loft, and she knew she needed to clear the area before she proceeded. A narrow, steep set of stairs led up to the darkened room. Sara unsnapped the flashlight from her duty belt, turned it on, and held it in her left hand. She again retrieved her revolver from her belt with her right hand and slowly ascended the stairs.

"Alaska State Troopers!" she called. "I'm Trooper Sara Byram. Is anyone up here?" She listened for a moment but heard nothing. "Show yourself now," she said and was relieved to note her voice sounded strong and official.

Sara reached the top of the stairs and shined her flashlight around an area filled with boxes and totes. A small bed, more like a cot, occupied the far corner of the loft. A tiny window allowed only a soft ray of light to enter the space. Sara carefully inspected the stacked boxes and totes but found no one crouched behind them. A pent-up breath escaped her lungs. Unless she'd missed some hidden room in the small cabin, she felt certain no other humans occupied the building. At least, she saw no live humans in the place.

She returned to the cabin's main floor and approached the man slumped in the chair next to the table. She donned her nitrile gloves and knelt on the floor in front of the body. The man she assumed was Sam Lutz had been shot once in the middle of the forehead. The gunshot stippling around the wound suggested someone had shot him at close range. Sara might have suspected suicide, but she saw no weapon near the body, and with this wound, Sam must have died instantly. He certainly didn't have time to shoot himself, hide the gun, and sit back down to die.

Sara stood and stepped back three steps. She pulled her small trooper-issued camera from her pocket and photographed the scene. She snapped photos of Sam's body slumped in the chair and of the wall behind him covered with blood splatter and what she thought must be brain matter. Her stomach roiled, and she ran outdoors and sprinted as far away from the crime scene as she could before she dropped to her knees and retched. She vomited the roll and coffee she'd eaten for breakfast and continued to heave even after her stomach was empty. Finally, she sat back against a tree and cried.

Sara loved her job, but the stress of the last day was finally hitting her. Eight people dead at the lodge, and now Sam Lutz. Who was the murderer, and when did he or she kill Sam? Mark had interviewed Sam at his cabin the previous afternoon, so someone had shot Sam between early afternoon yesterday and sometime this morning. If the murder occurred after Patterson flew to town with the Bartlett children and Deb's boyfriend, then Sam's murder would clear all their most obvious suspects. She reminded herself that Sam's murder would only clear Brian, Deb, and Jason from killing Sam—not from killing the people at the lodge—but she knew the murders must all be related.

Perhaps Brian, Deb, or Jason had had time to murder Sam before they flew to town with Patterson. It wasn't as if they were under constant surveillance.

Sara knew she needed to let Patterson know immediately about Sam Lutz. The sat phone was back at the lodge, so she climbed to her feet, her legs still trembling. She found the path and began to walk. The rain felt good, and she welcomed the chill. As she regained her strength, she quickened her pace and began to run, her eyes planted firmly on the ground, sighting troublesome branches and rocks in her path.

When she reached the front door of the lodge, she bent over to catch her breath, bracing her hands on her thighs.

"Sara?" Gary Reeves approached her. "Are you okay?"

Sara looked up at him, still too winded to talk. Once her breathing slowed, she said, "He's dead. Someone shot Sam Lutz in the head."

CHAPTER 19

Sunday, September 7th

10:23 a.m.

Patterson opened the door to the conference room and entered. Deb Bartlett had arrived ten minutes late for her 10:00 a.m. interview, so Patterson had let her sit in the room alone for several minutes. He needed to let her know she was not calling the shots in this interrogation. He now noted he'd wasted his psychological maneuvering on Deb. She sat at the far end of the conference table, hunched over her phone, and didn't even seem to hear Patterson enter the room.

"Hello, Deb," Patterson said.

Deb looked up, a dazed expression on her face as if she'd forgotten where she was. "Hello, Sergeant," she said and then slid her phone into the large leather handbag sitting on the table next to her.

"How are you this morning?" Patterson asked. He reminded himself to have patience with this young woman. Someone had brutally murdered her parents, and if she and her boyfriend weren't the ones who'd killed them, then she must be struggling to cope with her loss.

Deb sighed. "I'm doing better, I guess." She rested her arms on the table. "Look, I know I said I'm happy my parents are dead, but that was a lie." She wiped an invisible tear from her face. "We didn't always agree on things, but I loved them."

"It's okay, Deb," Patterson said. "In moments of stress, people say things they don't mean. I try not to read too much into it." He realized he was lying to Deb. Someone's first response to news of a relative's or friend's murder never told the entire story, but it did provide valuable information.

"What types of things did you and your parents fight about?"

Deb said nothing for a moment, and then she laughed. "You name it, and we fought about it. I was not a model daughter. I rebelled at a young age, and I did everything my parents told me not to do—drugs, alcohol, sex, body piercings, tattoos—I did them all. The more my parents scolded me, the worse I behaved. I thought I was hurting them, but I know I was really hurting myself."

"Did you fight with them two nights ago when you went to dinner at the lodge?"

"Oh yes, but I have to thank Brian," Deb said. "He's usually the golden child, but he threw such a tantrum about Mom and Dad selling the lodge that I got off easier than usual. After Brian stormed out of the lodge, though, they let me have it."

"What did they say to you?"

"The usual stuff," Deb said. "Dad accused me of stealing from them, and Mom pleaded with me to break up with Jason."

"What did your dad accuse you of stealing?"

"This time, it was Mom's turquoise and diamond earrings." She shook her head. "I'm sure they're here at the house in town. Why would she bring something so ridiculous as expensive earrings out to the lodge?"

"Have you ever taken anything from your parents?"

Deb said nothing for several seconds. "In the past, I've taken some of Mom's jewelry, and I stole a few guns and other things." She shrugged. "I'm an addict. When I was using, I'd do anything for drug money. I did plenty of things I'm not proud of."

"You're clean and sober now, though?"

"I am," Deb said, "and I hope to stay that way. I haven't stolen anything from my parents in over two years. Every time they misplace something, they blame me."

Patterson noted Deb's use of the present tense when referring to her parents. "What about Jason?" he asked.

"What about him?" Deb's voice raised an octave, and she seemed ready to fight to protect her boyfriend.

Patterson decided to poke. "I've heard Jason is a drug dealer. Is this true?"

Deb leaned back hard in her chair. "No, it's not true. He used to sell drugs, but he saw the light, and he doesn't want to go to jail. His dream is to get training and become a diesel mechanic. Those guys make big money working on all the fishing boats around here."

"Were you with Jason all night when you returned to the cannery after having dinner with your parents?"

Deb hesitated a beat too long before answering. "Sure," she said. "Jason picked me up at the lodge, and we were together the rest of the night."

Patterson let her statement hang in the air, but Deb held his gaze, defiant. He could not contradict what she'd said, so he changed the subject. "Deb," he said, "who do you think murdered your parents and their guests?"

Deb deflated and seemed to get smaller. She ran her fingers through her blonde hair, which hung in clumps around her face. "I don't know," she said. "Brian was furious when he left, and he inherited my dad's violent temper. I think they left the lodge to Brian in their will, so maybe he thought if he killed them before they had a chance to sell it, he'd get the place free and clear."

"Do you know what else was in their will?"

"No," Deb said. "I have no idea. I just remember them telling Brian a few years ago that they were planning to leave the lodge to him."

"Do you think Brian could kill your parents?"

"I want to say no," Deb said, shaking her head, "but the truth is, I don't know."

"Is there anyone else you suspect?"

Deb shrugged. "My dad made plenty of enemies, but I can't imagine anyone hated him enough to brutally murder him and my mom and then kill the guests." She paused for a minute. "You think the killer used an ax?"

"We think your parents were murdered with an ax or something similar. We'll know more after the medical examiner finishes their autopsies."

"Someone must have hated them to kill them with an ax." Deb shook her head again.

"Yes," Patterson said. "Your parents' murders were personal."

"Sergeant, I didn't much like my dad, and I know he didn't care for me. I think he stopped loving me a long time ago." She paused. "But I did love my mother. We fought, but we also had good times. I would never hurt her. I wouldn't hurt either of them."

"What did you think about your parents leaving the lodge to Brian in their will?"

"It upset me when I first heard the news, but I got over it. When I wasn't high, during periods of relative clarity, I understood why my parents didn't trust me. I'd done nothing to earn their trust. My problem with them, especially with my dad, was that they didn't support me. They never tried to find me help. A doctor recently diagnosed me as bipolar, and he gave me medicine that makes me feel so much better. Why didn't my parents take me to a psychologist the moment I began to act out? Where were they? Why weren't they paying attention to me? I don't care about their money or their stinking lodge. They should have done a better job as parents." Tears spilled from Deb's eyes, and she grabbed a tissue from the box on the table.

"Did you express these feelings to your parents?"

Deb wiped her eyes and fought to regain her composure. A sad smile curved her lips. "I screamed my feelings at them several times. I know my mother felt bad and said she should have noticed sooner and got me help."

"And your father?" Patterson asked.

Deb shook her head. "He didn't care. Dad only worried about himself. He was not a nice man, and I don't think I'll miss him."

"What can you tell me about your parents' relationship?"

Deb shrugged. "I don't think it was great, but I haven't spent much time around them in years, and they rarely fight in front of Brian and me. Dad puts Mom down, and she ignores him, but I know she lets him have it when they're alone. I overheard her lay into him a few times."

Deb was again referring to her parents in the present tense. She came across as truthful and unfiltered, but Patterson felt she was hiding something. He wanted to hit her harder on the subject of Jason's whereabouts on the night of the murder, but he didn't want her to warn Jason about his suspicions.

CHAPTER 20

Sunday, September 7th

10:40 a.m.

"I'm going for a walk," Elle said as she grabbed her jacket and headed for the door.

Susan looked away from the television for a moment. "Can I go with you?" she asked.

"I need to be alone for a few minutes," Elle said. "I won't be gone long."

"Okay," Susan said in a small voice.

Elle thought Susan was about to cry, and she nearly gave in to her request. She hurried out the door before she agreed to allow Susan to tag along. Elle was tired of being cooped up with the girl. Susan was so needy and wanted to follow Elle everywhere. Susan was seventeen years old, but sometimes she acted as if she were twelve. Elle didn't have the mental strength to support Susan through this crisis. Elle knew she was hanging on to her sanity by a thread. She couldn't take care of herself and Susan too.

The day felt chilly and gloomy. A light rain dampened her hair, and she pulled up her hood. Her chest billowed with pressure, and she felt ready to explode. She craved pain. She wanted to run the razor blade across her thigh. She needed the release, but she knew she should stop cutting herself. The doctors had told her that cutting was a manifestation of her mental illness. When she felt the need to cut, she should seek help from a psychologist. This was Kodiak, though. She had no idea where to find a good psychologist here.

If she asked for help, she knew the police would suspect her of the murders. Maybe they already suspected her. *Do they know about my past? Have they heard about what I did to my sister or the girl in the bathroom? Do they know how crazy I am?*

She could never hurt Jules and Bob, though. They had been very good to her, and she loved her cooking job at the lodge. Both Jules and Bob praised her meals, and the guests tipped her well. *I could never hurt anyone again, could I?*

Why didn't she remember anything from the night of the murders? Elle recalled making dinner, and Jules asking her to give the family some privacy. Did she go straight to bed? Did she read or listen to music? Why couldn't she remember? She didn't remember hurting her sister or the other girl either. Was she doing it again?

Elle couldn't take it. She returned to the small house she currently shared with Susan.

"You weren't gone long," Susan said as Elle entered the front door.

Elle said nothing but hurried toward her bedroom.

"Are you okay?" Susan called after her.

Elle slammed shut her bedroom door and rushed into the bathroom. She removed the small case from the drawer where she'd hidden it. She pulled a clean razor blade from the kit, pulled down her pants, and slid to the floor. She pushed hard as she ran the razor across her thigh. She laid her head against the wall and let out a long breath. The pressure in her chest momentarily eased.

CHAPTER 21

Sunday, September 7th

11:24 a.m.

Jason Caine arrived twenty minutes late for his interview. Patterson knew the young man was trying to make a statement with his late arrival, but the move only served to anger him. If Jason had any sense, he'd know this interview would prove much easier for him if he showed common courtesy and respect. Patterson doubted Jason Caine ever did anything the easy way, though.

Patterson wanted to let Jason stew for a while, but he didn't have time to play mind games. It would soon be noon, and he needed to get back out to the Bartletts' lodge. Besides, he had no reason yet to hold Jason, and if the young man wanted to, he could simply walk out of the conference room and leave.

As soon as Brie called to tell him she'd escorted Jason to the interview room, Patterson jumped up from his desk, grabbed his notebook, and headed for the door. Just as Patterson's hand closed on the doorknob to the interview room, Brie called his name.

"Sir!" Brie rushed down the hall toward him, her face pale. "It's Sara on the phone. She needs to talk to you right away."

Thoughts swirled in Patterson's head. Something must be wrong, but what was it? *Did they find the murderer?* Sara was headed out to talk to Sam. Did he attack her? Patterson immediately regretted not insisting that Sara take another trooper with her. The young trooper was intelligent and capable, but had she run into danger? Did something happen at the lodge while she was gone? He refused even to entertain that idea. He didn't ask Brie questions. Instead, he raced toward his office and his phone.

"Patterson!" he barked into the phone.

"Sir," Sara said. Her voice sounded unsteady, but the background noise on the satellite phone made him uncertain of his assessment.

"What is it, Sara?"

"It's Sam Lutz."

He waited for her to continue, but all he heard was her heavy breathing through the phone receiver. Finally, he said, "What about Sam?"

"He's dead, sir. Shot in the head."

This possibility hadn't occurred to Patterson. "Murdered? Where did you find him?"

"In his cabin, sir. Sitting at the table."

Patterson now clearly heard the tremble in her voice. "Sara, are you up to going back to Sam's cabin?"

"Yes, sir," she said without hesitation.

Patterson knew Sara would never admit how shaken she was to have found Sam's body. "Wait until Patrick and Joe finish in the log cabin, and then I'd like the three of you to return to Sam's cabin. Take the trail, not the boat, and look around on your hike. I don't know what you're looking for, but note it and mark it if you see anything unusual. Once you get to Sam's place, concentrate on the area around and in his cabin. Of course, I want you to inspect his body, but don't laser focus on it."

"Yes, sir," Sara said.

"Mark was in Sam's cabin yesterday. I'll be out there in two hours, and I'll bring him with me. Maybe he can tell us if anything seems out of place in the cabin. We'll land at the lodge and bring the skiff over to Sam's place."

"Yes, sir," she said again.

"Are you sure you're okay with going back to Sam's? I understand if you're not, and I won't think any less of you. I can send Peter with the other guys."

"No, sir," she said. "I want to go back. I'm fine, honestly."

"Okay. I'll see you soon."

Patterson pushed back in his desk chair. The bodies were piling up. Mark had interviewed Sam at his cabin around noon the previous day, so Sam was murdered sometime within the last twenty-four hours. Patterson had brought Brian, Deb, Jason, Elle, and Susan to town with him, and Mark had been with Tim and Georgie Fairweather. And then he'd escorted Tim to Kodiak. Either one of these people had murdered Sam before they left Kanuk Bay, or none of them was the murderer. Another possibility was that the person who murdered Sam was someone other than the perpetrator who'd committed the killings at the lodge. He rejected this idea because it seemed so preposterous. *Sam must have possessed incriminating evidence against the person who murdered the Bartletts and their guests, and the killer silenced him.*

Patterson pushed out of his chair and tried to refocus his mind on Jason Caine. He wanted to grab Mark and fly out to the lodge immediately, but Jason was here, and he didn't want to miss his opportunity to interview him. For now, Patterson would stick to the murders at the lodge. He didn't yet have enough information about Sam's death to ask questions about it. He hoped the ME would be able to narrow down the time interval when Sam had died. The time of Sam's murder could point this investigation in a new direction. Right now, Patterson considered Brian, Deb, Jason, and Tim Fairweather his primary suspects. But if the ME determined Sam was murdered sometime late Saturday afternoon or night or even Sunday morning, then these suspects would all have alibis, at least for Sam's death.

Jason Caine sat on the far side of the conference table, back against the wall, eyes closed. Patterson could tell he wasn't asleep, but the young man didn't open his eyes when Patterson entered the room.

"Jason." The word came out louder than Patterson had intended, and he took a steadying breath.

Jason's shoulder-length hair hung in greasy clumps, and Patterson wondered if he or Deb ever showered. Her hair also had been dirty, but at least Deb had smelled okay. Patterson could detect Jason's body odor from across the room. He chose a seat at the head of the table, several chairs away from him.

Jason sat forward, and Patterson noted the grease stains on his black sweatshirt. What did Deb see in this guy? Jason pushed his hair off his face and settled his black eyes on Patterson. He attempted to look bored.

"I don't know why I'm here," Jason said. "I have nothing to say."

"Tell me about the night of the murders."

"I wasn't there."

"What time did you pick up Deb at the lodge?"

Jason shrugged. "A little before nine p.m., I guess."

"What was Deb's demeanor like?"

"What do you mean?" Jason crossed his arms over his broad chest and narrowed his eyes.

"Was she upset, was she happy, what was her mood?"

"Well, first of all," Jason said, "she wasn't covered with blood. She was angry and upset, like she always is when she spends time with her family."

"Why was she angry?" Patterson's patience was nearing the breaking point.

"How would I know?"

"Look, Jason," Patterson said, "the sooner you answer my questions, the faster we'll get done here."

Jason pulled at a strand of hair. "Deb's parents hated me, and I hated them. According to Deb, we put her in the middle." He shrugged. "I guess it's true, but how could I like her dad? He didn't respect me." Jason spread his hands. "I did nothing to the man, but he banned me from his house, and he and Deb's mom tried to fill Deb's head with all kinds of bad nonsense about me."

"What type of nonsense?"

Jason sat forward, elbows on the table. He said nothing for several moments and then replied, "Stuff, that's all. I don't want to get into it." He shook his head. "Look, I haven't always been an upstanding citizen, but everyone makes mistakes. I'm working hard now to turn my life around."

Jason's statement rang false to Patterson. Maybe people could change, but Patterson felt Jules and Bob Bartlett were right to try to warn their daughter against hanging out with Jason Caine. They'd likely watched Deb screw up her life time after time, and then, when she'd finally seemed at the point of turning things around, she'd taken up with a loser like Jason Caine.

Patterson focused on his line of questioning. "What did Deb say to you when she left the family dinner?"

Jason shrugged. "She didn't say much, except that she hated her parents. She said her dad accused her of stealing things again, and she said they asked a bunch of questions about me, wanting to know what I was doing and how I was treating her."

"Was Deb madder than usual with her parents?"

Jason looked directly into Patterson's eyes. Sweat gleamed on his crooked nose. "She wasn't mad enough to kill them."

"What did you and Deb do after you left the Bartletts' lodge?"

"We went back to the cannery. It was dark, and I could barely see where I was going."

"What did you do at the cannery?"

Jason exhaled a loud breath, tilted his head, and stared at Patterson. "We went to our room," he said. "What else would we do?"

"I have no idea what else you would do, Jason," Patterson said. "Did you and Deb remain together for the rest of the night?"

"Yes, we were together at all times."

Patterson didn't believe him. The words seemed rehearsed and unnatural coming out of Jason's mouth. Patterson hadn't believed Deb when she said she'd spent all night with Jason, and now, he was getting the same feeling from Jason's reply to the question.

"You didn't split up for any reason after you got back to the cannery?"

Jason said nothing but just shook his head.

"Did Deb steal anything from the lodge?"

"No," Jason said. "She used to steal things, so every time her parents misplaced something, they thought she took it. Her dad had to apologize to her a couple of months ago, when he accused her of stealing a gun and then remembered he'd left it in town. Almost every time she saw them, they blamed her for stealing something."

"What did they accuse her of stealing the last time she talked to them?"

Jason shrugged. "She didn't say. When Deb gets mad, she stops talking."

Patterson told Jason not to leave town. As soon as he walked out of the conference room, Patterson returned to his office and opened the window to breathe fresh air. Patterson could picture Jason and Deb murdering her parents and shooting the guests, but if they were the murderers, then how and when did they kill Sam?

CHAPTER 22

Sunday, September 7th

12:13 p.m.

After clearing his head, Patterson searched for Mark Traner and found the young trooper sitting at his desk, writing notes.

"Have you found anything of interest?" Patterson asked when Mark looked up from his computer.

"Not yet, sir. I'm just starting to look into everyone's background."

"Did you hear about Sam Lutz?"

"Yes, sir." Mark shook his head. "We hauled everyone to town. Who killed him?"

"I don't know," Patterson said. "We need to think about where everyone was before we flew them to town."

"Deb and her boyfriend were at the cannery and had access to a boat. They could have gone to Sam's cabin and shot him."

"Yes," Patterson said, "and the same goes for Brian. He had a skiff."

"I don't see how Tim Fairweather could have come all the way into the bay and made it back to his place before I interviewed him," Mark said.

"Not unless he's lying about his timeline. Maybe he didn't leave the cannery until midmorning, and he killed Sam before he went home."

Mark shrugged. "If that's the case, we should be able to find witnesses at the cannery who saw him there later in the morning."

"Did Georgie say what time Tim arrived back at their cabin?"

Mark shook his head. "I didn't ask her. I didn't think it mattered what time he returned home. I was only worried about his timeline for the previous night."

Patterson nodded. "We'll need to talk to Georgie Fairweather again, and I want you to canvass the cannery workers soon. Right now, though, I'd like you to fly out to the lodge with me. We'll meet Sara at Sam's cabin. You've been there before, so you'll be able to tell us if something seems out of place."

"Sure," Mark said, the tone of his voice indicating his eagerness to get away from desk duty. "How is Sara doing? She's the one who found Sam, right?"

The question surprised Patterson. Ever since Mark had lost a friend and fellow trooper a few months earlier, he'd kept his distance from the other officers, and Patterson felt he was afraid to get close to anyone in fear of losing him or her again. Patterson worried about Mark, but maybe the trooper was recovering from his loss. He seemed genuinely concerned about Sara.

"She sounded a bit shaky on the phone when she called with the news," Patterson said, "but you know Sara. She's tough. She'll come around."

Mark laughed. "Yeah, she's tough, all right." He grinned.

Patterson heard a note of admiration in Mark's voice, or was it something more? He wanted Mark to form bonds with his colleagues, but he did not want a romance to form between his officers. Patterson pushed the notion to the back of his mind. He didn't have time to think about office politics right now.

Mark grabbed his jacket, and Patterson stopped at his office to get his coat. He closed his eyes to think about what they would need when they got to Kanuk Bay and then told Mark to grab some evidence bags and a body bag. At the rate they were going through body bags, he'd have to start requesting them by the pallet load.

Patterson closed his office door and walked toward the front lobby.

"Sir," Brie said when he rounded her desk, "Rick has something for you. He's headed up from the lab now."

"Can it wait until I get back?"

Brie shook her head. "He said it's important, and you'd want to see it before you left."

Patterson sighed. Rick was a young lab tech who was a wizard with technology. He spent most of his time servicing the computers in the building, but he loved computer forensics. While Patterson appreciated his enthusiasm, he knew Rick thought every detail he uncovered, no matter how mundane, would break the case. Patterson wanted to get out to Sam's place instead of standing around for a long-winded explanation about how Rick had uncovered a string of unimportant texts.

The young tech ran down the hall, his mop of curly blond hair bouncing. When he reached Patterson, he was too winded to speak, so instead, he shoved a cell phone into Patterson's hands.

Patterson looked down at the blurred image on the phone. He reached into his shirt pocket, pulled out a pair of reading glasses, and again looked at the phone. He regretted thinking Rick would waste his time. The tech was right to show him this as soon as possible.

"Whose phone is this?"

"Bob Bartlett's, sir."

"Interesting," Patterson said. He looked over the top of his glasses at the young tech. "Good work, Rick, and thank you for bringing this to me right away."

"I thought you'd want to see it. Do you know who it is?"

"I think I do," Patterson said without further explanation. "Please blow up this photo and print it, and let me know if you find anything else." He handed the phone back to Rick.

Rick reached for the phone but stood still, his attention focused on Patterson. He was probably hoping for more information about the people in the photo, but Patterson didn't plan to provide him with what he wanted. Patterson had no wish for a rumor to spread through the trooper unit and then out into the public. He trusted Rick, but the kid was young and enthusiastic. Nothing good would come from telling him details he didn't need to know.

"Thank you, Rick," Patterson said again. "That's all for now."

"Yes, sir." Rick turned quickly to head back to the lab and nearly bumped into Mark, whose arms were full of evidence bags and a body bag.

Mark turned and watched Rick's fleeing form. "Who lit a fire under him?"

"Young Rick discovered something interesting," Patterson said. "I'll tell you about it when we're on our way." He looked at Brie. "Is Brad on duty today?"

"Yes, sir," Brie said. "He ran out to grab some lunch, but he should be back in a few minutes."

"As soon as he gets back—and this is a priority—I want him to chase down Tim Fairweather, bring him here, and hold him."

"Should he lock him up, sir?"

"If necessary," Patterson said, "and it probably will be necessary."

"Where will Brad find Mr. Fairweather?" she asked.

"I hope he hasn't flown back to his cabin," Patterson said, "or worse yet, left the island. He has a place here in town. Find his town address and then call the charter companies to see if he's made reservations to fly back to his cabin."

"Yes, sir. I'm on it."

"This is top priority, Brie. Send Brad right back out the door when he gets here."

"I will, sir."

Patterson looked at his watch and then called Kodiak Flight Services and pushed back the plane charter to 4:00 p.m. If it left town at 4:00 p.m., it would get to the Bartletts' lodge at 5:00 p.m. Patterson hoped an extra hour would give them enough time to finish up at the lodge and process Sam's place.

Once Patterson and Mark were in the SUV heading for Trident Basin, Mark asked, "Didn't you interview Fairweather last night?"

Patterson nodded, his eyes on the road. "I did, but I now have proof Mr. Fairweather lied to me."

"What type of proof?" Mark asked.

Patterson hesitated a moment. He glanced at Mark. "For now, let's keep this between the two of us, okay?"

"Of course, sir."

"Young Rick is looking through the two cell phones and a laptop I brought back to town with me from the lodge. They have a desktop computer we need to get today. Don't let me forget it."

"Okay," Mark said.

"On Bob Bartlett's cell phone, Rick found a photo of a woman who looks like Jules Bartlett, and she's in bed with another man."

Mark whistled, and then the full implication seemed to hit him. He turned sideways in his seat and stared at Patterson. "No way. Tim Fairweather?"

"I'm sure it was Fairweather in the photo," Patterson said. "I only know what Jules Bartlett looked like from the family pictures I saw at the lodge, but the woman in the compromising photo has long, dark hair just like Jules Bartlett."

Mark sat back in his seat. "This shines a new light on the investigation."

"It does, but how, when, and why would Tim Fairweather kill Sam Lutz? And I do believe Sam's murder is related to the rest of the murders."

"For that matter," Mark said, "why would Tim Fairweather kill the guests at the lodge? I can understand a love triangle, but the poor guests didn't have anything to do with it."

Patterson shook his head. "I don't know, unless the guests saw him at the lodge, and he killed them to eliminate witnesses."

"I guess the same could apply to Sam too," Mark said. "If Sam saw his boat at the lodge, or their boats passed each other in the bay, maybe Fairweather feared Sam would say something to us."

"Why wait until after we interviewed Sam to murder him, though?"

Mark shook his head. "Nine people murdered in the wilderness on an island. You'd think we'd find the killer in a matter of hours."

"I hope we do, but geography is not on our side with this one. It's an hour plane ride every time we want to revisit the crime scene or interview another suspect."

"Maybe we'll find something at Sam's," Mark said.

Patterson laughed. "Yes, maybe Sam kept a diary of all his inner thoughts and suspicions."

CHAPTER 23

Sunday, September 7th

1:20 p.m.

On the plane ride out to the lodge, Patterson asked Mark for his thoughts on the case. Patterson respected Mark, and the trooper often offered valuable insights.

Mark spoke into the microphone on his headset. "I think this Fairweather lead looks promising," he said. "He has a bad temper, and if Bob Bartlett took the photo on his phone and then confronted Fairweather, I could see Fairweather's anger turning to murder."

"But why would he also kill Jules? He liked her at least enough to have sex with her."

Mark shrugged. "Maybe Jules left Fairweather and went back to her husband, so Fairweather hated them both."

"What do you think about the Bartlett children as suspects?"

"Deb and her boyfriend check all the boxes," Mark said. "They had means, motive, and opportunity."

Patterson nodded as he nosed the plane through a steep mountain pass. The wind currents through this pass had rattled his teeth the previous evening, but now they encountered only smooth air. "I don't care for Jason, and I certainly understand why the Bartletts didn't want him around their daughter," he said.

"Do you think Jason abuses Deb?"

Patterson glanced over at him. "Why do you ask?"

"I noticed a bruise on her arm when we interviewed her at the cannery."

"I missed it," Patterson said. "Good catch. I want to talk to both Deb and Brian again, together this time, so I'll take a closer look at Deb."

"Why do you want to interview them together? Didn't you just talk to them today?"

Patterson nodded. "During their interviews, they each pointed the finger at the other one. It'll be interesting to see what they do when I put them in the same room."

While the wind was calmer than it was on the previous evening, a low overcast forced Patterson out of the passes, and he had to skirt the west side of the island. A drizzle pelted the plane, and as the visibility decreased, Patterson turned his full attention to navigation.

Forty minutes later, they finally touched down in the cove in front of Bear Creek Lodge. Patterson idled up to the dock, where Trooper Reeves stood ready to greet them.

"How is everything here, Gary?" Patterson asked.

"No excitement at the lodge, but I guess you heard about what Sara found."

"Yes. Has she left yet to return to Sam's cabin?"

"She and Patrick and Joe headed that way"—Gary consulted his watch—"about forty-five minutes ago."

"Were they finished in the guest cabin?"

"Yes, sir," Gary said. "Jill and her crew are nearly done processing the main cabin, and Jill said she'll be finished by the time the others get back from Sam's place."

"What about the Bartletts' cabin cruiser? Has anyone taken a look inside it?"

Gary nodded. "Sara and Patrick went out to the boat this morning, but they didn't find anything of interest."

Patterson nodded. "Mark and I are taking the skiff to Sam's, and when we return, we'll pack up things here. The KFS plane should be here around five p.m."

"Yes, sir," Gary said. "I'll tell the others."

Since Mark had been to Sam's place the previous day, Patterson asked him to run the outboard. Patterson had checked the tide book and knew the tide was falling. When they reached the beach in front of Sam's cabin, they tied the skiff to the long running line and pulled the boat away from the beach to keep it floating while the tide ebbed.

When they reached the cabin, Patterson found Joe Wilson and Sara Byram in the main room. Joe squatted, and Patterson guessed he must have been looking for trace evidence on the floor. Sara focused on the body of the sixty-year-old man slumped in the chair, sitting next to a small table.

Patterson took in the scene. "Did you find the murder weapon?"

Joe looked up at Patterson. "No, sir. Unfortunately, I don't see the smoking gun, unless it's one of the guns over there in Sam's case."

"Bring all his guns to town," Patterson said. "I don't think you'll find much trace evidence on the floor, but be sure to dust the table, chairs, and doorknob for prints."

He turned aside. "Sara, have you found anything on Sam? Is the body in rigor?"

"Yes, sir," she said. "As a rough estimate, Sam must have died between the time Mark talked to him and late last night."

Patterson nodded while he considered the time frame. "Did you find anything in his pockets?"

"Just a handkerchief."

"How many shots?"

"Just one," she said. "There's quite a bit of stippling, so the killer must have been within three feet of Sam when he"—she paused for a moment—"or she pulled the trigger."

"In this tiny cabin, the shooter couldn't have been too far from Sam when he fired," Mark said.

"He just sat there," Sara said.

"What do you mean?" he asked.

Sara looked up at him. "He didn't try to run or wrestle the gun away from his killer. He just sat there, took the bullet, and died."

"The shooter must have taken him by surprise."

"Or he knew the person and didn't think the individual would kill him," Patterson said.

"I think you're both right," Sara said. "I've been running this through my mind, and I believe the killer surprised Sam, but Sam knew the person, so Sam wasn't frightened by their sudden appearance."

Patterson noted strands of auburn hair pulled free from Sara's bun. Her hands shook as she talked, and redness rimmed her brown eyes. He knew better than to ask her if she was okay, especially in front of Joe and Mark, but maybe he would find a way to question her later. Finding a murder victim would rattle any officer, but discovering a recent homicide victim in the middle of the wilderness when she was alone must have terrified her.

Patterson considered the implications of Sam's murder. If someone had murdered Sam the previous afternoon or evening, then the killer was either still in the vicinity, or Patterson or someone else had flown the perpetrator to town. *Did Brian, Deb, or Jason have time to murder Sam before flying to Kodiak?* he thought. *The timing would be tight but not impossible. Deb and Jason were late arriving at the lodge for the flight to town. Did they stop at Sam's cabin and shoot him before heading to the lodge?*

"Is Patrick outdoors checking around the cabin?" Patterson asked after thinking things through.

"Yes," Joe said. "Sara told him to bag the ax."

Patterson nodded. "I'll find him. Mark, will you stay here and look through Sam's things? I don't know what you're looking for, but bag any personal paperwork and anything else you feel we should take a closer look at."

"Yes, sir," Mark said.

Patterson found Trooper Patrick Little by a stack of logs behind Sam's cabin. With gloved hands, Patrick was sliding a long-handled ax into an evidence bag. He looked up as Patterson approached.

Patterson smiled at the young trooper. "I see you found Sam's ax."

"Yes, sir. This ax is the only one I see."

"I doubt Sam used this ax to murder the Bartletts, and then someone else murdered him, but we can't discount anything at this point. Have you found anything else?"

"No, sir, but I just started looking," he said. "We didn't see anything unusual on the trail between the Bartletts' lodge and Sam's place. I walked the trail slower than Sara and Joe and searched for evidence."

Patterson nodded. "Good job, Patrick. I'll circle the cabin and see if I notice anything, and you continue to search the woods around the cabin." Patterson had no idea what they were looking for, but he didn't want to miss anything that could point to the killer's identity.

By 4:30 p.m., Patterson felt they'd searched every inch of Sam's cabin and the surrounding woods. They all worked together to slide Sam's body into the bag and then carry him down to the boat. Next, they transported the bags of evidence they'd collected to the skiff, and then Mark piloted the boat with everyone on board back to the Bartletts' lodge. Just as they were tying up to the dock, the Kodiak Flight Services turbine Beaver circled overhead and landed.

There wasn't enough room at the dock for another airplane, so the turbine Beaver pulled up to the beach. Steve Duncan, the owner of the charter service, crawled out of the pilot's seat.

Steve looked at Patterson and nodded his head in greeting. "Is the tide still falling?" he asked.

Patterson looked at his watch. "It won't be low for over an hour. We'll make room for you at the dock. I can move my plane to the end."

Patterson, the troopers, and the crime scene techs loaded the evidence bags and their camping gear into the planes. Mark reminded Patterson about the desktop computer, and Joe and Jill unhooked it and carried it to the plane.

Duncan untied the turbo Beaver and departed with Jill, Joe, Peter, and Patrick. Patterson, Mark, Andy, and Sara stood on the dock.

Patterson looked at his three troopers. "I'm sure we forgot something," he said, "but this will have to do for now."

CHAPTER 24

Sunday, September 7th

7:45 p.m.

It was 7:45 p.m. when Patterson and his crew returned to trooper headquarters with their piles of evidence. There was no late flight to Anchorage on Sundays, so they would have to wait until the first flight in the morning to send Sam's body to the medical examiner.

Patterson gave Mark the grim task of sorting through Sam's paperwork to find his next of kin. If they couldn't find the information there, they would have to depend on one of the techs to uncover it on Sam's notebook computer. Patterson told Mark to go ahead and make the death notification call if he found contact information for a relative or even for one of Sam's friends. While Patterson normally liked to personally notify relatives as soon as possible, after passing along the grim news to three distraught families recently, he'd decided to delegate the task this time.

Helen was at the dispatchers' desk when Patterson entered trooper headquarters. "Dr. Libby wants you to call him right away," Helen said as soon as Patterson opened the door, her gruff voice betraying a lifetime of smoking cigarettes.

Patterson looked at his watch. "Does he want me to call him at home or wait until morning?"

Helen shook her head. "He said to call him on his private number as soon as you can."

"Do you know if Brad found Tim Fairweather?"

Helen nodded. "Mr. Fairweather is in the holding cell, and he's none too happy about it."

Patterson smiled. "Good."

He shut his office door, sat in his desk chair, and dialed Dr. Harold Libby's number.

"Sergeant Patterson," Libby said when he answered the phone. "I'm glad you got back to me this evening. We finished the posts on your eight victims."

"What did you find, Doctor?"

"Six were shot with a .44 caliber gun. I recovered four of the bullets, but two exited the skulls. Did you find them at the crime scene?"

"Yes," Patterson said. "Our techs found two bullets at the scene."

"As you know," Dr. Libby said, "the other two victims were bludgeoned to death with what I believe was a large ax or a similar instrument. It was a heavy, sharp implement, and I think an ax best fits that description."

"I saw the scene, and I concur. I think the killer used an ax and was very angry."

"Definite overkill," Libby said. "The shootings appear sterile in comparison. I couldn't determine how many times the killer struck each victim with the ax, but Julia Bartlett had more wounds than her husband. Perhaps Julia was the primary victim, or maybe the killer got tired after striking her so many times, so he delivered fewer blows to her husband. After all, swinging an ax requires a great deal of energy."

"Good point," Patterson said. "The number of wounds each victim sustained may or may not be important. Perhaps the murderer was exhausted after using an ax on the Bartletts, so he or she killed the guests with a gun." He paused a moment and then asked, "Did you find anything else, Doctor?"

"Yes," Libby said. "I discovered something surprising and a fact I thought might steer the course of your investigation."

I could certainly use some help right now."

"Julia Bartlett was three months pregnant," Libby said. "I thought this might be an important find in a woman her age."

"Jules Bartlett was pregnant? Wasn't she too old?"

"No," Libby said. "Apparently not."

"How old was she?"

"She was forty-six, but she obviously hadn't gone through menopause yet."

Patterson thought about the image he'd seen on Bob Bartlett's cell phone. "Can you get a DNA sample from the fetus and do a paternity test?"

"You don't think her husband was the father?"

"Possibly not," Patterson said. "She was involved with another man."

"I'll need this man's DNA."

"I'll get it for you."

"I can put a rush on it," Libby said, "but the results will take at least two weeks."

"I know," Patterson said, "but if this case ever goes to trial, the paternity of the baby might play into it."

"As soon as I receive the possible father's DNA from you, I'll send it and the DNA from the fetus to the lab."

"I have a question for you," Patterson said. "The guests were all shot in the head, but no one seemed to wake up as the killer walked through the cabin and methodically killed them."

"Yes. This is one of the things I wanted to talk to you about. I found traces of feathers in some of the wounds, and I assume the killer used a pillow as a sort of silencer. Did you find a pillow at the scene?"

"We did," Patterson said, "and I know the pillow would muffle the sound of a shot, but it still would be fairly loud. It should have at least awakened the other occupants of the room."

"My thoughts exactly," Libby said. "I ordered tox screens on blood samples from all the victims, but it'll be a few days before I get the results."

"Thank you, Doctor. I can't help but think the guests were drugged. But who could have done it?"

"Ah," Libby said, "I just find the 'what.' You, sir, find the who and how."

Patterson laughed. "By the way, I'm sending you another patient in the morning."

"Another murder there? Before long, there won't be any people left on your island."

"I think this one's related to the others. This victim was a neighbor of Bob and Jules Bartlett. He was one of my main suspects in their murders until one of my troopers found him dead in his cabin this morning."

"Was he shot?" Libby asked.

"Shot in the head."

"Good," Libby said with a dry laugh. "I hope I've done my quota of posts on hatchet murders this year."

"Yes," Patterson agreed. "I've had my fill of those too."

CHAPTER 25

Sunday, September 7th

8:20 p.m.

Tim Fairweather sat ramrod straight in a wooden chair in the interrogation room. His black eyes fixed on the door when Patterson entered.

"You have no right to treat me like this," he said.

Patterson sat in the only other chair in the room and wasted no time. "I saw a photo of you today, Tim."

Fairweather ran his right hand through his hair. "So what?" he said, his voice quieter.

"I don't think it was a photo you posed for," Patterson said. "I'd label it a candid shot."

Fairweather shifted in his chair. He said nothing.

"One of the interesting things about this photo," Patterson continued, "is who you're with and what you're doing, but the most intriguing point is where we found the photo."

"I don't know what you're talking about," Fairweather said in a whispery voice. Sweat dripped down his forehead.

"I think you know exactly what I'm talking about, Tim. Yesterday, you told me you didn't know Jules Bartlett very well, but from the photo I saw, you knew her intimately."

Tim Fairweather let out a heavy breath and sat back in his chair. "Just tell me what you saw, okay?"

"I saw a photo of you and Jules in bed together, and the photo was on Bob's phone."

"All right." Fairweather stared at the floor. "Jules and I had an affair, and Bob caught us."

"How?" Patterson asked. His question surprised him, but he realized it had been at the back of his mind ever since he'd seen the photo on Bob Bartlett's phone. "How do you have an affair in the middle of the wilderness? Your cabin is, what, thirty miles from the Bartletts' place?"

"About twenty-five miles," Fairweather said.

"When did you get to know Jules Bartlett, and how did you have an affair at her lodge? I assume she was rarely ever alone out there."

Fairweather sighed. "Jules and I were both stuck in unhappy marriages. We had a lot in common. It wasn't just sex. We spent most of our time together talking."

"Tell me how it started."

Fairweather mopped the sweat off his face with his handkerchief, and he looked up, his gaze unfocused. "A couple of years ago, Jules and I were both stuck at the cannery for the night. Bob dropped Jules off to catch the afternoon flight to Kodiak, and I was also planning to fly to town. Fog moved into town, though, and they canceled the flight. The cannery had plenty of open rooms, so we just stayed there for the night." His lips curled into a sad smile. "We sat at the same table for dinner in the mess hall and started talking. At first, we just chatted about superficial things like the weather and fishing. Then, we finally started talking about our lives. Our past. Our present. Our hopes for the future." Fairweather chuckled. "We stayed up all night talking, and we exchanged email addresses. Then, we started chatting by email, and finally, one night that fall, Jules told me that Bob was going to town for a few days, and she invited me to drop by the lodge for dinner. She was there alone. They didn't have guests, and Deb and Brian were both in town."

"How often did the two of you get together?"

"Not often," Fairweather said. "Whenever Jules knew she'd be alone at the place, she'd send me an email, and I'd slip over there if I could get away."

"Wasn't your wife suspicious?"

"Nah," Fairweather said. "She's always happy to get rid of me. I don't have a happy home life, Sergeant."

"Why not get a divorce, then?"

Fairweather shrugged, his eyes again focusing on Patterson. "I guess I'm lazy." He laughed. "Or, maybe I'm afraid Georgie would shoot me if I asked for a divorce."

"Did Georgie know about your affair with Jules?"

Fairweather nodded. "Oh, yes. Bob wasted no time telling Georgie after he caught us."

"When and how did he catch you?"

"A little over a month ago," Fairweather said. "Bob was suspicious of Jules, so he told her he was taking the boat to town, but instead, he came back to the lodge that night. When he saw my boat there, he snuck into the house and took the photo."

"Then what happened?"

"We got into a fight," Fairweather said. "He didn't even give me time to put on my pants before he pulled me out of bed and started hitting me. By the time we finished fighting, we were both bloody and bruised."

"What did Jules do while the two of you were fighting?"

"At first, she tried to stop us, but Bob backhanded her, and she crawled into the corner and cried." Fairweather tapped the table and looked into Patterson's eyes. "If I'd had a weapon on me, I would have killed Bob Bartlett that night." His black eyes blazed. "I've never hated anyone so much in my life."

Fairweather's frank admission surprised Patterson. "Did you kill him?"

"No," he said. "I could never hurt Jules. I loved her." Tears trickled down his cheeks. "I've never loved anyone as much as I loved Jules."

Patterson wasn't sure he believed him. Passion could be a powerful motive for murder. "Were Elle and Susan at the lodge when all this happened?"

Fairweather shook his head. "They had a short break between guests, and Elle and Susan went camping for two nights. I think Jules talked them into the camping trip so that we would have the lodge to ourselves."

"I assume when Bob Bartlett punched you at the cannery, his anger had more to do with your affair with his wife than with your boats banging against each other on the running line?"

Fairweather shrugged. "I heard him yell at Jules, so I told him she deserved someone better than him. He disagreed with me."

"How did Bob tell your wife about the affair?"

Fairweather sighed. "He emailed her. A real classy move on his part."

Patterson didn't bother pointing out that having an affair was hardly a classy move either. "How did Georgie respond to the news?"

"She threatened to kill me. Sergeant, my wife is a much more violent person than I am."

"Are you suggesting that she murdered the Bartletts and their guests?"

Fairweather shrugged. "No," he said. He rubbed his head and then raked his fingers through his hair. "Georgie might kill me, but she could never hurt anyone else."

"Did she confront Jules?"

Fairweather nodded. "One time when we were at the cannery, Georgie and Jules ran into each other in the store."

"What happened?" Patterson prodded when Fairweather didn't continue.

"I didn't see it, but Georgie told me she threatened to kill Jules if she didn't stay away from me." Fairweather dropped his head in his hands and massaged his temples.

Tim Fairweather's bravado had faded. It was as if someone had stuck a pin in him and let out all the air. Patterson watched the man deflate.

Fairweather mopped his face with his handkerchief. "Georgie wouldn't kill Jules, would she?"

Patterson studied the man. Was this an act? Was he trying to blame his wife, or was he genuinely concerned by the possibility that Georgie could have killed the Bartletts?

"After Bob caught you and Jules together, did you end your affair with Jules?" he finally asked.

Fairweather leaned back in his chair, his eyes directed at the table. "I was in love with Jules Bartlett. I begged her to leave Bob and told her I would divorce Georgie. I wanted us to be together."

"But Jules wanted something else?"

"Jules emailed me three days after Bob caught us." He shook his head. "She said she and Bob had decided to give their marriage another try." He crossed his arms over his chest. "I don't know how many times Jules told me she hated Bob." Fairweather lifted his gaze to meet Patterson's eyes. "I think Bob threatened her with something. I can't think of any other reason she'd agree to stay married to him."

"You think he threatened her with violence?"

Fairweather shrugged. "I don't know if it was violence or something else. Maybe he convinced her she would get nothing if she left him. From some of the stories Jules told me, I know Bob Bartlett could be very manipulative."

"Tim," Patterson said, deciding it was time to drop the bombshell, "did you know Jules was three months pregnant?"

Fairweather held Patterson's gaze but said nothing for several seconds. "Yes," he finally said in a hoarse whisper.

"How and when did you find out?"

"She emailed me with the news a few days ago."

"Did she know who the father was?"

"Jules was certain the baby was mine."

"What did you do when you heard the news?"

"Nothing," Fairweather said. "Jules asked me not to respond to her email because she was afraid Bob would see my reply."

"Did she mention what she planned to do about the pregnancy?"

"No," Fairweather said. "She said she was confused and needed to think. I planned to talk to her as soon as I had a chance, but ..." He shrugged.

"Did Georgie know Jules was pregnant?"

Fairweather shook his head. "No," he said. "Jules said she hadn't told Bob, and I certainly didn't tell Georgie. Georgie was already on the warpath. She would have killed me if she knew about the baby."

"What did you want Jules to do about the baby?"

"I wanted her to keep it," he said quietly. "I wanted us to be a family."

"Did Deb or Brian Bartlett know about your affair with Jules?"

Fairweather shrugged. "I couldn't say," he said. "If so, they never said anything about it to me."

"Do you get along with Sam Lutz?" Patterson asked.

The swift change of subject seemed to confuse Fairweather. "Sam? I barely know him. Why?"

"Mr. Fairweather, I'd like to get a DNA sample from you. Would you consent to allow one of our techs to swab your cheek?"

"Why?" Fairweather asked again.

"We want to determine the paternity of the baby Jules was carrying."

Fairweather exhaled a tired sigh. "Sure," he said. "I don't see why the identity of the baby's father matters now, but you can take my DNA. If Georgie hears about the baby, though, you will be responsible for my murder."

CHAPTER 26

Monday, September 8th

9:00 a.m.

At nine o'clock the following morning, Patterson sat across the conference room table from a trembling Elle Chaplin. A paper cup of coffee sat untouched on the table in front of her.

"How are you doing, Elle?" The question was not just a nicety. Her appearance alarmed Patterson.

Elle's red-rimmed, puffy eyes suggested she had been crying a great deal. Her unfocused stare signaled a lack of sleep.

"I'm okay," Elle said, her voice low and robotic.

"Have you taken any medication, Elle?" Patterson asked.

Elle slowly shook her head. "Just Tylenol."

"Have you been sleeping?" Patterson had seen her only two days earlier, but in that time, she looked as if she'd dropped ten pounds. Her gray sunken face worried him.

"A little," Elle said. "I slept a few hours last night."

"You don't look well. Would you like to see a doctor? We can run you to the emergency room at the hospital."

Elle's eyes widened, and she shook her head furiously. "No," she said. "I'm fine. I'm just sad."

"Do you feel like talking to me?"

"Sure," Elle said. "I'll tell you what I can."

"I'm sorry to make you remember the horrible events you witnessed a couple of days ago," Patterson said, "but I need you to tell me everything you did and saw the morning you found Jules's and Bob's bodies."

137

Elle inhaled sharply, but she nodded her head.

Patterson watched her. Elle seemed to be carrying a great weight. *Does she know who murdered the Bartletts and their guests? Is she trying to protect him or her?* Patterson didn't want to push her too hard. She seemed fragile and about to break. On the other hand, if she was hiding something, he needed to know what it was.

"You woke up at five a.m.," Patterson nudged.

Elle nodded. She stared at the table while she talked. "I always get up at five to bake the sweet rolls for breakfast. I have two hours to myself before anyone else gets up."

"Susan doesn't go to work when you do?"

"No," Elle said. "Susan comes downstairs at seven to set the table and help me in the kitchen. Bob usually gets up then, too, and Jules comes out a little later. Mornings are hectic because, in addition to breakfast, we need to pack lunches for the guests, and Bob and Jules get the fishing gear and bait rounded up for the day."

"When do the guests come down to the main cabin?"

"They usually start trickling in around seven thirty, but sometimes they come down earlier and get coffee," Elle said. "I always have two large carafes of coffee and one of hot water ready for anyone who wants it."

"Two days ago," Patterson said, bringing the interview back to the morning of the murder, "did Susan come downstairs at her usual time?"

"Yes. We were busy in the kitchen, and I glanced at the clock and realized how late it was. Bob usually turns on the generator by seven." She shrugged. "I just thought he and Jules overslept. It's late in our season, and we're all tired."

"Tell me again what you did," Patterson said.

Elle took several deep breaths, exhaling slowly. "I knocked on their door, and when they didn't answer, I opened the door a slit and called to them again several times. Then, I walked into their room and saw the blood." Tears dripped down her face.

Patterson pushed the tissue box toward her. "Take your time," he said.

Elle mopped her face. "As I told you before, I tried CPR on Bob. He was on his back, so I ran over to him and put my hands on his chest, but ..." She began to sob and covered her face.

Patterson waited. He hated making Elle relive this nightmare.

"Bob's face was gone. He looked like a monster, and he felt cold. Jules felt cold, too, and the blood was already starting to dry." Elle's voice dropped to a whisper. "There was nothing I could do."

"Of course not," Patterson said. "Jules and Bob suffered catastrophic wounds. I'm sure they died instantly. You couldn't have revived them. Don't blame yourself for this, Elle."

"Maybe if I'd checked on them sooner."

Patterson shook his head. "If they felt cold to you, they died several hours earlier."

Elle slowly nodded her head.

"What happened next?"

"What?" Elle looked at him, her face blank.

"When you decided you couldn't help Jules and Bob, what did you do?"

Elle's gaze dropped to the table. "I shut their bedroom door and went back to the kitchen. I think I was in shock. I told Susan they were dead and told her to run up and check on the guests."

"What was Susan's reaction?"

Elle remained silent for several seconds. "I don't remember," she finally said. "I don't think she said anything. I had blood on me, so I must have scared her." She shook her head. "I don't remember."

"What's the next thing you recall, Elle?"

Elle crossed her arms over her chest and hugged herself. "I remember Susan telling me the guests were dead. She said we had to call the troopers, and she said the killer could still be nearby." Elle looked up at Patterson. "I hadn't thought about the killer still being there. I grabbed the satellite phone and found the number for the troopers, and then Susan and I waited in the great room for you to arrive. I got one of Bob's shotguns and loaded it, just in case."

"What about Susan?" Patterson asked. "Didn't she also want a gun?"

Elle shook her head. "She said she was afraid of guns, so she just stayed next to me."

"Are you and Susan close?"

Elle shrugged. "She's a kid," she said. "I like her, but she's too immature to be my friend. I think of her more like a little sister."

"What can you tell me about the Bartlett family dinner the evening before the murders?"

Elle remained silent.

"Elle?" Patterson watched as she squeezed herself tighter. *What isn't she telling me?*

"Jules asked me to make enough food so she, Bob, Deb, and Brian could have a family dinner after the guests ate," she said. "The last time they had a family dinner, Jules invited Susan and me to join them, but this time, she made it clear that she wanted to have a private family dinner. She told us to clean the dishes after the guests ate and then go to bed, and she would clean up after the family. Susan and I started to set the table for the family, but Jules got kind of mad and told us to go to bed and give the family some privacy."

Patterson tapped the table while he thought about how to proceed. "Elle," he finally said, "I know you're very loyal to Jules and Bob, but you and Susan lived in their home and worked in their kitchen. I'm sure you know a great deal about the Bartlett family's interactions and tensions." He tried to look into Elle's eyes, but they remained fixed on the table. "I need to know what was going on in that family. Can you help me?"

After several seconds of silence, Elle said, "I don't know what you mean."

Patterson sighed. Elle was not making this easy. "Did Jules and Bob seem to get along well with each other? What about the kids? Did Brian fight with his parents, and what about Deb? I know she had a rocky relationship with her mom and dad, and she and Brian don't even seem to like each other."

"I try not to eavesdrop," she said.

"Elle," Patterson said, "I'm sure you know more than you're telling me. I need your help to catch the murderer."

"Bob wasn't very nice to Jules, especially this summer," she finally said. "He always put her down and loved to point out her mistakes. He blamed her for everything."

"How did Jules respond to his criticism?"

"She ignored him. I know she didn't love him anymore." Elle's eyes slowly met Patterson's. "One time, she told me she didn't think she would be at the lodge next summer."

"Do you think she planned to divorce Bob?"

She shrugged.

"Elle," Patterson said, "did Tim Fairweather ever visit the lodge?"

Elle's gray face flushed pink, and she quickly looked down again. "A few times," she said.

"Tell me about his visits."

"It's none of my business."

"Elle," Patterson said, "do you want us to find the person who brutally murdered Jules and Bob and shot the guests?"

"Yes, but ..." Elle began.

"Then you need to tell me what you know."

"I don't know anything." Elle's voice was so low Patterson could barely hear her. "Mr. Fairweather came to the lodge three or four times when Bob was in town running errands. He came in mid-June and then again a couple of times in July, and I guess once in early August." Elle paused a moment and then added, "Bob hated Tim Fairweather, but Mr. Fairweather and Jules were friends."

"What did Fairweather and Jules do when Tim came to the lodge?"

Elle shrugged. "Jules would make him dinner, and they'd spend the evening together."

"Did he spend the night?"

Her pink face deepened to red. "The last two or three times he spent the night, but I haven't seen him since early August. He didn't come over the last time Bob was in town."

"Did something happen between Tim and Jules?"

Elle shrugged again. "Susan and I knew not to hang around when Mr. Fairweather was at the lodge. We gave Jules and him space. Jules told us never to mention his visits to Bob."

"What do you think Bob would have done if he knew Tim Fairweather was visiting his wife?"

"Bob had a bad temper," Elle said. "I don't know what he would have done."

"How did Bob and Jules get along with Brian?"

"Fine," Elle said. "I think they planned for him to take over the lodge soon."

"Did you hear rumors about them selling the lodge to someone else?"

Elle shook her head slowly, but Patterson didn't believe her. "What about Deb?" he asked.

"Deb fought a lot with her parents," Elle said. She seemed to relax once the focus of Patterson's questions had shifted from Brian to Deb. "She had a drug problem, and she was always stealing stuff from her mom and dad to support her habit."

"What kind of things did she steal?"

"Money, if she could find it, but Bob usually put cash in the safe in his office. She also took jewelry from Jules, and once, she stole a valuable gun Bob had in a display case in his office. Bob had to go to town and buy it back from the pawnshop." Elle shook her head. "He was furious."

"Did Deb ever steal anything from you?"

"Bob told us to hide our cash," Elle said, "but I don't have anything worth stealing."

"Deb told us she's clean and sober. Do you think that's true?"

Elle nodded. "I do. She's been much nicer to everyone this summer, and her mind seems clearer. She isn't stoned all the time."

"Was she still stealing things?"

Elle sighed. "I don't know. Jules lost some jewelry and blamed it on Deb, but I think Jules misplaced it. She said she lost a bracelet, a necklace, and some turquoise and diamond earrings, but I don't remember seeing her wear that jewelry this summer. She rarely ever wears jewelry at the lodge. Why would she? We don't get dressed up there. Besides, except for the earrings, Jules said the missing jewelry wasn't valuable, so why would Deb steal it if she couldn't sell it for much?"

"What do you think happened to the jewelry?"

"I think Jules left it at her house in town," Elle said. "I don't think she ever had it out at the lodge. She just got confused."

"When did she tell you she lost the jewelry?"

She looked at the ceiling, lost in thought for a moment. "She lost the bracelet and necklace in mid-July and the earrings sometime in late August, I think. She blamed Deb, because both times, she noticed the jewelry missing soon after Deb had been at the lodge for dinner."

"Did Jules confront Deb?"

"Both times, and she and Deb got into screaming matches," Elle said. "I was surprised when Jules said Deb was coming to the family dinner the other night, because after Jules accused her of stealing her earrings a couple of weeks ago, Deb said she would never step foot in the lodge again."

"Tell me about your relationship with Brian," Patterson said to switch gears.

The light turned off in Elle's eyes. She'd relaxed while talking about Deb, but at the mention of Brian's name, she hugged herself tightly and said nothing.

"Elle, I get the feeling you care about Brian."

She shrugged, her eyes focusing on the table. "We're friends. That's all."

"Have you talked to him since you've been in town?"

Elle shook her head, and tears spilled from her eyes.

Patterson could see he was losing her, so he changed topics again. "On the night of the murders, you said you served dinner to the guests, cleaned up the dishes, and then left the Bartletts alone so they could have a private family dinner."

Elle nodded, her eyes still downcast.

"Did you go to your room?"

Another nod.

"Did you hear any noises coming from downstairs?"

"Like what?" Elle looked at Patterson, her eyes wide.

"Raised voices, perhaps. Did the Bartletts get into a fight at dinner?"

"No," Elle said. She grabbed a tissue and wiped her nose, but she did nothing to stem the flood of tears flowing down her face.

"What about later?"

"What do you mean?"

"Elle, someone brutally murdered the Bartletts. Did you hear any unusual noises?"

Elle buried her face in her hands and sobbed.

Patterson looked at her with concern. He wasn't sure what to do, so he watched Elle cry for several minutes.

Finally, Elle dropped her hands and looked at Patterson. "I can't talk anymore," she said. "I want to leave."

"You're free to leave at any time. Maybe we can chat again when you feel stronger."

Elle stood and took a step, but her legs buckled, and she grabbed the wall for support.

Patterson jumped to his feet and headed for her. He grabbed her arm to support her. "Are you sure you're okay?"

Elle nodded and pulled her arm away from Patterson. He watched her leave the conference room and then walk unsteadily down the hall. He thought about the interview. He'd learned a great deal from Elle, but he was most interested in what she hadn't told him. Maybe Susan could help fill in the blanks.

CHAPTER 27

Monday, September 8th

9:43 a.m.

Patterson watched Susan Pack walk down the hall and then ushered her into the conference room. She wore an ankle-length lavender dress dotted with small, yellow flowers. Her long, dark-brown hair hung down her back in a single braid.

"What did you say to Elle?" Susan asked him. "She's really upset." Her wide eyes looked up at his face.

Patterson hadn't noticed Susan's green eyes when he'd talked to her at the lodge. "I didn't mean to upset Elle," he said. "She seems very fragile. You two are staying in the same house. How is she doing?"

Susan shook her head as she took a seat at the table. "Not very well. I've never seen her like this. I guess seeing the Bartletts' dead bodies freaked her out."

"I imagine so," Patterson said. "What about you? How are you doing?"

"Okay, but I want to go home and see my boyfriend."

"We'd like you to stay in town for a few more days, and then you can go home."

Susan slowly nodded. "Will I be able to get the rest of my stuff from the lodge?"

"Sure," Patterson said. "We'll arrange for you and Elle to fly out to the lodge and get your things."

Susan sat with her hands primly folded on the table while she watched Patterson.

"Susan," he said, "I'd like you to tell me about the morning when you found the bodies."

"I already told you all that."

Patterson took a steadying breath. "I know you did, but I'd like to hear it again."

Susan shrugged. "Okay."

"What time did you get up that morning?"

Susan produced another shrug. "The usual time, I guess. I'm supposed to be downstairs by seven to help Elle."

"What was Elle doing when you came downstairs?"

"Making cinnamon rolls. The kitchen smelled so good."

"What did you do?"

"I started setting the table."

"Did you and Elle talk?"

Susan frowned. "I don't remember," she said after several seconds. "I doubt it, though. Elle isn't much of a morning person, so I usually keep to myself."

"Is she cranky in the morning?"

Susan nodded. "Very."

"Tell me what happened next."

"I did my job," Susan said. "I straightened up the great room and put the syrup and butter and other breakfast stuff on the table. I made sure the coffee carafes looked clean, and I set out plenty of cups for the guests." She paused. "Then, I went back to the kitchen to get honey for the table, and Elle noticed how late it was. I think it was seven thirty, and Bob hadn't started the generator." She shook her head. "I don't ever remember Bob oversleeping."

"Then what?" Patterson urged when Susan stopped talking.

"Elle said she'd better wake up Bob and Jules, so she walked down the hall to their room. I heard her knock on the door and call their names."

When Susan paused again, Patterson nodded to encourage her to continue.

Susan placed her hands flat, palms down on the table, and spoke in a steady voice. "I didn't hear anything for a few minutes, and then

Elle ran into the kitchen." Her eyes widened. "She was covered in blood, and it scared me."

"Did she scream when she found the bodies?"

"I didn't hear a scream," Susan said.

"What did Elle say to you?"

Susan closed her eyes for several seconds and then opened them again. "I think she said something like, 'They're dead,' and then she told me to go up and check on the guests."

"Take me through exactly what you did next, Susan, and it's important you tell me everything, even the smallest details."

Susan blinked her eyes. "Everything?"

Patterson nodded.

"I put on my boots and jacket," Susan said, "and I walked up to the cabin. There was a heavy overcast, and it was kind of dark. I remember I wished I'd brought my headlamp."

"Did you hear anything?"

"The leaves rustling. It was breezy." She paused. "I thought it was strange, though, because I didn't hear any noises from the guest cabin or on the trail. I sometimes have to wake up a group when they oversleep, but we had three different couples in camp, and I couldn't believe they would all oversleep."

"When you reached the cabin, what did you do?"

"I knocked on the sliding glass door for the first room. Each room has a separate outdoor entrance."

Patterson nodded. He had noted this when he was at the lodge.

"The curtain was shut, so I couldn't see through the glass door," she continued. "I knocked several times, and I thought maybe they were out hiking or in the great room talking to some of the other guests." She paused and took several deep breaths. Her eyes remained glued on Patterson's face. "I slid open the door and peeked around the curtains ..."

When Susan stopped talking, Patterson urged her to continue. "What did you see?"

"They were still in bed."

"Which couple was this?" he asked. The information probably didn't matter, but he realized that he'd paid little attention to the guests

147

in his haste to concentrate on the Bartletts. The Bartletts seemed to have been the targets of the murders, but Patterson had been a cop long enough to know that tunnel vision led to mistakes.

"The Brites were in the first room," Susan said.

"The couple from England?"

Susan nodded. "They were stuffy, but they seemed nicer than the Steins or the Weisses. Art and Fran Weiss from Atlanta were rude and ordered Elle and me around."

"When you saw the Brites still in their bed or beds, what did you do?" Patterson asked.

"Beds," Susan said. "The first room has twin beds, and the other two rooms have queen beds."

"What did you do then?" he asked again, trying to steer Susan back onto the subject.

"I called their names, but they didn't move, so I walked into the room and tiptoed toward the beds. That's when I knew," she said, her voice just a whisper.

"What did you know?" Patterson asked. He was sure he knew the answer, but he wanted Susan to tell him this story in her words.

"Someone shot them. I could see the holes in their heads."

"Did you check on the other guests?"

Susan nodded. "They were all dead."

"Susan, were the doors between the individual bedrooms and the great room open or closed when you arrived at the cabin?"

She squeezed shut her eyes for several seconds. "Closed," she finally said.

"You're sure?"

She nodded. "I opened them, but I don't think I closed them again."

"Did someone take your fingerprints when you arrived here today?"

"Yes. Why do you need them?"

"Your fingerprints will be on the doorknobs in the cabin, but if we know they belong to you, we can exclude them."

Susan nodded again.

"After you discovered the guests were dead, what did you do?"

"I was a little freaked," she said. "I ran down to the lodge as fast as I could and told Elle." Susan reached up and tugged on her braid. "Elle didn't seem to know what to do. I think she was in shock, so I told her I thought we should call the troopers. After that, we just stayed together and waited for you."

"Was Elle still wearing her bloody clothes when you got back to the lodge?"

Susan shook her head. "No, she must have changed. I didn't even think about it until you asked her if she got blood on her when she tried to give Bob and Jules CPR." Susan paused a beat. "I don't understand, though. How did she get blood on her clothes? Shouldn't it have dried by the time she found them?"

Patterson shook his head as well. "Some of it was dry, but it takes a long time for pools of blood to dry."

"I was scared," Susan said, "but Elle was freaked out. I've never seen her like that."

"Tell me about the night before the murders."

"There's not much to tell," she said. "After Elle and I cleaned up the dishes from dinner, Jules asked us to go to our rooms so that the Bartlett family could have a private dinner. I was tired, so I went to bed."

"Did you hear any noises after you were in bed?"

"Just Elle."

"What do you mean. What was Elle doing?"

Susan shrugged. "Nothing. I heard her come and go to her room a few times. It sounded like she was walking past my room, but she must have been going to the bathroom."

"Her room is between your room and the bathroom?"

Susan nodded.

"But she would walk past your room to go down the stairs," Patterson said.

"Yes," Susan said, "but Jules asked us to give the family privacy, so she wouldn't have gone downstairs."

"What about later in the night? Did you hear any strange noises then?"

"I didn't hear the murders," Susan said. "I don't know why, but I didn't hear anything."

Patterson studied his notes and considered what else he wanted to ask Susan. "What can you tell me about the Bartlett family?"

"This is only my first summer," she said. "I don't know them very well."

"You've been around them for a few months now, though. Give me your impressions. Start with Jules and Bob."

"Jules was nice, but she didn't think I should have a serious boyfriend. I got tired of her bugging me about it, but I know she was just trying to help me."

"And Bob?"

A slight smile creased Susan's mouth. "He had a temper," she said. "He taught me a lot about filleting and packaging fish, but he didn't have much patience. He expected me to learn it right away. He was surprised I knew how to use a hammer and a saw, though, and he complimented my strength."

"Did your parents teach you how to build things?"

Susan nodded. "We didn't build our house, but we built all the sheds, and I helped build my brother's house. He just lives down the road. I know how to use a power saw and a level and everything." Susan's green eyes shined.

"But Bob had a short fuse?" Patterson asked to return to the subject.

Susan nodded. "I learned not to let him hurt my feelings, though."

Patterson smiled. "You are wise beyond your years," he said. "How did Bob treat Jules?"

"He put her down all the time. Elle and I felt sorry for her, but she got him back?" she said, a question in her voice.

"How did she get him back?"

"She had an affair," Susan said.

Patterson was surprised she had volunteered this information. "Who with?"

"Tim Fairweather."

"Did Bob know about this affair?"

Susan shrugged. "I don't know."

"You didn't hear them fighting about it?"

"Sometimes I heard raised voices in their bedroom, but they never really fought in front of us. Bob said mean things to Jules in front of us and even in front of the guests, but they never yelled at each other." She shrugged again. "I could tell they weren't getting along, though."

"When was the last time Tim Fairweather came to the lodge?"

Susan lifted her hands from the table and placed them in her lap. "I don't know. It's been a while—maybe a month?"

"Did Brian Bartlett get along with his parents?"

At the mention of Brian's name, Susan wrinkled her face. "Most of the time," she said.

"What do you mean by 'most of the time'?"

"He came to the lodge several times this summer, and he and his dad would talk outdoors or even go out on the boat."

"Could you hear what Brian and his dad talked about?"

"Not really," Susan said. "One time, I saw them out on the boat, and they were fighting."

"How could you tell?"

"Brian was throwing his arms around while he talked, and I could hear his voice way in onshore. I couldn't hear what he was saying, but I knew he was mad. Then"—Susan's eyes shined as she relayed the story—"Bob grabbed Brian's shirt by the neck, and I thought he was about to punch him, but Brian stiff-armed him and pushed him away." She giggled. "I think Bob realized Brian would wallop him if they got into a fight."

"But you don't know what they were fighting about?"

"I think they were arguing over the lodge."

"Why do you think they were fighting about the lodge?"

"Earlier that day, Brian ate lunch with Jules and Bob, and I heard Bob tell him that he and Jules were planning to sell the lodge," she said. "They told Brian he could buy the lodge at full value, but they couldn't afford to give him a deal, and they certainly couldn't give him the lodge."

"What did Brian say?"

"Not much. I think he was stunned. I heard him ask why they wanted to sell it now, but I didn't hear what Bob and Jules said."

"Do you like Brian Bartlett?" Patterson wasn't sure why he'd asked the question, but by the way Susan talked about Brian, he had the feeling she didn't care for him, and he wanted to know why.

Susan shook her head. "Not really," she said. "He's a spoiled brat. Did he think his parents would just hand him their business?" She shook her head. "He's also a bully, and he says mean things to Elle and me. I don't know what Elle sees in him."

"Does Elle like Brian?"

Susan put her right hand over her mouth. "I shouldn't say anything."

"Susan," Patterson said, "I won't tell Elle what you say to me, but I need to know everything I can about Brian and Deb Bartlett."

Susan paused for several seconds and finally said in a soft voice, "I think Elle loves Brian. I saw them kissing the other night, and I noticed every time he came to the lodge, she'd run upstairs and put on makeup."

"How do you think Brian feels about Elle?"

"It's so sad," Susan said. "I think it's just a fling for him. He hasn't even called her since we got to town, and I think that's one of the reasons she's so upset."

"Has Elle talked to you about him?"

Susan shook her head. "No, Elle is very secretive."

"What do you think about Deb Bartlett?"

"I don't know her very well," Susan said, "and I doubt she even knows my name. Whenever she comes to the lodge, she and her parents fight."

"What do they fight about?"

"About everything. Deb uses drugs, she has a scuzzy boyfriend, she has piercings and tattoos her mother doesn't like, and she's always stealing things."

"Deb says she's no longer using drugs," Patterson said. "Do you think she still is?"

Susan shrugged. "I have no idea. As I said, I've barely ever talked to her."

"Tell me about Sam Lutz," Patterson said.

"Sammy? What about him?"

"I understand he and Bob had a big fight?"

Susan giggled again. "Bob caught Sammy window peeping."

"Sam said he was watching a deer. Do you think that's true?"

Susan shrugged. "Maybe."

"Susan, we found Sam dead in his cabin yesterday. Someone murdered him."

Her head recoiled as if Patterson had slapped her. "Sammy is dead?"

Patterson nodded.

"Was he murdered by the same person who killed Jules and Bob?"

"We don't know," Patterson said, "but right now, we assume he was killed by the same person or persons who murdered everyone at the lodge."

"Didn't one of the troopers question Sam on Saturday?"

Patterson nodded.

"The killer was still in the area then?" Susan hugged herself.

"We think the killer was either still in the area, or he or she left and came back to kill Sam."

"Who would do that?" Susan's wide, green eyes studied Patterson's face.

"We're trying to figure that out," Patterson said.

"Did you tell Elle about Sammy?" she asked.

"No," Patterson said. "She ran out of here before I had the chance."

"She liked Sammy. She'll be so upset. Should I tell her?"

"You can tell her about Sam if you want to. She'll hear the news soon anyway."

"I think Elle should see a doctor."

"Why do you say that?"

"She's acting weird."

"I think she's just upset about the murders."

"I know," she said, "but I think it's something more than that. I think she knows something, and she's keeping it inside. She needs to talk to someone, and she won't talk to me."

Patterson excused Susan and watched the thin girl in the baggy dress walk down the hall. He returned to his office and called the front desk. Irene, the senior dispatcher and receptionist, was on duty this morning, and Patterson told her to have one of the troopers give Elle and Susan a ride back to Brie's house.

"Have the officer take them to the store if they need groceries," he added.

"Yes, sir," Irene said. She lowered her voice to a whisper. "I don't know what you said to Elle, but she's very upset. She looks like she's about to faint."

"Do you think she should see a doctor?"

"I offered, and she said no."

"That's all we can do."

As soon as Patterson disconnected with Irene, he called Sara's cell phone.

"Sara, where are you?" he asked.

"I just arrived at headquarters, sir."

"Would you come straight to my office, please?"

Two minutes later, Patterson heard a knock on the door and asked Sara to enter. "Have a seat, Sara," he said.

Sara's hair was pulled back as usual in a tight bun, her cheeks flushed, and her brown eyes blazed with anticipation. "Sir?"

"I just interviewed Elle and Susan, and Elle told me something interesting."

"What?"

"She said Bob Bartlett has a safe in his office."

Sara stiffened.

While Sara was only one of the team members who'd spent the night at the lodge to sift through the entire crime scene, Patterson knew she would take his words as a personal rebuke. He also knew she would not get defensive and offer up excuses. He was not happy to learn his troopers had supposedly combed over the scene and managed to miss something as important as a safe. *What else did they miss?*

"In the office?" she asked.

"Yes," Patterson said.

"Do you know where in the office?"

"No, but I think I need to send a team out there to do a more thorough job, don't you?"

"Yes, sir." Sara's posture remained rigid, her eyes fixed on Patterson's face.

"Would you like to head up that team?"

"Very much so, sir, and I apologize for not doing a good job the first time."

"I'll send Jill with you. Do you think the two of you can find the safe?"

"Yes, sir."

Patterson felt bad about laying the blame for missing the safe at Sara's feet. The troopers and crime scene techs had probably been looking through the office when Sara went to Sam's cabin and discovered him dead. He imagined the crew was so concerned with collecting computers, phones, and financial records that they didn't bother searching for a safe. Still, it was a big miss, and Sara was part of the team, so she deserved a measure of the blame. He would be sure also to let the rest of the team know they had erred. Sara was a good trooper, and Patterson felt she would move up the ranks quickly. She would learn from this mistake.

"I don't have time to fly you out there today, but I'll have Irene set up a charter with KFS. She'll let you know the time."

"Should we try to open the safe?" Sara asked.

"Not unless you conveniently find the combination somewhere," he said. "Even then, I would prefer you bring the safe back here to open it. We need to protect the integrity of the evidence. I would guess it's a small safe. If it's a built-in safe, give me a call, and we'll need to come up with another plan."

"Yes, sir."

"Have the pilot stand by. I want to get that safe back here right away. You let me know if you think we need to spend more time going through the lodge."

Sara nodded and stood. Patterson watched her leave the room, her body rigid with tension.

CHAPTER 28

Monday, September 8th

11:02 a.m.

Elle ran to her bedroom, slammed the door, and threw herself onto the bed. Susan didn't seem to get the hint. A few seconds later, Elle heard her soft knocks on the door.

"I want to be alone for a while," Elle called.

"Are you okay?" Susan asked through the closed door.

"I'm fine, just tired."

"What did Sergeant Patterson say to you to upset you so much?"

"Not now, Susan."

Susan finally got the message, and a few seconds later, Elle heard the muffled sound of the television in the living room. Elle could finally cry in peace.

Within a matter of minutes, Elle drifted into a troubled sleep. Images raced through her mind and tumbled into a nonsensical nightmare. She saw her sister fighting against the hand holding her down and struggling to get to the surface for a gulp of air. Then, she saw the girl's bloody face in the bathroom, followed by so much blood and the unrecognizable faces of Bob and Jules. A moment later, it was her sister whose face was smashed and bloodied as she lay on the bed, stiff and cold.

A scream awakened Elle from her nightmare, and then Susan threw open the bedroom door and rushed to her.

Elle sat and pushed her back against the headboard. "What is it?" she asked.

"You were screaming," Susan said. "Are you all right?"

Elle rubbed her hand over her head. "I'm okay. I just had a nightmare."

"What about?"

"It doesn't matter," Elle said. She paused for several seconds and then asked, "Susan, the night everyone was killed, did we go straight to bed after we cleaned up the kitchen?"

"You don't remember?"

"I guess I fell asleep right away," Elle said. "I don't remember doing anything else, and I know I was tired."

"No," Susan said. "I heard you come out of your room at least twice."

"You did?" Elle thought she was going to be sick. *Why don't I remember?*

"I thought you were listening to the Bartletts from the top of the stairs," Susan added.

"No, I wouldn't do that," Elle said. *Would I?*

Susan shrugged. "Maybe you were just going to the bathroom, but it sounded like you walked past my room, and you were gone quite a while. I heard you walk back down the hall and shut the door to your room."

"What time did you hear me?"

Susan pulled on her braid and gave Elle a curious look. "The first time was about twenty minutes after we went to our rooms, and then I heard you again in the middle of the night." Susan's eyes widened. "Maybe it wasn't you the second time. Maybe it was the murderer."

"Tell me exactly what you heard the second time," Elle said.

Susan shrugged. "I heard someone in the hall, that's all. I just assumed it was you."

"Were they going toward the stairs or up the hall toward my room?"

Susan squinted her eyes. "Toward the stairs, I think, but I can't be sure. I was barely awake." She paused a moment. "Do you think it was the killer?"

"I don't know," Elle said. "I have to go to the bathroom. I want to take a shower. I'll talk to you later."

Susan started to walk toward the bedroom door but then stopped and turned around. "Did you hear about Sammy?"

"What about Sam?"

"Someone killed him," Susan said.

A loud siren sounded in Elle's head. Susan was still talking. Elle could see her lips moving, but she couldn't hear what she was saying. The loud sounds blaring in her head drowned out everything else.

Elle rushed to the bathroom and dropped to her knees in front of the toilet. She retched the meager contents of her stomach into the porcelain bowl. *Someone killed Sammy? When? Why? Why can't I remember? Has it happened again?* She couldn't stand Bob, and she'd hated the way he treated Jules. She'd thought she and Jules were close until she'd overheard what Jules said to Brian. Elle had planned to talk to Jules, but she hadn't had the chance. *I could never hurt them, though, and I would never hurt Sammy, would I?*

Elle stood under the water in the shower, alternating the temperature between hot and cold. She knew she needed to pull herself together, and she had to stop doubting herself. She hadn't had a problem in several years, and she did not plan to end up in the hospital or, worse still, in prison.

Elle climbed out of the shower. She pulled on her underwear and bra, and she slid her arms into the sleeves of her white blouse and buttoned it. She stared at her pale face in the mirror and struggled with her inner demons. She then opened the drawer and slowly removed the small black case. She sat on the floor and zipped open the case. Just the sight of the pack of razor blades eased her breathing. She removed a blade and took several deep breaths to steady her shaking hands. Slowly and deliberately, she drew the blade across her right thigh. She watched the crimson blood flow from the cut, and then she pressed toilet paper to her leg so that the blood wouldn't run onto the floor. She relaxed her head against the cool wall, closed her eyes, and sighed. For a few moments, anyway, her mind became blissfully blank. Her stress vanished, and she felt in control of her emotions.

Elle sat motionless for more than ten minutes, but then the fears and uncertainties again began to gnaw at her. Her past haunted her. When she'd overheard Jules and Brian talking a few days earlier, Jules's words had upset her, and they'd made her cry. She didn't remember feeling angry, just hurt, and she'd planned to talk to Jules about the matter.

Elle looked down at her leg, where blood still oozed from the cut. She checked her kit, but she'd already used her last Band-Aid. She held the toilet paper to her bloody leg and walked into the bedroom. She hoped she still had the extra box of Band-Aids in her pack. She unzipped the front pocket but found nothing other than two pens and a small notebook. She opened the large main pocket and began pulling out the contents onto the floor. She dug deeper into the recesses and removed smaller items.

When a sparkly item fell to the floor, Elle stopped her search for bandages and picked up the small round object for a closer examination. Her hand froze a few inches from her face, and Elle sat firmly on the floor. Air rushed from her lungs. The small, round diamond and turquoise loop stared up accusingly from her hand.

Why is Jules's missing earring in my backpack?

CHAPTER 29

Monday, September 8th

2:02 p.m.

Patterson sat in the conference room with Troopers Peter Boyle and Mark Traner and lab technician Rick Hanson. Rick was their tech guru, and he had already impressed Patterson by finding the compromising photos of Jules Bartlett and Tim Fairweather on Bob's phone. Of course, this feat required nothing more than scrolling through the images on Bob's phone, but Patterson knew Rick possessed a much broader skill set.

"Have you found anything interesting on the desktop or laptop computers?" he asked Rick.

He nodded. "It appears that Bob mostly used the desktop, and Jules used the laptop. I found lots of deleted emails on the laptop between Jules and Tim Fairweather." Rick shrugged. "They weren't sexting each other or anything. The emails are mostly cryptic, but you don't have to be a genius to read between the lines and see they were having an affair. I'll print off the emails for you," he added, "but it's obvious this was more than just an affair."

"What do you mean?"

"They were in love. Fairweather states that he wants to divorce his wife in one email, and he hopes Jules will consider leaving Bob."

"Good work, Rick," Patterson said. "Please print off those emails for me. Have you found anything else worth noting?"

"The financial stuff," Rick said, pushing his wire-rimmed glasses up on his nose. "I gave it to Angie because finances aren't my thing."

"You're more of a relationship guy, eh, Rick?" Peter said, and Mark laughed.

Patterson ignored Peter's jab. "What about the finances?" he asked.

"From first glance, it looked to Angie and me like the Bartletts were in serious debt. Angie should have more soon."

"Have her write a report on it."

Rick nodded. "Yes, sir."

"That's all for now, Rick," Patterson said. "Good work."

Rick shut his notebook and nodded to Patterson as he left the room.

Patterson looked from Mark to Peter. "I don't think I need to tell you guys how important it is to wrap up this case as quickly as possible. We have one or possibly two murderers who have killed nine people, and they're out there somewhere, possibly with more victims in their sights."

The two troopers nodded.

"I want background checks on everyone, including the victims, maybe especially the victims. The affair between Jules and Tim Fairweather looms front and center, but we can't let it be the only focus of this investigation." Patterson stood and walked to the whiteboard at the back of the room. He wrote the names of the victims on the board. "Peter, I want you to start with our list of victims, including the six guests. At this point, I don't believe they were the focus of these murders. They were unfortunately just in the wrong place at the wrong time." He narrowed his eyes at him. "We need to keep an open mind, though. Maybe you'll learn something about one of the guests to change the investigation completely."

"Yes, sir," Peter said. "I find the murder of Sam Lutz especially interesting, though. If we can find how he fits in with the other victims, perhaps he'll be the key to solving this."

"I agree," Patterson said. "I also want you to look into Sam's background, especially his relationship with the Bartletts. We know he and Bob Bartlett got into a huge argument this summer. Bob thought Sam was watching Jules with binoculars, but Sam said he was watching something else. Something was going on there."

"What do you want me to do, sir?" Mark asked.

"I'm getting to it," Patterson said. "But, first of all, Peter, ask Patrick to help you background check the victims, okay?"

"Yes, sir," he said.

Patterson turned back to the whiteboard and began a new list. He wrote the names Deb Bartlett, Brian Bartlett, Jason Caine, Tim Fairweather, Georgie Fairweather, Elle Chaplin, and Susan Pack. He tapped the board. "These are the people we know had access to the lodge on the night of the murders. Mark, I want you and Sara to take a hard look at each of these individuals. Do they have a police record? Do they have any record of violence?" Patterson shrugged. "Were they ever tardy for school? I want you to dig into every last detail of their lives."

"Yes, sir," Mark said. "But Georgie Fairweather was all the way out at her cabin the night of the murders."

"She claims she was alone at her cabin the night of the murders," Patterson said, "but she had a skiff, she had weapons, she had a great motive, and Georgie reportedly has a hot temper."

Mark nodded. "Yes, sir." He paused. "What about the captain of the boat Susan mentioned? The one who yelled at Bob."

"I've asked Bart to talk to him," Patterson said. "At this point, I think he's a long shot, but if Bart feels he warrants a closer look, we'll fly out there and find him."

"Do you think Elle and Susan are viable suspects?" Peter asked.

Patterson shrugged. "They were at the lodge during the murders, and they survived without a scratch. We have to consider them." He tapped Elle's name on the board. "Also," he said, "I don't think Elle is telling me everything. I think she knows more about the family dynamics than she's saying, but she is very fragile. I want to talk to her again soon, but next time I'll ask Sara to sit in on the interview with me. I think Elle might respond better to her."

The two troopers began collecting their things, preparing to leave the conference room.

"Guys," Patterson said, "we need to work fast. For now, this case is your only assignment."

CHAPTER 30

Monday, September 8th

3:04 p.m.

Patterson's desk phone chirped, and he looked up from the stack of printed emails he was reading.

"Sara's calling on the sat phone," Irene said, and before he could respond, she was connecting him to Sara.

"Sir," Sara said, "Jill and I found the safe. It's bolted into a recess behind the large family photo in the office."

"I remember the photo," Patterson said. "Can you remove it?"

"You have to open it to remove the bolts." Sara laughed and added, "But opening it won't be a problem because someone taped the key to the back of the safe."

"Really? The key is taped to the safe?"

"To be fair, it took us a while to find the key. It was taped underneath the safe on the back side. Luckily Jill has small hands, or we never would have found it. We were just trying to figure out how the safe was bolted down when she found it there."

"Have you opened the safe?"

"No, sir, I wanted to get your permission to open it, so we can unbolt it and bring it to town. Or, we can just bring the contents of the safe to town."

"Is the safe fairly small?"

"Yes, sir," she said. "We can bring the entire thing to town if you want."

"Unbolt the safe and bring it all to town," he said. He didn't want to have to fly back to the lodge the following day if they learned about a document sealed under the safe lining. Besides, the chain of custody would remain intact if Sara transported the safe and its contents together.

"Disturb the contents as little as possible," he added. "We'll take a closer look once you get it here. Oh, and Sara ..."

"Yes, sir?"

"Have Jill dust the front of the safe for prints before you open it."

"Yes, sir, she's already dusted but didn't find any usable prints."

Two hours later, Patterson met the two women at the floatplane dock. He helped them put the heavy safe in the back of the SUV, and they returned to trooper headquarters. They placed the safe on the table in the evidence room, and Sara took the key from her jacket pocket and opened the lock.

Patterson donned nitrile gloves and removed five envelopes from the safe. Four were full of money, and the fifth, a legal-size envelope, held the wills of Bob and Jules Bartlett plus a third document.

"Count the money, Jill, and we'll log it into evidence," he said. "Also, send the envelopes to the crime lab in Anchorage and have them check for prints. I know you're perfectly capable of pulling prints from an envelope, but I don't want to cut any corners here. Let's involve the official crime lab people."

Jill nodded. "Yes, sir. I'll send the envelopes to them right away."

"Tell them to put a rush on it," he said. "Also, take a careful look at the safe, and make sure we didn't miss anything. Check the lining and see if it's secure and double-check that no one's tampered with it."

Patterson returned to his office and sat at his desk. He still wore the nitrile gloves, and now, he carefully unfolded the first will and began to read.

Except for the boat, Bob Bartlett had left the bulk of his estate to Jules. He left the boat to Brian. He had a $50,000 life insurance policy, which would go to Deb. Patterson assumed the boat must have been only in Bob's name because Jules mentioned nothing about the boat in her will. She wanted her $50,000 insurance policy divided equally between her two children. Both wills referred to additional $30,000 life insurance policies to be used for burial expenses.

Patterson read the third document last, and it was by far the most interesting of the three. It was another will, but it covered the event in which Bob and Jules died simultaneously. Patterson guessed the Bartletts had created this document in case of a plane crash, a boat disaster, or a fire. He doubted they imagined dying at the hands of an ax-wielding maniac.

If both Bartletts died at nearly the same time, then they'd leave the lodge, the boat, and all the contents of the lodge to their son, Brian. They'd bequeath their house in the town of Kodiak to Deb, and they'd leave one $50,000 life insurance policy to Deb and the other to Brian.

Patterson still wore his nitrile gloves, and he had only touched the edges of the document, but he knew he should have slid the pages of the wills into clear plastic bags before he looked at them. He now walked downstairs to the lab and asked Jill to accompany him back to his office.

Patterson pointed at the wills on his desk. "Carefully copy these wills and then send the originals to the crime lab," he said. "We'll need to check them for prints."

Jill slid the three documents into evidence bags. "I'll let you know when they have the results, sir," she said.

A moment later, Patterson's phone rang.

"Sir, this is Joe Wilson from the lab."

"Go ahead, Joe."

"We collected four notebooks from Sam Lutz's cabin."

"I wasn't aware you found notebooks."

"Mostly, it's just bookkeeping. Sam apparently did a fair amount of trapping, and the notebooks list his sales and expenses, but I did find something interesting in his most recent notebook?" he said, a question in his voice.

Patterson waited impatiently for Joe to continue. "Yes?"

"It seems like Sam was watching someone."

"I don't understand," Patterson said.

"He lists dates, times, and coordinates where someone he refers to as 'the subject' buried things."

"You'll have to do better than that, Joe." Patterson massaged his neck. "I don't know what you're talking about."

"I'm not sure I do, either," Joe said. "Let me give you an example. On July fourteenth, he writes, 'Subject buried unidentified object near old shed,' and then he lists the latitude and longitude."

"How many of these notations did he make?"

"I've found six so far," Joe said. "The latest one was three weeks ago."

"Does he ever identify what the subject buried?"

"Out of the six I've found, he lists two as suspected cash and two more as jewelry."

Patterson rubbed his chin. "I need to see this notebook as soon as you're done with it."

"Yes, sir," Joe said. "I'll bring it to your office within the hour."

Patterson dropped the phone handset into the cradle and then sat back in his chair. Who was burying things near the Bartletts' lodge, and did it have anything to do with the murders? Did these notations explain who Sam was watching when Bob Bartlett accused him of window peeping?

CHAPTER 31

Monday, September 8th

12:03 p.m.

Elle ripped things from her pack until she found the matching earring. These were the earrings Jules thought Deb had stolen from her room a few weeks earlier. *How did they get in my pack? Did I put them there?* She began to shake violently. She pulled her legs up to her chest and pushed back against the wall. She remembered her bloody leg too late and looked down at the streak of blood on her white blouse. She buried her face in her hands and cried.

Elle wrapped more toilet paper around her cut and checked the medicine cabinet in her bathroom for a Band-Aid. She didn't find any, so she rifled through the bathroom drawers but still found nothing. She pulled on a pair of jeans, changed her bloody blouse, and walked down the hall to the living room, where she found Susan sprawled on the couch, watching TV.

"Do you have any Band-Aids?" Elle asked.

Susan unlocked her eyes from the TV and looked at Elle. "Sure," she said. "Did you hurt yourself?"

"I cut my leg while I was shaving," Elle said.

Susan frowned at Elle and then pushed herself off the couch. "I have some in my bag," she said.

Elle followed Susan to her bedroom and watched while she reached into the closet and unzipped her blue backpack. Susan pulled a box of Band-Aids from the bag.

"How many do you need?" Susan asked.

"Maybe two."

"Are you okay?" Susan asked after handing the Band-Aids to Elle.

"I'm fine. I'm just tired. I think I'll rest for a while."

"You can talk to me," Susan said. "You can tell me what you're feeling."

"Thanks," Elle said. "Maybe later."

"Can I ask you something?" Susan asked.

"What?"

"Why did you yell at Jules?"

"I don't know what you're talking about," Elle said. "I never yelled at Jules."

Susan stared at Elle for several seconds. "Yes, you did. The day before the murders, I heard you screaming at Jules, but I couldn't tell what you were saying. I was outside, and I heard it."

Elle took a step back from Susan. "I need rest," she said and then fled to her bedroom, slamming the door behind her.

Elle threw herself on the bed and began to sob. She forgot about bandaging her leg and fell into a restless sleep.

Before long, Elle slipped into the same terrible nightmare she'd had the previous night. The faceless stranger entered Jules and Bob's bedroom. The couple lay on their bed, sound asleep. The stranger advanced slowly toward Jules's side of the bed and raised his arm in the air. He held an object that looked like an ax. Slowly and methodically, he swung the instrument toward Jules's head.

Elle awoke with a start. She stared at the ceiling. Was it possible she had heard the killer murder Jules and Bob? Maybe she heard a noise and went downstairs to check it out. Perhaps she saw something and blocked it out of her mind. Maybe she saw the killer. An image of Brian swam through her mind, but she pushed it away. She refused to believe Brian could kill his parents.

CHAPTER 32

Monday, September 8th

5:10 p.m.

The pain in Patterson's neck began the slow march up the back of his head. He checked his watch and sighed. It was 5:10 p.m. already, and he felt as if they had accomplished nothing on the case today. They had bits and pieces of information, but none of it seemed related to each other.

Sam's notebook represented his current puzzle piece. The lab tech, Joe Wilson, had marked eight entries in the book with yellow tape flags. Patterson was now reading through them, but they made no sense, and he doubted they related to the murders. In between recording sales and expenses for his fur-trapping business, Sam had jotted down poems in the notebook. Between his stanzas of homespun rhymes, he'd listed the coordinates where his "subject" had buried either cash, jewelry, or unknown objects. Joe had thoughtfully plotted Sam's reference points on a map, and Patterson referred to the map as he read about each burial. Most of the burials were on or near the Bartletts' property, and Patterson knew they needed to return to the lodge to check the spots. Perhaps he would send two of his troopers the following day. These mysterious burials seemed like a wild goose chase, though, and he hated to expend money and human resources on them. If only he'd had this information before Sara and Jill had returned to town.

Patterson put Sam's notebook aside. He took a bottle of aspirin from his top desk drawer and popped three in his mouth. Patterson then sat back in his chair and closed his eyes. He wanted to go home and take a nap, but he also wanted to feel he'd accomplished something on this case today. Still, his head hurt too much to think clearly.

By the following morning, he hoped to know more once his troopers reported on their background checks for the primary persons of interest in the case. Maybe then, he would have a good lead and a suspect worthy of most of his focus. The most likely candidates were Tim Fairweather, the Bartlett kids, and Deb's boyfriend, Jason, with an emphasis on Tim Fairweather and Jason Caine.

Patterson slid Sam's notebook into his bottom desk drawer and locked the drawer.

When he passed Irene's desk, he told her he was leaving for the day and asked her to inform Brie when she arrived for her shift to call him if anything happened on the case.

When he got home, Jeanne met him at the door with a hug and a kiss.

"Wow, what did I do to deserve this?" he asked.

"I have news," Jeanne said.

"Good news, I hope. I don't need more bad news today."

"I hope you think it's good news," she said. "I'm pregnant."

Patterson could not force a smile, and he watched Jeanne withdraw from him. The pounding in his head increased.

"I was afraid you wouldn't be happy," she said, tears spilling from her eyes.

Patterson reached for his wife. "You know I want us to have a child, hon, but I'm just worried about you."

The Pattersons had been trying to have a baby for seven years, and two years earlier, Jeanne had started fertility treatments. She'd finally gotten pregnant in the spring, and she seemed happier than Patterson had ever seen her. When Jeanne miscarried in June, she plummeted so low that she nearly took her own life. He dreaded stepping onto that roller coaster again, and he feared what Jeanne would do if she lost another baby.

"I know," Jeanne said. "I'd given up on getting pregnant ever since the miscarriage and didn't think I could without the fertility treatments, but lately I've had morning sickness, so I did a test this afternoon." She offered a tentative smile. "I have a good feeling this time," she added quickly.

Patterson pulled his wife to him and hugged her. "You haven't seen a doctor yet?"

"No," she said, "but I'm sure I'm pregnant."

"Make an appointment right away, okay?"

"I will," Jeanne said. "Try to be happy about this."

"Promise me you'll start seeing a therapist again," he said.

"You think I'm going to have another miscarriage, don't you?" Jeanne pulled away from Patterson and frowned up at him.

Patterson chose his words carefully. "I hope you don't." He paused and added, "But I'm scared what will happen if you do."

Jeanne's face fell. "You're right," she said and then backed up a step. "I'll call tomorrow and make appointments with my doctor and my therapist."

After Jeanne's sobering news, Patterson's head screamed with such ferocity that he knew he could not eat a bite. He told Jeanne he needed to lie down and rest a few minutes. The next thing he knew, his alarm sounded its 6:00 a.m. wake-up call.

CHAPTER 33

Tuesday, September 9th

7:10 a.m.

Elle made herself toast with peanut butter for breakfast. Susan was already up and planted on the couch in front of the television. Instead of a morning show or the news, Susan was watching the cartoon channel.

Elle sat in an overstuffed chair and tried to focus on SpongeBob.

"It's beautiful out," Susan said. "Do you want to go for a walk?"

Elle tried to think of a way to decline Susan's invitation, but she admitted to herself that she had nothing else to do, and she could use the fresh air.

"Sure," Elle said, "as soon as I finish my toast."

Fifteen minutes later, the two young women left the house. The air smelled like autumn, with a hint of wild cranberries and decaying leaves. The sun was still low on the horizon and provided little heat. A thick dew clung to the grass, and Elle pulled her jacket tight and zipped it. She turned her face to the sky and inhaled a deep breath.

"It's nice, isn't it?" Susan said.

"I love fall," Elle said.

"Did you sleep better last night?" Susan asked. "I didn't hear you yell."

"I know I screamed yesterday, but have I been yelling a lot while I sleep?"

Susan shrugged. "Just since we got to town."

"Did I say anything?" Elle was almost afraid to hear the answer to the question.

"Two nights ago," Susan said, "you yelled something about Jules."

"What did I say?"

"I couldn't make it out, but I could tell you were mad at her."

"You must be wrong. I wasn't mad at Jules."

"Then why were you yelling at her the day before she died—the day before someone killed her?"

"I don't remember yelling at her," Elle said. "You're wrong."

"I heard you," Susan pushed.

"I don't want to talk about it," Elle said, "and unless you change the subject now, I'm going to turn around and go back to the house."

"Okay. I won't talk about it."

Susan remained quiet for the next several minutes, and then she began skipping like a little kid. Elle reminded herself that Susan was barely more than a child. She was happy when Susan skipped several paces in front of her. She wanted to enjoy the crisp autumn air and not think about the murders for a few minutes. Susan finally stopped and waited for Elle to catch up with her.

"Have you talked to Brian since we got to town?" she asked.

"No," Elle said. "Why?"

"I'm just curious about what the troopers have told him and Deb."

"I don't think the troopers know much," Elle said. "I wonder if they think the Bartletts' killer is the same person who shot Sam."

"How do you know Sam was shot?" Susan asked.

"Didn't you tell me that?"

Susan shook her head. "Sergeant Patterson didn't tell me how Sam was killed."

"I must have just guessed he was shot," Elle said. *Why do I think Sam died from a gunshot wound?*

"I wonder if they suspect Brian or Deb of killing everyone?" Susan said.

"Why would they suspect Brian?" Elle snapped the words at Susan, her hands on her hips.

"Sorry." Susan slowed her pace and walked beside Elle. "I don't know why you always defend him," she said softly. "He was mean to you the other day at the lodge when the troopers were there."

"I don't always defend him," Elle said, "and he was upset the other day. He'd just found out someone murdered his parents."

Susan shrugged. "But he hasn't called you since we got to town."

Elle sighed. "He has a lot going on in his life. Besides, we're not a couple. He doesn't owe me anything." The tears rimming her eyes caused her words to ring false.

"Do you think Deb and Jason killed Jules and Bob?" Susan asked.

"I have no idea who killed them," Elle said. "Nothing makes sense." She pushed the memory or the nightmare she'd had the previous day from her mind.

Susan's eyes widened in excitement. "We have to find out what happened at the family dinner. It just makes sense. Bob or Jules must have said something to upset Brian and Deb so much that one or both of them killed their parents."

"I don't think so," Elle said. "I know Brian isn't a murderer, and I don't think Deb could kill her parents, especially with an ax."

"Jason could, though," Susan said.

"I don't know," Elle said. "Maybe. I don't want to talk about this, Susan."

"Okay, but if you talk to Brian, will you tell me what he says?"

"Sure," Elle said. She had no intention of telling Susan what she and Brian talked about, if they ever spoke to each other again. The quickest way to shut up Susan, though, was to tell her what she wanted to hear.

Elle tried to enjoy the autumn air, but Susan had ruined her walk by talking about Brian and the murders. Elle felt relief when they returned to the house, and she shut herself in her bedroom.

Elle tried to read, but she couldn't keep her mind on the book. Next, she attempted to sleep, but she only tossed and turned. She checked her watch. It was nearly 10:00 a.m. She called Brian's cell phone and waited while it rang.

Brian answered on the third ring. "Elle?"

Since cell phones didn't work in the wilderness at the lodge, Elle rarely talked to Brian by phone, but they'd exchanged numbers the previous fall.

"Sorry to bother you," Elle said quickly. "I just wanted to know how you're doing?"

"I'm fine, Elle," Brian said, "but you need to leave me alone."

His words stung, and Elle didn't know how to respond.

"What happened during your family dinner the night before your parents died?" Elle's words surprised her.

"Elle, not now."

"Susan said she overheard your dad tell you they were planning to sell the lodge to someone else."

Brian didn't respond.

"Did you fight about selling the lodge during dinner?"

"Elle, this is none of your business," he said, carefully enunciating each word.

"I heard what your mom said the other day," Elle said. She fought back the tears, but she felt them trickle down her cheeks. "She told you that she thought you could do better than me."

"Elle," Brian sighed. "I'm sorry you heard that, but she didn't mean anything. She was just concerned about your past."

Elle felt herself go cold. She'd told Jules about her problem childhood in the strictest of confidence. Jules had no right to tell Brian.

"Elle, are you still there?"

"Yes," Elle said, but her reply sounded more like a croak than a word.

Brian said nothing for several seconds, and while she waited, Elle's mind raced. No wonder Brian wanted nothing to do with her. How could Jules tell him her secrets?

"Elle," he said, "you didn't hurt my parents, did you?"

"What?" Elle thought she must have misunderstood him.

"Look, I'm sorry, but I know you can be violent," Brian said. "You have been violent. You didn't … kill them, did you?"

Elle ended the call and threw her phone as hard as she could at the bedroom door. She immediately heard Susan running down the hall.

Susan threw open the bedroom door. "Are you okay?" she asked. "What happened?"

CHAPTER 34

Tuesday, September 9th

7:45 a.m.

Patterson reached trooper headquarters at 7:45. He sat at his desk and reviewed the stack of call slips Irene had handed him on his way past her desk. Nothing looked pressing, and unfortunately, nothing suggested a new lead in the case. He removed Sam's notebook from his desk drawer and began reading through it. A pilot's journal had recently helped Patterson solve a murder, but he didn't think they would be as lucky with Sam's notebook. For one thing, the book was not a daily diary but more of an accounting journal peppered with excerpts of Sam's creative writing. Sam had apparently fancied himself a poet, and maybe this stuff was good. Patterson knew he was no judge of poetry. Jeanne liked poetry, so perhaps he should read some of this to her and see what she thought about its quality.

Sam's observations about someone hiding things appeared at random moments throughout the book. The references bore dates beginning in July and ending September 1st. Sam didn't provide much information, but Patterson doubted he had ever planned to show this book to anyone. The notations were probably only meant for himself, so he could remember what day and where he saw this individual hiding things. Sam had not even indicated whether the person was male or female. Patterson didn't like to leap to conclusions, but the obvious assumption was that Deb was hiding things she'd stolen from her parents. He planned to talk to Deb and Brian again this afternoon, so he'd ask Deb point-blank if she hid stuff in the woods.

Just as Patterson was shutting Sam's book, a knock sounded on his door.

"Come in," he called.

Joe Wilson stepped into Patterson's office and closed the door behind him.

"Sir," Joe said, waving a stack of papers at Patterson, "I stayed late last night and uncovered a bunch of emails from the desktop computer. They were deleted but still on the hard drive." He walked forward and set the stack of papers in the middle of Patterson's desk.

Patterson sighed as he considered the daunting task of reading through what must have been two hundred or more emails. "Did you read them?"

"No, sir," Joe said. "I didn't have time, but I printed all of them."

"Are you still working on the computers and phones?"

"Yes, sir, but I haven't found anything interesting yet."

Patterson thanked Joe for his hard work and then bundled the stack of pages and headed down the hall to the large room where his force had their desks. When he entered the room, he saw only Mark Traner and Gary Reeves.

"Gary," Patterson said, "how are you this morning?"

The trooper looked up from the cup of coffee he was sipping. "Fine, sir."

Patterson handed the computer pages to him. "These are deleted emails from the desktop computer at the Bartletts' lodge. I'd like you to go through them and let me know if you find anything interesting."

"Yes, sir," Gary said.

"How are you doing on the background checks?" Patterson asked Mark.

"I'm making progress."

"Are Patrick, Peter, and Sara here yet?"

"I don't know about Patrick, but I saw Peter and Sara a minute ago."

"Give me a call once they're all here. I want to meet in the conference room."

Twenty minutes later, Patterson sat at the head of the table in the conference room, with Sara and Peter seated on one side of the table and Patrick and Mark on the other.

"I plan to bring in Brian and Deb again this afternoon and question them together," Patterson said to start. "There doesn't seem to be much love lost between the two of them, so I hope by pitting them against each other, I can learn more about the Bartlett family dynamics. Which one of you looked into their backgrounds, and what can you tell me?"

"I took Deb, and Sara checked out Brian," Mark said.

"You start, Mark," Patterson said.

The trooper cleared his throat and looked at his notebook. "Deb has a long record. Her juvenile record is supposed to be sealed, but I talked to some of the patrolmen who arrested her. She had a prescription drug problem and then a romance with heroin." He shook his head. "She did the usual things to support her habit, including shoplifting, robbery, and prostitution. She spent most of her teens in and out of rehab facilities."

"What about her parents?" Patterson asked. "Did they do anything to help her?"

Mark shrugged. "Again, this information is just hearsay, but according to my sources, her parents put her in a treatment facility down in Seattle three times. Deb escaped from the place once, and the other two times, she started using again as soon as she was released. After she turned eighteen, her parents washed their hands of her."

"What about her police record as an adult?" Patterson asked.

"More of the same," Mark said, "but the detective I talked to said she believed Deb was trying to get sober. She's stayed out of trouble for the past eighteen months."

"And her boyfriend, Jason?"

The trooper shook his head. "That guy is a loser. He's been arrested multiple times for everything from selling drugs to robbery and domestic abuse. One woman even accused him of rape, but the charges didn't stick."

"Was the domestic abuse against Deb?" Patterson asked. He wasn't surprised to learn about Jason's propensity for violence, but confirmation of his abuse pushed him to the top of Patterson's list of suspects.

"No," Mark said. "Jason beat his former girlfriend so badly that she ended up in the hospital. She pressed charges at first but then dropped them. At least she had enough sense to break up with him, though." Mark shook his head again. "It wasn't his first charge of domestic abuse. It was his third, and he was convicted once."

"Did your detective friend tell you if she thinks Jason's still dealing drugs?"

"She feels certain he's still in the drug business, but he hasn't been busted selling drugs in over two years."

"Did you get a feel for Deb's relationship with her parents?"

"I've been trying to run down Deb's friends," Mark said, "but most of them are drug addicts. I just found a girlfriend who was an addict, but she's been clean and sober for three years. She and Deb are still close. She says Deb is doing well and is better now than she has been in a year. She was worried, though, about what Deb might do in the wake of her parents' murders."

Patterson nodded. "Good work. Did you ask her about Jason Caine?"

"I asked, but she said she'd never met him."

"Sir, have you gotten the tox screens back on the guests yet?" Patrick asked.

"No," Patterson said, "but I hope to have them soon."

"I still don't understand why none of the guests heard anything," Patrick said. "They all looked like they were sound asleep when the murderer shot them."

"The shooter did muffle the gun with a pillow," Sara said.

"Still," Patrick said, "you'd think at least one of them would have heard something."

Patterson nodded. "I agree with you, Patrick. We'll see what the tox screens say." He looked at Sara. "What did you find out about Brian?"

"The thing that jumped out to me about Brian," she said, "is he is in debt up to his eyebrows."

"The fishing boat?" Patterson asked.

Sara nodded. "Two years ago, he paid nearly $300,000 for it and another $100,000 for a commercial salmon permit."

Peter laughed. "Talk about bad timing. Salmon fishing's been a bust the last two years."

"Yes," Sara said, "and the harbormaster told me Brian doesn't use the boat for any other fishery such as halibut or cod."

"How is he making payments?" Patterson asked.

"This is just a rumor, but the harbormaster told me he heard Brian's father bought the permit for him, and he made the first few boat payments. Daddy must have stopped paying, though, because Brian hasn't made any payments lately, and he's about to lose the boat."

Patterson rubbed his chin. "If a judge determines the wills we found in Bob Bartlett's safe are legitimate, then Brian stands to inherit the lodge from his parents."

"Interesting," Mark said. "Brian's parents conveniently died just before they had the chance to sell the lodge to someone else and erase Brian's inheritance."

"Maybe the kids teamed up to kill their parents," Peter said.

"They both had reasons to want their parents dead," Patterson said. "Good work, Sara. Keep digging. We need to talk to Brian's crewmen. Maybe they can give us a feel for the relationship between Brian and his parents." Patterson glanced down at his notes. "What about the Fairweathers?" He looked from Mark to Sara. "Did either of you have a chance to look at them?"

Mark and Sara glanced at each other and laughed. "Wow!" Sara said. "Those two are something else."

"They have a nice cabin in Kanuk Bay and a house in town," Patterson said. "How do they pay for it all? Are they retired?"

"I've been trying to get a handle on their finances, but they don't bank anywhere in town," Sara said. "I know Tim was a contractor in Kodiak and Georgie worked at the hospital as a receptionist. I think Tim made a bundle of money, and they both retired early. They live in Kanuk Bay in the summer and Kodiak in the winter." She looked up from her notes. "One of their neighbors told me they also have a condo on Maui."

"Do you think they made their money legitimately?" Patterson asked.

Sara shrugged. "I haven't found anything to suggest otherwise."

"I checked with Kodiak police, and I gave Bart a call," Mark said. "KPD has a record of twenty-three reports of domestic abuse calls from their residence here in town."

"Who was the reporting party?" Patterson asked.

"Georgie placed sixteen of the calls, and Tim made seven reports. Bart said the same thing. He's taken numerous calls from one or the other claiming abuse."

"Is there any evidence that Tim has physically abused Georgie?"

"Not really," Mark said, "but I'm sure there's more than enough verbal abuse to go around. The officer I talked to with KPD told me that the domestic abuse calls started about four years ago. He said they initially took them seriously and hauled Tim away to jail the first three times. Then, Tim placed the next call, and he was bleeding. They said Georgie went at him with a steak knife, but she didn't do much damage, and Tim declined to press charges."

"How long have these two been married?" Patterson asked.

"Twenty-eight years and seven months," Sara said.

"Officer Downs told me that he believes they reached the point four or five years ago, after they'd both retired, when they should have divorced. Instead, they've clung to this toxic relationship. Downs said he expects one of them to kill the other, and his money is on Georgie to win the battle."

Patterson tapped his pen on the table. "If Georgie is in danger, KPD shouldn't take this so lightly."

"That's just it, though, sir," Mark said. "Both Downs and Bart think Georgie is the aggressor, and Tim is the victim."

"I don't know Georgie Fairweather," Patterson said, "but Mark, didn't you describe her as meek?"

The trooper shrugged. "Yes, and I have trouble believing Georgie is the dominant partner in the relationship, but that's how Downs and Bart see it."

"If Georgie has a violent temper," Patterson said, "then I wonder what happened when Bob Bartlett told her about Jules and Tim's affair."

"I asked both Downs and Bart that question, and they both gave me the same answer. They said they were surprised Tim is still alive."

Patterson nodded slowly. "Tim might still be alive, but Jules isn't."

"Do you think Tim Fairweather's life is in danger?" Sara asked.

"He didn't tell me that he was worried about his safety," Patterson said. "Has he flown back to his cabin yet?"

The four troopers all shook their heads.

"I think he's planning to fly back home sometime today," Patterson said. "We need to question Georgie Fairweather."

"We still have the same problem with her," Mark said. "Her cabin is an hour away from the Bartletts' lodge, and if she's the murderer, she would have had to travel back and forth in the dark."

"Not easy, but not impossible," Patterson said. He sipped his coffee while he stared at his notes. "Who else do we have?" he asked. "Peter, Patrick, did you find anything of interest on the six guests?"

"No, sir," Peter said, "but it's tough to find much on foreigners. I googled the Brites and the Steins, and the only thing I learned was that Henry Stein is a controversial financier in Berlin. He certainly has enemies, but I can't imagine any of them following him to a remote area of Kodiak Island to kill him. I found nothing of interest about the Brites, and Patrick looked at the Atlanta couple."

"Art and Fran Weiss," Patrick said. "By all accounts, they were pillars of the community."

Patterson shrugged. "The guests are a long shot, but we needed to check." He looked around the table at his troopers. "Did you learn anything else?"

Sara said, "I have one thing, sir. Elle Chaplin."

"What about her?"

"She has a sealed juvenile record in Indiana," she said. "I haven't found anyone willing to talk about it yet, but I did learn she spent several years locked up."

This news surprised Patterson, and he began to wonder about the source for Elle's current fragile state. Maybe she'd experienced a traumatic past with law enforcement, and memories of past events haunted her now. "Keep digging," he said. "You can always find some-one willing to talk. Try past teachers or schoolmates."

"Yes, sir," Sara said.

"What about Sam Lutz?" Patterson asked. "I can't figure out how he fits into all of this. From the notations in his journal, Sam was spying on someone who was hiding cash or jewelry. Was this why the murderer killed him, or did Sam see something the night of the murders?"

"I looked into Sam," Peter said. "The guy is clean. He has no re-cord of any type. He was a financial analyst with a big New York firm, and he must have done well. He retired at thirty-eight and built a small cabin in Alaska." He shrugged. "I guess everyone has a dream."

"No sign anyone has ever accused him of being a sexual predator or a Peeping Tom?" Patterson asked.

"Absolutely not. My feeling is that the murderer killed Sam be-cause he thought Sam saw him or her either coming or going to the lodge the night of the massacre."

"Or the killer is the same person who Sam was watching hide things," Mark Traner said, "and the murderer knew Sam was already suspicious of him or her."

"If Mark is right," Sara said, "then Deb, either alone or with the help of Jason, is our likely suspect. We know Jules and Bob accused Deb of stealing from them."

"Okay, people," Patterson said, "we have work to do here. Right now, we have too many good murder suspects." He looked at Sara and said, "Sara, keep digging into Elle. Also, go to Brie's house and talk to Elle and Susan, together and separately. Push harder on what they know about Sam. Was he watching someone? When did they last talk to Sam? Just because Bob told Sam to keep his distance doesn't mean Elle and Susan didn't walk over to Sam's place now and then."

"Yes, sir."

"Mark, you and I are going back out to Kanuk Bay and find out whatever we can about the Fairweathers and the Bartletts. The bay covers a large area, but it's like a small town. We'll talk to the can-nery workers. Did everyone there know about Jules and Tim's affair?

I doubt Georgie kept her mouth shut after Bob told her. Also, we need to question Georgie, either in Kanuk Bay or here in town. I want to know what she has to say, and I want to learn what it takes to make her angry. From your description of her, I can't see her wielding an ax in a fit of fury, but maybe I'm underestimating her strength. I'd like to take a closer look."

Patterson nodded to Peter. "Peter, talk to the Bartletts' neighbors and friends here in town and ask about all the members of the family." He swung his gaze to Patrick Little. "Patrick, do the same thing with the Fairweathers. They must be obnoxious people to have as neighbors, so I bet you can find someone who'll talk about them."

"What about the residents of the village of Kanuk Bay? Shouldn't we interview them too?" Peter asked.

Patterson nodded. "The residents of Kanuk are on my list, but they aren't at the top. Bart said the Bartletts rarely came to Kanuk, so I doubt the residents could tell us much about what happened at the lodge on September sixth."

"There's no store in Kanuk, and I'm not sure you can even get fuel there," Patrick said. "The Bartletts could get everything they needed at the cannery, and the cannery is closer to the lodge."

"From what we've learned about Bob Bartlett, though," Sara said, "I bet he managed to make some enemies in Kanuk."

Patterson nodded. "We can't overlook the village."

"What time do you want to leave, sir?" Mark asked.

Patterson looked at his watch. "Let's plan to leave here at noon. I need to do a few things here first."

"Yes, sir."

"Are you heading back to your desk?" Patterson asked Mark.

He nodded.

"Tell Gary I'd like him to bring the emails to my office once he's read through them."

CHAPTER 35

Tuesday, September 9th

9:25 a.m.

As soon as Patterson returned to his office, he placed a call to Brian Bartlett and told him he would like for him and his sister to come to trooper headquarters as soon as possible. He then called Deb and told her the same thing. He hoped to get the interview underway because he wanted to leave for the Aktuvik cannery by noon. The afternoon forecast called for showers and twenty-knot winds out of the northeast, but the wind was supposed to increase to thirty-five knots by midnight, when the showers would become steady rain. Patterson didn't mind flying in twenty-knot winds, but the weather could rapidly deteriorate if the system arrived sooner than expected.

Patterson called Irene and told her to let him know when the Bartlett siblings arrived.

A few minutes later, he heard a knock, and Gary Reeves opened the door, a bundle of papers in his hands.

"Have you read through those already?" Patterson asked.

"I skimmed," Gary said. "I need to look through them more carefully, but I knew you'd want the high points."

Patterson smiled and sat back in his chair. "Good man. Have a seat."

Gary sat in the chair in front of Patterson's desk and rested the stack of papers on the desk. He handed the top two pages to Patterson. "I think these two will interest you," he said.

Patterson put on his reading glasses and quietly examined the pages. He then let out a low whistle and nodded. "Yes, indeed.

Either Tim Fairweather was lying to me, or he wasn't aware of what his wife knew."

"She definitely knew Jules was pregnant, and she knew Bob suspected Tim was the father," Gary said.

"From what I've heard about Georgie Fairweather, I assume she discussed this matter with her husband," Patterson said.

Gary laughed. "It's a wonder he's still alive."

Patterson shook his head. "I guess we'll have to haul Tim back in here again. It would be easier just to keep him locked up."

He again glanced at the two emails. The first was from Bob to Georgie telling her about Jules's pregnancy. The second was from Georgie to Bob, and it simply said, "I'll kill them both."

"Thank you, Gary," Patterson said. "Mark and I plan to speak with Mrs. Fairweather this afternoon, and these emails will come in handy."

"Yes, sir," Gary said. "I'll go through the rest of these again."

"Let me know if you find anything of interest, and sort the emails into piles of junk, business, personal, and so on."

Patterson watched Gary leave and shut the door behind him. *Could Georgie Fairweather be our murderer?* He reminded himself to keep an open mind. Mark's description of Georgie was that she was plump and meek, but he knew looks could be deceiving.

Twenty minutes later, Irene called him. "Brian Bartlett has been here about five minutes, and his sister just arrived."

Patterson told Irene to show them to the conference room and offer them coffee or water. He then consulted his notebook and thought about what he wanted to ask the younger Bartletts. He believed it was possible that either Brian or Deb could have murdered nine people, but which one was guilty, or were they both innocent? Or were they both guilty?

Deb Bartlett sat on the far side of the conference table in the left-hand corner, while Brian sat on the near side in the right-hand corner. Deb stared at her phone, and Brian stared at his folded hands, resting on the table. Patterson sat at the end of the table next to Brian.

Patterson thanked Deb and Brian for meeting with him so quickly. He noted that Deb looked clean this morning. Her blonde hair hung just past her shoulders, and makeup muted the acne scars on her face. He couldn't tell whether she was wearing a skirt or pants, but a dark-green knit blouse accented her green eyes and slim figure. The long sleeves of the blouse hid any possible bruises on her arms. Brian wore a sweatshirt and jeans, his curly, blond hair tousled.

"Have you learned anything about who murdered my parents?" Brian asked.

"*Our* parents," Deb corrected him.

"Whatever," Brian said.

Patterson shook his head. "I'm afraid we don't have anyone in custody yet," he said, "but we're getting closer. We've been searching through your parents' computers and phones." He looked from Brian to Deb. "We've found a few interesting things."

"Like what?" Deb asked.

"Did you two know that your mother was having an affair with Tim Fairweather?"

"No way," Deb said. "That guy is crazy. Mom would never have anything to do with him."

Brian said nothing but returned his gaze to his hands.

"Brian?" Patterson asked. "Did you know about the affair?"

Brian remained silent for several seconds and then released a long sigh. "I knew," he finally said.

"What?" Deb said. "You're lying."

Brian stared at his sister. "If you weren't obsessed with yourself all the time, maybe you'd notice what's going on around you."

Patterson held up his hands. "Let's keep this civil," he said. "How did you know about the affair, Brian?"

"Dad told me. He said he and Mom were getting divorced."

"Why, so she could marry Tim Fairweather? Give me a break," Deb said and then jumped to her feet.

Brian shrugged. "That's why they wanted to sell the lodge. They needed to split up their assets."

"They didn't say anything about it at dinner," Deb said, balling her hands into fists.

"Please," Patterson said. "Sit down, Deb."

Deb slowly sat in the chair, but her posture remained rigid.

Patterson watched Deb resume her seat, wondering how to phrase his next question to keep her from jumping up and leaving the room.

"Deb, you need to remain calm," he said. "I understand I have difficult questions, and I'm sure they'll upset you, but I need your help to find the murderer."

Deb said nothing, but she stared at Patterson.

Patterson returned his attention to Brian. "At the lodge, you told me you didn't know if your parents were planning to divorce."

Brian shrugged. "I didn't see how their relationship could matter. I still don't."

"Why don't you let me worry about what matters," Patterson said. "Your job is to tell me the truth."

"I thought I'd talked Dad out of selling the lodge," Brian said. "I was surprised when he mentioned it at dinner."

Patterson again looked from one Bartlett sibling to the other. "Did either of you know your mother was a little over three months pregnant?"

The color drained from Deb's face, and she sat back so hard in her chair that she nearly tipped it over. Brian again remained silent, not reacting to the question.

"Did you know about the pregnancy, Brian?" Patterson asked.

Brian's gazed remained focused on his hands, but he slowly nodded. "Dad told me."

"What?" Deb sat forward and slapped her hands on the table. "Why didn't anyone tell me? A few months ago, Mom told me she thought she was going through menopause."

Brian glared at his sister. "If you'd pay attention, you'd know what's happening around you," he said again.

"Shut up, Brian," Deb said.

"What did your father tell you about the pregnancy, Brian?" Patterson asked.

Brian's eyes dropped again. "Tim Fairweather was the father."

"Why did he think Fairweather was the father?" he asked.

Brian now glared at Patterson. "Why do you think? She was having an affair with Fairweather, and she and Dad hadn't had a sexual relationship in months."

"Did you ask your mother about the affair or the baby?" Patterson pressed.

Brian shook his head. "No," he said. "I didn't blame Mom for finding someone else. Dad could be mean, and he treated Mom like crap. She wanted something better, but why Tim Fairweather?" He glanced at Deb, who was now crying. "Fairweather is crazy, and he has an explosive temper. She traded down from Dad by choosing Fairweather, and the guy is married." A dark cloud fell over Brian's face. "I couldn't believe I was about to have a brother or sister who was his kid." He nodded to Deb. "And I thought *she* was a worthless sibling."

"I hate you, Brian," Deb said, nervously pulling at her hair.

"What's on your arm?" Brian asked. He stood and walked toward his sister.

Deb immediately dropped her arms underneath the edge of the table. "None of your business."

"Let me see your arm," Brian demanded.

Patterson knew he should stop this confrontation, but he was curious to see what would happen. After all, the reason he'd put the two siblings in the same room was so he could study their interactions.

Brian grabbed Deb's arm and pulled.

"Stop! You're hurting me!"

"Show me," Brian said. He continued to pull at Deb's arm until she jerked it from underneath the table and slammed it on the surface. The bangle on her arm bounced.

Brian stared at the enameled copper bracelet encircling Deb's left wrist. "It's Mom's. You stole it from her!"

"I did not," Deb said. "She gave it to me last year."

"You're lying," Brian said. "You're always stealing her jewelry."

"Not since I quit using," Deb said.

"A couple of weeks ago," Brian said. "Mom accused you of stealing her earrings."

"I didn't take her earrings." Deb slammed her fist on the table again. "She must have lost them."

"Yeah, right."

"Sit down, Brian," Patterson said.

Brian returned to his seat but continued to glower at his sister.

Patterson decided he should change the subject. "We've been going through your parents' financial records, and they were carrying a lot of debt. Was their lodge in trouble? Were they having trouble booking guests?"

"They were in debt because they spent all their money on Brian and his ridiculous boat."

"Shut up, Deb. What about paying for all your trips to rehab?"

"They paid for rehab twice," Deb said. "Once I reached eighteen, they refused to give me a penny."

"Yeah," Brian said. "They were sick and tired of paying for your drug abuse. At least I was trying to make something out of my life."

"You thought they should hand over the lodge to you. Why did you deserve the lodge? Why shouldn't I get it?"

Brian huffed out a sarcastic laugh. "What would you know about running a lodge?"

"As much as you do!" Deb yelled.

"Okay, pipe down." Patterson pretended to be annoyed by Brian and Deb's argument, but their jealousy and anger fascinated him.

"You killed them to get the lodge," Deb said, her voice barely above a whisper, but she enunciated each word as her eyes shot arrows at her brother.

Brian sucked in a tight breath but said nothing.

Patterson paused, waiting for the pair to say something else, but Deb's furious accusation ended their conversation.

"Did either of you know about your parents' wills?"

Neither Brian nor Deb responded to the question.

"Brian, did your parents tell you what was in their wills?" Patterson asked.

Brian looked at him. "I know they had their wills done a couple of years ago," he said. "They told me I would inherit the lodge."

Interesting, Patterson thought. *Before, Brian told me he didn't know what his parents had put in their wills.* "Did you know what else you would get or what Deb would inherit?" he asked.

Brian's gaze once again dropped. "No, they only told me about the lodge. Once they decided to sell the lodge to someone else, they probably changed their wills, though."

Patterson didn't believe Brian. He suspected he not only knew the entire contents of their wills, but he also knew they hadn't yet changed them.

"What about you, Deb?" Patterson asked. "Do you know what your parents put in their wills?"

Deb shook her head. "My father told me several years ago that he was disowning me, so I'm sure they left me nothing." She shrugged. "I don't want their money, anyway."

"Can either of you tell me anything about your father's feud with Sam Lutz?"

After several moments of silence, Brian said, "I have a theory. I think Dad suspected Mom was having an affair. The night he caught her and Fairweather together, he was supposed to be in Kodiak. He told Mom he planned to fly from the cannery to town, so he used the skiff to get to the cannery. Instead of getting on the plane, though, he snuck back to the lodge and caught Fairweather in bed with Mom."

When Brian stopped speaking, Patterson nodded for him to continue.

"I think up until the time he saw Mom in bed with Fairweather, Dad believed she was having an affair with Sam Lutz. When Dad saw Sam looking through binoculars at something or someone near the lodge, he exploded and told Sam to never come near the lodge again."

Deb nodded. "It makes sense," she said. "I didn't understand why Dad went ballistic on Sam. He didn't even give Sam time to explain himself. He just assumed the worst of him. If he thought Mom and Sam were having an affair, though, of course he'd be furious with him."

"As you both know, the killer or killers murdered Sam only hours after murdering your parents and the others at the lodge. We've been looking through Sam's things and trying to understand why he was also murdered." He looked from Brian to Deb. "In a notebook of poems, Sam made several notations about someone hiding items—money, jewelry, things of value—near the lodge. Does this mean anything to either of you?"

Deb slowly shook her head.

Brian said, "Deb?" He stared at her.

Deb whipped her head toward Brian and said, "It wasn't me, okay?"

Deb turned toward Patterson. "I didn't take anything from Mom this summer, and when I did steal from her and Dad, I certainly didn't hide what I took. I sold it. I needed money for drugs, so I stole things. What would be the purpose in burying the items I took?"

"So you could retrieve them when no one was watching," Brian said. "We're on to you, Deb. You might as well quit lying. The bracelet on your arm tells the truth."

Deb folded her arms across her chest and stared at the wall.

"You've had a few days to think," Patterson said. "Do either of you suspect who the killer or killers are?"

Deb looked at Patterson. "Yes," she said. "He's in this room."

"Nice, Deb," Brian said and then looked at Patterson. "I think you need to take a closer look at my sister's boyfriend."

CHAPTER 36

Tuesday, September 9th

11:30 a.m.

Fog hung low over the town of Kodiak as Patterson warmed up the Beaver's engine. Mark sat next to him, strapped into his seat with his headphones in place. Patterson talked to the tower and two other pilots who had just returned to town, and they all reported he would need to fly around Spruce Cape instead of through the mountain passes near Kodiak. They said the fog had dissipated from Port Lions south, and at that point, he could fly inland and cut through the passes for the remainder of his trip.

Right now, calm winds prevailed over most of the island, but the wind was supposed to increase steadily as the day progressed. He and Mark had gotten out of the office by 11:20 a.m., but by the time he'd warmed up the plane and flown the longer, more circuitous route to the south end, it would be nearly 1:30 p.m. before they reached Kanuk Bay. He hoped to finish interviewing Georgie and the cannery workers by 5:00 p.m. so he and Mark could get back to town by 6:30 p.m.

Mark remained silent for the first twenty minutes, and Patterson knew his trooper was smart enough to let him concentrate on flying beneath the low-hanging fog and clouds. Without being told, Mark looked down through his window, watching for boats entering the port. While they were flying well above the mast height of a salmon seiner, Patterson might have to maneuver around the ferry if it picked this moment to traverse the narrow inlet accessing the port. Once they passed Port Lions, the ceiling lifted to 2,500 feet, and Patterson felt the muscles in his shoulders relax.

Mark's gaze lifted from his window, and he settled back in his seat. After a few moments, he asked, "Where are we going first?"

Patterson spoke into the mike on his headset. "Let's stop at the Fairweathers' cabin first. I want to land there while it's still calm enough to leave the plane at the beach. Also, I hope Tim hasn't returned home yet, and we can talk to Georgie without him looking over her shoulder. If Tim's already there, we might have to bring Georgie back to town with us."

Mark nodded. "It'll be tough to get Tim to leave the room if he's there."

Patterson and Mark traveled in silence for the next twenty minutes. Patterson flew through the inland passes when he could, but the wind was already getting bumpy, and the rough air in the passes made him nervous. He finally flew back to the coast. This track would take at least thirty minutes longer, but it would provide a smoother ride.

"Who do you want to talk to at the cannery?" Mark hadn't spoken for so long that his sudden question surprised Patterson.

"As many people as we can in the time we have," he said. "I'll start with the manager and the office staff while you question the crew. We won't have time to talk to everyone, but we should get a feel for what they know and if they have any suspicions about who the murderer is."

"Do you want me to ask if they knew about Fairweather and Jules?"

"Yes," Patterson said. "We need to find out if the affair was common knowledge. Also, do they remember seeing Tim Fairweather at the cannery the night of the murders, and did Deb and Jason remain at the cannery after returning from the lodge around eight thirty p.m., or did anyone see them leave in a skiff later in the evening? According to Deb and Jason, they remained together all night after Jason picked up Deb from the lodge, but I don't believe them. Maybe we can find someone who saw Jason or Deb leave the cannery alone." Patterson paused a moment and then added, "Let's also ask if anyone saw Georgie and Jules or Georgie and Bob interacting."

"What about Tim and Bob or Tim and Jules, for that matter?" Mark asked.

"Yes," Patterson said. "I imagine most of the cannery workers won't have much to say about the Fairweathers or Jules and Bob, but they should have opinions about Jason and Deb. Didn't Tim Fairweather say he and the cannery mechanic are friends? Make sure you talk to him again and find out what he has to say about the night of the murders. Ask him again when he last saw Tim. What did Tim talk about, and does he think Tim left the cannery that night. He's an important witness."

Mark nodded. "The mechanic's name is Jim Chase. Maybe he's remembered something since I talked to him the other day."

"It would also be nice if we could learn what time Tim left the cannery the morning after the murders," Patterson said. "He said he ate breakfast and left a little after six a.m. and went straight home, but can anyone back up his claim?"

"If he ate before he left, someone should have seen him in the mess hall," Mark said.

"This weather is supposed to deteriorate, so I want to head back to town no later than five p.m. We won't have time to talk to everyone. I would start with the mechanic, the people who worked near Jason and Deb, and the cafeteria staff. The people on the food line can hear all the gossip, and gossip is good. It might not be usable in a court of law, but it could point our investigation in the right direction."

"Yes, sir," Mark said. "I'll be happy to fly out here again to talk to anyone we miss today."

Patterson nodded. "Let's see what we learn today, and then we'll decide if we need to do a more thorough canvass."

A slight chop creased the surface of the water when Patterson landed in front of the Fairweather cabin. The appearance of the sky concerned him more than the waves, though. He could land in much rougher sea conditions than this, but the dark sky threatened worse to come. He wouldn't feel happy until they'd landed in Kodiak and he'd tied the plane to the dock.

Mark helped Patterson secure the Beaver to a tree on the bank above the beach. No one came to the beach to meet them, which either meant that no one was home or the Fairweathers did not welcome their intrusion.

Patterson led the way up to the cabin. Georgie Fairweather soon approached them on the trail, a shotgun held firmly at her side.

"Mrs. Fairweather," Patterson said. "I'm Sergeant Patterson with the Alaska State Troopers, and I believe you've already met Trooper Traner."

"I know who you are," Georgie said, jerking her head at Mark. "He took my husband away, and he hasn't returned yet."

"He's not in custody, ma'am," Patterson said. "He's free to come home at any time."

"He's supposed to come home this afternoon," Georgie said, "but you gave him a free trip to town, and he'll leave me alone out here by myself as long as he can."

Patterson was happy to hear Tim Fairweather had not yet returned from town. If she cooperated, he and Mark would be able to interview Georgie without her husband's interference. "If" was the operative word, though. Right now, the woman held a shotgun and looked none too happy to see them.

"We have some questions for you, Mrs. Fairweather, if you can spare us a few minutes," Patterson said.

Georgie stood her ground for several more seconds and then turned and headed for the door. "Call me Georgie," she said.

Once inside the cabin, Georgie offered the men coffee and ushered them into the main room, where the large picture windows provided the perfect view of the gathering storm clouds.

Patterson and Mark sat on the couch, and Georgie took a seat in a chair facing them. "I don't know what I can tell you," she said. "I already told you Tim wasn't here on the night of the murders. I can't give him an alibi."

"We want to talk to you about your whereabouts the night of the murders," Patterson said.

"Me? Why?"

"Ma'am, we know about Tim's affair with Jules, and we know Bob told you she was pregnant."

Georgie's gray eyes narrowed, her posture rigid.

Mark had described Georgie as meek and overweight, but this was not the Georgie Fairweather he observed. While she could stand to lose a few pounds, her pink T-shirt displayed well-formed biceps, and ever since he'd first met her, Patterson had detected a smoldering rage boiling just beneath the surface.

"Yeah, I knew about the affair—so what? It wasn't Tim's first indiscretion, and it won't be his last."

"How did you feel about Jules?" Patterson asked.

"How do you think I felt?" Georgie quietly enunciated each word, her face burning red.

"I know I wouldn't be happy," he replied.

Georgie snorted a laugh. "Exactly, I wasn't happy with the perfect Mrs. Bartlett. Why don't you ask me if I hated her enough to kill her?"

"Did you?" Patterson asked.

Georgie cocked her head to one side and studied Patterson for several moments. "I smiled when I heard someone whacked Jules to death with an ax. I bet her face doesn't look so pretty now. But I wasn't the one who did it. Besides, why would I kill Bob? I had nothing against him."

Anger burned in Georgie Fairweather's pebble-gray eyes. Blotches of red covered her cheeks and neck, and her hands were clenched into fists. She frightened Patterson, and he began to feel sorry for Tim. He had doubted that Georgie was the aggressor in her toxic relationship with her husband. After meeting her, though, he believed she could be responsible for at least half the domestic abuse in this marriage. If he were married to Georgie Fairweather, Patterson doubted he would be able to close his eyes to go to sleep at night. No wonder Tim sometimes slept at the cannery.

"What did you say to your husband when you found out about the affair?" he asked. Tim Fairweather was lucky his wife hadn't served him a lethal dose of cyanide in his morning coffee.

Georgie shrugged. "I told him I'd leave him if he ever strayed again, and he promised he wouldn't. What else was there to say about it?"

Patterson knew Georgie did more than let Tim off with a gentle warning. He pushed harder. "Did Tim have feelings for Jules?"

197

"No," Georgie said a little too quickly. "He said it was just sex, nothing else. I'm the only woman he loves."

Yeah, right. "Did Tim and Jules end the affair before Jules was murdered?"

"Oh, yes," Georgie said.

"What about the baby?" Mark spoke for the first time.

Georgie widened her eyes and looked at him. "What about it? It wasn't Tim's."

"Ma'am," Patterson said, "we know Bob Bartlett sent you an email telling you he believed the baby was Tim's."

Georgie shrugged. "It doesn't matter now."

Patterson studied Georgie for several seconds and wondered if he should take her to town and lock her in a jail cell. *What will happen when Tim returns from Kodiak? Will she shoot him in his sleep?*

"I see you have two small boats on your running line," Patterson said. "Do they both run?"

Georgie shrugged. "The last time I checked, but you'd have to ask Tim. I don't pay much attention to the boats."

"But you're comfortable running a boat?" Patterson asked.

Another shrug. "Not really," she said, "but I can run one if I need to. I'm not a mechanic, though, so I don't like to take the skiff by myself."

Patterson nearly laughed at Georgie's attempt to paint herself as a damsel in distress. He didn't buy the act, and he bet she wouldn't think twice about motoring the boat to the Bartletts' lodge in the dead of night. He could almost envision her wielding an ax to kill Jules. From looking at the position of the bodies, he believed the murderer had killed Jules first and then turned his or her attention to Bob. Dr. Libby said Jules had received more blows than Bob. *Maybe Jules was the primary target. If Georgie committed the murders, then perhaps her only reason for killing Bob was to eliminate a witness.* Patterson didn't know why Georgie would kill the guests, but he doubted the act would bother her.

Patterson looked at Mark. "What would you like to ask, Mark?"

The trooper cleared his throat. "Did you ever confront Jules about the affair?" he asked.

Georgie pushed back in her chair, but her posture remained rigid. She seemed to consider her reply. "I talked to her once at the cannery," she finally said.

"What did you say to her?" Mark urged.

"I told her to keep her hands off my husband."

"And what did she say?" he asked.

"She didn't say anything."

"Georgie," Patterson said, "do you think your husband killed the Bartletts?"

She returned her gaze to Patterson. "I don't know why he would kill Jules, because he liked her well enough to sleep with her. He hated Bob Bartlett enough to kill him, though, and I can see Tim murdering the guests out of spite."

"Georgie," Patterson said, attempting to soften his tone, "does Tim abuse you?"

Georgie snorted and then shrugged. "We fight hard, Sergeant. Sometimes Tim wins, and sometimes I do."

"We heard about your radio call a while back, announcing your husband was in his boat, armed and dangerous. Were you trying to get him killed?"

Georgie laughed. "It doesn't matter now. We made up."

"What time did Tim return to your cabin on Sunday morning?" Mark asked.

"The day after he spent the night at the cannery?" Georgie asked. Mark nodded.

She shrugged. "He was home when I got back at a little after two p.m."

Patterson and Mark shared a look.

"Where were you?" Patterson asked.

"I was deer hunting that morning, Sergeant."

"You took a skiff?" Patterson asked. *Didn't she just tell us that she doesn't like to take the boat on her own?*

"Yes, Sergeant," Georgie said. "I didn't take it far, though. I only went about a mile down the beach, and then I hiked up into the woods."

"Did you get a deer?" Patterson asked.

Georgie shook her head. "I didn't see any bucks," she said.

"Why didn't you tell us this before?" Mark asked.

Georgie shrugged. "You didn't ask."

Patterson considered Georgie's words. She'd returned to her cabin only a short time before Mark and Bart had arrived to question Tim. Not only were the Fairweathers unable to provide each other alibis for the murders at the lodge, but they also could not swear to their spouse's whereabouts during the window of time when someone murdered Sam.

"Do you often go hunting alone?" Patterson asked.

"I usually go alone," Georgie said. "Tim isn't much of a hunter."

Patterson thanked Georgie for her time. She walked the men to the door, and Patterson saw her standing on the path watching Mark and him as they untied the plane, turned it around, and jumped on the floats.

Patterson turned his attention to the ocean and noted the small waves lapping over the pontoons. The storm was quickly approaching.

CHAPTER 37

Tuesday, September 9th

2:40 p.m.

"What do you think about Georgie's claim that she was deer hunting the morning after the murders?" Mark asked once he and Patterson were alone in the cockpit of the plane.

"I'm not sure what to make of it," Patterson said, "except that either Georgie or Tim could have killed Sam Lutz."

Mark nodded. "Unless we can more accurately pin down Tim's movements, neither one of them has a decent alibi for the approximate time of Sam's murder."

Patterson nosed the plane into the wind and mounting waves. When they were a few feet off the water, a gust jolted the plane.

"I don't want to spend more than an hour at the cannery," he said. "We need to get back to town before this front arrives."

Fifteen minutes later, Patterson landed the plane in the protected cove in front of the cannery. Mark jumped from the pontoon, the water lapping at his hip boots as he tied the Beaver to the running line in front of the office.

"Is the tide falling?" Mark asked Patterson when he joined him on the beach.

"Yes, we'll need to pull the running line out a ways."

Mark untied the running line and pulled on it until the plane bobbed in the gentle waves several feet from shore.

Patterson walked over to Mark and gestured with his chin to the building at the top of the beach. "I'll start with the office staff. Why don't you find Jim Chase? He's had time to think, and maybe he can tell you more about Fairweather's movements on the night of the murders and the next morning. We'll meet back here in an hour."

"Yes, sir," Mark said.

Ten minutes later, Patterson sat across a desk from Cy Darvon, the cannery manager.

Cy shook her head after Patterson introduced himself and told her he wanted to ask a few questions related to the murders at the Bartletts' lodge.

"It's horrible," Cy said. Her close-cropped gray hair framed a tanned face with pale-blue eyes. Lines creased her forehead and the corners of her eyes and mouth. She wore no makeup. "I'm not sure how I can help you, though," she continued. "As you know, the Bartletts were not commercial fishermen. They did not sell to this cannery."

"No," Patterson said, "but their son sells to you."

Cy bent her head toward her right shoulder, conceding the point. "Ask your questions," she said. "I'll tell you what I know."

"I'll start with the most obvious question. Do you know anyone in this bay who would want to murder the Bartletts?"

Cy sat back in her chair and crossed her arms over her ample stomach. She regarded Patterson for several moments. "No, sir," she finally said. "The Bartletts occasionally came to the cannery to buy supplies and fuel. I knew them well enough to say hello, but otherwise, we never crossed paths."

"How well do you know their son?"

"Brian?" Cy shrugged. "I deal with him a bit more often than I did his parents, but I don't know him well."

"What about their daughter, Deb, or her boyfriend, Jason Caine?"

Cy nodded slowly. "I am not the cannery foreman, so I don't often deal directly with the cannery workers. I don't know that I've ever held a conversation with Deb, but Jason's another matter."

"How so?"

"I phoned Mr. Caine yesterday and told him he is no longer welcome at Aktuvik Fresh Seafoods."

202

Patterson opened his notebook. "Why did you fire him?"

"The foreman found a stash of drugs in Caine's locker next to the processing room in the plant."

"What kind of drugs?"

"I'm not an expert," Cy said, "but the foreman told me he had a variety—everything from pot to heroin and prescription drugs. He was selling them and had a lucrative business going behind the scenes." Cy shook her head. "I would love to drug test all the workers, but I'm afraid I'd lose most of my crew. I guess it's a case of 'live and learn.' Next year, I'll drug test everyone before we pay to fly them out here to the cannery."

"Do you have any idea if Deb Bartlett was taking drugs?"

Cy shrugged. "I wouldn't be surprised, but I don't have proof. You'll have to talk to Walter Xander, the foreman, to find out more about Deb."

"Did you see either Deb or Jason return from the lodge on the night of the murders?"

Cy shook her head. "I usually eat dinner in the office and then head straight to my little home. I try to hide from the cannery for a few hours."

"How well do you know Georgie and Tim Fairweather?"

Cy puffed up her cheeks and expelled a long breath. "Those two," she said. "I know them better than I wish I did. Tim spends one or two nights a week here at the cannery, usually getting our mechanics to help him work on one of his outboards. He sells fish to us occasionally but not often. I finally told Jim Chase, the head mechanic, that he and the other guys could only help Fairweather on their time off." A slow smile spread across Cy's face. "I think Fairweather hangs out here to get away from his wife. She is crazy as a loon."

"Why do you say she's crazy?"

"Have you heard about the recent radio call when she announced to the bay that her husband was in his skiff and was armed and dangerous?"

"Yes," Patterson said. "Bart told me."

"She may as well have said, 'Shoot him on sight.' I predict one of those two will kill the other one unless they get a divorce."

"Tim claims he was here at the cannery the night someone murdered the Bartletts and their guests," Patterson said. "Do you remember seeing him here?"

"I heard he was here that night, but I didn't see him. He tries to stay out of my line of sight. I think he's worried I'll kick him out of here, and he knows I told the mechanics they could only work on his stuff on their own time."

"Do you think Tim Fairweather could be our murderer?"

Cy's gaze drifted from Patterson's face to a point above and beyond his head. She appeared lost in thought for several moments while she weighed his question.

"I honestly couldn't say," she finally said. "If you're asking me whether he could have left the cannery, murdered the Bartletts, and then returned, I'd say yes, absolutely. Between the cannery workers and the fishermen, there's activity around the cannery all night long. No one would think twice about a skiff coming or going." Cy paused a moment. "But if you're asking me whether he's capable of murder, I don't know him well enough to say."

"Did you know Tim Fairweather and Jules Bartlett were having an affair?"

Cy slowly nodded. "I heard the rumor yesterday. To be honest, someone told me several weeks ago that Fairweather was having an affair with someone and that Georgie was on the warpath. I suspected the lucky woman was someone here at the cannery. I didn't know it was Jules Bartlett until yesterday." Cy chuckled. "I shouldn't criticize the dead, but Jules Bartlett had bad taste in men. From what I've heard, Bob Bartlett was a bully, and Tim Fairweather is an idiot."

Patterson laughed. Cy offered a refreshingly honest take on the men in Jules's life.

Cy sat forward and tapped the desk with the ballpoint pen she held in her right hand. "I just remembered something, and it makes perfect sense now. Georgie Fairweather and Jules Bartlett got into a shouting match at the cannery store three or four weeks ago."

"What was the fight about?"

"I don't know," Cy said. "Georgie has an explosive temper and a hair trigger. I assumed Jules took the last head of lettuce or something equally egregious. You should talk to the store manager, Fred Kapp. He can tell you more than I can about the incident."

"What about Georgie? Could she murder someone?"

"Bingo," Cy said. "If you're looking for a likely suspect, I think you just found her. She is a nasty woman with a terrible temper. She once let loose on me because she thought we charged too much for fuel. The woman scares me. She looks harmless, but she is strong. I've watched her throw a fifty-pound bag of flour over her shoulder and haul it to their boat. I would not underestimate her."

After thanking Cy for her time, Patterson left the cannery office and hazarded a nervous glance upward. Dark clouds sped across the sky, and he felt a knot form in his stomach. He checked his watch. He'd told Mark to meet him at the plane in an hour, but it had only been twenty-five minutes. He walked down the boardwalk to the small store. He entered and shut the door behind him.

The store was nearly empty. One shopper roamed the aisles, and a middle-aged man with a receding hairline stood behind the cash register near the door.

Patterson held out his hand to the man at the cash register. "I'm Sergeant Dan Patterson with the Alaska State Troopers. You must be Fred Kapp?"

"Yes, sir," Kapp said, extending his hand for a firm shake with Patterson. "What can I do for you this afternoon?"

Patterson lowered his voice. The shopper was searching the shelves for something at the far end of the store, but the small space yielded little privacy. "I'm investigating the murders at the Bartletts' lodge," he said.

Kapp nodded his head. "Terrible," he said.

"I was just talking to Cy in the office, and she said Georgie Fairweather and Jules Bartlett got into a nasty argument here in the store a few weeks ago. Did you witness the argument?"

Kapp nodded again. "About three weeks ago," he said. "It wasn't much of an argument. It was mostly Georgie screaming at Mrs.

Bartlett." Kapp shook his head. "It scared me. I was afraid Georgie would pull that gun she always carries and shoot Jules Bartlett and possibly everyone else in the store."

"Georgie carries a gun with her?"

Kapp nodded once again. "She always carries a huge, knitted shopping bag. When I ring up her groceries, she removes the gun from the bag, lays it on the counter, puts the groceries in the bag, and places the gun on top of the groceries." He shrugged. "I assume she wants it handy in case she needs it. Considering her bad temper, though, the gun frightens me. I'm afraid she'll shoot me just because she thinks her grapes cost too much."

"What was the fight with Jules about?" Patterson asked.

"The store was fairly full at the time," Kapp said, "so I wasn't paying much attention to the women at first. One of the other shoppers later told me that Georgie approached Jules and whispered something to her, and Jules whispered something back. By the time I realized anything was wrong, Georgie was screaming at Jules, and her face was bright red."

"What was she screaming?"

"At the time, I thought she was saying, 'Leave it alone,' but I now believe she said, 'Leave *him* alone.'"

"What did Jules Bartlett say?"

"I think Jules was scared and embarrassed," Kapp said. "She took several steps back from Georgie, and then she turned and ran out of the store. She came back about twenty minutes later, once Georgie was gone, and finished her shopping."

"What was Jules's demeanor when she returned?"

"She was upset. She just grabbed what she needed, paid for it, and left. Mrs. Bartlett was usually very friendly, but she was quiet that day, and she'd smudged her makeup. I could tell she'd been crying."

"Before she ran out of the store, did Georgie say anything else to her?"

"Yes," Kapp said, nodding slowly. "As Mrs. Bartlett ran toward the exit, Georgie screamed, 'I'll kill you!'"

CHAPTER 38

Tuesday, September 9th

3:23 p.m.

Patterson next walked to the cafeteria. He knew Mark would have his hands full with the mechanic and the line workers and wouldn't have time to question anyone else.

"We're not open yet," someone called from the kitchen as soon as Patterson opened the door.

"I just want to talk to you," he said.

A young man with a bad case of acne pushed through the kitchen door and stared at Patterson, carefully taking in the uniform. He stood in the doorway, frozen in place. The kid wore a hair net and a white apron.

"Who is it, Gerald?" a deep, female voice asked.

When he didn't reply, the woman yelled, "Gerald!"

Gerald regained his ability to move and speak. "The police," he said.

"What?" the woman asked.

Suddenly, a large woman appeared in the doorway behind Gerald.

"Get out of my way." She pushed Gerald aside, and he crept back into the kitchen.

The woman approached Patterson. "How may I help you?"

Patterson introduced himself and told her he was investigating the lodge murders.

"I'm Shirley Myers," the woman said. "I'm the head cook here at the cannery."

Shirley stood nearly six feet tall. A mesh net covered her short dark hair, and something yellow stained her apron. The apron strained to cover her ample form.

She moved aside. "Come in," she said. "I don't know anything about the murders, though, so I don't see how I can help you."

"I know working in the cafeteria, you're in contact with the cannery staff, and I'm sure you hear plenty from the workers."

Shirley shrugged. "Not really," she said. "I try not to listen. I keep my head down and do my job."

"Did you know Bob and Jules Bartlett?"

She shook her large head. "I never met them."

"What about Tim and Georgie Fairweather?"

"Mr. Fairweather sometimes eats here," she said, "but I've never had a conversation with him. He seems nice enough. He always compliments my cooking, which is more than I can say for the hyenas who work here. I don't know his wife."

"Have you heard any rumors about Jules Bartlett and the Fairweathers?"

Shirley stuck out her bottom lip and shook her head.

"What about Deb Bartlett or Jason Caine?"

"I know them both, and I don't care for either one of them," Shirley said, her tone matter of fact.

"Why don't you like them?" Patterson asked. This lady did not give up information easily.

"Deb feels entitled. She's a princess, and I hate princesses, but I cannot guess what she's doing with a loser like Jason Caine. That guy is a thug."

"A thug?" he asked, urging Shirley to continue.

"About a week ago, I saw him threaten another worker with a knife, and it wasn't the first time I've seen him threaten someone."

"I've heard a rumor that Jason deals drugs. Is it true?"

"Gerald!" Shirley bellowed to her assistant.

The young man slowly pushed through the swinging door to the kitchen.

"Get over here," she said.

Gerald approached, and Patterson could see his body trembling. What had this kid done to make him so nervous around the police?

"The sergeant here wants to know if Jason Caine deals drugs."

Gerald locked eyes with Shirley, and the two seemed to share an unspoken conversation.

"Tell him what you know," Shirley ordered.

"Yes, ma'am," Gerald said. He looked at Patterson, and then his gaze fell to the floor. "Yes, sir, Jason Caine is a drug dealer. He sells to the workers here at the cannery and some of the fishermen when they come into the cannery. I hear he makes a fortune."

"Have you seen him sell drugs?" Patterson asked.

Gerald and Shirley again shared a long look.

"I caught young Gerald buying Oxy from Caine one day," Shirley said. "I convinced him not to do it again."

Gerald again looked at the floor and began to shake even more violently. The moment was so comical that Patterson had to suppress a laugh.

"Did either of you see anyone leave the cannery late on the night of the murders?"

Shirley laughed. "Sergeant, Gerald and I go to work at four a.m. We don't stay up late."

"What about on your way to work, then. Did you see anything suspicious?"

"No, sir," Shirley said.

Gerald shook his head.

"Do you remember if Tim Fairweather ate breakfast here on Sunday morning?" Patterson asked.

Shirley looked down at the floor for several seconds while she considered Patterson's question.

"I think he stopped by before breakfast and grabbed a sweet roll," she said. "I was busy, though. I can't be sure I saw him." She looked at her assistant. "Do you remember, Gerald?"

Gerald shook his head.

"Have you heard any rumors about the murders or who the murderer might be?"

Shirley remained silent for several seconds and finally said, "Most people here think Jason and Deb committed the murders."

CHAPTER 39

Tuesday, September 9th

2:53 p.m.

Elle's phone buzzed, awakening her from a deep sleep. She checked her watch and was surprised to see she'd slept for over two hours, and for a change, she couldn't remember having a nightmare once she'd fallen back asleep.

"Hello?" she said.

"Did I wake you?" a deep voice asked.

Elle sat bolt upright in bed, trying to clear her mind. Less than six hours earlier, Brian Bartlett had told her to leave him alone, so why was he calling her?

"What do you want?" She was happy to hear the tone of annoyance in her voice. Maybe she was already getting over Brian.

"Elle," Brian said, "I'm sorry. I've been a jerk, and I know it." He paused. "This has all been so horrible, though. Not only were my parents murdered, but I have to deal with the lodge."

"I thought you wanted the lodge," Elle said.

"Not like this. Along with the business comes all the debt, and believe me, there's plenty of debt. I met with Mom and Dad's attorney today, and I think I'll have to sell it just to get out from underneath."

"I'm sorry, Brian. I don't know what to say."

"Would you like to go out to dinner tonight?"

Brian's question surprised Elle. "I didn't think you wanted to hang out with me right now."

"I don't know why I said such a stupid thing," he said. "I could use someone to talk to, and I miss you."

"I miss you too." As soon as the words left her mouth, Elle regretted them. Brian's words sounded right, but she didn't hear any emotion behind them, and she wondered what his real motive was for asking her out to dinner. Elle knew she should stand her ground, tell him she was tired, and refuse his invitation. She couldn't do it, though. She wanted to see him.

Elle didn't know how long she'd been sitting in bed clutching her phone when Susan knocked softly on her door and called her name. She'd accepted Brian's invitation to dinner, ended the call, and then what? Her mind was a blank.

"Go away," she said. "I'll be out in a while."

"The lady cop is here and wants to talk to us."

"What?" Elle felt her heart rate quicken.

"You need to come out here now," Susan said.

"I'll be right there." Elle's pulse pounded in her ears. *Why do the troopers want to talk to me again? Do they have evidence against me? Have they found out about my past?* She hurriedly slipped into her shoes and ran a comb through her hair. By the time she reached the living room, she found Susan and the trooper named Sara sipping coffee and chatting like old girlfriends.

When Elle entered the room, Sara stood and held out her hand. "Hi Elle," she said. "I came by to check on you and Susan. Do you have everything you need here?"

Elle shrugged. "We're fine." The words came out as a dry croak.

"You want a cup of coffee or some water, Elle?" Susan asked.

"Water," Elle said.

Susan ran to the kitchen and filled a glass with tap water. She handed it to Elle and then returned to sit on the couch. Elle sat in the chair across the room from the sofa, and Sara joined Susan on the couch.

"Elle," Sara said, "Sergeant Patterson told me you left trooper headquarters in tears yesterday. How do you feel now?"

Elle sipped from the glass of tepid water. "Better," she said. "This is all so upsetting."

Sara smiled, and Elle thought her big, brown eyes looked kind.

"I'll be honest with you," Sara said. "I've never been involved in investigating a crime scene as horrible as the one at the lodge. I didn't even know Jules and Bob Bartlett, and I was very upset. I can't begin to imagine how you two must feel."

"It's awful," Susan said.

"You ladies have had some time," Sara said. "Have you thought of anything that could point us toward the killer or killers?"

Elle shook her head, and Susan said, "Not really."

"Does 'not really' mean you have thought of something?" Sara asked Susan.

Susan looked down at her feet and said nothing.

"When was the last time either of you saw or talked to Sam?"

Susan and Elle looked at each other and shrugged. "It's been a while," Elle said. "Bob banned him from coming to the lodge."

"Did you ever walk over to Sam's place to say hi?" Sara asked.

Elle and Susan shook their heads. "Bob told us to stay away from him," Elle said.

"According to some notations in one of Sam's journals, he saw someone hiding money and jewelry," Sara said. "Do either of you know anything about that?"

"Hiding it where?" Susan asked.

"I think mainly in the ground," Sara said. "From what he wrote, it seems Sam watched someone dig holes and bury money and jewelry."

"Deb sometimes stole things," Susan said. "Maybe she buried what she stole."

Sara looked at Elle. "Do you know anything about stolen and buried objects?"

Elle felt her face get hot. "I have no idea," she said, her eyes fixed on the floor.

"Sergeant Patterson asked me to talk to each of you alone. Would that be all right? Do you feel up to it?" Sara again directed her questions to Elle.

"I guess so," Elle said. "We can go to my bedroom."

"Why don't you wait for me in your room, and I'll talk to Susan first," Sara said.

Elle returned to her room and shut the door. What did Sara want to ask her? She forced herself to breathe evenly, and she tried to think calm thoughts. She wanted to go into the bathroom and run a razor blade across her thigh, but she knew she couldn't cut herself now. *You can do it after the cop leaves*, she promised herself.

Elle looked around the room. Was there anything here she didn't want the cop to see? She'd carefully hidden Jules's earrings in her bag, but what if Sara asked to look in her bag? She closed her eyes and again forced herself to breathe in and out slowly. *Sara can't look through my stuff without a search warrant. Can she?*

Elle waited for what seemed like hours, and then she heard a soft knock on the bedroom door.

"Come in," Elle called.

Sara pushed into the room and shut the door behind her. "Brie has a nice little house, doesn't she?"

"I'm happy she let us stay here," Elle said. "I'd hate being stuck in a motel room."

Elle sat at the head of the double bed, and Sara sat near the foot.

"Elle," Sara said, then paused. "Do you have any idea who would want to kill the Bartletts and Sam?"

Elle felt the tears bubble from her eyes, and she grabbed two tissues from the box on the bedside table to wipe her face. She slowly shook her head. "No," she said, her voice a whisper.

Sara smiled. "I don't want to drag this out too long, because I know it's tough for you to think and talk about the murders."

"I just keep seeing Jules and Bob when I went into their room to check on them." Elle began to sob. "I'll never be able to forget what I saw."

Sara scooted closer to Elle and put her arm around her. Elle leaned against her. She wanted to tell Sara her fears and how she couldn't remember much from the night of the murders. Elle knew Sara was not her friend, though. She had to stay strong and get through this interrogation.

When Elle finally stopped crying, Sara moved away from her. "I'm going to ask you a few questions, Elle, and if you don't want to answer them, you let me know. I don't want to upset you any more than you already are, and you're free to tell me to leave at any time. Do you understand?"

Elle nodded.

"When we do an investigation into a murder, we have to look at everyone who was close enough to commit the crime. We look the hardest at family members, but in this case, we also need to consider you and Susan."

Elle felt herself trembling and wondered if Sara could see her shaking. She nodded at Sara and fought to control her terror.

"As you might guess," Sara continued, "I learned you have a juvenile record."

Elle hugged herself as tight as she could. She knew Sara expected her to say something, but she remained quiet.

"Your record is sealed, as it should be," Sara said, "but do you want to tell me about it?"

Elle knew she should say something, but she simply shook her head back and forth.

"Nothing?" Sara prodded.

Again, Elle shook her head.

"Is there anything else you want to tell me?" she asked.

"I want to be alone," Elle said.

CHAPTER 40

Tuesday, September 9th

3:07 p.m.

Mark had to ask three people before he finally located Jim Chase. The mechanic was down in the engine room on the salmon seiner *Mystique*, working on a faulty starter. One of the boat's crewmen yelled down into the gaping hole in the deck, and a few moments later, Chase climbed out of the engine room, wiping his hands on a towel. Chase wore dirty Carhartt coveralls and a cap so grease-stained that Mark could not make out the logo on the front.

"I'll come to you," Chase called up to Mark on the dock. He stuffed the rag in his pocket and began climbing the steep ladder bolted to the side of the dock. He grabbed the top handrails, pulled himself up onto the wood-planked surface, and held out a hand to Mark.

Mark accepted the firm handshake, trying not to think about how much grease had just transferred from Chase to him in the process.

"Good afternoon, sir," Chase said. "What can I do for you today?"

"I'm following up on our last conversation, Mr. Chase," Mark said. "Have you heard anything about Tim Fairweather's movements three nights ago?"

"The night of the murders," Chase said.

"Yes, sir."

Chase slowly shook his head. "I asked some of the younger guys if they saw anyone leave the cannery in a skiff around midnight or later, but no one noticed one way or the other. One guy remembered

216

seeing Deb Bartlett return to the cannery with her boyfriend around nine p.m., but no one saw Fairweather leave in his boat."

Mark doubted he would be lucky enough to find someone who remembered a blood-drenched Tim Fairweather returning to the cannery in the middle of the night. Still, the fact that no one remembered seeing a boat leaving the cannery late at night meant little to their investigation. Mark knew boats came and went from the cannery every hour of the day and night, so Tim, Deb, Jason, or Deb and Jason could have maneuvered without anyone noticing.

"Did you see Jason or Deb Bartlett by themselves after they returned to the cannery on the night of the murders?"

Chase shook his head. "I didn't see either one of them," he said.

"I did," a young man with long blond hair and a beard working on the back deck of the *Mystique* called up to Mark.

"Which one of them did you see?" Mark asked the crewman.

"Jason. I was watching TV in the rec room around midnight, and Jason showed up. I remember because there were five or six of us in there watching an old *Star Trek* movie, and Jason wanted us to change the channel. We told him to get lost, and he left."

"And you're sure this was the night of the murders?" Mark asked.

The man nodded. "It was Friday night."

"What is your name?"

The man stared at Mark for a moment and then shrugged. "Steve Wright," he said.

Mark wrote the information and the young man's name in his notebook and then returned his attention to Jim Chase. "What about the next morning? Did you notice what time Fairweather left the cannery to go home?"

"No," Chase said. "I didn't see Tim the next morning."

"Sir," Mark said, "did Tim Fairweather say anything to you about Jules Bartlett?"

Chase again shook his head. "No. Her name never came up while we were talking."

"What about Bob Bartlett?"

Chase chuckled. "Oh, yes," he said. "Tim had nothing good to say about Bob Bartlett, and the other night he went on a rampage about the man."

"What did he say?"

Chase folded his arms across his chest, blew out a breath, and stared at the dock for several seconds.

"To tell you the truth, I was only half listening to him. He thought Bob was a bully and a thief. He claimed Bob stole one of his subsistence crab pots, and he said he saw his pot at the lodge one day."

"Did he say why he was at the Bartletts' lodge?"

Chase seemed lost in thought for several more seconds but then said, "I never asked him why he was there. As much as he disliked Bob Bartlett, I doubt he was there for a social occasion."

"He never said anything about how Bob treated Jules?"

"I don't remember him ever saying anything about Jules," Chase said.

"Did Tim talk about his wife?"

Chase barked a laugh. "Yes," he said. "He talks about her all the time. I get the feeling he both hates and fears Georgie, and he probably should."

"Why do you say he probably should?" Mark asked.

"I've seen Tim with a black eye more than once. He always makes up an excuse, but I'm fairly sure Georgie punches him in the face regularly." Chase paused for a moment and then added, "She tried to get him killed a few weeks ago. Have you heard about her radio call? She announced to everyone in the bay that Tim was armed, dangerous, and unstable."

"I heard," Mark said. "Did Tim mention the incident to you?"

"I asked him," Chase said, "but he wouldn't talk about it."

"Did you know Tim and Jules Bartlett were having an affair?"

Chase shook his head. "No way," he said. "Tim Fairweather and Jules Bartlett?"

"Yes, sir," Mark said.

"Did Bob know?"

"Yes," Mark said. "He knew."

Chase whistled. "Tim didn't say anything to me about the affair. No wonder Georgie wants to kill him."

"Do you have any thoughts about who killed the Bartletts and their guests?" Mark asked.

"Until now, I would've said Jason Caine," Chase said, "but if I were you, I would not overlook Georgie Fairweather."

"Georgie was out at her cabin the night of the murders," Mark said. "Do you think she could have motored to the lodge, committed the murders, and then returned to her place in the dark?"

"Absolutely," Chase said, not even pausing to think about his answer. "Georgie Fairweather is a strong, capable woman with a mean streak."

CHAPTER 41

Tuesday, September 9th

3:38 p.m.

Mark shook hands with Jim Chase, handed him a business card, and asked Chase to give him a call if he heard anything more about the night of the murders. As Mark walked down the dock back toward the cannery office, a gust of wind slammed into him so hard that he nearly lost his balance. He'd planned to interview the cannery foreman next, but he decided instead to find Patterson to see if he wanted to head back to town. They'd been at the cannery for an hour, and the leading edge of the storm had arrived.

Mark found Patterson on the beach, tending to his plane in the mounting surf. Mark ran down the beach to help him, and Patterson told him to jump in the plane. Mark hopped onto the float and slid into the front passenger seat of the aircraft. Patterson climbed into the pilot's seat, started the engine, and quickly powered away from the rocky beach.

Both men donned their headsets, and Patterson said, "I think the storm's already here."

"The wind came up in a hurry," Mark said.

"I don't want to attempt to fly back to town in this. Let's fly over to the Bartletts' lodge. It should be protected in this wind, and we can wait out the storm there."

"Yes, sir," Mark said.

As soon as they were airborne, a gust of wind buffeted the plane, and Mark watched Patterson struggle to gain altitude. Mark didn't mind waiting for the wind to calm before they flew back to town, but he was less enthusiastic about spending the night at a lodge where someone had recently murdered eight people.

Mark's stomach clenched when Patterson turned the plane in a tight circle. Mountains lined both sides of the deep, narrow bay, and the de Havilland Beaver gyrated in the wind. The plane slowly lost altitude and skimmed across the small waves in front of the Bartletts' lodge.

"It is much calmer here," Mark said.

Patterson nosed the plane toward the dock. "Yes," he said, "but if the wind switches a few degrees to the west, this cove will take a straight hit. I'll spend the night in the plane to keep an eye on it, but there's no reason you can't stay in the lodge."

"Sir?" Mark glanced at Patterson. "Isn't the lodge still a crime scene?"

"Most of it is," Patterson said, "but you can sleep on the couch in the great room. For now, let's tie the plane to the dock and put a few extra lines on it."

After the plane was secure, Patterson said, "Hang on a moment—I need to call headquarters and have Irene cancel my flight plan. Then, before it gets dark, I want to walk around the grounds. According to Brian Bartlett, his parents owned another ax, one with a blue handle. Let's see if we can find it."

"Yes, sir," Mark said. He unbuckled his seat belt, stepped out onto the float, and leaped to the dock. He began securing the plane lines to the cleats.

"Do we need to worry about the tide?" Mark asked when Patterson joined him.

"I believe it'll be low around eight p.m., but we have fairly small tides right now, so the plane should be fine here. Even if it goes dry, it won't matter as long as it doesn't pound against the beach in the surf. I'll keep an eye on it. The plane is my first responsibility until we get back to town."

They walked up to the lodge, and Patterson extracted the front door key from his jacket pocket. As soon as they entered the great room, Mark smelled the coppery aroma of blood. He checked himself.

Did he smell blood, or was he imagining the smell? He considered asking Patterson if he smelled blood, too, but he thought better of it. He didn't want his boss to believe he was uncomfortable about returning to a crime scene.

"It's chilly in here," Patterson said. "I think we can turn on the heater without compromising the scene. I should probably also run the generator for a few hours. I'm sure the batteries need a charge. I hope we're nearly done with our investigation here at the lodge, but it seems as if every time I consider releasing the scene, something else happens to make me think we need to take a closer look."

"Sara was upset about missing the safe," Mark said.

"It wasn't her fault," Patterson said. "I sent her to talk to Sam while the others finished processing the scene." He shrugged. "To be honest, I probably would have overlooked the safe too. Sara and Jill said it was hidden behind a painting. While we're here, though, let's take a closer look at the office and see if we missed anything else."

"Yes, sir," Mark said.

Mark found the oil heater and set the thermostat to sixty-eight degrees. Meanwhile, Patterson checked out the kitchen. When he returned to the great room, he told Mark he'd found peanut butter, jelly, bread, and coffee.

"That works for me," Mark said.

"Let's search for the blue-handled ax first," Patterson said. "We can look outdoors and in the two sheds while it's still light. If we don't find it outside, we can search through this building tonight." He paused for a moment. "I thought of something else," he said. "While we're here, I'd also like to chase down the GPS coordinates marking the locations where Sam Lutz watched someone hide something."

"Do you have those coordinates with you, sir?"

"No, but I'll call Sara on the sat phone. She can give me the coordinates."

Mark nodded. "Yes, sir, I'll start searching for the ax."

Mark started with the two small sheds. One held gardening and yard-maintenance supplies, such as a lawnmower, rakes, fertilizer, and a weed eater. The small space appeared neat, with the hand tools carefully hanging on the wall. It took Mark only a few minutes to decide the ax was not in this shed.

The second shed proved more problematic. This space was the catch-all for everything from old pots and pans to tents and camping gear. Mark even found a scuba tank in the corner of the shed. He rummaged through the shed for ten minutes, and although he couldn't swear the ax wasn't hidden somewhere among the various odds and ends, he didn't think the shed warranted more of his time at present. He wanted to search as much of the property as he could before the daylight faded.

Mark walked toward the woodpile and chopping block, where Susan had led Patterson to show him the other ax. He looked around the area but saw nothing of interest. He stretched his back and surveyed the grounds. He doubted he would find the ax in the guest cabin. If it were up to him to dispose of a bloody ax, he'd take it out in a boat and drop it in three hundred feet of water. If that's where the blue-handled ax had ended up, they would never find it.

Maybe the killer didn't have the time to dispose of the ax properly. Perhaps he found a temporary hiding place for the weapon and planned to return for it later.

Mark stepped up onto the boardwalk leading from the main cabin to a set of stairs down to the beach. Stacked logs lined this side of the building. A wooden structure supported a metal roof to cover the firewood, providing some protection from the wet Kodiak climate. As Mark stared at the logs, he realized this would be the perfect temporary hiding place for a bloody ax. If the assailant hadn't had time to dispose of the ax, perhaps he'd stuffed it between or behind the logs until he could return for it and permanently get rid of it.

Mark put his head next to the lodge wall and attempted to look behind the stack of logs, but the chunks of wood abutted snuggly against the wall of the building, leaving no room to hide anything. He then walked along the front of the woodpile, hoping to see the handle of an ax protruding from the logs. When this effort failed, he sighed.

There was only one way to determine if the killer had hidden the ax in the pile of stacked logs.

He began at the edge of the pile nearest to the front of the lodge and removed the logs from the stack one by one, carefully inspecting the spaces revealed after he'd pulled each chunk of wood from the pile. After a few minutes, Mark removed his jacket and wiped the sweat from his forehead. He was beginning to think this was an exercise in futility and wondered if he should instead spend his time searching elsewhere on the property. Still, he'd started this project, so he might as well finish it.

When he was approximately halfway through the pile, he looked behind him at the destruction he'd wrought. He'd thrown the logs to the other side of the boardwalk, where they huddled in a jumbled pile. It would take someone over an hour to restack this pile, and he hoped that someone would not be him. His back already complained from his actions of the past half hour.

When he was over two-thirds of the way through the pile, Mark hit pay dirt. Three logs from the top, nestled in a perfect little hollow between two chunks of firewood, he found a large ax with a blue handle. He stared at the object in wonder. By now, he'd exhausted any vestige of hope that this project would yield results. He'd kept going, though, because he was too stubborn to quit.

Mark pulled his camera from his pocket and photographed the ax where it lay. Brown spots covered the handle, and the blade looked as if someone had dipped it in a can of rust-colored paint. He had no doubt this was the murder weapon. He also knew proper police procedures. He should now don his nitrile gloves, remove the ax from the woodpile, and carefully bag and tag it. He decided not to touch it, though, until Patterson could look at it. This tool was essential to their investigation, and it would be a valuable piece of evidence if this case ever went to trial. He didn't want to make a mistake with how he handled the chain of custody.

As Mark stared at the ax and wondered what to do next, he heard footsteps on the walk. He looked up and saw Patterson approaching him from the direction of the guest cabin.

"You've been busy," Patterson said. "Did you find anything?"

"Yes, sir." Mark tried not to smile, but he failed.

Patterson walked up and stood beside him. He let out a long, low whistle."Nice job, Trooper Traner," he said. "I'd say you found the murder weapon, or at least, the weapon used to kill Bob and Jules Bartlett."

Mark nodded. "It's covered with blood," he said. "It was certainly used to kill something."

"Did you take photos?"

"Yes, sir."

Patterson pulled his camera from his pocket. "Let me get some too," he said. "I'm glad you left it where you found it. If necessary, we can now both testify about where the weapon was hidden."

Once they'd carefully bagged and labeled the ax, Mark carried the package down to the plane and placed it on the floor behind the front passenger seat. After he shut the plane's door, he heard a loud wind gust barrel down the mountain on the opposite shore and blast the ocean, exploding into several waterspouts. Patterson was right. This small cove was currently protected from the blunt force of the wind, but if the wind direction shifted just a few degrees, they would take a direct hit, and then, how would they protect the plane?

When Mark returned to the lodge, he found Patterson making himself a peanut butter and jelly sandwich. A pot of coffee simmered on the stove.

"Help yourself," he said, gesturing to the open jar of peanut butter. He handed Mark a section of paper towel. "Here's your plate."

Once the coffee had finished perking, Patterson and Mark took their meager meal out to the front porch to eat. Mark got the impression that Patterson didn't feel any more comfortable in the lodge than he did.

"Great job on finding the ax," Patterson said. "I hope the lab guys can pull some prints from it."

"Me too," Mark said. "A fingerprint or two would make our job much easier." He suddenly realized he hadn't asked Patterson about what he'd found. "Did you locate the GPS points Sam noted in his journal?"

Patterson swallowed a sip of coffee and nodded. "I found two places where the soil looked recently disturbed. The others must have been older because vegetation had already grown over the areas."

"This place is a jungle. Things grow fast," Mark said.

"I took the small pack shovel I keep in the plane and dug at each location, but I didn't find anything."

"Weird," Mark said.

Patterson nodded. "I'm beginning to think the GPS points in Sam's journal have nothing to do with our investigation, but at this moment, I don't know what is or isn't important."

"Maybe we'll get useful forensic evidence from the ax," Mark said.

"Yes," Patterson said. "I'd like to get the ax on its way up to the state crime lab this evening, but I guess it'll have to wait until tomorrow."

Mark told Patterson what he'd learned from Jim Chase and the crewman on the *Mystique*.

"Interesting," Patterson said. "I suspected Deb and Jason were lying when they said they spent the entire evening together after they returned to the cannery, and now we have proof." He shrugged. "Of course, it might have been an innocent lie to give each other an alibi, but at least we now know Jason could have returned to the cannery without Deb knowing where he went."

"Chase thinks Georgie could be the killer," Mark said.

"Yes," Patterson said. "We can't forget about her. The cannery supervisor and the store manager also mentioned Georgie's terrible temper."

Patterson and Mark ate their sandwiches and sipped coffee in silence for a few minutes. When Patterson finished his sandwich, he wiped his mouth. "I called the office on the sat phone," he said. "Irene said the weather's closed in, and she can barely see across the street."

Mark groaned. "Do you think it'll improve by tomorrow?"

"The wind's supposed to die down, but according to the forecast, we can expect heavy rain all day. I hope it lifts enough for us to sneak into town."

As if to refute Patterson's comment, a big gust of wind rattled the front windows of the lodge.

Patterson stood. "I think I'll head down to the plane before the sea conditions worsen here in the cove."

"I hope you don't get seasick," Mark said. "You'll be rolling around all night if you sleep in the plane."

"I won't get sick, but I probably also won't get much sleep." Patterson nodded to the front door of the lodge. "Will you be okay sleeping in there? I'm not sure I would be crazy about sleeping near a murder scene."

"I'll be fine," Mark said. He didn't want to spend the night alone in the lodge, but he wasn't about to admit his apprehension to Patterson.

"We didn't get a chance to go through the office," Patterson said. "Would you do that before you go to bed?"

"Yes, sir."

"Turn on the VHF radio in the lodge," Patterson said. "Channel sixty-nine. If I have a problem with the plane, I'll give you a call."

Mark watched Patterson as he walked down the trail to the dock. He slowly stood, grabbed his and Patterson's coffee cups, and pushed through the front door and into the great room. He turned on the four table lamps and the ceiling light, but the room still seemed gloomy. The VHF radio sat on a shelf by the gun case. Mark turned it on and adjusted the dial to channel sixty-nine. He then went into the kitchen, washed the two cups, cleaned out the coffeepot, and got it ready for the following morning. He knew if the weather improved, Patterson would want to leave soon after first light, so he planned to get up before daybreak and start the coffee.

Mark flipped on the overhead light in the office and looked around the small room. He had no idea what Patterson hoped to find here. While the crime scene techs had overlooked the wall safe, they had thoroughly processed the rest of the office. Still, he had nothing else to do this evening, and he doubted he would get much sleep. He spent the next two and a half hours examining old receipts, check stubs, and correspondence. He noted that the only thing of interest was the large checks Bob had written to Brian over the past three years. It seemed that Brian needed his parents' money to keep him in the commercial fishing business. Had Bob Bartlett recently told Brian he would no longer back him? If he had, then it would add another motive for Brian to murder his parents and inherit the lodge before they could sell it.

At 8:40 p.m., Mark stood and stretched. He'd looked through every drawer and file cabinet in the office and had little to show for his effort. He flipped off the office light and returned to the great room. It was nearly dark outside, but Mark heard the wind and rain pelting the front windows. He wondered how Patterson was faring in the plane.

The temperature in the room had warmed and now felt comfortable. Mark considered looking for a blanket, but he rejected the idea since he wanted to touch as little as possible in the lodge. If he got cold during the night, he could cover himself with his jacket.

Mark searched through the magazines in the basket near the couch until he found a fishing magazine. He reclined on the sofa and tried to concentrate on an article about the best lures for halibut fishing. After twenty minutes, he drifted off to sleep.

The sound of a human voice jarred him to consciousness. He jumped to his feet and looked around the room, startled. Several moments later, he realized the voice was coming from the VHF radio.

"Bartletts' lodge, VPSO office Kanuk Bay, can you read me, Sergeant?"

Mark hurried to the radio and keyed the mike. "Kanuk Bay, this is Officer Traner."

"Yes, sir," Bart responded, his voice taut. "Would you or Sergeant Patterson give me a call on your sat phone?" He paused a moment. "This is a high priority."

"I'm here, Mark," Patterson said through the radio. "I'll call him."

Mark put on his jacket, slid into his rubber boots, and headed out into the storm. The wind-driven rain hurt as it pelted his skin, and he wished he had his raincoat. The rain would drench him by the time he talked to Patterson and returned to the lodge.

The dock bucked and gyrated in the building seas, and he understood why Patterson had insisted on spending the night in his plane. His headlamp did little to illuminate the dock in the pounding rain, but he found his way to the Beaver, tied near the end of the dock. Patterson had added more lines to secure the plane.

Patterson stood on the outside float of the plane, the sat phone held to his ear. Mark climbed through the passenger door and waited for Patterson to finish his conversation with Bart.

A few minutes later, Patterson climbed into the plane and slammed his door shut, rain dripping from his hat and coat. He slid his head-lamp off his hat but didn't turn it off. He placed it in the seat next to him. "You won't believe what's happened now."

CHAPTER 42

Tuesday, September 9th

6:47 p.m.

Susan was not happy to hear that Elle planned to go out to dinner with Brian and leave her alone in the house.

"I won't be gone long," Elle said. "You can text me if you get scared, and I'll come back."

"But what about you?" Susan asked. "Do you think you can trust Brian? Maybe he's planning to take you into the woods and kill you."

"Brian wouldn't hurt me," Elle said. "Don't be ridiculous."

"You should take a gun."

"I don't have a gun." Elle put her hands on Susan's shoulders. "I'll be fine. I won't be gone long. Brian just wants to talk to me and apologize for ignoring me."

"Promise me you'll take your can of bear spray," Susan said, her green eyes wide.

"Okay," Elle said. "I promise to take bear spray if you promise to calm down."

Elle watched through the front window as Brian's gray pickup pulled in front of their house. She smiled at Susan. "I'll be back soon."

When Elle saw large tears roll from Susan's eyes, the pressure inside her started to build. Why wouldn't Susan leave her alone? She couldn't stand this stress.

Elle hurried down the front steps. A light rain pelted her head. She opened the passenger-side door of Brian's truck and slid onto the seat.

"Are you okay?" Brian asked. "You look upset."

"It's Susan," Elle said. "This whole thing has made her very clingy."

"She didn't want you to go out for dinner?"

"She wants me to spend all day and night with her," Elle said. "I hope Patterson lets her fly home soon. She needs her family and her boyfriend."

"How are you doing?" Brian asked. He shifted into drive and slowly pulled forward down the street.

"I'm okay." Elle tried but failed to keep her voice from shaking.

"You don't sound fine."

"How are you and Deb? How did it go with Patterson?"

"Deb is up to her usual games. We've met with Patterson twice, once individually and once together."

"Why did he question you together?"

"I think he wanted to watch each one of us throw the other one under the bus."

"What do you mean?"

"Deb tried to make me look guilty, and I suppose I did my share of trying to pin the murders on her."

"Do you think Deb murdered your parents?" Elle asked.

Brian shrugged. "I don't know. I think Jason could be responsible, and maybe Deb helped him."

"Has Deb started taking drugs again?"

Brian shrugged again. "She says she's clean and sober, but she's a professional liar, so I don't know."

"Where are we going?" Elle asked.

"Are you in the mood for sushi?"

"Sure," she said.

"Kodiak Hana it is, then."

Brian and Elle stood in line for twenty minutes before a table became available. The waitress seated them by the window, and Elle looked down at the channel and the boats coming and going from the Kodiak boat harbor. The rain was coming down harder now. She saw a Steller sea lion churn up the water in search of its next meal, and in the distance, at the edge of the fog, three sea otters floated placidly on their backs.

"It's a great view," Elle said.

"It's even nicer when the weather's good," Brian said. He pointed to the deck outside the window. "Sometimes eagles perch on the railing."

The waitress took their orders and brought Brian a beer. Brian had asked Elle if she wanted a beer or glass of wine, but Elle said she only wanted water. She needed to have her wits about her tonight. She didn't want Brian to think she was unstable or that she cared too much about him. She was beginning to realize he didn't like any sign of weakness.

Elle looked out the window while Brian sipped his beer. She tried to think of something to say to him, but her mind was blank.

"Can I ask you something?" Brian asked.

Elle was relieved to have Brian take the lead in the conversation, but her stomach churned in anticipation of his question. "Sure," she said.

Conversations buzzed from the other tables. Elle could tell that none of the other diners were paying attention to them, but Brian lowered his voice and leaned across the table toward her. "Who do you think did it?"

"Did what? You mean who do I think killed your parents?"

Brian nodded. He seemed to be watching her too closely. Was this a trick question? Did he suspect her?

Elle shrugged. "I don't know," she said. Her gaze dropped to the table. "I guess Jason could have done it, but I can't imagine Deb being involved."

"Why didn't you and Susan hear anything?" he asked.

Elle felt the tears on her cheeks and knew she was about to melt into a sobbing mess. She stiffened her muscles and forced herself to take deep breaths. She held the glass of water to her mouth with a shaking hand and took a long swallow. Brian watched her every movement.

"I don't know," Elle said. "I guess I was tired." She thought of Susan telling her that she'd heard her in the hallway during the night. *Why can't I remember getting up to go to the bathroom? Or did I get out of bed for some other reason?*

The waitress brought their food, and Elle relaxed a fraction while Brian turned his attention to his plate of sushi. Elle took one bite of her Kodiak roll but felt her stomach turn a flip and knew she would not be able to eat.

"Aren't you hungry?" Brian asked after his plate was nearly empty.

"I guess not."

"Elle, you need to eat," Brian said. "At least have some rice."

Elle dutifully lifted some rice to her mouth with her chopsticks. She forced herself to swallow and then took another drink of water.

"Don't you like the food?"

"Sure, it's great. I'm just not hungry. Do you want my dinner?"

"No," Brian said. "Take it home to Susan."

"I don't know why I didn't hear the killer." The words tumbled from Elle's mouth, and she wished she could grab them back. This time she couldn't stop the stream of tears. She jumped up from the table and ran to the bathroom. She wished she'd brought a razor blade with her to dinner.

By the time Elle returned to the table, Brian had paid the bill, and a box holding Elle's dinner sat on the table. Elle slid into her jacket, and she and Brian hurried through the pelting rain to Brian's truck. He turned on the engine but made no move to leave the parking lot.

He turned toward Elle and held her hand. "I didn't mean to upset you," he said. "I'm just trying to make sense of everything."

Elle nodded. "I know," she said. The tears began again, and she pulled a tissue from her purse and wiped her face. "I would never hurt your parents."

"Of course not," Brian said, but his words sounded flat.

"I loved your mom," Elle said. She shrugged. "Even if she didn't love me."

"I'm sorry you heard her tell me about your past," Brian said. "She thought the world of you, but I think she was worried you could be mentally fragile."

Elle fought to hold back the sobs. "Do you think I'm fragile?"

"Right now I do, but it's reasonable for you to be upset."

"I didn't hurt them." The words came out as a whisper, and Elle didn't know if she wanted to convince Brian or herself.

"Of course not," he said. "I wonder, though, why didn't you tell me about your childhood?"

Elle wiped her face and steadied her breathing. "I didn't want to scare you away," she said. "I would have told you eventually."

"It's okay," Brian said. He dropped Elle's hand and pulled out of the parking lot.

Elle stared at the wiper blades as they drove through the streets of Kodiak.

CHAPTER 43

Wednesday, September 10th

12:15 a.m.

"Dead?" Mark asked.

"That's what Fairweather said."

"Did he say what happened?"

Patterson let out a long breath, pulled his handkerchief from his coat pocket, and began mopping his face. "Tim must have arrived home soon after we left their cabin. He said Georgie was furious when he got there, but her anger intensified as the evening progressed. Around eight p.m., she pulled a gun on him, and he said he barricaded himself in their bedroom and stayed there for two hours. At first, Georgie tried to break into the room, and she even shot at the door several times. Finally, she stood outside the door and screamed at Tim."

"Did Tim have a gun on him?" Mark asked.

Patterson nodded. "He keeps a handgun in a drawer in his bedside table. He said he armed himself and hid on the far side of the bed, where he felt he had the best chance of avoiding a stray bullet. Tim told Bart that he has never been so terrified in his life."

"If this story is true, I'd be scared too," Mark said.

"A little after ten p.m., Georgie wound down. Tim said he waited another hour, but he decided to leave the bedroom when he didn't hear any sounds. He assumed he would find Georgie asleep on the couch. He said after one of her rants, she usually passes out on the couch and sleeps like a baby."

"But, he held on to his gun just in case she wasn't asleep?" Mark asked.

Patterson nodded. "He said Georgie was waiting for him, and as soon as he left the bedroom, she ambushed him. He claims she shot at him but missed, so he shot her."

"He killed her with one shot?"

"I don't know," Patterson said. "Bart said Tim was vague about how many times he shot her."

"What do we do now?"

"Bart told him not to touch anything and said the troopers would head his way at first light if the weather improves. Bart said he called trooper headquarters, and Brie told him we were at the lodge."

"Did Bart believe Fairweather's story?"

Despite the tragic situation, Patterson felt himself smile. "I asked Bart the same question, and he said he believed Tim Fairweather shot and killed Georgie, but he had a tough time imagining Fairweather cowering behind his bed for two hours."

"I guess we can't do much until morning," Mark said.

"I think the wind has calmed a bit, but it's going to have to improve more than this, or we'll be stuck here tomorrow."

As if to punctuate Patterson's point, a series of large waves slammed into the dock, causing the plane to buck and pull against the lines tying it in place. Patterson heard the lines strain and expected one to snap at any moment.

"Can Bart get to the Fairweathers' place by boat?" Mark asked.

"No," Patterson said. "Bart said sea conditions are not good for boat travel."

"At least Fairweather's stuck at his cabin in this storm," Mark said, "but he has all night to manipulate the crime scene to match the story he told Bart."

Patterson nodded. "It'll be hard to know what we should and shouldn't believe when we analyze the scene."

"Do you think Tim killed the people here at the lodge?"

"He's at the top of my list," Patterson said. "What do you think?"

"Until now, I would've put my money on Jason Caine and possibly Deb Bartlett, but now, I'm not so sure." Mark shrugged. "But why would Fairweather kill Jules Bartlett? You said Dr. Libby told you that the killer hit her more times with the ax than he hit Bob. I thought Tim said he was in love with Jules Bartlett."

"One thing I've learned over the years," Patterson said, "is that love can easily become hate, and they are both powerful emotions."

"You think Jules rejected Fairweather, and he was so angry he went to the lodge and murdered her and Bob?"

"I think it is possible," Patterson said. "Mind you, I haven't yet ruled out Jason Caine or the Bartlett children."

"I looked through the office tonight," Mark said. "I found the paperwork to back up what Angie discovered on the computer about the Bartletts' financial situation. Bob invested a lot of money in Brian's fishing operation. If his parents suddenly cut him off, he had plenty of motive to kill them, especially if he thought they were about to sell the lodge."

"Interesting," Patterson said. "Good work. Did you bag the relevant documents?"

"Yes, sir."

Patterson stared straight ahead for several seconds and then said, "If the weather improves by morning, I'd like to fly out to the Fairweathers' cabin. I'll take Tim back to town and put him in a jail cell, where we can keep an eye on him." Patterson looked at Mark. "Would you mind staying at his cabin to begin processing the scene? I hate to leave the place unguarded until we have the chance to take a good look at it. We'll have a difficult enough time trying to figure out what's real and what's been fabricated by Fairweather, but if news of the murder gets out, and it will, we might also have curious fishermen or villagers popping by to take a look at the carnage."

"Sure," Mark said. "I'll stay at the cabin."

"I'll return with a crime scene tech as soon as possible."

"What time is it?"

Patterson shined his headlamp on his watch. "It's 12:43 a.m. Why don't you head back to the lodge and try to get some sleep. We'll see what daylight brings us."

CHAPTER 44

Wednesday, September 10th

7:27 a.m.

Patterson was standing on the dock in the morning gloom, trying to stretch out the kinks in his back, when he saw Mark walking in his direction. The trooper held a thermos bottle in one hand and two plastic thermos cup lids in the other.

"I thought it would be okay to borrow a thermos from the lodge," Mark said.

"As long as it's filled with strong coffee," Patterson said.

"Yes, sir," Mark said. "What's the news from town? Is it flyable?"

"Three miles' visibility," Patterson said. "As long as it's okay between here and there, I think I can sneak into town."

"What about the wind?"

Patterson gestured to the placid water in the cove. "It's like this in town. I haven't talked to Bart this morning, but unless there's a big swell in front of the Fairweathers' cabin, we should be able to land there."

"Are you ready to leave yet?"

"As soon as you are," Patterson said. "We have a long day ahead of us, and the weather is not on our side."

"I'll run back to the lodge and grab the papers I took from the office."

"I have a partially smashed granola bar for you for breakfast," Patterson called after him.

Mark turned around and smiled. "Sounds delicious."

Twenty minutes later, they were airborne. Patterson didn't like the low ceiling and visibility, but he'd flown in much worse. He wanted to get Tim Fairweather to town as soon as possible. As it was, nothing they found at the crime scene would provide good evidence in court because Fairweather had had all night to manipulate the scene. He hoped Fairweather would confess to shooting Georgie in the heat of the moment, but from what Bart had said, it sounded as if Tim was already angling for self-defense and justifiable homicide.

Patterson had been second-guessing himself ever since Bart called to tell them about the killing. *Should I have removed Georgie from the cabin when I had the chance?* He reminded himself that he'd had no cause to force Georgie to leave against her will. From everything he and Mark had learned, though, they knew the Fairweathers' marriage was a powder keg ready to blow at any minute. *Is Tim Fairweather telling the truth? Did Georgie attack him, or did he simply grow tired of her, shoot her, and then manufacture his narrative of self-defense?*

An ocean surge pushed up onto the beach in front of the Fairweather cabin. Patterson circled to better gauge the conditions.

"The plane will get beat up if we leave it on the beach long," he said. "Let's get Fairweather into the plane, and then we can run up and take some photos of Georgie's body. I want to fly her back to town so we can send her up to Anchorage to the ME as soon as possible. I have a body bag in the rear of the plane we can use."

"Yes, sir," Mark said. "Did I also see extra evidence bags in the back of the plane?"

Patterson nodded. "I have an empty duffel bag back there too. Do you have your camera?"

"I do." Mark patted his jacket pocket.

Tim Fairweather met the plane when it pulled up to the beach. The man looked as if he had aged ten years overnight. His short, black hair ringed his face in spikes, and from his red, puffy eyes, Patterson could tell he'd been crying.

"Mr. Fairweather," Patterson said after he'd jumped off the float of his plane. "I want you to go back to town with me, now. Do you need anything from your cabin before we leave?"

The question seemed to puzzle the man. He stared at Patterson for several moments and then slowly shook his head.

240

Is he on drugs? Patterson didn't plan to take chances. As Mark was making his way to the beach with the body bag, evidence bags, and duffel, he told him to get his handcuffs.

"I know this won't be comfortable," Patterson said to Fairweather, "but we're going to put handcuffs on you for the flight to town."

Fairweather said nothing but meekly complied by holding his hands behind his back.

"I'll cuff them in front of you, sir," Mark said. "It'll be more comfortable for sitting in the plane."

Once he'd secured Fairweather's hands, helped him into the plane's front passenger seat, and fastened his seat belt for him, Mark tied the plane to the running line in front of the Fairweathers' cabin. The two troopers then hurried inside.

They found Georgie's body faceup on the floor at the edge of the main room. She had obviously suffered at least one bullet wound through her chest. From the gaping hole, Patterson thought it looked as if her husband had shot her twice in the chest. Blood smeared her blue sweatshirt and pooled around her body. Tim had apparently left her where she fell. Patterson was relieved to see that Tim hadn't covered his wife's body with a sheet or blanket, a move that would have contaminated her body with transfer particles.

Both troopers snapped several photos of Georgie where she lay, and then they rolled her into a body bag. The two men struggled to lift the bag and carry it out of the cabin and down to the plane. Patterson estimated that Georgie's body weighed at least 160 pounds, and they nearly dropped her when they lifted her from the float into the rear of the Beaver. They pushed her up onto the seat, and Patterson fastened two seat belts around the bag.

Patterson glanced at Tim in the front of the plane. He was not watching the troopers move his wife's body but instead stared straight ahead.

Mark untied the plane from the running line, and Patterson and Mark then turned the plane around so the nose pointed away from the beach. Patterson climbed back up onto the float while Mark held on to the plane.

Patterson reached inside the cockpit and pulled out the small case with the satellite phone. He tossed it to Mark. "Call if you need anything," he said. "I'll get a crime scene tech or two out here as soon as possible."

Patterson slowly idled away from the beach. "You okay there?" he asked Fairweather.

Fairweather offered a slow nod, but all the fight was out of him. "I didn't mean to kill her," he said.

For the next hour, Patterson focused his attention on flying. There was no wind as he made his way north toward the town of Kodiak, but visibility deteriorated from bad to worse the closer he got to town, and rain pelted the windshield most of the way. The fog forced him to fly around the outside of the island instead of flying over the mountains. He talked to another pilot, who told him the visibility in town had dropped to less than a mile.

Patterson's stomach burned as he stared out the window, watching for other planes. He announced his position over the radio every few minutes. He considered asking Fairweather to help him keep an eye out for other air traffic, but when he glanced over at his prisoner, he saw his closed eyes and open mouth and realized the man was asleep. *How do you fall asleep after murdering your wife?*

Patterson's shoulder muscles finally relaxed when he idled up to the floatplane dock in Trident Basin. Troopers Sara Byram, Andy Marrs, and Peter Boyle waited on the dock to greet him.

Patterson handed over Tim Fairweather to Peter and gave the bagged ax and financial papers from the lodge to Sara. Once Peter had secured Fairweather in his trooper SUV, he returned to the plane and helped Patterson, Sara, and Andy carry the body bag to Sara's SUV. Patterson told Sara and Andy to fill out the necessary paperwork and get Georgie's body on the next flight up to Anchorage. If they hurried, they should be able to get her on the 11:30 a.m. flight.

Patterson told Fairweather to get some rest and said he would interview him in a few hours.

After his troopers left with their assignments, Patterson fueled the plane and then drove home to take a shower and change his clothes.

He fantasized about a nap, but he had no time for sleep at this point in the investigation.

CHAPTER 45

Wednesday, September 10th

11:28 a.m.

Patterson arrived at trooper headquarters a little before 11:30 a.m. He smiled at Irene. "Anything going on this morning?"

"Bad car wreck out near Pasagshak this morning," she said. "Patrick should be there by now."

Patterson nodded. As much as he wanted to put all his troopers on the lodge murder case, he knew other bad things would continue to happen on the island. They could not ignore them. "If he calls in, patch it through to me, please," he said.

"I've had two calls from reporters this morning," Irene said. "They asked about rumors of a mass murder, so I guess the news is finally getting out there."

"What did you say?"

"I said you weren't available to comment."

Patterson smiled. "Let's make sure I'm not available for a while."

He asked one of his young troopers to escort Tim Fairweather to the interview room and then went to his office to leave his coat and get a notebook. He grabbed two bottles of water and then headed for the interview room.

Tim looked defeated. He sat slumped in the chair, elbows on the table, and his head cradled in his hands. When Patterson entered the room and shut the door, Fairweather slowly sat straight and stared at him.

Patterson pointed to a camera in the corner of the room near the door. A light at the top of the camera flashed red. "Is it okay with you if I record this interview?"

Fairweather nodded.

"I need a verbal response," Patterson said.

"Yes," Fairweather said.

Patterson sat in the chair at the small table. "I'm going to read you your rights," he said, sliding a small card from his billfold. He'd memorized the words on the card long ago, but his mind was so fuzzy this morning that he knew it was wise to read them so he wouldn't forget any part of the Miranda warning. Nothing could get a case kicked out of the system faster than a police officer's faulty recitation of Miranda.

Once he'd finished reading Tim Fairweather his rights, he asked him if he would like to call an attorney.

Fairweather shook his head. "I didn't do anything wrong," he said in a low voice.

"Tell me what happened," Patterson said.

"Georgie finally snapped."

"Start with when you got home."

Fairweather let out a long sigh and rubbed his eyes. "I guess my plane landed about an hour after you left, or maybe less. Georgie was still hot about you being there, and she started screaming at me the minute I stepped onto the beach."

"About what?" Patterson asked when he failed to elaborate.

Fairweather sighed again. "About everything," he said. "She said I brought the police into our lives." He let out a dry laugh. "Considering how many times Georgie has called the police on me and lied to them …" He shook his head. "I told her she was ridiculous."

"What else?"

"The whole affair," Fairweather said. "I guess your questions brought up all those bad memories for her. She was most upset when you confirmed Jules was carrying my baby. I didn't know Bob had told her about the baby. She never said anything to me. I didn't even know Jules told Bob she was pregnant." Tears streamed down his cheeks. "Georgie and I never had kids because I didn't want any, so it was tough for her to hear I'd gotten Jules pregnant."

"I see," Patterson said. He felt sorry for Georgie Fairweather, and for a moment, he wished he were sitting here interviewing her about murdering Tim instead of the other way around.

"I tried to calm her down," Fairweather continued, "but she just kept screaming. She asked me if I loved Jules, and at first, I told her not to be silly. She kept pushing, though, and I finally lost my temper and told her the truth."

"What did you say, Tim?"

Fairweather wiped at the tears on his face, and Patterson handed him a tissue from the box on the table.

"I told Georgie I loved Jules more than I had ever loved her," Fairweather said.

"I'm guessing she didn't take that well."

Fairweather shook his head. "It was a stupid thing for me to say, but she made me so angry. I lost my temper."

"What happened next?"

"I guess she had a gun in the pocket of her sweater. I don't know, but suddenly, she had a gun in her hand, and she fired it at me. As soon as I saw the weapon, I leaped to the side, so she missed, but she fired again." Fairweather stared at Patterson, his bloodshot eyes open wide. "She wanted to kill me."

"Why didn't you run out the door, jump in your boat, and get away from her?"

"Georgie was standing between me and the door." Fairweather shrugged. "Even if I could've gotten to the beach, the boats were on the running line. She would have shot me before I could've pulled one to shore."

"Okay," Patterson said. "So what did you do?"

"I ran to the bedroom. I had a small handgun by my side of the bed and a twelve-gauge shotgun in the closet. I didn't want to hurt Georgie. I didn't want to kill her, but I had to protect myself."

Fairweather's words and actions seemed so sincere that Patterson wanted to believe him, but if the man was a psychopath, he could probably mimic regret even if he didn't feel any.

"I locked the door and drug the heavy chest of drawers in front of it. Then I hid behind the bed, as far from the door as I could get." Fairweather took a long drink from the bottle of water. "Georgie kept yelling, and then she tried to bust through the door. When she couldn't break down the door, she shot at it several times, and then she shot through the wall."

Fairweather sat forward and rested his forearms on the table. He lowered his voice. "I was scared for my life, Sergeant. I've seen Georgie mad plenty of times, but I've never seen her like she was last night. She was beyond reasoning."

"Did she continue to shoot at the wall?"

"For a while, but then she just yelled at me. She went on and on for over an hour, reciting every wrong, real or imagined, from our marriage."

"What exactly?" Patterson asked.

"She called me every name in the book, and then she told me all the things she's done for me and all the sacrifices she made to be my wife." Fairweather slowly shook his head. "I know I'm not a model husband, but Georgie and I had many good years before our marriage started coming apart."

"What happened to it?" Patterson asked. He was not a marriage counselor, but he was curious.

A sad smile curved Fairweather's lips. "We retired and started spending all of our time together. I think we both began clinging to a marriage we should have ended years ago."

"What happened last night after Georgie stopped yelling at you?"

"Usually, when Georgie goes on one of her rampages, she finally runs out of energy, and she goes to bed and sleeps for twelve hours. Last night, after she finally quit yelling, I waited for over an hour, and I didn't hear a sound." He shook his head. "At first I was relieved, but then I started to worry that Georgie had hurt herself. I decided I'd better check on her. I thought she was probably asleep, so I tried not to make too much noise. I had to slide the chest away from the door, though, and it's heavy. She probably heard me push it across the floor."

Fairweather stopped talking, so Patterson nudged him forward. "And then you left the room?"

"Yes." Fairweather shook his head rapidly several times as if trying to snap out of a trance. "I grabbed my handgun just in case she started shooting at me again, and I walked out into the hall. I went into the main room and didn't see Georgie at first, but then she let out a hideous scream and came running at me. She had her gun pointed at my chest." Fairweather began to cry. He grabbed several tissues from the box and mopped at his face. "I shot her," he said.

"How many times?"

"Only once," Fairweather said. "She died instantly."

"I didn't take the time to examine her wounds," Patterson said, "but it looked like you shot her more than once."

Fairweather didn't respond to Patterson's comment but continued to cry and wipe his face with the tissues.

Patterson waited for Fairweather to regain his composure and then said, "You've had time to think about it now, so who do you think murdered Bob and Jules Bartlett and their guests?" Patterson hoped the sudden change of subject would throw Fairweather off balance.

Fairweather paused for several seconds as if thinking about the question. "I think Georgie killed them."

"Did she tell you she murdered them?"

"No," Fairweather said, "but she was so angry at Jules; I know she wanted to kill her."

"Why would she murder the guests?"

Fairweather shrugged. "I don't know, but Georgie wasn't in her right mind."

"It's convenient for you to blame Georgie when she isn't here to defend herself."

"I hope she didn't do it," Fairweather said. "If she murdered all those people, then I'm partly responsible for their deaths because my affair with Jules ignited Georgie's rage."

"How many shots do you think Georgie fired in your general direction last night?"

"I don't know. It seemed like twenty or more, but it was probably only ten or twelve."

"Is Georgie a good shot?"

Fairweather nodded. "She's good. She loves to hunt."

Patterson studied Fairweather. "Your wife was a good shot, and she fired at you at least ten times. How is it you managed to avoid a bullet?"

"I guess I got lucky," Fairweather said, "but most of the time, she was firing through a door or a wall. She couldn't see where I was hiding in the bedroom."

"Georgie told us that she wasn't at your cabin when you returned from the cannery the morning after the murders."

Fairweather nodded. "That's right," he said. "She was out hunting."

"Did you see her skiff on your way back to your cabin?"

"No," Fairweather said. "She told me she left the boat in a cove about a mile past our place. I wouldn't have seen it unless I went in that direction."

"So, Georgie had no idea what time you arrived home the morning after the murders?"

"I was back at our cabin a little after eight a.m."

"So you say."

Fairweather shrugged. "Why would I lie?"

"Mr. Fairweather," Patterson said, "I have ten victims on my hands, and I think it's possible you killed all of them."

Fairweather slumped back in his chair and shook his head. "You're wrong," he said. "I only killed Georgie."

CHAPTER 46

Wednesday, September 10th

11:00 a.m.

Elle had the dream again where she stood over the Bartletts in their bed and swung an ax at their heads, blood flying everywhere. She'd awoken at 4:00 a.m., drenched in sweat. She ran to the bathroom and heaved into the toilet until she had nothing left in her, and then she grabbed a razor blade and cut her thigh several times, watching the blood while it spread across her leg. She didn't have a Band-Aid, so she dabbed at the mess with toilet paper.

She remembered how she'd felt after hitting the girl in the bathroom at school. She'd thought everyone was lying to her because she couldn't remember the incident, and how do you forget hitting someone so many times that you knock her out, and both of you are covered with her blood? To this day, she couldn't remember hitting the girl. At the time, her bruised knuckles and bloody clothes were the only things that made her believe what the adults were telling her.

If she hurt Jules and Bob, though, then where were her bloody clothes? She'd gotten her clothes bloody when she'd tried to perform CPR on Bob, but those were the only bloody clothes she had. Maybe she hadn't been wearing clothes. The idea came to her in a rush. Perhaps she'd simply showered away the blood. She didn't know. She couldn't remember anything. She needed help but knew she couldn't ask for any. If Sergeant Patterson found out about her past, he would suspect her of murdering Jules and Bob.

Elle cleaned the dried blood from her legs and returned to bed. She immediately fell into a deep, dreamless slumber and didn't wake until she heard Susan pounding on her door.

"What is it?" Elle called.

"I'm just checking on you," Susan said. "It's eleven o'clock. Are you still in bed?"

"Go away," Elle said. "I'll be out in a while."

Why couldn't Susan give her some space? Elle didn't know where she would go when this was all over, but she would be glad to get away from Susan.

Elle tried but failed to fall back to sleep. She stood under the shower for twenty minutes, letting the water pelt her face. Her mind felt clearer this morning. She hoped Sergeant Patterson would find the real killer soon, so she could stop doubting herself and get on with her life. She decided she would move to a city and begin seeing a psychologist again. Elle wanted to find her inner strength and maybe even some happiness.

She threw on blue jeans and a flannel shirt and raked her fingers through her short hair. She was just about to leave her room when her phone buzzed.

She grabbed the device and checked the screen. "Brian?" She wasn't sure she would ever hear from him again.

"Have you heard the news?" he asked.

"What news?"

"Tim Fairweather murdered his wife last night."

"Why?" Elle didn't know Tim Fairweather well, and she'd never met his wife.

"I heard he's claiming self-defense."

"How do you know?" she asked.

"I just talked to Sergeant Patterson, and he told me."

"He called to tell you about Georgie Fairweather?"

"I called him," Brian said. "He has the computers and notebooks from the lodge, and I have to contact the rest of the summer guests to tell them the lodge is closed. I called to ask him if I could come by and copy down the information I need. He said I could, and then

I asked him how the case was going. He told me Tim Fairweather killed Georgie last night. Fairweather's claiming self-defense."

The news was terrible, and Elle didn't understand why Brian seemed so happy about it. "What does this have to do with the murders of your parents?"

"Don't you see? Tim must have murdered them, too, and now he's in jail here in Kodiak."

"Has he confessed?" Elle didn't want to burst Brian's bubble, but just because Fairweather killed his wife didn't mean he murdered nine other people.

"I don't know if he's confessed yet, but this is great news, Elle. We'll all be able to go back to our lives soon."

After she disconnected with Brian, Elle sat on the edge of her bed. Brian had seemed almost giddy with the news about Tim Fairweather killing his wife. Was he relieved because he thought the troopers caught the person who murdered his parents or was he relieved because they were no longer focusing on him as a suspect? Or perhaps Brian was happy because he no longer thought she'd murdered his parents. Elle hoped the troopers had the murderer, but she felt it would take a leap of logic to believe Tim Fairweather murdered everyone at the lodge simply because he killed his wife.

Elle unlocked and opened her bedroom door. For a change, she didn't hear television sounds coming from the living room. She wandered through the rooms of the empty house and was surprised to see that Susan had cleaned the place. She saw no dirty dishes in the kitchen, and it looked as if Susan had swept the floor.

She was beginning to wonder where Susan was when the front door opened, and she breezed through it.

Instead of wearing one of her long dresses, Susan wore sweats this morning. She'd pulled her long hair into a ponytail, and her bright-pink cheeks suggested she'd been exercising.

"Were you jogging?" Elle asked.

Susan nodded and fought to catch her breath. "It's nice out," she said. "I had to get out of this place for a while. It's depressing in this house."

"Did you eat the food I brought you last night?" Elle asked.

Susan nodded again. "It was good. Why didn't you eat it?"

"I guess I wasn't hungry."

"How did it go with Brian?"

"Fine," Elle said. "We mostly talked about the murders." She had no intention of telling Susan what she and Brian had discussed. "Did you hear about Georgie Fairweather?" she asked.

Susan shook her head and sat on the couch.

"Her husband killed her last night."

"Wow!" Susan said. She reached back and tugged on her ponytail. "How did you find out?"

"Brian called this morning. He just heard the news from Sergeant Patterson before he called me."

"What happened?" Susan's large, green eyes searched Elle's face.

"Tim Fairweather said it was self-defense," Elle said.

"I bet his wife found out about him and Jules."

"Maybe," Elle said, "but I think we should keep that idea to ourselves."

"Do you think he killed the Bartletts?" Susan asked.

"I don't know, Susan."

"Maybe Sergeant Patterson will let us leave the island now." Susan stood and began to pace. She seemed to be in her own world and not even listening to the answers Elle gave to her questions.

"Listen, Susan," Elle said. She waited until Susan had stopped pacing and looked at her.

"What?"

"Just because Tim Fairweather murdered his wife does not mean he killed Bob, Jules, Sam, and the guests."

"There can't be two murderers in Kanuk Bay," she said. "Do you think?"

Elle rubbed her head. She could feel the migraine starting to form. She hoped Tim Fairweather was the murderer. Nothing would make her happier than to learn someone she barely knew had committed the gruesome crimes and was now in custody. She wanted to believe Fairweather had killed Jules and Bob, but she couldn't believe it until Sergeant Patterson told her it was true.

CHAPTER 47

Wednesday, September 10th

2:10 p.m.

Peter Boyle, Sara Byram, Gary Reeves, and Andy Marrs sat at the conference table with Patterson. Bottles of water, a carafe of coffee, and sandwiches filled the middle of the table.

"As I'm sure you know," Patterson said, "Mark, Jill, and Joe are at the Fairweather cabin working the latest crime scene, and Patrick has his hands full with a car wreck. I thought the rest of us could put our heads together and see what we have so far."

"I can start," Sara said. "I called the cannery and asked them to pass along a message to Brian's crewmen to call me as soon as possible, but I haven't heard from any of them yet."

Patterson nodded. "If they don't get ahold of you soon, you might have to fly out there to talk to them. Last night, Mark found financial information in the lodge's office clearly showing that Bob was financing Brian's commercial fishing business. We know Brian had a good motive for killing his parents. He wanted the lodge and needed the money. I'd like to hear what Brian's crewmen have to say about Brian's relationship with his parents, and I'd also like to know if Brian was on the boat when they returned from their poker game at the cannery."

"I talked to the Bartletts' neighbors here in Kodiak," Peter said. "I interviewed the neighbors on either side of them and across the street." He checked his notes. "The Bartletts have lived in that house for the last twenty-seven years."

"What did you learn?" Patterson asked.

He shrugged. "The neighbors all seemed to like Jules and Bob, but I got the feeling they didn't know them very well. One neighbor said they were friendly but private."

"What about the kids?" Patterson asked.

"The people who live across the street have only been there about five years," Peter said. "They see Deb and Brian come and go, but they don't know them. The neighbors on either side were a different story, though."

"How so?"

"They said the Bartlett kids were spoiled and out of control in their younger years. Whenever their parents went off the island somewhere and left the kids alone, either one or both of them threw a nonstop party until Mom and Dad returned. One neighbor said she talked to Jules and Bob about the situation, but they told her, 'Kids will be kids,' and they acted as if there was nothing they could do to control the behavior of their children. This lady said one of the other neighbors called the police about four days into one of Deb's never-ending parties, and Bob was furious with the woman when he got home."

"What about lately?" Patterson asked. "Did the neighbors say anything about Brian's or Deb's recent behavior?"

Peter shook his head. "No, they said neither Brian nor Deb live at home anymore, but they see them come and go."

"Patrick was assigned to interrogate the Fairweathers' neighbors, so I'll talk to him later," Patterson said. "Mark found what we believe was the ax used to murder the Bartletts. It was hidden behind the stack of logs outside the lodge."

"Did it have blood on it?" Gary asked.

"It was covered in blood and tissue, and I've already sent it to the crime lab. I hope we can get fingerprints or the killer's DNA from it."

"I find it interesting that the killer used a weapon he or she found at the scene to murder the Bartletts," Andy said. "Does it mean these murders were done in the heat of the moment and were not premeditated?"

"Good point, Andy. I was wondering the same thing," Patterson said. "If the killer used Bob Bartlett's missing .44 to shoot the guests, then it appears he or she found both weapons at the crime scene. I don't want to read too much into this, but it does make me wonder if the killer got mad at Bob and Jules and suddenly decided to start killing everyone with whatever weapons were at hand."

"But why did the killer spare Elle and Susan?" Peter asked.

"The murderer must have either liked them or forgot about them," Gary said.

"I learned something interesting," Sara said. "It's probably not relevant, but I think we should consider it."

"What is it?" Patterson asked.

"Remember I told you that Elle has a juvenile record in Indiana? I couldn't find anyone in law enforcement in Indianapolis who would talk about her record, so today, I went over to Brie's house, where Elle and Susan are staying. I talked to each of them separately, and I asked Elle what she did to get in trouble." Sara shook her head. "She wouldn't tell me, so when I got back to my desk, I called some of the older teachers at Elle's old grade school, and I finally found one woman named Louise Block, who seemed more than happy to talk."

"Was Elle one of her students?" Andy asked.

"No, she didn't know Elle, but she'd heard the stories," Sara said. "She said when Elle was around ten years old, her family took a vacation at the Texas coast. Elle and her little sister were playing in the surf, and Elle pushed her sister underwater and held her there until she stopped struggling to get to the surface. Elle's dad noticed what was happening a little too late. The sister survived, but she has some brain damage."

"Wow," Peter said. "Elle seems so sweet and meek."

"It sounds like an accident to me," Andy said. "What happened? Did her parents report her to the police?"

"Yes," Sara said, "but they urged a judge to place Elle in a psychiatric hospital for four years. She was in high school by the time she got out."

"The poor kid," Peter said. "She must have felt guilty, and instead of helping her cope, her parents dumped her in a psych ward?"

"I asked Ms. Block why Elle's parents had convinced the judge to send her to a psychiatric hospital, but she didn't know. Her take on the situation was that they should have left her in the hospital a while longer."

"Why?" Patterson asked.

"Seven months after she left the hospital and returned to school," Sara said, "Elle beat up a girl in the bathroom, and the girl's injuries were so severe that she spent two weeks in the hospital."

"What started the fight?" Peter asked.

Sara shrugged. "Neither the girl nor Elle remembered anything about the fight."

"I can understand why the girl didn't remember," Patterson said. "She probably had a traumatic brain injury, but Elle couldn't remember the event either?"

"She said she couldn't remember," Sara said. "According to Ms. Block, none of the faculty at the school believed her, and when Elle's mother told the principal about the incident with Elle's sister, the principal asked the parents to remove Elle from the school."

"What happened to her?" Andy asked.

"She went back to the psychiatric hospital until she graduated from high school," Sara said. "Ms. Block didn't know what happened to her then, but I followed her trail to Indiana University, where she got her bachelor's degree in accounting. During her time in college and since, she's worked as a bartender, waitress, and cook at several different places, including Connecticut, New Mexico, Seattle, and Anchorage. This was her third year with the Bartletts."

"Great work, Sara," Patterson said. "Maybe we need to stop walking on eggshells around Elle and interrogate her harder next time."

"If we're looking for an unhinged individual, I guess Elle Chaplin fits the bill," Peter said.

"Maybe," Sara said. "I think this new information shines a different light on Elle, but I find it difficult to believe she could take an ax to her employers."

Patterson shook his head. "Someone like Elle can lose their temper and do the unthinkable, but it's never neat and clean. If Jules or Bob said something to upset her, she might have killed them with an ax in a fit of rage, but the other scene makes no sense."

"The guest cabin?" Gary asked.

Patterson nodded. "Those killings were methodical and sterile. I'm not saying Elle couldn't have killed the Bartletts and their guests, but the murders of the guests didn't look like the work of an unhinged mind." He held up his hands. "Just a thought," he said. "Just because it looks strange to me doesn't mean it didn't happen."

"I think it's interesting that Elle lied about her past," Sara said. "She told me she grew up here and there, but she spent her entire childhood, including college, in Indiana."

"She probably didn't want us to find her juvenile record," Peter said.

"Should I bring Elle here so that you can interrogate her again?" Sara asked.

"Let's hold off until we get back the tox screens for the Bartletts and their guests. Meanwhile, Sara, I would like you to keep an eye on Elle and Susan."

"Sir?" she asked.

"I don't mean I want you to sit in a car outside the house where they're staying, but give them a call this afternoon and see if they need anything. Talk to Susan if you can and ask how Elle is doing. I think we need to keep an eye on Elle, so she doesn't hurt herself or someone else."

"The problem with Elle or Susan as suspects is that they didn't have the time or opportunity to kill Sam Lutz," Peter said.

Gary cleared his throat. He looked at Patterson. "I don't know about Susan, but Elle took a walk after you told her to pack her things. I know because she went out the front door and walked past me."

"How long was she gone?" Patterson asked.

"Over an hour," he said.

Patterson stroked his chin. "Interesting."

"I'll keep an eye on her, sir," Sara said.

Patterson nodded and looked at Trooper Boyle. "Peter, how do you feel about going through Brian Bartlett's finances? Sara's already looked at them, but I'd like you to take a deeper dive into how much he owed and when he's likely to lose his boat. You can get Angie to help you." He added, "Was he desperate enough to kill his parents so he could inherit the lodge before they had a chance to sell it?"

He turned to Sara and said, "Run down the Bartletts' attorney. Is the will we found at the lodge their last will, or did they file a more recent one? Just because we found a will in their safe doesn't mean it's the newest version."

"Yes, sir," she said. "When do you expect Mark and the others to return to town?"

"They're supposed to come back this afternoon," Patterson said, "but if this fog doesn't lift, they'll have to spend the night at the Fairweathers' cabin."

CHAPTER 48

Wednesday, September 10th

2:48 p.m.

"Dr. Libby wants you to call him," Irene Meadows said as soon as Patterson left the conference room.

Patterson sat in the desk chair and rubbed his eyes, trying to clear his brain fog. He needed a nap, but he wasn't going to get one today. He dialed Dr. Libby's cell phone number and waited while the phone rang.

"Libby," a deep voice said.

"Doc, this is Dan Patterson. I have a message to call you."

"Sergeant," Libby said. "Yes, I got back the tox screens you wanted, and I thought you'd find the results interesting."

"Let me guess: the guests were sedated."

"Bingo," Libby said. "The Bartletts also had traces of zolpidem tartrate in their systems."

"Speak English, Doc," Patterson said.

"Your murder victims all ingested a healthy dose of Ambien within hours of their deaths."

"Interesting," Patterson said. "In other words, they were drugged."

"I think so."

"Were the dosages high enough to kill them?"

"No," Libby said, "but they would have slept through the night."

"I guess we now know why none of the guests responded to the first gunshots in the cabin."

"Even if one of the guests awoke, they would've been groggy and confused with so much Ambien on board."

"Thank you, Doctor. You've cleared up one mystery for me," Patterson said. "Do you have the results back from Sam Lutz? Was he also drugged?"

"No," Libby said. "No drugs in Mr. Lutz's system. Just a fatal gunshot wound."

"Has our latest murder victim arrived in your lab?"

"Yes," Libby said, "and that's my other reason for calling. One of my colleagues is finishing the post on Georgina Fairweather."

"That was fast."

"We started as soon as she arrived," Libby said. "I thought I should get on it right away so you can catch this murderer. When one of my assistants told me your tox screen results were back, I let the assisting pathologist take over the autopsy so I could call you. I think we've already found everything relative to Georgina's death."

Patterson let out a long sigh. "I know who killed Georgie. Her husband did it, but I don't know yet if he's our guy for the other murders. Did you find anything of interest when you examined her body?"

"Nothing in addition to the obvious," Libby said. "Four bullets contributed to the death of Georgina Fairweather. Two through the chest, and two in the back."

"In the back?"

"Yes," Libby said. "It looks like she was facing her attacker when he shot her the first two times, and then, as she turned and tried to flee, the assailant shot her two more times. The last two rounds entered through her back. I think any one of the four shots could have proven fatal, and she didn't stand a chance after suffering all four wounds." Libby paused a moment and then added, "I can go into more detail if you would like."

"Not necessary, Doctor. I'll wait for your report," Patterson said. "Your findings are interesting, though, because Georgie's husband claims he shot her once in self-defense."

Libby said nothing for several seconds, and Patterson was beginning to think he'd disconnected when he said, "Sergeant, you know as well as I do that once a perpetrator's adrenaline starts flowing, he often continues to shoot or stab. I had one case up here where a man was coming at his wife with a baseball bat. He was about six feet away from her, and she emptied the gun into his chest. It was overkill, but I also believe it was self-defense."

"Maybe," Patterson said, "but I'm already suspicious of Tim Fairweather's self-defense claim. After hearing about the two bullets he shot into Georgie's back, I don't buy self-defense. I think I'll have another chat with Mr. Fairweather."

"Do you have any other questions?" Libby asked.

"Yes," Patterson said. "Can you tell me if the gun used to kill Georgie Fairweather was the same weapon the killer used to murder the guests at the lodge?"

"It's the same caliber," Libby said. "I'll let the ballistics expert here at the lab examine the bullets and see what he thinks."

After Patterson disconnected, he sat back in his chair. What happened at the Fairweather cabin last night? Did Georgie tell Tim she knew he was the murderer? Maybe she had some sort of proof, and Tim killed her to keep her quiet. The victims were all drugged, though. How did Tim Fairweather manage to slip them Ambien? Another thought suddenly occurred to Patterson. Were Elle and Susan also drugged? If they were, it might explain why they didn't hear the murders.

Patterson called Sara and asked her to come to his office. Sara had a sharp mind, and he wanted to bounce this new information off her.

She sat in the chair in front of Patterson's desk and listened while he told her what Libby had said about the Ambien and Georgie Fairweather's autopsy.

"Everyone was drugged," Sara said, slowly nodding her head. "Now we know why the other guests didn't react to the first shot."

"Yes," Patterson said. "Also, Elle clearly can't remember much about the night of the murders. I thought it was strange, but maybe she and Susan were also drugged."

"But who could have drugged them, and how?" she asked.

Patterson shrugged. "This should narrow our suspect list, but Deb and Brian came and went from the lodge. I don't know how they would do it, but I suppose they could have drugged everyone."

"It seems less likely that Tim Fairweather would've had the opportunity to drug the Bartletts and their guests."

"Just when I thought we had our guy," Patterson said and then sighed. "He might not be responsible for the lodge murders, but Tim Fairweather murdered his wife."

"What about Jason?" Sara asked. "Does this move him down our list?"

"Not necessarily," Patterson said. "He could have convinced Deb to hand out Ambien-laced cookies or something similar to the Bartletts and their guests."

"Maybe we should look for someone who has a prescription for Ambien," Sara said.

"Do we have a list of the medicines found in the bathrooms at the lodge?"

"We do," Sara said. "I'll check it, but it still won't tell us if Deb or Brian has a prescription."

Patterson ran a hand through his hair. "I guess I'll need to get Elle and Susan back in here. Elle's the cook, so she should know if someone brought food or drink to the lodge and shared it with everyone."

Sara nodded. "Elle should know what one thing everyone ate and drank. Unless the killer drugged multiple items."

"I think I'll visit Elle and Susan and have a chat with them. Maybe they'll remember a food item someone brought to the lodge. I'd like you to come with me, Sara."

"Yes, sir," she said.

"Elle is very fragile, and I think I intimidate her. She responds better to you." Patterson looked at his watch. "I have a few other things to do. Let's leave here at 3:15 p.m., and meanwhile, I'd like you to check the list of medicines found at the lodge to see if anyone there took Ambien."

Patterson fought against fatigue. He poured himself a cup of strong coffee and hoped it would clear the cobwebs in his brain. He needed to find the brutal killer who'd murdered nine people before he or she struck again. *If Tim Fairweather murdered those at the lodge, how did he drug them? When would he have had the opportunity?* Bob

Bartlett certainly would not have welcomed Fairweather at the lodge. Deb, Brian, Elle, and Susan theoretically could have slipped a doctored cookie or drink to the guests, but how could they be sure the guests or the Bartletts would eat or drink enough of the drug to cause them to sleep soundly?

Patterson rubbed his temples. Maybe Elle and Susan would provide them with more insight.

CHAPTER 49

Wednesday, September 10th

3:15 p.m.

Sara was waiting by Patterson's trooper SUV at 3:15 p.m. He unlocked the doors to the vehicle, and they both climbed into the SUV.

"Did you check the list of medicines?" he asked.

"Yes, sir," Sara said. "Jules had Ambien in the medicine cabinet in the bathroom in the master bedroom. The bottle was nearly empty, but she refilled the prescription three months ago, so there's no way to know if she took the pills or if someone stole them from her."

"Ambien is a common sleep aid," Patterson said. "I imagine the killer could have gotten it from several places."

"The real puzzle is, how did the killer deliver the drugs to the Bartletts and their guests? What one thing did they all eat or drink?"

Patterson pulled over in front of Brie's house and parked by the curb. He and Sara walked up to the front door, and he knocked.

Susan looked more than ever like a little girl when she opened the front door. Her long hair was in disarray, and she rubbed her eyes and blinked at Patterson.

"Did we wake you?" he asked.

"I guess I fell asleep watching TV," Susan said. She stood aside and let Patterson and Sara enter.

"Is Elle here?" Patterson asked. There was no sign of her in the small living room.

"She's in her bedroom," Susan said. "I can get her if you want."

A few minutes later, Elle followed Susan into the living room. She looked alert, and Patterson thought she also seemed ready to bolt if necessary. Patterson scolded himself. Elle was mentally fragile, but despite her past, he had no reason to suspect she could be responsible for the murders of nine people.

"Hi Elle," Patterson said. "We've learned a few more things about the murders, and we have some questions for you and Susan."

Patterson motioned for Elle and Susan to sit on the couch. He took the chair across from the sofa, and Sara pulled a chair from the small dining room table into the living room and sat next to him.

Susan relaxed against the back of the couch, but Elle sat forward, her hands on her thighs.

Patterson nodded to Sara to take the lead. He wanted to observe Elle and Susan while Sara questioned them.

"The medical examiner tested the blood of the Bartletts and the guests," Sara said, looking back and forth from Elle to Susan. "He called Sergeant Patterson this afternoon and told him that everyone had Ambien in their systems when they died. Do you know what Ambien is?"

Susan shook her head, but Elle said, "I do. I took it for a while, but I didn't like the way it made me feel."

"How long ago did you take it?" Sara asked.

Elle's face flushed red. "A couple of years ago," she said.

Sara nodded. "Susan, Ambien is a sleeping pill, and we think the killer gave it to the Bartletts and the guests so they would fall into a heavy sleep, making it easier for him or her to control."

"You mean easier to kill," Susan said.

Elle gave Susan a sharp look.

"It's okay," Sara said. "You're right, Susan. The Ambien made it easier for the killer to murder them. They were groggy and not as likely to fight back."

"How did the killer give the drugs to everyone?" Susan asked.

"That's what we're trying to figure out," Sara said. "Can either of you remember a food or drink, perhaps something like cookies, that someone brought into the lodge shortly before the murders?"

Susan and Elle looked at each other.

"Deb brought brownies from the cannery," Elle said. "I doubt she made them herself, though."

"Brian brought a case of his home-brewed beer," Susan said.

Elle glared at Susan, and Susan quickly looked down at her hands.

"We usually set out appetizers for the guests," Elle said. "Sometimes I make smoked salmon spread, or we lay out an assortment of cheese and crackers, but the evening before the murders, Jules told me she had the appetizer ready."

Elle paused and seemed lost in thought.

"What did Jules put out for the guests?" Sara finally asked.

Elle looked at Susan, and Susan shrugged.

"Now that I think about it," Elle said, "it was kind of strange. She put out wild game sticks, like pepperoni sticks."

"What type of wild game?" Patterson asked.

"Mountain goat and deer," Elle said. "I have no idea where they came from. I'd never seen them before."

"What about you, Susan?" Sara asked. "Do you know where Jules got the wild game sticks?"

Susan shook her head. "They looked homemade. To be honest, they didn't look very good. They were kind of pale. I have no idea where Jules got them."

"Did you eat one of the sticks, Elle?" Patterson asked.

Elle shook her head. "I was busy cooking dinner when Jules put them out for the guests."

"What about you, Susan?" Patterson asked. "Did you try the sticks?"

Susan wrinkled her nose. "No, they looked gross."

"Did you ask Jules about the sticks, Elle?" Sara asked.

Elle shrugged. "I was swamped at the time and didn't think much about them."

"Did the guests eat the sticks?" Patterson asked.

Elle shrugged again. "I didn't notice," she said.

"I heard the British couple talking to the American couple about the sticks," Susan said, "but I don't know if the Germans tried them."

"What about the brownies?" Patterson asked. "Did everyone eat those?"

"I think so," Elle said. "I'd made pie for dessert, but when Deb brought the brownies, I used them for dessert instead and saved the pie. I planned to serve the pie the next night." She wiped a tear from her cheek. "I guess it's still in the refrigerator."

"Do you remember any of the guests saying they felt tired?" Patterson asked.

"Bob had led them on a long hike to go bear viewing," Susan said, "so I think they were all tired."

"Did the guests go back to their cabin right after dinner?" Patterson asked.

Susan nodded. "They didn't even sit around the table and talk like they usually do."

"Jules was happy they left so soon, so she could get the table ready for the family dinner," Elle said.

"Did Jules and Bob eat with the guests or with their kids?" Patterson asked.

"With their family," Elle said.

"Did you two eat brownies?" Sara asked.

Elle and Susan nodded.

"I took mine upstairs with me," Susan said.

"I ate mine when I was dishing them up for dessert for the guests," Elle said.

"Were there enough brownies for the family to eat?" Sara asked.

Elle nodded. "I doubt Deb had one, though. She never eats sweets."

"Were there any brownies or wild game sticks left after everyone ate their dinner?" Patterson asked.

Elle slowly shook her head. "I don't remember seeing any brownies the next morning," she said. "There should have been two or three left, but Jules probably sent the leftovers home with one of her kids."

"What about the wild game sticks?" Patterson asked.

Elle looked at Susan. "I don't know what happened to those. Do you?"

Susan shook her head. "I think they all got eaten," she said.

Patterson thanked Elle and Susan for their time. Susan again asked if she could home, and Patterson asked her to be patient for a few more days.

"Did the crime scene techs inventory the refrigerator?" Patterson asked Sara on the way back to trooper headquarters.

"They did, and I checked the list this morning," Sara said. "I'll double-check when I get back to my desk, but I don't remember brownies or meat sticks on the list. I guess they could have overlooked them, though."

"We know who brought the brownies," Patterson said, "but I wonder where Jules got the wild game sticks."

CHAPTER 50

Wednesday, September 10th

4:35 p.m.

Patterson tried to organize the facts surrounding the murders in Kanuk Bay. Except for the existence of the Ambien, Tim Fairweather seemed like the most obvious suspect. If he'd somehow given Jules Ambien-laced wild game sticks, then he was their guy. Patterson had heard nothing, though, to suggest Fairweather and Jules had seen each other in over a month. Perhaps they'd met somewhere to talk about the baby.

On the other hand, it was also possible someone had injected Ambien into the brownies. Even if they hadn't made the brownies, Deb or Jason could have added an Ambien-laced layer of frosting to the treats.

The beer also presented a possible vehicle for the Ambien, but did everyone drink the beer? Patterson knew he should send someone back to the lodge to collect all the leftover food and drinks. If Brian brought a case of beer to the lodge, there should still be some left.

Maybe the Ambien came from another source, and if so, then either Elle or Susan served it to the guests. Elle admitted she'd once had a prescription for the drug. Could she be responsible for killing the Bartletts and their guests? Did she hike to Sam's cabin and kill him before Patterson flew her and the others to town?

Patterson's desk phone rang, and he snapped up the receiver: "Patterson."

"Sir, this is Jill from the lab," Jill Clafflin said. "I have some results here for you."

"I'm glad to hear you made it back from Kanuk Bay," Patterson said. "I was afraid you'd be stuck out there all night. What do you have for me?"

"I had some lab results waiting on my desk when I returned," Jill said, "and I thought I should call you right away."

"I appreciate it," Patterson said. "Go ahead."

"The lab found two clear prints on the papers I sent them from the Bartletts' safe," Jill said. "One print was on the envelope, and the other was on the first page of the wills."

"Did both prints belong to the same person?"

"Yes, sir," she said. "Both prints belonged to Deborah Bartlett."

Patterson sat back in his chair. He'd expected Jill to say the prints belonged to Brian Bartlett. Deb had lied to him when she'd said she didn't know anything about her parents' wills. He wondered how Deb had managed to handle the will if it was locked in the office safe. Did she rifle through the safe when it was open, or did she know her father had taped the key to the back of the safe?

"That's all I have, sir," Jill said.

Patterson realized he hadn't spoken in several seconds. "Thanks, Jill," he said. "Let me know when you get more lab results."

He rubbed the back of his neck. Just when he felt they were closing in on a suspect, new evidence seemed to point at someone else. Deb, Jason, or both Deb and Jason could easily be their killer or killers. Now he would have to bring Deb back in for more questioning and find out why she'd lied to them about knowing what was in her parents' wills.

A knock on his office door rescued Patterson from his dark thoughts. "Come in," he called.

The door swung open, and Mark Traner walked into the room.

"I'm glad you made it back to town today," Patterson said. "The last time I talked to KFS, they were on weather hold."

"It wasn't pretty," Mark said. "I don't think we ever had more than two miles' visibility on the flight to town."

"Did you finish with the crime scene?"

Mark nodded. "Thanks for sending Joe and Jill. It went fast with their help."

"Did you find anything of interest?"

"We found nine shotgun blasts in the walls and door of the bedroom," Mark said, "and someone also shot the chest of drawers, but when we dragged the chest in front of the door, the holes didn't line up."

"Do you think Fairweather staged the scene?"

Mark shrugged. "I think it's possible."

"Dr. Libby says Tim used a .44 caliber gun to shoot Georgie. Did you find it?"

Mark nodded. "The same caliber used to murder the lodge guests and to kill Sam Lutz."

"You brought the gun to town with you?"

"Yes, sir. I'll send it to the crime lab."

"I think you and I should interview Mr. Fairweather together."

"Yes, sir."

Patterson had Tim Fairweather escorted to the conference room, where he and Mark met him a few minutes later.

Tim Fairweather looked as if he had aged another ten years over the last few hours. His hair spiked from his scalp, and his red eyes made him look like a demon. Patterson placed a bottle of water on the table in front of him.

"Mr. Fairweather," Patterson said, "Trooper Traner just returned from your cabin, and he found some troubling inconsistencies between the evidence and your story."

Fairweather said nothing. He pointed his face toward Patterson, but his eyes looked unfocused. If Patterson didn't know better, he would have thought he was on drugs.

Patterson nodded to Mark. "You tell him what you found."

"We found nine shotgun blasts to the wall and door of your bedroom," Mark said, "and there were holes in the back of the chest of drawers, but the holes in the chest didn't line up with the holes in the door."

As Mark spoke, Fairweather's head slowly swiveled from Patterson to Mark, but he said nothing.

"Mr. Fairweather," Patterson said, "are you under the influence of narcotics?" Patterson couldn't imagine where Fairweather would have found drugs, but he didn't seem to be tracking correctly.

Fairweather shook his head twice in reply to Patterson, and then he said, "It happened like I said it did. I don't know why the holes don't line up. Maybe the chest was at an angle to the door when Georgie shot it."

"Mr. Fairweather," Patterson said, "the medical examiner told me that you shot Georgie four times, and two of those shots entered through her back. That doesn't sound much like self-defense to me."

Fairweather returned his gaze to Patterson, his eyes narrowed. "I want to call my lawyer."

Patterson sighed. The interview was over, and they wouldn't be able to talk to Fairweather until the following day, with his lawyer present.

CHAPTER 51

Wednesday, September 10th

4:40 p.m.

Elle blew on her spoonful of soup and then carefully swallowed it. This afternoon was the first time she'd felt like cooking since the murders. It was such a relief to know Sergeant Patterson didn't suspect her of killing the Bartletts. He thought the killer had drugged everyone with sleeping pills. Someone had drugged her, and that's why she didn't remember anything after dinner. She wasn't going crazy.

"This is good," Susan said.

"It's just potato chowder," Elle said. "Brie doesn't have much food here. I guess we'll have to go grocery shopping if we stay here much longer."

"I hope they let us leave soon," Susan said. "Stan wants me to come home."

"It sounds like Sergeant Patterson is making progress on the case. At least now he knows we were all drugged."

"I don't think the drugs were in the brownies," Susan said.

Elle's hand froze before the next spoonful reached her mouth. "Why not the brownies?" she asked.

"I ate a brownie, and it didn't make me tired," Susan said.

"How do you know? You went to bed right after you ate it."

"I was awake for a long time, though. I had trouble going to sleep that night. If the drugs had knocked me out, I wouldn't have heard you wandering the halls."

"I wasn't wandering the halls," Elle said. The soup suddenly tasted sour.

"I'm not saying everyone wasn't drugged," Susan said. "I just don't think the drugs were in something I ate." She shrugged. "Maybe the wild game sticks were drugged. I didn't eat any of those."

"Neither did I," Elle said. Her mood began to plummet into darkness again. Elle couldn't remember eating or drinking anything other than the brownie and a glass of iced tea. If the brownies didn't have Ambien in them, then maybe she hadn't swallowed the sleeping medicine. This thought brought her back to where she was before the troopers came to talk to her and Susan. Why couldn't she remember anything after she'd gone up to her room that night?

CHAPTER 52

Wednesday, September 10th

6:08 p.m.

The fragrant aroma of stew greeted Patterson when he walked through the front door of his home. Jeanne had the small television in the kitchen tuned to the evening news, and she stood at the center work island tearing lettuce for a salad.

She smiled up at Patterson as he walked toward her and planted a kiss on the top of her head. "It smells great in here."

"I hope you have time to sit down and eat this evening," Jeanne said. "Dinner's ready as soon as you are."

"I thought you had to work all day?" Patterson said after he'd eaten half a bowl of stew.

"I traded with Ann. I had a doctor's appointment at three."

"What did the doctor say?" Patterson suddenly had no appetite.

"I'm two months pregnant," she said. "The doctor took blood for tests, and I got an ultrasound." Jeanne smiled at Patterson, "So far, so good. Everything looks normal."

Patterson felt his stomach drop. The tests had all looked normal last time too. Would Jeanne survive another miscarriage? She'd nearly killed herself the last time.

"I know you're worried, and so am I." Jeanne shrugged. "I'll get through this no matter what happens. I promise." She reached for her husband's hand. "I think the risk is worth it, hon. I really want to have my own baby."

Patterson forced a smile, but he couldn't eat another bite. He wanted a child, but he did not wish for Jeanne to endure what she had a few months earlier.

"How is your case going?" she asked. "Are you any closer to finding the killer?"

Patterson sighed and pushed the bowl of stew away from him. "Not really."

"Do you want to tell me about it?"

Patterson started to shake his head, but he knew he wanted to unburden himself, and Jeanne would never repeat anything he told her.

For the next twenty minutes, he talked, and Jeanne listened. He felt exhausted after he'd finished, but he knew he would be able to sleep.

Jeanne asked few questions, but tears trickled from the corners of her eyes. She lightly rested her hand on her husband's arm. "I don't know how you do what you do."

"Sometimes neither do I. This is the worst case I've ever investigated."

Patterson went to bed early and immediately fell into a deep sleep. His buzzing phone awakened him at 3:12 a.m. He grabbed the offending device and hurried out of the bedroom so that he wouldn't bother Jeanne.

"Sir," Brie said, sounding tense, "I just received a call from Elaine Peterson, the dispatcher with the Kodiak PD. KPD responded to a call at the Bartlett residence about twenty minutes ago."

Patterson's mind cleared in an instant, and he was awake and alert. "What happened?"

"Jason Caine beat Deb Bartlett, and she's being transported to the hospital."

"How bad?" Patterson asked.

"She's nearly dead," Brie said. "The responding officers thought this incident might be related to the murders at the lodge, so they told Elaine to call us with any news."

"Thanks, Brie," Patterson said. "I'm on my way to the hospital."

"Should I send anyone else?" Brie asked.

"I assume KPD took Jason into custody?" Patterson said.

"Yes, sir," Brie said.

"We'll talk to him tomorrow," Patterson said. "You don't need to send anyone to the hospital. I doubt Deb is conscious, but if she is, I want to be there to hear what she says."

Patterson hated second-guessing himself, but he wished he'd gotten Deb away from Jason and brought her in the previous evening to question her about the fingerprints on the will. Still, he'd had no reason to detain her, and after the interview, she would have gone home to her boyfriend.

When Patterson arrived at the hospital, the ER staff was busy preparing Deb for transport to Anchorage and more specialized medical care. The ER doctor allowed Patterson into the room but told him to stand back. If a nurse hadn't told Patterson that the patient in the bed was Deb Bartlett, he would never have recognized her swollen, discolored face.

"She has three broken ribs and internal bleeding," Dr. Floyd told him. "She also has intracranial bleeding." He turned to Patterson and shook his head.

Patterson watched the staff work for several more minutes, but he could see Deb wasn't going to regain consciousness anytime soon, if ever. He left the ER room and exited the hospital. *Where was Brian? Didn't he hear the fight?* Patterson thought both Deb and Brian were staying at their parents' house.

Patterson pulled up the phone number for Brian Bartlett and pushed send.

The phone rang six times before a groggy voice said, "What?"

"Mr. Bartlett, this is Sergeant Patterson. Your sister is in the emergency room at Providence hospital."

Brian didn't immediately respond, and Patterson wondered if he'd disconnected.

Finally, Brian said, "Why?"

"She's in critical condition," Patterson said. "She and Jason got into a physical altercation."

Brian groaned. "I told her to stay away from that loser. Where is he now?"

"He's in custody at the Kodiak Police Department," Patterson said. "The emergency room staff is stabilizing Deb so that they can ship her up to Anchorage."

"I'm on my way," Brian said.

Less than fifteen minutes later, Brian pulled into the hospital parking lot, and Patterson escorted him into the hospital emergency room. Brian took one look at Deb's swollen face and started to cry.

Brian's emotional display surprised Patterson, because he'd expressed no emotions when informed of his parents' murders.

Patterson introduced Brian to the ER staff, and a clipboard full of papers for him to sign suddenly appeared. A nurse explained the do-not-resuscitate directive, then asked Brian to sign it if he did not wish for them to start CPR if his sister's heart stopped beating.

Brian took a step back from the nurse. "You think she might die?" he asked.

Patterson thought Brian should realize this possibility just by looking at his sister.

"I'm not saying she's going to die, sir," the nurse said, "but it's better to have the directive in place in case something does happen."

Brian scribbled his signature on the DNR form as well as on several other documents. Once he'd finished with the paperwork, he slowly approached his sister. Patterson watched him mumble a prayer and then extend his right hand toward Deb's face, withdrawing it before he touched her.

The doctor placed his hand on Brian's shoulder. "The medevac plane is ready, so we're going to transport Deb to the airport and fly her up to Anchorage, where an ambulance will take her to Alaska Regional Hospital. The staff there will call you later this morning with more information on her condition."

Brian looked helpless as he watched the orderlies wheel Deb out of the emergency room. He turned and looked at Patterson, tears streaming from his eyes. "Let me at him," he said. "I'll get rid of him once and for all."

"Let's go down to the cafeteria," Patterson said. "I'll buy you a cup of coffee."

Brian followed quietly behind Patterson. Once he'd paid for them, Patterson started to hand Brian his cup of coffee, but when he noticed how much his hands were shaking, Patterson carried both cups to a small metal table in the far corner of the room.

"Are you okay?" he asked Brian. Brian looked so pale that Patterson feared he would faint at any moment.

Brian wiped his face with a napkin. "Deb is all I have left," he said. "She can't die."

"Were you staying at the house with Deb and Jason?" Patterson asked.

Brian shook his head. "I stayed there the first night, but I can't stand that pig. I've been crashing at a friend's place."

"Do you have any idea what might have set Jason off? Why would he hurt Deb?"

Brian shrugged. "Who knows? Jason has a bad temper. He and I almost got into a fight because I told him to clean up his dirty dishes." He shook his head. "I knew he'd hurt Deb at some point, but I didn't think it would be this bad. I should have protected her."

For the first time since he'd met him, Patterson felt sympathy for Brian Bartlett. He couldn't help but wonder, though, where this grief was when he'd first heard about his parents' deaths.

"You want to know who murdered my parents and their guests?" Brian asked. "It was the same guy who just tried to murder my sister."

"Why do you think Jason killed your parents?"

"Because they didn't like him, or because Deb would inherit some money if my parents died. You saw Deb. He didn't need much of a reason to resort to violence."

Patterson agreed. Jason Caine had an anger issue. "Do you have any evidence that Jason murdered your parents?"

Brian slowly shook his head. "No, but I'm convinced he did it. Even before this, I suspected Jason, but now, I'm sure of it."

"Do you think Deb had anything to do with the murders?"

"No," Brian said. "I think it was all Jason. He probably waited until Deb fell asleep and then took the boat back to the lodge and killed everyone. Probably something Deb told him my parents said set him off."

"We think the crimes were premeditated," Patterson said. "The medical examiner found traces of the sleep medication Ambien in all the victims."

This news seemed to confuse Brian. He sat back in his chair and regarded Patterson. After a few moments, he said, "Deb brought brownies to the lodge."

"Did you eat a brownie?" Patterson asked.

Brian shook his head. "I got into a fight with Dad and left before dessert. Deb doesn't like sweets, so she wouldn't have eaten one either." He paused a moment. "If the brownies were laced with Ambien, then Jason drugged them without Deb knowing. There's no way Deb would conspire to murder my parents and the guests. Deb just wanted my parents to love her. She didn't want to kill them." Tears again streaked down Brian's face as he wiped furiously at them with a napkin.

Patterson arrived home at 5:30 a.m. He saw no reason to go back to bed for an hour, so instead, he climbed into the shower and stood under the hot water. *Did Brian Bartlett just pull off an Oscar-worthy acting performance, or is he innocent of the murders of his parents, their guests, and Sam Lutz?* Patterson knew he couldn't yet mark Brian off his list of suspects. He reminded himself that while Brian had seemed upset to learn his sister might die, he didn't have the same reaction when Patterson informed him that someone had murdered his parents.

Patterson agreed with Brian, though. Jason Caine had a temper, and after seeing what his fists had done to Deb, Patterson found it easy to imagine Jason swinging an ax at the heads of Jules and Bob Bartlett. He could have doctored the brownies to drug the Bartletts and their guests, and if Jason was still dealing drugs, he probably knew how to score Ambien. It was not hard to believe Jason could have slipped away from the cannery for a few hours to commit the murders. Perhaps Sam Lutz saw Jason that night, or maybe Jason thought Sam had some other reason to suspect him of the murders, so he killed Sam too.

Jason Caine checked all the boxes. *Did Deb suspect him, and is that why he nearly beat her to death?* Perhaps she'd threatened to take her suspicions to the troopers. Or maybe Deb was in on the murders, but her conscience was now bothering her, so she'd told Jason she planned to confess.

If Jason was the killer, Patterson knew they needed more evidence to make a solid case against him. Perhaps they could get Jason to confess if they went at him hard, but Patterson doubted he would cave under questioning.

CHAPTER 53

Thursday, September 11th

4:12 a.m.

Whack. Whack. Whack. Blood flew everywhere. Elle released a savage yell as scarlet splattered her naked body.

"Elle. Elle, wake up. It's just a nightmare." Susan gently patted her back.

Elle awoke with a start and scooted toward the headboard. She couldn't breathe. There wasn't enough oxygen in the room.

"Are you okay?"

Susan's voice sounded low and steady, and Elle tried to latch on to it. She gradually slowed her breathing.

Susan crawled onto the bed beside Elle, and Elle leaned against her.

"It was just a nightmare," Elle said.

"What was it about?" Susan asked.

"I don't know. I can't remember," she said. She reached for her bottle of water on the nightstand and took a long, slow drink. She could feel her heart rate beginning to slow.

"Why don't you go back to sleep," Susan said. "I'll stay here with you for a while."

"Okay," Elle said. She hated that she wanted Susan to stay with her, but maybe her presence would keep the demons at bay.

Elle scooted back down on the bed and laid her head on her pillow. Susan crawled under the covers beside her. Elle turned on her side, and Susan slid over next to her and put her arms around her.

She didn't think she would be able to fall asleep, but Susan's body next to hers felt oddly comforting, and she soon began to drift. She was nearly asleep when she heard Susan's whispered words.

"Thank you for not killing me," she said.

CHAPTER 54

Thursday, September 11th

7:34 a.m.

Patterson arrived at trooper headquarters a little after 7:30 a.m., and he immediately called the hospital in Anchorage for an update on Deb Bartlett's condition. He was expecting to have to cut through a mountain of red tape, but he got straight through to a surgery nurse.

"Kodiak told us you'd be calling to check on her," the nurse said. "She's been in surgery for a little over an hour. The doctor removed her spleen and is now making other repairs. His biggest concern is intracranial swelling and pressure, but so far, she remains critical but stable."

Patterson thanked the nurse and disconnected. If Deb survived, he knew he would need to ask a trooper from the Anchorage post to question her at the hospital. Even if she did survive this trauma, though, she could have brain damage, and she almost certainly would have some memory loss about what had happened to her.

Patterson next called the Kodiak Police Department and asked to speak to the detective working the Jason Caine case.

"Powers," a deep male voice said a few minutes later.

Patterson knew Craig Powers and felt he was competent but not brilliant. He asked about Jason Caine and if the detective had interrogated him yet.

"I wasn't on duty when they brought him in," he said. "I just got handed the case when I arrived a few minutes ago."

Patterson explained his interest in Jason Caine and asked if he could be present for the interview.

Powers paused a beat, but he must have realized Patterson deserved a seat at the table. After all, the troopers were up against the wall trying to solve the murders of nine people.

"Can you get over here in the next few minutes?" Powers asked.

"I'm on my way," Patterson said.

Twenty minutes later, Patterson followed Craig Powers into an interview room at the Kodiak PD. Jason Caine sat next to the small table, his handcuffed hands resting in his lap.

Jason smelled terrible and looked even worse. His black hair hung in greasy clumps around his face, and his red eyes suggested he either had a hangover or was coming down from a high. He glared at Patterson, who took a seat on a folding chair in the corner of the room. Powers sat at the table with Jason.

Powers introduced himself and read Jason his Miranda rights. Jason acknowledged that he understood his rights, but to Patterson's relief, he did not request an attorney.

"So, you're a tough guy," Powers said.

Jason said nothing.

"You like beating up your girlfriend?"

Jason's gaze dropped to the table. "How is Deb?"

"Nearly dead," Powers said. "She might not make it through the day."

Jason did not reply.

"This isn't the first time you've beaten up a girlfriend," Powers said. "Does it make you feel like a real man to use your fists on a woman?"

Jason responded with a slight shrug.

Patterson's instincts told him Powers was going at Jason too hard. Jason would lawyer up before they got anything useful out of him.

"Tell me what Deb said or did to make you want to beat her to death," Powers said.

Jason said nothing, so Powers stood, punched the table with his fist, and then leaned down until he was within a few inches of Jason's face. "What set you off!" he yelled.

Jason pulled away from Powers. "She's just been moody since her parents got murdered."

Powers fell back into his chair with a thud. "How dare her," he said. "What right does she have to be a little moody after she learns someone hacked her mother and father to death with an ax?"

Jason did not seem to pick up on Powers's irony. "Yeah," he said. "She's in a bad mood all the time."

"Does Deb suspect you're the one who killed her parents?"

Patterson fought the urge to jump up and tell Powers to worry about his own case. Powers didn't know enough about the murders at the lodge to question Jason on the subject.

Jason stared at the table and didn't respond to the question.

"Look," Powers said. "Even a loser like you doesn't beat someone to within an inch of her life simply because she's in a bad mood. What did you and Deb fight about?"

"I'm not talking to you," Jason said.

Wonderful. Patterson was not impressed with Detective Powers's interrogation skills, and he'd grown tired of playing nice. "Can I ask you a few questions?" Patterson asked.

Powers's head whipped toward Patterson with a glare, but Patterson ignored the policeman and concentrated on Jason.

Jason glowered at Patterson. "I'm not answering any questions about what Deb and I fought about."

Patterson jumped in before Powers could stop him. "Do you know where Deb got the brownies she brought to the lodge for dinner the evening before her parents were killed?"

Jason's face turned a darker shade of red. "How would I know? From the mess hall or the store, I guess. I don't know anything about them."

Patterson found Jason's reaction interesting. He'd thought the question might have confused him. An innocent man would wonder why the cop had asked him about brownies in the middle of an interrogation, but instead of confusing him, the question seemed to have angered him. On the other hand, everything seemed to anger Jason.

"Did you or Deb know what was in her parents' wills?" Patterson asked. "Did she have any idea what her mom or dad planned to leave her?"

"No," Jason said. "Deb told me her parents were leaving everything to Brian. If you want to know who killed them, you need to talk to him."

Got you, Patterson thought. "If Deb didn't know what was in her parents' wills, why were her fingerprints on them?"

Patterson didn't think Jason's face could get any redder, but he was wrong.

"If she looked at the wills, she didn't tell me," Jason said, his gaze firmly fixed on the floor.

"You know what I think, Jason?" Patterson asked. "I think Deb told you she would inherit some money and a house if her parents both died. You thought if Deb inherited, then you would inherit, because even though you aren't married, what's hers is yours, right?"

Jason remained silent and did not look at Patterson.

"I have a witness who says he saw you by yourself, without Deb, around midnight at the cannery on the night of the murders. You and Deb lied when you said you were together all night. I believe you drugged the brownies Deb planned to take to the lodge for dinner, and then, once Deb fell asleep, you returned to the lodge and murdered everyone."

"You're wrong," Jason said. "You don't know what you're talking about."

"Last night," Patterson said, "Deb finally figured out you were the murderer, and she planned to turn you in, so you lost it and tried to beat her to death."

Jason's eyes slowly lifted from the floor until he met Patterson's gaze. "I got nothing to say to you."

CHAPTER 55

Thursday, September 11th

9:20 a.m.

Patterson knew he should feel relief. His two main suspects for the murders were now in jail and off the street and out of the wilderness. He didn't have anything solid on either one of them, though, and the lack of evidence bothered him.

Fairweather had admitted he'd killed his wife, and the only question was whether he'd murdered her because he was tired of her or whether he'd murdered her in self-defense. He had a motive for killing Bob Bartlett, but why would he murder Jules or the guests or Sam?

Jason Caine was mean and hated Deb's parents. Patterson could imagine Jason swinging the ax. Jason might have killed the guests because he despised Brian Bartlett. If Brian inherited a lodge where six guests had been murdered, he would possibly have a tough time securing future bookings. Getting back at Brian seemed like a crazy reason to murder six strangers, but no one had a good reason for murdering the guests. If Deb survived her injuries, maybe she'd finally tell the truth about Jason's involvement.

Someone knocked on Patterson's closed office door.

"Come in," he called.

Sara marched into his office, holding a notepad in her hand. This morning her hair was pinned in a bun, as usual, and her brown eyes burned with focus.

"Good morning, Sara," Patterson said. "Do you have something for me?"

"Sir," she said, "I finally got ahold of Elle's mother in Indiana."

Patterson nodded for her to continue.

"She said Elle had a troubled childhood, but she hasn't had any problems since she went to college."

"We knew this information already, didn't we?" Patterson asked.

"When I first told Mrs. Chaplin who I was and where I was calling from, she said, 'What has she done now?' Then she seemed to catch herself. After that, she said all the right things, but she sounded nervous." Sara's face blushed. "I know it isn't much, but I got a weird feeling from the woman."

Patterson nodded. Maybe he wasn't looking seriously enough at the other possible suspects in this case. He knew he needed to be careful not to wear blinders. "Let's bring her in for questioning again," he said. "Do you feel comfortable questioning her by yourself? She responds better to you."

"Yes, sir," Sara said. "Do you want me to go get her?"

"Send one of the other troopers to pick her up," Patterson said, "and don't give her any warning. I hate to traumatize her more than necessary, but if she's our killer, then we can't afford to be too gentle with her."

"Yes, sir," Sara said.

"Put her in the interrogation room, and let me know before you start questioning her. I want to watch the interview from the observation room."

Sara nodded. "I'll jot down a few notes, and then I'll send someone to get her."

CHAPTER 56

Thursday, September 11th

11:12 a.m.

Patterson watched Elle through the one-way glass window. She looked at her phone and then put the device on the table and hugged herself. Next, she stood and paced, and then she retook her seat. He hoped Sara wouldn't leave Elle by herself too long. Sometimes you wanted to make your suspect sweat for a few minutes, but Elle was so fragile that Patterson feared she'd unravel if Sara waited too long.

The door to the interrogation room opened, and Sara entered. She handed Elle a bottle of water, and she opened another bottle and took a long drink before sitting in the vacant chair at the table.

"Thank you for coming in, Elle," Sara said.

"I don't think I had a choice."

"Of course you have a choice," Sara said. "You're not under arrest, but we appreciate all the help you've given us with this case. I just have a few more questions for you."

Elle's shoulders lowered a fraction. "I'll tell you what I know."

"What do you think happened the other night at the lodge?"

"What do you mean?" Elle began tapping her fingers on the table, and then she pulled the offending hand to her body and hugged herself.

"The night someone murdered Jules and Bob. What do you think happened?"

"I don't understand," Elle said. "I guess someone whacked Jules and Bob with an ax and then shot the guests."

"Do you have any idea who killed them?"

291

Patterson noticed Elle's leg begin to shake. "I think Jason did it. I heard he nearly killed Deb last night."

"Where did you hear that?" Sara asked.

Elle's face flushed scarlet, and her eyes ping-ponged around the room. After several moments, she said, "Brian told me," her voice only a whisper.

"How did he tell you?"

"He called me this morning," Elle said. "We're friends."

"You think Jason murdered everyone at the lodge by himself?"

Elle shrugged. "I don't know," she said. "Why are you asking me this?"

"Elle," Sara said, "as I told you before, one of our jobs as troopers is to look into the backgrounds of everyone close to the victims. We take a hard look at anyone, no matter how innocent they seem, who had access to the victims and the crime scene. Do you understand what I'm saying?"

Patterson watched Elle as Sara spoke. The color drained out of Elle's face so fast that he expected her to faint. Instead, she gripped the edge of the table and stared at Sara's face.

Sara continued: "I talked to people in your hometown, and I heard about the problems you had as a child. I understand you had some flashes of violence, coupled with memory loss of certain events."

Elle's mouth opened, but she didn't say anything.

"Do you want to tell me what happened?" Sara asked.

Elle's mouth snapped shut, and she looked down at her hands. She was quiet for so long that Patterson didn't think she was going to respond, but then she said, "Those things happened a long time ago. I was different then."

"What do you mean you were different then?"

Elle shrugged. "I've had therapy," she said. "I went to college. I've worked at several jobs. I'm fine now. I don't have blackouts anymore."

"But you told Sergeant Patterson that you don't remember much of anything from the night of the murders."

"Someone drugged me with sleeping pills," Elle said.

Sara put her arms on the table and leaned toward Elle. "Listen, Elle," she said in a soft voice, "you have to look at this from our perspective. You were the cook at the lodge, and you had access to all the food, so you could have slipped the drugs into anything. Susan thought she heard you walking in the upstairs hall in the middle of the night, but you say you don't remember anything."

Elle jumped up so quickly she knocked over the chair she'd just vacated. "I loved Jules. I wouldn't hurt her," she said. Tears gushed from her eyes, and her body began to shake so violently that she gripped the wall for support.

Sara bolted from her chair and hurried to support Elle. "I know this isn't easy, Elle, but we need to get to the bottom of these terrible murders."

"I didn't hurt anyone!" Elle sobbed. She pulled a handful of tissues from her pocket and held them to her face.

"May I take you to the hospital?" Sara asked. "I think you need to see a doctor."

Elle furiously shook her head. "I want to leave. I'm not answering any more questions."

Sara looked toward the one-way glass and shook her head. She walked Elle back to the table, picked up the overturned chair, and told Elle to sit for a few minutes and drink some water. "Once you feel a little stronger, I'll have someone take you back to the house."

CHAPTER 57

Thursday, September 11th

12:07 p.m.

Elle burst through the door of Brie's house and ran to her bedroom. Out of the corner of her eye, she saw Susan sitting on the couch, and she knew she must have been talking to her. All Elle could hear, though, was a roar in her ears.

Elle slammed the bedroom door shut and engaged the lock. She threw herself on the bed and sobbed.

"What happened?" Susan's voice sounded a long way off, but Elle could hear her knocks on the bedroom door, so she must've just been in the hall.

"Go away, Susan," Elle said. "I'll talk to you later."

"Are you okay?" Susan asked. "What happened?"

"I'm fine," Elle said. She put the pillow over her head and pushed it against her ears until Susan's voice was a muffled blur.

They think I killed everyone at the lodge. The troopers' suspicions wouldn't have scared Elle so much if she knew they were wrong, but she feared they were right. *How did Jules's earrings get into my bag? Did I steal them? Why can't I remember?* Elle had been furious with Jules when she'd overheard her tell Brian he could do better than Elle for a girlfriend. Had that set her off? *Did I drug the food with Ambien? Did I stand over Jules and Bob and hack them to death with an ax? Could I do something so terrible?*

Elle rushed to the bathroom and heaved into the toilet. She pulled her kit from the bathroom drawer but then remembered the Ambien.

She grabbed her small bag from the bedroom and searched through it until she found the ziplock bag containing her medicine. Her hands shook as she fumbled with the bottles of pills. She found the bottle of Ambien, pulled off the lid, and stared into it in disbelief. There was only one pill in the bottle. She hadn't taken Ambien in several months, but Elle knew she should have at least half a bottle of pills left. What had she done with them?

Tears streamed down Elle's face as she took off her pants and sat on the floor. It would take more than one cut to quiet her demons today. She sliced each of her thighs and watched the blood stream over her legs and onto the floor. She leaned her head against the wall and sobbed until she felt some relief.

She could imagine herself bringing down the ax on Jules's and Bob's heads with long, solid whacks, using the same motion Bob had taught her to use when splitting wood. Bob had also taught her how to shoot, and she'd fired his .44 Magnum before. Did she use it to murder the guests? Elle could feel her fragile grip on her sanity slipping.

CHAPTER 58

Thursday, September 11th
2:05 p.m.

Patterson, Mark, Sara, Peter, and Gary sat around the conference room table. "I think Jason is our guy," Peter said.

Patterson nodded. "He had means, motive, and opportunity."

"The trifecta," Andy said, "and we know Deb lied when she said he was with her all night after they returned to the cannery, so he doesn't have an alibi."

"I think both Caine and Fairweather make better suspects than Elle," Sara said, "but something about Elle troubles me."

"What is it?" Mark asked. "Her past?"

"Not just her past," Sara said. "I think she doubts her innocence."

"Yes," Patterson said. "I noticed the same thing during your interview. Elle can't remember anything after she went upstairs on the night of the murder. Since she lost her memory during two previous episodes of violence, she's worried it happened again, and she thinks, this time, she did something truly horrible."

"Should we bring her in and hold her?" Peter asked. "Is she a possible danger to herself or Susan?"

Patterson let out a long breath. "We don't have reason yet to detain her. I'd love to have a psychologist talk to her, but she says she doesn't want help."

"What's our next move?" Andy asked.

"I just talked to an ICU nurse at Alaska Regional in Anchorage," Patterson said. "She said Deb Bartlett is still unconscious but stable. I hope she wakes up soon and wants to talk to us."

"I hope she can remember what she and Jason fought about," Sara said.

Patterson nodded. "It might not have anything to do with our case, but something caused Jason to fly out of control, and I'd like to know what it was."

A sharp knock on the conference room door caused all five troopers to turn and look at the closed door.

"Yes?" Patterson called.

Jill Clafflin stepped into the room. "Sergeant," she said, "I just received some results from the crime lab, and I think you should take a look at them."

"Thanks, Jill," Patterson said. "I'll come down to the lab as soon as we finish here."

"Sir," Jill said, "I don't think this should wait."

CHAPTER 59

Thursday, September 11th

2:18 p.m.

Patterson walked out into the hall with Jill, who handed him a piece of paper. "Sandy, the lab tech in Anchorage at the crime lab who analyzed the blue-handled ax, called me a few minutes ago. They found a partial fingerprint on the ax, and they found a match right away. Sandy sent the report, and I knew you would want to see it immediately."

Patterson looked down at the paper Jill had handed him and read the lab results. His pulse beat a drum solo in his ears as he rushed back into the conference room. He looked at his troopers. "Grab your vests and meet me in the parking lot. I hope this goes peacefully, but you should prepare for a hostage situation."

CHAPTER 60

Thursday, September 11th
2:17 p.m.

Elle awoke and looked down at her legs. The sight disgusted her. Blood still oozed from both cuts, but she'd cut too deeply on her right leg, and she knew it would continue to bleed for some time. She needed to ask Susan for another Band-Aid, and she would be full of questions. She thought Susan already suspected her of cutting herself, and she would never believe Elle again cut herself shaving.

She wrapped a coil of toilet paper around each leg and then carefully pulled up her jeans. She walked out of her room and into the hall. She heard the television in the living room, and it sounded as if Susan was watching her cartoons. Elle believed she would lose her fragile grip on her sanity if she didn't get out of this house and away from Susan soon.

Elle walked into the living room and was just about to call Susan's name when she saw Susan herself passed out on the couch. Elle stopped, turned, and tiptoed back down the hall. Maybe she wouldn't have to ask Susan for another bandage. She'd seen Susan take the last Band-Aid from her small bag, and Susan didn't need to know if Elle took another one.

Elle quietly entered Susan's bedroom and walked toward the closet. The closet door stood open a crack. The door squeaked as Elle tried to open it more. She looked behind her to make sure Susan wasn't standing there. She knew she would not be happy to find her snooping through her things.

The blue bag sat on the floor just inside the closet. Elle zipped it open and stuck her hand in the bag, searching for the box of bandages. Her hand closed around a hard metal object. Elle slid the bag from the dark closet and into the ray of light shining through the window.

She fought back nausea as she tried to make sense out of what she held in her hand.

"What are you looking for?" Susan's voice came from behind Elle.

Elle's head whipped toward her young helper. Her eyes focused on the large kitchen knife Susan held in her right hand.

CHAPTER 61

Thursday, September 11th

2:24 p.m.

Mark Traner climbed into one SUV with Patterson, while Peter, Andy, and Sara jumped in another vehicle. Patterson drove as fast as he dared through the streets of Kodiak.

"There must be some kind of rational explanation," Mark said.

"I can't think of one, can you?" Patterson asked.

"She's just a kid," Mark said.

"She's a very disturbed kid." Patterson glanced at the rearview mirror to make sure Peter was following close behind him.

"When we get there," Patterson said, "remember, she probably still has the gun she used to kill the guests, and we have to assume she won't hesitate to shoot us."

"If we're right, she's already murdered nine people," Mark said.

Patterson pulled up in front of Brie's house and parked by the curb. Peter pulled in behind him. Patterson sent Andy to the rear of the house, and he asked Sara to watch the left side of the house while he positioned Peter on the right side. Patterson didn't want Susan to run out the back door or slide out of a side window. He and Mark drew their weapons and walked up the front porch steps. Patterson knocked on the door, and then the two troopers carefully stood to either side of the doorway. When no one answered his knock, Patterson rapped his knuckles on the door again.

CHAPTER 62

Thursday, September 11th

2:25 p.m.

Elle pointed the .44 Magnum at Susan. "Stop right there," she said.

Susan smiled. "It's not loaded, Elle. It wouldn't be safe to keep a loaded gun in my bag."

Elle dropped the gun and began to tremble. She knew she needed to say or do something to keep Susan from plunging the knife into her. "Why?" she asked.

"I did us a favor," Susan said. "Bob and Jules are not nice people. I hate them both, and I am so sick and tired of Jules telling me to dump Stan." Susan took a step closer to Elle. "It's none of her business who I date."

Elle noted Susan's use of the present tense. Susan's eyes looked dead. *Have they always looked like that?* She knew she had to keep Susan talking until she could think of a way to get past her and out of the house.

"Why the guests?" she asked.

"Did you hear what that Weiss woman said to me?" Susan took another step closer to Elle. "She told me I didn't know how to clean a bathroom."

Elle pushed against the bedroom wall. She was moving away from the bedroom door instead of toward it. Maybe she could talk some sense into Susan and get her to back down.

"What about the other guests?" Elle asked.

Susan shrugged. "Unless they needed something, they never talked to me. They didn't even know I was there. They were like all the other guests we had this summer."

"Susan, it was our job to take care of them. Bob and Jules paid us to look after the guests."

"You wouldn't understand," Susan said. "The guests respect you because you prepare their meals, but they just thought of me as a slave."

Elle wanted to lecture Susan about the hospitality industry, but she knew this was not the place or time. "Why hurt Sammy?" she asked.

A tear trickled from Susan's right eye. "I liked Sammy," she said, "but he was too nosy. I had to shoot him, or he would have told the troopers to suspect me of the murders."

"Why?" Elle asked.

"I took some of Jules's jewelry," Susan said. "I knew Jules would think Deb took it, and she would never suspect me." A slight smile curved her lips. "Whenever I took something, I buried it, and one day, Sammy saw me burying one of Jules's silver necklaces. He told me he'd tell Jules if I didn't put it back where I found it."

"Did you put it back?" Elle wondered how long she would be able to distract Susan. She knew Susan was stronger than she was, so she didn't like her chances if it came to a struggle to control the knife.

Susan nodded. "I put it back in Jules's jewelry case, but I took it again a few days later and buried it. I saw Sammy watching me a few times when I walked in the woods, and I'm fairly sure he saw me bury something else."

"Were you who he was watching when Bob thought he was window peeping on Jules?"

"I think so," Susan said. "I buried something up by the old shed that day, and I think Sam was watching me through his binoculars. He never said anything, though."

"How much stuff did you bury?"

Susan shrugged. "Not much. I dug up the last two items the day before the murders."

"You put the earrings in my bag," Elle said.

Susan nodded. "I'm sorry."

"I don't understand when you had time to murder Sam. The troopers interviewed him at his cabin at the same time Sergeant Patterson was talking to us."

"When Sergeant Patterson told us to pack our stuff, I realized I couldn't leave Sammy alive. I was worried he'd already told the troopers about me burying Jules's jewelry, but if he hadn't told them yet, I knew he would eventually."

"So, you hiked to his place and shot him?"

Susan giggled. "You were walking in the woods," she said. "I almost ran into you. I had to hide behind a tree." She shook her head, a smile still on her face. "Sammy didn't even hear me coming. He told us about what a great tracker and outdoorsman he was, but I snuck into his cabin and shot him before he even knew what happened."

"How could you kill nine people?" Elle asked.

Susan smiled. "I did all of this for us, Elle. You are like a sister to me. I could have killed you too. You were out cold the night of the murders, but I didn't want to hurt you. I wouldn't hurt you now if I didn't have to."

"You drugged everyone with my Ambien, didn't you?"

"I didn't think you'd mind," Susan said. "I sprinkled it on the brownies and then added more frosting from a can we had." A tear trickled down Susan's cheek. "I feel terrible about Snowball, though. I didn't know she was under the covers with Jules and Bob. I must have accidentally hit her with the ax."

Elle thought about what Susan had done. Not only had she murdered nine people, but she'd also played mind games with Elle, trying to make her believe she was the killer. Elle felt her fear morph into red-hot anger. She charged at Susan, catching her off guard.

Susan nearly dropped the knife but then recovered it and plunged it into Elle's shoulder.

Elle heard the scream, but it took her several seconds to realize it was coming from her.

CHAPTER 63

Thursday, September 11th
2:37 p.m.

Patterson heard a scream. He and Mark looked at each other, and Patterson nodded to him. The trooper stood back and kicked hard at the front door. The door frame cracked as the wood splintered. Patterson spoke into the radio on his vest.

"We're going in," he said to his other troopers. "Hold your positions, but prepare to provide backup."

Patterson led the way through the small house, and Mark followed closely behind. They heard Susan and Elle before they saw them. Elle sobbed while Susan hummed a tuneless melody.

Patterson nodded toward the bedroom, and Mark gave two sharp bobs of his head. Gun firmly gripped, Patterson quickly walked past the bedroom door, and he and Mark took up positions on either side of the doorway.

"I'm sorry I hurt you," Susan said, "but soon, you won't feel anything."

"Drop it!" Patterson said. He held the gun on Susan as he edged into the room.

Mark also pointed his gun at Susan when he walked into the room.

Susan stared at the two troopers for a moment and then dropped the knife. "I'm so glad you're here," she said. "Elle was about to shoot me."

"Hands behind your back, Susan."

Mark moved to cuff Susan while Patterson called for an ambulance.

Patterson dropped onto the floor beside Elle. She'd lost some blood, but a shoulder wound wouldn't kill her. He spoke soothing words to her while he applied direct pressure to her injury. A few minutes later, he heard the approaching sirens.

CHAPTER 64

Thursday, September 11th

7:10 p.m.

Patterson looked up at the sky as he left trooper headquarters. They were losing several minutes of daylight every day now, and soon he'd be leaving work in the dark. A brisk wind rattled the dried leaves on the trees, sending a wave of them swirling in the air with every gust. Wispy cirrus clouds raced across the blue sky, hinting at high winds aloft. Autumn was in full swing, and winter was quickly approaching.

When Patterson entered his house, he smelled pork chops, baked apples, and stuffing. His stomach rumbled. Jeanne had prepared the perfect fall meal.

She greeted him with a bottle of beer as soon as he walked into the kitchen. She clinked her glass of water against the beer. "Congratulations on closing another case," she said.

Patterson kissed his wife and then sat on a kitchen stool. "I don't feel good about this one, Jeanne."

She tilted her head to one side as she regarded him. "Why not? You locked up a mass murderer this afternoon."

"She's a kid," Patterson said. "How can a seventeen-year-old girl carry such hate, and why would she think it was okay to solve her problems by killing people?"

Jeanne shook her head. "I hope we do a better job raising our child."

Patterson gave Jeanne a sad smile. He didn't have the energy to think about her pregnancy.

Jeanne seemed to pick up on his mood and quickly changed the subject. "Poor Brie. How will she ever live in her house again after a mass murderer stayed there?"

Patterson nodded. "Boyle said that once we release the house as a crime scene, he and some of the other troopers will go in and clean up Elle's blood before Brie sees it."

"Still, I couldn't live there again. Maybe we should invite Brie to stay with us for a while until she decides what she wants to do."

Patterson pulled his wife to him. "You are such a good person. I'll ask her if she wants to stay with us, but I imagine she'll stay with her parents if she doesn't want to move back into her house."

"How is Deb Bartlett doing? Have you heard lately?"

Patterson shook his head. "She's still in a coma. Jason will do some time for this one."

"What about Tim Fairweather?" Jeanne asked.

"He's being charged with second-degree murder. I think he'll have a hard time convincing a jury that he killed Georgie in self-defense."

Tears trickled from Jeanne's eyes. "I get so sick of it—domestic violence against women—it never ends. I hope the two of them spend the rest of their lives in prison."

Afterword

Kodiak Island, Alaska's Emerald Isle, sits off the southern coast of Alaska, 250 miles (402 kilometers) southwest of Anchorage. The town of Kodiak lies on the northwestern edge of the island. Kanuk Bay, the setting for this novel, exists only in my imagination, and I have placed it near the southern end of Kodiak Island. Aktuvik Fresh Seafoods Cannery and the village of Kanuk Bay also are not real places. Brian and Elle share dinner at Kodiak Hana, an actual and popular restaurant located above the channel entrance to the Kodiak boat harbor. Be sure to check out Kodiak Hana the next time you visit the island.

The Massacre at Bear Creek Lodge began as a game in the Facebook portion of the Readers and Writers Book Club. I wrote the beginning chapter and then asked club members to comment and vote on what they thought should happen next. I hoped to create an interactive book-writing experience, but I did not plan to turn the project into an actual novel. By the time the game fizzled, though, I'd written the first quarter of a novel, and I decided to continue with the story. During the book club game, I asked participants to enter their names for a drawing to become a character in my book. Debbie Semrau, the drawing winner, graciously loaned her first name to the Bartletts' daughter, Deb. Thank you, Debbie!

My husband and I own a small, remote lodge on Kodiak Island, and I based the doomed lodge in this novel on our home. The similarities end there, though. Mike and I bear no resemblance to Bob and Jules Bartlett, and no character in this book represents a real person. When an author writes a novel, her life experiences and acquaintances

309

tend to creep into her writing, but I have not consciously based any of my fictional characters on a living human being.

Jane Marcus did not appear in this novel, and I know some readers will be disappointed not to see her. Jane does dominate my next book, though, and her curiosity will again lead her into danger. Will she survive her next brush with death? You'll have to wait and see.

Thank you, Evan and Lois Swensen, at Publication Consultants, for your guidance and assistance. From the cover artwork to the interior design, the folks at Publication Consultants create beautiful books and run a well-oiled operation. Thank you to my fellow authors at Author Masterminds for your inspiration and support. I look forward to our weekly meetings.

Thank you, Bill Siever, for your editing wizardry. You make me a much better writer.

A very special thank-you to my husband, Mike, who always supports my writing and podcasting endeavors, no matter how crazy. He reads everything I write and listens to all my podcast episodes. He is also my weapons and logistics expert.

I have written four previous novels: *Big Game, Murder Over Kodiak, The Fisherman's Daughter,* and *Karluk Bones.* I've also written the nonfiction book *Kodiak Island Wildlife.* You can find my books at amazon.com, barnesandnoble.com, authormasterminds.com, and other online booksellers.

If you enjoy reading true-crime stories about Alaska, be sure to sign up for my monthly newsletter at https://mailchi.mp/e34d-98f1a569/alaska_mystery_newsletter. If you prefer to listen to your true-crime stories, check out my podcast, *Murder and Mystery in the Last Frontier,* at https://murder-in-the-last-frontier.blubrry.net.

I invite you to join me on Facebook at https://www.facebook.com/wildernessauthorrobinbarefield and on Author Masterminds at https://authormasterminds.com/robin-barefield.

Thank you for reading.

www.ingramcontent.com/pod-product-compliance
Lightning Source LLC
Chambersburg PA
CBHW051519260626
47170CB00003B/697